DARCY BY ANY OTHER NAME

Laura Hile

Copyright © 2016 by Laura Hile.

All rights reserved. No part of this publication may be reproduced, distributed or transmitted in any form or by any means, including photocopying, recording, or other electronic or mechanical methods, without the prior written permission of the publisher, except in the case of brief quotations embodied in critical reviews and certain other noncommercial uses permitted by copyright law. For permission requests, write to the publisher at the address below.

14280 SW Wildhorse Way
Beaverton, Oregon 97008
www.laurahile.com

Publisher's Note: This is a work of fiction. Locales and public names are sometimes used for atmospheric purposes. Any resemblance to actual people, living or dead, or to businesses, companies, events, institutions, or locales is completely coincidental.

Book Layout ©2013 BookDesignTemplates.com

Cover Design by Damonza

Darcy By Any Other Name/ Laura Hile. -- 1st ed.
ISBN 978-1530600366

For my mom, Janet, with love.

*Follies and nonsense,
whims and inconsistencies
do divert me, I own,
and I laugh at them whenever I can.*

JANE AUSTEN, *PRIDE AND PREJUDICE*

Contents

1 ANY SAVAGE CAN DANCE 1
2 A FINE FIGURE OF A MAN 15
3 HIT OR MISS 29
4 BAREFACED QUESTIONS 37
5 RUFTY TUFTY 53
6 WHIRLIGIG 71
7 SUCH AMIABLE QUALITIES 79
8 WHAT I SUFFER 97
9 PETTICOAT WAG 113
10 STEP STATELY! 129
11 ROSE IS RED, ROSE IS WHITE 141
12 NO HUMOR AT PRESENT 155
13 TO CROWN THE WHOLE 167
14 A FINE THING 183
15 PICKING OF STICKS 195
16 DRIVE THE COLD WINTER AWAY 209
17 CHEERILY AND MERRILY 225
18 A PARSON'S FAREWELL 241
19 THE JOVIAL BEGGARS 261
20 NEW, NEW NOTHING 281
21 VERY LIVELY HOPES 291

22 OF MEAN UNDERSTANDING	307
23 A FINE COMPANION	321
24 MORE SECRETS THAN ONE	331
25 A MATTER OF PRIDE	343
26 RAG, TAG, AND BOBTAIL	353
27 IF ALL THE WORLD WERE PAPER	365
28 FAULTS ON ALL SIDES	381
29 TOPSY-TURVY	393
30 DECKED IN THE GARB OF FANCY	403
31 FOR A KINGDOM	415
32 CERTAINLY VERY LITTLE	423
33 BUT LOOK AT HOME	433
34 LET SOLDIERS FIGHT	441
35 RANTING, ROARING, RATTLING BOYS	453
36 OF CHEQUERED FORTUNE	467
37 FIELDS OF FROST	483
38 HE KNEW NOT HOW	491
39 PAST ENDURANCE	499
40 TUTOR OF TRUTH	515
41 PERILS OF MEN	523
42 GIVE ME LEAVE	537
43 TOLLING THE BELL	557
44 MY REASONS I'LL OWN	567

45 'Tis Certain So	583
46 Fain I Would	595
47 Jump at the Sun	605
48 Turn of the Tide	625
49 Epilogue: Upon A Summer's Day	641

1 Any Savage Can Dance

Fitzwilliam Darcy's gaze swept the Netherfield ballroom. A stout fellow, his clothes shrieking of the parsonage, was urging Elizabeth Bennet to join him in the dance. Darcy's smile threatened to become a smirk. He'd seen the man earlier, bumbling through dances he did not know, skipping and cavorting like a mooncalf. Apparently Miss Elizabeth would have no more.

Should Darcy ask her for another dance? Hardly! They'd danced earlier, and everything Darcy said she deliberately misunderstood.

Perhaps this was just as well. After all, what was she to him but the second-eldest Miss Bennet? Even in his thoughts—especially in his thoughts! —he would allow this beguiling young woman no quarter. Yet like a moth drawn to flame, here he was thinking about her, observing her.

That parson, or whoever he was, was mightily attracted. His smiling attempts at raillery spoke volumes. Why hadn't he the sense to conceal his infatuation? Did he not realize that he was making an idiot of himself? She so obviously did not wish to speak with him.

And yet this was the sort of fellow that Elizabeth—no, the second-eldest Miss Bennet! —was likely to marry. Truth, Darcy reminded himself, must be faced. And so he studied the parson's flushed, well-fed cheeks and promising double chin.

That a person like this (Darcy could hardly call him a man!) might wed adorable, intelligent Elizabeth was revolting. But such was the way of the world, his world, and it happened every day. Darcy drew a long breath and averted his gaze.

Presently he heard a cough and the words "Hunsford" and "Lady Catherine de Bourgh." Why, the unknown clergyman was no longer at Elizabeth Bennet's side, he was here at Darcy's elbow. And he was making a very low, very formal bow.

"My dear Mr. Darcy," said he, "far be it from me to thrust myself upon your notice. However—"

Did this person, whose surname was Collins, intend an introduction? Darcy was too astonished to reply.

"I have been so fortunate as to be distinguished by the patronage of your esteemed aunt," said he, "whose beneficence has preferred to me the rectory of Rosings

Parish." Mr. Collins paused to draw breath and displayed a fine set of teeth. Had he come to the end of his speech? Darcy hoped so.

But no, Mr. Collins had more to say, and his plump fingers became busy in a hand-washing motion that Darcy found repellent. "And in such a capacity," said Mr. Collins, "I must set social niceties aside and take it upon myself—for indeed, it is my solemn duty as a clergyman—to convey to you the tidings that, as of Monday last, your aunt was in excellent health."

Mr. Collins paused and smiled expectantly. Darcy said nothing.

The silence, which Darcy meant to become awkward, was quickly filled. "Lady Catherine, as you know," said Mr. Collins, "is a most distinguished and worthy patroness, and I am humbled and gratified by her notice. And I am most honored to make myself known to you, her distinguished nephew. Such an august lineage is yours, and such a distinction is mine, to serve—"

There followed more praise of his aunt. Darcy endeavored to stem the flow with a quelling look, but it was no use. Mr. Collins would talk, tossing out compliments with abandon.

At last there came an opening. "My venerable aunt," said Darcy crushingly, "is known for her powers of discernment. I am certain she could never bestow a favor unworthily."

This was the wrong reply to a simpleton like Collins. He responded with delight, not chagrin, and resumed talking. At last, with a gesture and another bow, Mr. Collins dropped a useful bit of information. Apparently he was related to the Bennets of Longbourn.

Didn't this cap all! As if Miss Elizabeth's mother and boisterous younger sisters were not enough, she must have this noxious cousin!

Darcy's lips curled into a sneer. After the slightest of bows to Collins, he turned away. Mr. Collins went immediately to Elizabeth's side, apparently to share his triumph, but Darcy did not wait to see her response. He had had quite enough of her family.

In fact, he'd had quite enough of Netherfield Park. Why in heaven's name had he convinced Bingley to take this estate? Anything—a cow herder's stone cottage shared with the cow! —would be preferable!

But no, when considering a property one took into account nothing of true importance. The size of the rooms, the condition of the park, the number of bedchambers, the state of the drains—what were these? What one ought to do, Darcy now realized, was examine the neighbors! Line them up, spend thirty minutes exposed to their chatter and flattery and hapless conversation, and then run like Hades in the opposite direction!

Darcy's next thought involved supper, but the sight of Charles Bingley in conversation with Miss Jane Bennet pulled him up short. Charles was all smiles, and with every glance he displayed his preference for Miss Bennet. She, of course, was loveliness itself. Darcy looked on for some minutes, wondering what peril Bingley would suffer. When they made for the supper tables, Darcy followed at a distance.

And who should be sitting there but the mother, Mrs. Bennet, deep in conversation. Miss Elizabeth, who sat beside her, was looking uncomfortable and no wonder; once again Collins was pressing his attentions. There was an empty seat at the opposite side of her table, one that would allow Darcy to observe Bingley's movements.

With narrowed eyes Darcy took a plate from the buffet and filled it. The noise in this room was almost painful, and yet he was able to catch some of Mrs. Bennet's conversation.

"Such a charming young man," she was saying, and Darcy knew at once that she was referred to Bingley. "And so rich. And living but three miles from us. And what a comfort to think how fond the two sisters are of Jane! To be sure, they must desire the connection as much as I."

Darcy stiffened. With precision he placed his fork on his plate.

"And what a promising thing," Mrs. Bennet continued, "for my younger daughters, as Jane's marrying so greatly must throw them in the way of other rich men." She patted her companion's arm with gloved fingers. "You have all my good wishes, my dear, to soon be as equally fortunate with your sweet daughters."

Miss Elizabeth, looking most uncomfortable, leaned to speak into her mother's ear.

"What is Mr. Darcy to me," cried Mrs. Bennet, "that I should be afraid of him? I am sure we owe him no such particular civility as to be obliged to say nothing he may not like to hear."

"For heaven's sake—" Darcy heard Miss Elizabeth whisper.

Darcy focused his attention on his plate. Elizabeth, at least, had not her mother's scheming qualities. But the elder Miss Bennet? Darcy's gaze traveled to where she sat with Charles Bingley. A very deep game this mother was playing, and Charles had taken the bait. Jane Bennet seemed an obliging girl, but what was her true nature? What young woman would not be enticed by an income such as Bingley's?

Singing was talked of, and presently another Bennet sister came forward, a girl whom Darcy had thought to be quiet and retiring. How mistaken he was! This girl was as fond of attention as the younger sisters, but she had no musical taste and even less ability. Her performance on the pianoforte was insupportable, and her singing was worse. Darcy kept his eyes averted, but Bingley's two sisters did not. There were whispers and looks between them, as if they took pleasure in Mary Bennet's display.

Her father finally put a stop to it in a most ill-mannered way. But what could one expect in such a place and from such a family?

And then Mr. Collins decided to have his say. "If I," said he, speaking in a voice that half the room could hear, "were so fortunate as to be able to sing, I should have great pleasure in obliging the company with an air; for I consider music as a very innocent diversion, and perfectly compatible with the profession of a clergyman."

Darcy could only stare. These sentiments were lifted directly from his aunt, who gloried in her unlearned abilities.

Mr. Collins went blithely on, as if Bingley's guests were rapt listeners to a favorite lecture: "The rector of a parish has much to do. In the first place, he must make such an agreement for tithes as may be beneficial to himself and not offensive to his patron. He must write his own sermons—"

Many gaped, others smiled. Mr. Bennet, Darcy noted, was looking particularly amused, though why he should be was puzzling. Did the man not see that Mr. Collins brought shame upon every member of his family?

At last, after a bow in Darcy's direction, Mr. Collins concluded his speech with more twaddle about the homage due to the provider of his preferment.

"Very sensible," Darcy heard Mrs. Bennet whisper loudly. "A remarkably clever, good kind of young man."

Darcy rose to his feet. He had had enough of this ball, of Collins, and of the entire Bennet clan. He strode through the drawing room, down the staircase, and out of the mansion. If the door had been unmanned by footmen, he gladly would have slammed it.

Once outside Darcy skirted the house and made for the ornamental garden. The sound of music and muted laughter followed. What a fiasco Bingley's ball had become! And it was all the fault of the guests.

Never did Darcy think to prefer the soulless anonymity of the London social set, but such was the case tonight. Bluff country gentlemen and ambitious mothers, all staring as if he were a prize stallion! One whisper about the extent of his income, and every person was on the hunt to become his friend.

Charles Bingley, of course, saw none of this. He was pleased with each of his new neighbors and thought them charming. Darcy's brow knit in a frown. What to do about Bingley? For plainly he must be extricated from Jane Bennet's charms. That she was a fortune hunter Darcy had little doubt. He had paid his sister's dressmaking bills long enough to know that Miss Bennet's lovely gown was no homemade affair, nor were any of her sisters' dresses. Their mother obviously spent money like water!

A crunch of footsteps on gravel caught his attention; had someone followed him? Darcy turned and saw the white of a clerical cravat. Indeed, he could hear Collins' reedy voice calling his name.

Darcy increased his pace and crossed the lawn, heading for the stone Folly. Perhaps he could lose Collins in the shadows? There was no question that the man would take a hint and go away.

Sure enough, on Collins came; Darcy could hear his mincing trot. "Oh, Mr. Dar-cy," he shrilled. "Forgive the intrusion, but—"

The chill air held the promise of rain, and something in Collins' tone told Darcy that he was cold and uncomfortable. So much the better! Darcy came to a halt beneath one of the Folly's arches and waited. The wind was picking up; fallen leaves swirled around his feet. Yes, a storm was definitely blowing in.

"I am reluctant to intrude," Mr. Collins wheezed out, for he was breathing heavily. "Most—reluctant."

The man had crossed the garden at a run! Was he now pretending this encounter was accidental? Not only was Collins impertinent, but he was also a liar. Darcy folded his arms across his chest.

And Elizabeth thought *him* condescending? Top-lofty? Impossible to please? Would that she could see his patience and forbearance! For her sake, Darcy would not give Collins the reply his arrogance deserved.

The man gazed at Darcy with a confiding smile. "I cannot think why, but I neglected to inquire earlier," he said, and paused mid-sentence.

Darcy knew precisely why: because the man was an idiot!

"Is there a message, good sir, that you would like me to convey to your esteemed aunt? I return to Hunsford on the coming Saturday."

Surely this was the slenderest pretext for conversation! It now occurred to Darcy that the man might be seeking a loan.

"Lady Catherine shall, I am sure," Mr. Collins went on, "be pleased to learn of your connection with my relations here."

"I have no connection with your family," Darcy snapped. "Or with any other in this district, save for the Bingleys." That wind was decidedly sharp. He could hear the rumble of distant thunder.

Collins gave a tittering laugh. "How can you say so, sir? You are quite the most sought-after guest, if what I hear from the ladies is to be believed."

Was the man actually winking?

There was a flash of lightning. Collins' confiding smile was back, displaying all of the man's teeth. Such a grin on the face of a cleric was singularly disturbing.

"Such condescension," Mr. Collins said, almost purring. "And such an honor, to have your august presence among us, Mr. Darcy."

The wind tugged at Darcy's coat. "Kindly stop blithering," he said, "and confine your interest to your own affairs." He paused, and then purposely added, "When you introduced yourself earlier, I fear I did not catch the name."

Two can play at lying, he thought.

But Darcy's snub was too subtle. "Collins," came the cheerful reply. "The Reverend William Collins." And he held out an ungloved hand.

Darcy ignored it. Nothing would be gained by encouraging the man's presuming habits. "Kindly convey my greetings to Lady Catherine," he said through shut teeth. "And mention to her, if you would, that her latest rector—which would be you, Collins—is more of a humbug than the usual."

Collins' smile became less confident. "Her latest rector?" he repeated. "But the preferment is for life."

Another bolt of lightning flashed, much nearer than the last. Thunder rolled, and the sound made Mr. Collins flinch. Darcy stood like stone, his eyes fastened on Collins' podgy face. He allowed himself a slight smile. "Nevertheless, I fear my Aunt Catherine runs through rectors at a famous clip."

This remark caught Collins off guard. His eyes widened. "My predecessors have—resigned?"

Darcy lifted his shoulders in a shrug. "Even a toad, when it is kicked enough," he said, "will sooner or later come to its senses and hop away."

"Kicked?" Mr. Collins repeated. "Did you say kicked?" He lifted his chin. "I do not think," he said primly, "that this is a proper way to speak of my beneficent patroness."

"Perhaps not," Darcy admitted. "I am forgetting myself, Mr. Collins, and am speaking as to an equal. For you, her dependent, it would most definitely be improper."

Again lightning flashed, this time with violent crash of thunder, and rain began to fall in large drops. Collins wore no hat and soon his doughy cheeks were wet and shining. Reluctantly Darcy stepped back to allow the man to join him under the shelter of the arch. Even so, there were many spiders' webs. Collins obviously disliked spiders. He twitched and brushed at his sleeves and shoulders.

A tremendous gust rattled the branches of the bare trees, bringing dead leaves and debris swirling through the arch. The rain pelted down, and another roll of thunder shook the garden. Somewhere a door slammed. Mr. Collins looked anxiously in the direction of the mansion, obviously wishing to make a run for it.

This, Darcy knew, would be extremely unwise, and he said so. Another strike of lightning crackled like gunshot. Darcy leaned against the side of the arch. "You have only recently come to the Rosings parish?" he said conversationally. For Miss Elizabeth's sake he should make an attempt.

"Why, er, yes." Collins got hold of himself soon enough. "And wondrously generous Lady Catherine has been," he went on, "inviting me to tea and dinner at the estate—" There was more in this vein. Darcy did not comment, even when the pelting rain changed to hail.

More flattery, more obeisance. Was this what people thought he enjoyed?

And why, in heaven's name, was he standing here conversing with this man? A stray thought appeared: had Collins resumed his hand-wringing? Darcy allowed his gaze to slide in Collins' direction. Of course he had!

DARCY BY ANY OTHER NAME

Where did his aunt find these fellows?

At last Darcy felt he had to say something. "Gratitude and humility," he offered, "are necessary requirements of your profession, especially in my aunt's eyes."

Collins' chin lifted. "Why, yes," he said. "Never forget that *the meek shall inherit the earth*, Mr. Darcy," he said primly. He laid a kindly pastoral hand on Darcy's shoulder.

Darcy shrank from the man's touch. How dared Collins quote a biblical text to him! Conversation was bad enough, but a thinly-veiled rebuke?

"Very true," Darcy replied through shut teeth, for how could he argue with theology? Nevertheless, the de Bourghs and the Darcys would inherit the landed estates. Collins, inept and bumbling, would be master of nothing!

Another gust of wind struck the Folly.

The sky flashed white. Bits of stone and mortar went flying, and thunder exploded. There was a second flash as lightning struck again. This time the very stones of the Folly were dislodged. Mr. Collins gave a shriek, and Darcy felt the push of his hands as the man shoved him aside.

Then Collins went down, a quivering bulk of wet and howling black wool. "Mercy," he screamed. "Mercy!"

Darcy was unable to prevent himself from falling. He hit the pavement heavily and knew no more.

2 A Fine Figure of a Man

There were sounds in the garden—shouts or calls, as if a shooting party had lost its way. But this could not be right, Darcy decided. No one would be hunting in the middle of the night. For it was night; the moon was shining—or was it a lantern? Darcy worked to untangle his thoughts. What had happened?

He must have fallen asleep, he decided. But was he now awake? He should be able to see and to move, and he could do neither. But he could hear.

And what he heard was the sound of wings. Birds, large birds—could they be ravens? Or vultures? —came flapping and hopping round. He could feel them pulling at his clothing with their beaks. They had voices, rough and shrill like crows. Were they crows?

"Is he dead? Is he dead?" they called to one another.

Of course he was not dead. Couldn't they see that? He now realized where he was lying—in the garden at Netherfield beside the Folly, or what remained of it. There had been a storm, hadn't there? With rain and lightning and hail. Darcy summoned his strength to drive the birds away, but could not. The crows continued to squawk and caw.

Corbies, said the voice of memory. These were not crows, they were corbies. Darcy knew a rhyme about corbies; he'd learned it as a boy.

As I was walking all alone, I heard two corbies making a moan;

Yes, that was it. These crows were certainly doing that.

One unto the other did say, "Where shall we go and dine today?"

Darcy knew the answer: they would dine on human flesh! In fact, he could hear Mrs. Allan chanting the rhyme in her raspy brogue. This, his rational mind added, was what came of having a Scot to mind young children! Gruesome rhymes at bedtime!

And Mrs. Allen would say the next bit slowly, as if relishing every word:

In behind that old turf wall, I sense there lies a new-slain knight;

And nobody knows that he lies there, but his hawk, his hound, and his lady fair.

But Darcy was not a knight! The rest of the story involved the crows plucking out the dead man's eyes and thatching their nests with his hair.

And o'er his white bones, when they are bare, the wind will blow forevermare.

Even now these words made Darcy's skin crawl.

Meanwhile, the birds around him were not silent. "But who is he?"

"Who? Who?"

Darcy struggled to work this out. Had the crows now become owls? Or were they men? Men, he decided, although how birds could become human was beyond him.

"He don't look dead. Ha, dead drunk, do ye think?"

"He's nobody I've seen before."

Darcy became aware of something else, the tang of tobacco smoke—someone had lit a pipe! These men were standing about and smoking? Calmly discussing him as if he were downed game or a tree stump?

"I'm Darcy!" he wanted to shout. "Confound it, I'm Darcy, and I'm not drunk!" But his voice would not work.

"He'll catch his death out here," another person said. "It's nigh unto freezing."

Finally, someone with sense!

"How long do you suppose he's been here?"

Darcy worked to remember. He'd come out of the house after the dancing to clear his thinking, and Collins had followed.

Collins. He had a list of gripes about Collins—and he had voiced a few to the man's face, hadn't he? Well, he oughtn't to have followed. Collins got what he deserved.

"Look here," someone said. "It's that parson! Him as is staying with the Bennets!"

Which meant that Darcy was experiencing a nightmare, for Collins was in it.

"Once the boys get back from carrying that Mr. Darcy into the house," someone said, "we'll have a go with this one."

"A shame about Mr. Darcy," another voice said.

Oh, a shame indeed, thought Darcy. But why didn't these men help him? And why didn't they know who he was?

"I'll throw out my back, I will, if we carry him."

"Carry him?" someone else said. "Are you daft?" Darcy tried to ignore the sneer in the voice.

"We'll need the pony cart if we're to haul him all the way to Longbourn. That's a good two or three mile, that is. He's no lightweight." Against the small of his back Darcy felt the nudge of a foot.

Why would they take him to Longbourn? Netherfield, Darcy protested. They ought to take him to Netherfield! Why couldn't they hear him?

"A regular bonehead, to be out in a storm like that. No sense, these gentlemen, for all their fine ways." Someone gave a push to Darcy's hip—was he trying to turn him over? A wave of pain surged through his shoulder and arm.

"Tsk, tsk, would you look at that. A case for Mr. Jones, this is," a voice said. "That shoulder don't look right. Broken bone, do you think?"

Darcy could feel the men's growing curiosity as they gathered round to see. Nausea followed the pain. Why wouldn't they leave him alone?

And then Darcy felt his head being lifted. He was being forced to drink—brandy? Liquid slid down his throat, and somehow he managed to swallow. The warmth of the liquor spread through his chest.

"It'll be a long wait," a voice said. "And a cold one."

Darcy found he no longer cared, so long as the pain stopped. The men continued to talk, but their voices slipped away. All was blissfully dark and quiet.

Sometime later—how long he did not know—Darcy became aware that the quiet had changed. This was no longer the silence of the garden, but that of a house. He drew a long breath and attempted to open his eyes. Somehow he hadn't the strength to do this. No matter, he was dry and warm. His left shoulder hurt tremendously. It was just as well that he could not move it.

He soon became aware of more sounds: the crackle and pop of a wood fire and footfalls on a wooden floor. He was not alone! Was a housemaid in the room? There, the chime of a spoon against a glass tumbler! Had someone brought in breakfast? That person was stirring...what? His coffee?

And there was more: the distinct rustle of cloth. Darcy strained to hear. He discovered that he could make out whispering voices. Again he struggled to open his eyes. Why was he so weak?

"Pray don't disturb him. Let him sleep, poor man."

This was a woman's voice; was she one of the Netherfield housemaids? And very sound advice she offered. Sleep would be most welcome, if the pain would go away.

"But his eyelids," said another voice. "Do you see? They're moving. So he isn't dead."

Of course he was not dead! And wasn't it humiliating to be the topic of conversation among servants?

"At least," the same voice continued, "he isn't dead yet."

Darcy did not like the emphasis she put on the word *yet*.

"Lydia, hush!"

Lydia? What was this? He knew no Lydia, save for Lydia Bennet, Elizabeth's pert sister. And this certainly could not be her. What would Lydia Bennet be doing at Netherfield?

Lydia (or whoever she was) went on speaking. "How Mama would rejoice if he were!"

If he were dead, did she mean? Why would a housemaid's mother be glad about that?

There was a pause, during which Darcy waited. "And he's been snoring so," she complained. "It's enough to wake the dead."

Darcy felt himself stiffen. He did not snore!

"Lydia, please," said the first voice. "He shall not die; he merely needs rest. Such a shocking accident," she added.

So there had been an accident. The storm, the Folly, the lightning. It was not a dream.

"But you must admit, Jane, that it would be a wonderful thing if he never woke up. He could not inherit then."

Was this Jane Bennet? No, it was impossible. But how could two of Bingley's maids be named Jane and Lydia?

No, this sort of coincidence was too much. He must be dreaming again. Yes, that was it, he was dreaming. For if Jane and Lydia Bennet were at his bedside, he could not be at Netherfield. But he must be at Netherfield. The corbies had said they had taken him there.

Corbies again. Was he losing his mind? They were men, he remembered. And they said they had taken Mr. Darcy to Netherfield.

"It makes no difference, Lydia. We would not benefit in the slightest. Some other male relation would inherit, that is all."

This was a new voice, and Darcy struggled to identify its owner. This was not Caroline Bingley's sophisticated drawl, though if he were at Netherfield she would certainly wheedle her way into his sickroom. Nor did she sound like Louisa Hurst.

Her voice was clear and pleasing. Could she be...Elizabeth? Elizabeth Bennet in his bedchamber? Darcy felt his heart give a thump. Since this was a dream, it was very possible!

"Poor man," the voice known as Jane said. "He's lost weight."

"As if losing weight could be a bad thing!" said Lydia. She gave a muted giggle. "Imagine what will happen if he continues this way. His clothes won't fit!"

"Lydia, really."

"But how shall we manage? Father won't lend him anything, not that I blame him. And can you imagine the talk if we trot into Meryton and place an order? Or have the tailor call to take measurements?"

There was a pause. "What a thought," she added. "Like measuring a corpse for a coffin." The relish in Miss Lydia's voice was unmistakable.

"He is not a corpse," said the unknown voice. "I daresay he will recover soon enough, once he regains consciousness, for then he'll be able to eat."

"And eat and eat and eat! Poor Mama, did you see her face when dear Mr. Collins consumed quite half the ham? Not to mention three helpings of bread pudding and most of the rum sauce."

What did Collins have to do with anything? And why should he eat half a ham?

"Mr. Collins eats like, well, like gentlemen do."

Jane, Darcy decided, was a natural diplomat. "He must keep up his strength, as they say," she went on.

"Indeed," said Lydia laughingly, "the man needs plenty of strength to haul about that stomach of his."

"Haul?" Jane's voice carried mild reproof. "Those officers are corrupting your speech, Lydia."

Lydia merely giggled. "Oh, lord, not even Denny eats like Mr. Collins does, and Denny is as thin as anything. Father says Mr. Collins eats like a poor relation."

"Father," said Jane, "has an appetite which is more refined than most. And Father enjoys poking fun, you know that."

Darcy heard a door open. "Girls! What is the meaning of this?"

All doubts were banished now. This was certainly Mrs. Bennet.

"I'm surprised at you, congregating in a gentleman's bedchamber. Most irregular!"

"It isn't as if he's a threat to our virtue, Mama." This was from Lydia. Darcy felt someone lift one of his eyelids. "See?" she said. "He's still out. Dead to the world."

There was a pause. "Perhaps," Lydia added hopefully, "he'll stay out and save us a world of trouble. I was just telling Lizzy, Mama, that he'll eat us out of house and home before he leaves."

Lizzy? Darcy's heart gave a thump, and he strained to hear more.

"We came in to change the bedding, Mama," he heard Elizabeth's voice say.

"As well you should," replied Mrs. Bennet. "Very right and proper, Lizzy. And if you happen to be here when he comes to himself, so much the better."

"Mama, really."

"You might give Mr. Collins a bit of encouragement. Think of what it might mean to your future—to all our futures."

"I am thinking of it, Mama." Elizabeth's tone was dry.

"Well!" Mrs. Bennet said. "Turning up your nose at a gentleman with prospects is most unhelpful. By your standards no one is good enough!"

Elizabeth must be standing very near to the bed, for Darcy heard her murmur, "Even Mr. Darcy."

"Mr. Collins' prospects," Mrs. Bennet went on, "are as good as anyone's! Without having to inherit Longbourn, he has quite a snug situation."

Darcy held his breath. Collins was to inherit Longbourn?

"You would do well to mind that, Lizzy," continued Mrs. Bennet, "before he slips through your fingers!" On the strength of this remark, Mrs. Bennet left the room.

"What I say is that his so-noble patroness, Lady Whoever-she-is, must be a penny-pincher." This was from Lydia. Darcy felt someone's fingers close around his wrist. "Look at the cuff of his nightshirt. Imagine, wearing something so frayed! Mama would never permit it." There was a pause. "Now I wonder—" she added.

There was a mischievous lilt in her voice. What was she planning?

"Do you suppose," said Lydia, "that the elbow has been patched as well?" Darcy felt the blankets being moved aside. Was Miss Lydia intending to have a look?

Just as quickly the blankets were twitched back into place. "Lydia, really," Jane chided. "Allow the man some dignity."

"Everyone deserves that," Elizabeth added. "Even Mr. Collins."

Collins again. Why must people keep bringing him up?

"But Lizzy," said Lydia, "this is our chance to check! Quick, where is his coat? What has he got in his pockets? How much money is in his purse?"

"Nothing that interests us."

"But Lizzy!" Lydia pleaded.

"Off with you," Elizabeth said, and Darcy could hear the smile in her voice. "I daresay the poor man can hear everything we say."

Lydia gave a giggle. "Oh, surely n—" she stopped mid-sentence. "My gracious," she said, in an altered tone. "His fingers are so fat. Like sausages."

There was another pause. "If he's so eager to find a wife," she added, "I wonder that he'll be able to get a wedding ring to fit!" And then Darcy heard Lydia's skipping step go out of the room.

"Will she never learn to hold her tongue?" This was from Jane.

"I think not. Shall I open the window a bit? It seems rather close in here."

Darcy heard the rasp of the sash being raised. At once the door came open and brisk footfalls crossed the room. "Merciful heavens, he'll catch his death," Mrs. Bennet's voice cried. The sash was then forced down.

"Mr. Jones is here to attend him. You'd best come away, girls, for that bone might need setting. Mr. Jones," she added, "is known for putting members of the family to use."

At this all the women went into motion, or so it seemed to Darcy.

"I am willing to assist Mr. Jones, Mama, if he requires it."

"No, Jane dear," said Mrs. Bennet. "That is for Lizzy to do." There was a pause.

"A ministering angel you'll be, Lizzy," she went on, and Darcy could picture her wide smile. "The first face to meet his eyes after his ordeal." And then Mrs. Bennet went out of the room.

"I am willing to assist you, Lizzy, if you wish it," said Jane. She did not sound at all willing, but Darcy had to admire her spirit.

He felt the bedclothes being smoothed—by Elizabeth?

"Better not," he heard her say. "I was there when he set John Miller's arm last year, and the first thing Mr. Jones did was to make poor John very drunk."

Elizabeth hesitated. "Can you imagine Mr. Collins in the same state?" she added.

Collins again. Yes, Darcy could imagine it all too vividly.

Both girls left the bedchamber. It was then that Darcy discovered something wondrous: he was able to open his eyes. A miracle, he could see! Eagerly he took in his surroundings.

The bedchamber was entirely new to him, small and sparsely furnished—and unlike anything at Netherfield, unless it belonged to one of the servants. The walls were painted, not papered, and an ancient wardrobe stood in the corner. On the dressing table rested a wide-brimmed parson's hat, though what it was doing here Darcy did not know.

His left arm, which was very painful, was bound with cloths, and he decided not to move it. He was able to lift his right hand, however. Carefully he brought it nearer in order to see. And then Darcy felt a wave of panic. Here was the frayed cuff of which Miss Lydia spoke!

And his hand—what had happened to his hand? His long, elegant fingers were now thick and squat—as fat as sausages!

In a panic Darcy strained to see his left hand. His signet ring, worn by his father and grandfather, was gone! And was that a wart forming on the back of his hand? *A wart?*

There were brisk footfalls in the corridor and the door came quickly open. "Well, well," said a hearty voice—Mr. Jones'? Darcy turned his head to see.

"You're awake. Very good, yes."

Mr. Jones was one of those bluff country fellows—stocky, grey-headed, and cheerful. His eyes looked Darcy over with professional interest.

Darcy found his voice. "Good—morning," he rasped.

"Good afternoon," supplied Mr. Jones. "You've slept rather a long time, you know."

"Have I? How long?"

Mr. Jones held up two fingers, as if Darcy were a child. "Almost two days."

As long as that? Darcy drew a ragged breath. Who had seen to his needs? Surely not Elizabeth or her sisters!

"However, now you are out of danger and on the mend, Mr. Collins," said Mr. Jones. "Let's have a look at that arm, shall we?"

3 HIT OR MISS

When Elizabeth came into the bedchamber, Mr. Collins was awake, and Mr. Jones was holding his wrist. "Ah," she heard Mr. Jones say. "Yes, yes. Very good. Very nice."

He moved his hand to Mr. Collins' forehead and then bent to peer into his eyes. "Quite," he said.

Elizabeth thought she heard Mr. Collins say, "Quite what?" This sort of response was typical of her cousin, but the dry tone he used was not.

Mr. Jones went on with the examination. "So the wrist was not involved," he remarked. "A disastrous injury, the broken wrist. Cripples one for life." His fingers began probing Mr. Collins' left arm. Presently Elizabeth heard a gasp.

"I take it this hurts, yes?"

"Rather," said Mr. Collins, between shut teeth.

"Don't mind me," encouraged Mr. Jones. "Shout and carry on all you wish. Helps with pain, don't you know."

"I rather doubt that," said Mr. Collins.

Elizabeth studied her cousin. His face was set and pale, his eyes were narrowed. This hardened expression was something new. Mr. Collins, who sighed over every little thing and multiplied sentences into paragraphs, should be wailing with impunity. Why wasn't he?

Elizabeth leaned against the wall beside the door. Should she go out or should she remain? Curiosity took the upper hand and she stayed. Then too, hadn't Mr. Jones requested her presence?

But she must have made a noise, for Mr. Jones looked round. Over the top of his spectacles he twinkled at Elizabeth. "Don't mind Miss Elizabeth," he said cheerfully to his patient. "She's an old hand at bone setting. Eh, Miss Elizabeth? Ha-ha, that's rather good. A hand at bone setting!"

Elizabeth did not know how to respond. Mr. Collins was looking both vexed and embarrassed, and Mr. Jones' grin seemed out of place. She felt a stab of pity for Mr. Collins. "I am," she said.

Mr. Collins cast another look in her direction. "Happy thought indeed," he said bitingly. "Might we get on with it, Jones?"

DARCY BY ANY OTHER NAME

"Yes, yes, of course." Mr. Jones' fingers continued probing. "Collarbone looks fine." He pushed up the sleeve of the nightshirt, exposing Mr. Collins' bare arm.

It was a large expanse of flesh. Elizabeth turned her gaze away.

"The humerus is bruised, but intact," Mr. Jones observed. "It will be some time until the swelling and discoloration disappear." He continued prodding. The examination must have been very painful, for several times Elizabeth heard a quiet moan.

"I hear you are quite the hero, Mr. Collins," Mr. Jones said conversationally. "Apparently Mr. Darcy, as is staying up at Netherfield Park, has you to thank for his life. You took the brunt of his fall."

Mr. Collins grimaced and said, "Huzzah for Mr. Darcy."

"And what is more, by breaking his fall you kept him out of harm's way. That toppled keystone is rather massive."

"Keystone?" said Elizabeth. She quickly closed her lips. She had not meant to say anything.

Mr. Jones was not put off by her interruption. "Indeed, yes," he said. "Part of the Folly was knocked clean down. The arch between John the Baptist and Moses, they say." He paused his examination to say, "Ha-ha. There's a theological profundity for you, Mr. Collins. Betwixt the old covenant and the new."

"And what would old Lady Mustow think?" he went on. "She's the one as had the Folly built, you know, with biblical characters all round. No Grecian gods and goddesses for her! Can't think how it came to fall. The wind would not account for it."

"It was struck by lightning," said Mr. Collins. "Twice."

"Was it indeed?" Mr. Jones looked at Mr. Collins over his spectacles. "That's quite a feat. Not supposed to strike twice in the same place, lightning. Or so they say."

"So they say," repeated Mr. Collins. "I take it that Mr. Darcy has made a full recovery?"

Mr. Jones hesitated. "Early days for that," he chirped. "Now then, about the business at hand."

Mr. Collins lifted his head. "Mr. Darcy will recover?" he repeated.

"In time, perhaps. Shall we just have a look at that shoulder?"

Mr. Collins glared at Mr. Jones. "I am not accustomed," said he, in a tone that brooked no argument, "to having my questions brushed aside. What of Mr. Darcy?"

Mr. Jones looked uncomfortable. Elizabeth held her breath, waiting for his answer. What had happened to Mr. Darcy? And why was Mr. Collins so insistent?

"As of this morning," said Mr. Jones, "Mr. Darcy has not regained consciousness. This could be a good omen, a sign that his body is healing—like yours, Mr. Collins."

Mr. Collins spoke slowly. "Is he expected to live?"

"We have every hope." Mr. Jones was now examining the contents of his apothecary bag. "I was not aware that you were acquainted with Mr. Darcy."

"Ah, but I am." Mr. Collins' lips twisted into a wry smile. "Rather intimately, in point of fact."

Elizabeth's heart leaped into her mouth. What new disaster was this? Would her cousin begin babbling on about Mr. Darcy?

"What Mr. Collins means," she said hastily, "is that he serves as rector to Mr. Darcy's aunt in Hunsford. And naturally, he is concerned—for the family."

"Ah," said Mr. Jones. "A professional interest; I quite understand. If Mr. Darcy takes, shall we say, a fatal turn, you'll have of plenty of time."

"Time for what?" Mr. Collins wanted to know.

"Why, to compose your funeral sermon. Or perhaps Dr. Bentley will do the honors. Now then." Mr. Jones resumed his prodding. "Ah-ha," he crowed. "Yes, it becomes clear. A dislocated shoulder is what you have and not a broken bone, Mr. Collins."

"Please stop calling me that."

Mr. Jones looked surprised. "Eh, very well," he said. "With this sort of injury, Mr. Col—eh, a-hem! —a fall or a blow causes the top of the arm bone to pop out of the shoulder socket." Mr. Jones' fingers pressed a sensitive spot, and Mr. Collins gasped.

"The shoulder is incredibly mobile, but the joint is, unfortunately, prone to popping out of place."

Elizabeth winced. She did not like the way Mr. Jones said the word popping.

"I am familiar with the injury." Mr. Collins' tone was grim. "I fell from a horse as a boy. Our farrier put my shoulder back."

"Handy fellows, farriers," Mr. Jones remarked. "Then you are aware of what must happen next. The pain, while severe, is short-lived."

"I quite understand."

Mr. Jones was now rubbing his hands together. "Right-ho," he said. "Miss Elizabeth, this is where you come in. If you would kindly fetch a tumbler? Not a teacup, but a nice large glass. Yes, there's a good girl."

Elizabeth hesitated. From the corner of her eye she saw Mr. Jones bring a bottle from his apothecary bag. "Now then, we'll do something about that pain."

"With brandy?" Mr. Collins sounded skeptical.

"Oh, yes. We'll get you properly dosed."

"Dosed," repeated Mr. Collins.

"Three sheets to the wind, as the sailors say. Plucky breed, sailors."

Elizabeth went quickly out. She found Jane waiting in the corridor.

"Mr. Jones is asking for a glass," Elizabeth whispered. "And Jane, it is rather dreadful, for Mr. Jones must jest and tease. I almost feel sorry for Mr. Collins."

Jane went at once for the glass.

When Elizabeth returned to the bedchamber she found a situation. Mr. Collins had his chin up, with a mutinous expression in his eyes.

Mr. Jones held the bottle aloft. "Now then, Mr. Col— ah, my good fellow," he said. "Shall we have at it?"

"I say again, brandy will not be necessary."

"You may well say that now. However, once I begin—" Mr. Jones winked.

Mr. Collins spoke with cold dignity, his words clipped and precise. "It has been my experience that as a deadener of pain, alcohol is vastly over-rated."

Mr. Jones looked at him over his spectacles. "You'd prefer laudanum? Very well, I can accommodate that."

"No laudanum. And she," he paused to nod to Elizabeth, "must go out. Her services will not be needed."

Mr. Jones stood gazing at his patient. To Elizabeth's surprise, he crossed to where she stood and took the glass.

"Did you not hear what I said?" Mr. Collins demanded. "No brandy!"

Mr. Jones laughed uneasily. "This is not for you, my dear fellow," he chirped. "This is for *me*!"

Jane was still in the corridor when Elizabeth came out. "The most perplexing thing," Elizabeth confided. "Under the duress of honest suffering, Mr. Collins reveals an entirely new personality. I marvel that he is the same man."

Jane linked her arm through Elizabeth's and together they descended to the ground floor. "What do you mean?"

"He is reserved instead of prosy and—how shall I say it? Courageous, if you will. Mr. Collins!"

Jane looked amused. "No compliments? No tedious speeches?"

"Not a one. He ordered Mr. Jones about—not that he doesn't deserve it! —and told him, bold as you please, to get on with it."

"Mr. Collins?"

"The very same. And he refused the brandy, as well as the laudanum."

"Perhaps we have misjudged him?"

Elizabeth's steps slowed. "I do not see how that is possible, for his character was clear. And now it—isn't."

She went on to describe the examination. "What is more, this is not the first time Mr. Collins has dislocated his shoulder. He said he fell off a horse as a boy."

"Oh dear."

"But Jane," said Elizabeth, "did he not tell Father that he'd never learned to ride? He said so at dinner that first night, I know it."

"There must be some mistake," said Jane.

"There must be," echoed Elizabeth, but she continued to frown. "Can a man be so changed by a blow to the head? I think not. And yet—"

4 BAREFACED QUESTIONS

As soon as Elizabeth and Jane came in, Lydia slewed round. "Is the bone set? Did he squeal like a pig?"

"Lydia," said Mrs. Bennett with dignity, "I do not think that is a proper way to speak of your cousin."

"You know he *did*, Mama!" Lydia turned back to Elizabeth. "How was it? Deliciously gruesome?"

Elizabeth turned to close the door. "Mr. Collins is now awake. He has dislocated his shoulder. Mr. Jones is putting it back into place."

"Poor Mr. Collins," said Mrs. Bennet, with another look to Lydia. "Such a fine young man. And what a miserable time of it. Confined to his bed, with nothing but beef tea."

"I wonder when he will be up and about." This was from Mary.

"If we are lucky," chirped Lydia, "not until it is time to return to Hunsford." Her grin became impish. "So much for his plan to find a wife!"

"It is a fine plan, Lydia, and a noble one," said Mrs. Bennet. "The poor man is in no state to issue a proposal. Yet."

"I wonder if Mr. Collins honestly wishes to take a wife," said Jane. "Remember his letter to Papa? He wished to heal the breach, to make amends for the injustice of the—."

Kitty interrupted. "Of course he wishes to marry! He wants Lizzy!" She and Lydia dissolved into giggles.

Mrs. Bennet was unmoved by their mirth. "What better way to make amends?"

"So we must put up with him, oh lord, for weeks and weeks!"

"That is quite enough, Lydia. Mr. Collins," said Mrs. Bennet, "is welcome to remain as long as his recovery requires. I daresay he will not be fit to travel for a very long time."

Elizabeth wandered to the window and looked out. "Father ought to write to Lady Catherine," she said. "I wonder if he has."

"Can you imagine the letter?" said Lydia. "My Dear Lady Catherine, we are keeping your favorite rector, who is rather the worse for wear, having survived a crushing blow from Mr. Darcy's person." Lydia put up her chin. "You needn't look at me like that, Lizzy. Hill said that's what happened."

"A terrific blow it was, according to Hill," said Kitty. "At Netherfield they are wondering whether Mr. Darcy will survive."

"And," added Lydia, "they're laying odds ten-to-one against him, er, according to Hill."

"Of course Mr. Darcy shall recover," said Kitty, around more giggles, "as it was he who fell on Mr. Collins and not the other way round."

Elizabeth found a seat on the sofa beside Jane. "I daresay our cousin will not soon forget Mr. Darcy," she remarked. "He has made, shall we say, an indelible impression?"

Presently the door opened and Mrs. Hill came to say that Mr. Jones would like a word.

"Please do not get up, Mrs. Bennet," said he, coming in. Mrs. Bennet motioned for Jane to procure a glass of sherry.

Mr. Jones held up a hand. "No, I thank you," he said pleasantly. "Mr. Collins is resting and should sleep for most of the afternoon. His arm is sound, but he's had a nasty knock on the head. Now injuries to the head, they are a bit difficult. The patient will sleep quite a bit and will wake feeling confused and out of sorts."

Elizabeth listened intently. Mr. Collins had certainly been out of sorts!

"Upon rising, he will have a headache. He will also be easily fatigued and will have difficulty remembering people and places. These effects are common and will subside."

Jane turned to Elizabeth, a question in her eyes.

"He knew me, sure enough," Elizabeth whispered.

"He will also have difficulty concentrating," Mr. Jones went on, "will feel mentally foggy, be more emotional, and more irritable."

Mr. Jones paused to smile at Elizabeth. "Our patient has certainly been exhibiting the latter, no?" He turned back to Mrs. Bennet. "Keep him quiet; feed him as much beef tea as he will take. If he desires something more substantial tomorrow, that will be fine."

"Hill," said Mrs. Bennet, "is adept at making gruel and blancmange."

"Very good, very nice," said Mr. Jones. "Mind you, physical and mental exertion could bring a return of any of the symptoms I mentioned. I advise a slow return to duties."

"Will Mr. Collins be able to travel soon?" said Mrs. Bennet. "His parish is in Hunsford."

"That remains to be seen. I will call again tomorrow, if I may. And do not hesitate to send for me if his condition worsens." Smiling, Mr. Jones made his bow and went out.

There was a short silence. "Your father won't like paying his bill," said Mrs. Bennet, "but it cannot be helped. Now then, of what were we speaking before he came in? Ah, yes, Mr. Collins and marriage. A most agreeable subject!"

"Mama," protested Elizabeth.

"No, we were speaking of Mr. Darcy," said Kitty, "and whether or not he will live."

"Mr. Darcy," scoffed Lydia, smiling at her mother. "What care we for Mr. Darcy?"

"Not a whit," said Mrs. Bennet. "But all the same, Mr. Darcy is Mr. Bingley's particular friend." She looked at Jane. "You might take the opportunity to call on his sisters."

"But Mama," Jane protested, "surely the household is in disarray."

"Indeed it is. But you are an *excellent* listener, Jane, and in times of trouble, people *enjoy* speaking of their worries and complaints."

"Would not a note of sympathy be in better taste?" said Elizabeth.

"I daresay it would." Mrs. Bennet became occupied with thinking. "And yet," said she at last, "the situation ought to be used to advantage. Jane, this afternoon," she paused to glance at the clock on the mantelpiece, "no, tomorrow, you will attend morning prayer. Mr. Collins—and Mr. Darcy too—are in need of prayer."

Jane's face flushed. "Very well, Mama," she said.

"A wearing task, I daresay, but you will not mind," continued Mrs. Bennet. "It is the right and proper thing to do." Her lips curved into a smile. "And we shall hope that word will come round to Mr. Bingley that you have interceded on behalf of his poor friend."

Jane sighed but offered no protest.

"You will accompany her, Lizzy, to pray for Mr. Collins," Mrs. Bennet went on. She paused to gaze at each daughter in turn. "My girls," she announced, "piety is a most endearing virtue."

"Then perhaps, Mama," said Elizabeth, "you ought to join us."

"Oh, I am *quite* overcome with seeing to Mr. Collins' care, thank you. No, you girls will do very well without me. And Jane," she added, "wear the periwinkle gown."

And so on the following morning, Mrs. Bennet's plan was carried out, and Jane and Elizabeth went to service to pray. Offering supplications, even silently, on behalf of these two men put Elizabeth's Christian charity to the test.

As the weather was fine, they had opted to walk. "I suppose venturing out has been beneficial," said Elizabeth, coming out of the church into the autumn sunshine. She linked her arm with Jane's.

"The sooner we arrive home the better I shall like it," confided Jane. "Oh, Lizzy, how uncomfortable this is!"

"I do feel rather like that Pharisee," Elizabeth agreed, "praying before men in order to be noticed."

Jane sighed heavily. "The most endearing virtues in the eyes of God," she said, "are yet unseen by men."

"Not if Mama has any say about it."

"Dear Mama. This was not," said Jane, "one of her better ideas. I would rather have prayed in a closet!"

She indicated her gown. "And if I am mourning Mr. Darcy's injury (and truly, I am most sincerely sorry for him!), should I not be wearing black?"

"But periwinkle is so much more becoming!" Elizabeth said, smiling. "And so it is left for me to wear black. On behalf of two men for whom I could not care less."

"I am persuaded you do not mean that."

"Not entirely," admitted Elizabeth. "Like you, I am sorry for Mr. Darcy, for surely he is in pain. And the sooner Mr. Collins is restored to health, the better it will be for us."

"For you," said Jane. "But not, I think, for Mama."

Now it was Elizabeth's turn to sigh. "Dear Mama," she said.

The sound of horses and carriage wheels came from behind. Jane hid her face beneath the brim of her hat. "Let us hope," she said in a low voice, "that it is no one we know."

But the chaise slowed as it passed and then drew up. It was an elegant vehicle, Elizabeth noted. She took a swift glance at the occupants. "A man and a woman," she said, "and well-dressed at that.

Jane kept her eyes averted. "Lizzy," she whispered. "Why has it stopped?"

"Hallo and good morning!" called a familiar voice. "Miss Bennet and Miss Elizabeth! Where are you bound? May we take you up?"

Jane took a peek. "Mr. Bingley," she whispered. "And his sister."

"Mama knows best," quipped Elizabeth. She lifted a hand and called, "Good morning!"

"How mortifying," murmured Jane.

"Chin up," Elizabeth whispered. "Leave this to me. You needn't speak unless you wish."

Mr. Bingley had come out of the chaise and was now strolling toward them. "Out and about, I see," he said. "Doing a bit of shopp—" He broke off speaking and his steps slowed.

Elizabeth followed the direction of Mr. Bingley's gaze. Ah, yes. He'd noticed the prayer books they carried. And she noticed something else: Charles Bingley had a sweet smile. He was probably blushing just as much as Jane, but more than admiration shone in his eyes. Here was sincere gratitude.

"Have you been to prayer service?" he said softly.

Elizabeth glanced to her sister. Did she wish to answer?

"The accident," Jane faltered, her eyes gazing into his. "Our cousin. And your poor friend." She paused. "I am so very sorry."

Mr. Bingley took one of Jane's hands in both of his. "God bless you," he whispered.

"It is the least we can do," said Jane.

Meanwhile Caroline Bingley was left to wait. The window came down. "Charles!" she called.

Mr. Bingley dropped Jane's hands. "My sister," he said. "I should not—" He glanced back. "Shall we join her?" He and Jane turned together, and Elizabeth followed.

"Caroline has been having a difficult time," Mr. Bingley explained. "First with Darcy's injury and now with the Hursts." He lowered his voice. "Mr. Hurst is a singular fellow, repelled by sickness and suffering. The point is, he is easily cast down."

He smiled at Jane. "I know you are not so, Miss Bennet, and can bear any hardship. But the long and short of it is that Hurst and Louisa are for London."

Jane was all sympathy. "Miss Bingley must be so disappointed," she said. "I daresay she depends upon her sister more than you realize. Indeed, without my sisters I would be very lonely. That is—" she stopped, flustered. "I mean, not that I would be unhappy without them, but..."

This was Elizabeth's moment to rescue Jane, and she greeted Miss Bingley with particular friendliness. Caroline looked taken aback, and then motioned for her brother to come near. She whispered something in his ear.

When he turned to them, Elizabeth noticed that his face was pink with pleasure. "May I invite you ladies to join us," he said, "for an impromptu luncheon?"

"Please say you will come," urged Caroline. "The Hursts are packing up, and without Louisa I am simply desolated." Her expression sobered. "There is no question that we shall go with them," she added, "though Mr. Hurst was most insistent."

"Not for anything will we leave Darcy," said Mr. Bingley. He handed Jane up, and Caroline made room for her. Elizabeth took the seat opposite, with Mr. Bingley beside her.

"You will be encouraged to know," said Jane, "that Mr. Collins has been awake since yesterday afternoon."

Caroline's smile was polite. "Mr. Darcy," she said, "can sometimes be roused to swallow a bit of broth, but then he lapses into sleep. And I do believe," she added, "that Mr. Darcy's injuries are much more extensive than Mr. Collins'."

Soon the chaise passed through the gates of the Netherfield estate and along the sweep of gravel drive. "There," said Caroline, pointing to a traveling coach waiting in front of the mansion. "Do you see? They are leaving."

"How you will miss your sister," said Jane.

"Then again, autumn is not the season for London," Caroline said bracingly. "One might as well molder away on one's country estate as anywhere. Although I must confess, I shall miss the entertainments: the opera, the theater, and the private balls with select friends." Caroline looked at Jane with an appraising eye. "I take it you have been to London?"

"Oh, yes. My aunt and uncle live there. How much I enjoy the Vauxhill Gardens, especially on a summer night."

"Vauxhill Gardens," repeated Caroline Bingley. She did not sneer, but Elizabeth knew exactly what she thought of Vauxhill Gardens. And also of visiting the Metropolis during an unfashionable season!

Elizabeth kept her gaze fixed on Netherfield's wide lawns and trees. Charles Bingley seemed content with silence, and so she was free to listen.

"Do you know," Caroline went on, "I have spent an hour searching the shops for one similar to this?" She indicated the paisley-figured shawl that graced her shoulders. "The finest silk chiffon, so soft," she paused to stroke it. "Imported from India, of course. The edging," she added, "is worked in genuine gold. But alas, my time was quite wasted. I ought to have known that Meryton would have nothing like it."

Jane's praise for the shawl was sincere, however Elizabeth noticed that she wisely did not touch it.

"Louisa loves it even more than I, and I was so hoping to find one like it." Caroline lowered her voice. "Charles did not wish to go out, but the need, as you see, was urgent. And now I have no parting gift for Louisa."

"Perhaps," said Jane shyly, "you might consider giving her this one?"

"Oh no," said Caroline, and Elizabeth could hear as well as see the curl of her lip. "A gift," she explained, "must be new."

"But as between sisters?" Jane suggested gently. "Mrs. Hurst might value it all the more because it has been yours."

Caroline Bingley's brows went up. "I daresay she would not! In our family we do not give such presents. A gift must be not only appropriate, but also costly. A true mark of affection, and not something discarded by its former owner."

"Oh," whispered Jane.

Presently Charles Bingley spoke. "I say, that's odd. We are being followed."

Since she shared the rear-facing seat, Elizabeth was able to see a barouche enter through the gates.

Bingley continued to frown at it. "Caroline," he said, "are we expecting anyone?"

Miss Bingley's look was scornful. "Do you mean now? Of course not."

The Bingley's chaise came to a halt in front of the mansion. At once the main door opened and Louisa Hurst came out.

"Caroline, dearest!" Mrs. Hurst cried, extending her hands to her sister. "There you are at last. I am simply desolated. Mr. Hurst says we must leave at once!"

As if on cue, Mr. Hurst's head appeared in the open doorway. "Louisa," he bellowed. "Do you intend to take all of these blasted bandboxes? A fellow could trip and break his neck! Come sort them out!"

"Oh dear," said Mrs. Hurst. "Excuse me," and she hurried away.

Mr. Bingley assisted each of the women to descend, but instead of going into the house, they stood watching the barouche approach. When it came to a halt, one of its footman jumped down and let down the steps.

Mr. Bingley's pleasant greeting received a curt nod. "Is this Netherfield Park estate?" said the footman. "Residence of the Bingleys?"

"I am Charles Bingley, and this is my sister."

The footman opened the door and relayed this information to the occupant. He slewed round. "One Mr. Darcy is a guest?"

"That he is," said Bingley. "But how on earth did you—"

But the footman cut him off. "Lady Catherine de Bourgh of Rosings Park," he announced. "Sent here from Longbourn House at the Master's recommendation."

Elizabeth looked to Jane. "Can he mean Father?"

The passenger was a woman, richly dressed in black—a widow? Her face held a pinched expression.

"Is this right?" she inquired of the footman, as he assisted her to descend. "Dear Fitzwilliam is convalescing here?" She peered up at the mansion.

Charles Bingley stepped forward. "How do you do, ma'am?" he said, and made a bow.

"Never tell me that you are Mr. Bingley," she said. "Mr. Bennet informed me that Netherfield had been taken by a family named Bingley, but you are just a youngster."

Bingley hastened to present his sister. She swept a gracious curtsy. "My brother and Mr. Darcy," she said, "are the very best of friends."

"I do not believe that for a moment," said Lady Catherine. "If your brother were half the friend he claims, why did he not at once apprise Mr. Darcy's family of his injury?"

Lady Catherine turned to Mr. Bingley. "A slop-shod way you have of handling correspondence, young man."

Charles Bingley began to stammer. "Indeed, ma'am, the apothecary says it's early days yet."

"Early days? Is this not *just* like a man? And so I must come myself, a journey of many miles, at great expense and inconvenience, to see how matters stand. If not for Mr. Bennet, cousin of my rector, I would know nothing. *He* had the decency to write."

Lady Catherine paused to draw breath. "My dear nephew at death's door with no one the wiser!" She threw a dagger glare at Bingley, drew out a handkerchief, and blew her nose.

Elizabeth and Jane exchanged a look. Lady Catherine's handkerchief was edged with black. Clearly she was expecting the worst.

"Not at death's door, ma'am, surely," protested Mr. Bingley.

Lady Catherine emerged from the handkerchief. "And my poor, dear, sweet Anne," she continued, "who may never see him again in this world! Is her happiness to be blighted by catastrophe?"

Suddenly Lady Catherine rounded on her driver, who stood respectfully beside the footmen. "You," she said, "shall send for Sir Henry Fleming, my personal physician, and convey him to this place."

"But our apothecary, Mr. Jones, is quite competent," said Mr. Bingley.

Again Charles Bingley underwent scrutiny. "I know what passes for medical care in these countrified places, and I will not have it!"

"But—" said Charles Bingley.

Just then Mr. Hurst came stumbling round the corner of the house, the capes of his driving coat flapping. "Bingley," he bellowed. "Where's that case of burgundy you promised me?"

Mr. Bingley looked from his brother-in-law to Lady Catherine and back again. His pleasant smile slipped.

"When a fellow travels," Mr. Hurst shouted, "he needs sustenance!"

Except Mr. Hurst said shush-tenance and swayed on his feet.

Lady Catherine took in his flushed cheeks and red nose. Her lips compressed. "I beg your pardon, young man?" she said to Mr. Hurst.

She rounded on Charles Bingley. "That man," she said, pointing, "has been drinking, and it is barely noon. Exactly what sort of establishment *is* this?"

5 Rufty Tufty

Darcy was feeling somewhat better. His head still ached and his stomach did too, for there were limits to what bone broth and gruel could do. By this time he had discovered the name of his jailer. Not Mrs. Bennet, who came in only to flutter and flatter and scold, but the formidable Hill.

Mrs. Hill was stout and capable, though she often wore a harassed expression. And no wonder! Serving under a mawkish and emotional tyrant would drive anyone mad. (Indeed, Darcy had learned her name not through introduction, but from hearing it echo through the house.) But Hill was one to stand her ground, and she would put up with no nonsense from Mr. Collins.

Darcy, however, was wise in the ways of her kind. Not for nothing had he endured nannies and nurses and governesses! She put him in mind of Mrs. Reynolds, his housekeeper at Pemberley, a gracious woman with a rhino's hide and a lamb's heart.

Darcy also knew that if provoked, Hill would take action, for he was wholly in her power. If she guessed his intention to escape the house (for he was keen to examine the scene of the accident), she would probably take away his clothes!

So in his guise as Collins, Darcy was mindful to be meek and pleasant. He drank every drop of broth, was effusive in complimenting the cook, made cow eyes of submission, and endeavored to be cheerful.

Here Darcy made an important discovery. By allowing Collins' body to do what came naturally, his lips formed Collins' simpering smile and his voice climbed to Collins' tenor whine. It was painful to hear, but convincing.

Darcy's eyes studied Hill as she moved about the room. In order to escape he might have to climb out a window and slide down the drain pipe. Not that he hadn't done this before, but how would Collins' flabby body respond? He'd caught glimpses of Collins' thighs, each one plump and rounded like the body of a seal. Could he climb with such legs? Could he manage to ride?

DARCY BY ANY OTHER NAME

Darcy watched Hill stir the coals and add wood to the fire. How many stone was Collins? Did the Bennets have a horse that would bear his weight?

Presently Hill went out, and at once Darcy sat up, wincing a little at the way his head hurt. Steeling himself against pain, he swung his legs over the edge of the bed. Secretly he had practiced standing to gain strength and balance. Now it was time to venture farther.

Darcy took a sliding step in the direction of the wardrobe. He found that by holding on to the bedstead and then bracing himself against the nearby wall, he could reach the wardrobe door. Hanging inside were a black frock coat and a single pressed shirt. The shelves held smallclothes, stockings, and a cravat, clean and nicely folded. Darcy gathered these and made his way back to the bed.

With a weather eye on the unlocked door, he managed to dress himself. The effort left him weary and winded. He glanced at the clock. No wonder, it was almost time for the midday meal—more bone broth. Wonderful.

One of the things he'd noticed about Collins' body was how hungry he was. Continually he was craving food, especially sweets. This, Darcy decided, was something that would have to change. He would not be a slave to a voracious appetite.

Darcy draped the frock coat over the back of the chair and eased into a reclining position. His first step toward escape had been accomplished.

When he heard the latch of the door, he immediately drew the blankets to his chin.

Hill came in bringing Mr. Jones. "Say now," the apothecary called. "This is fine! You've got your color back, Mr. Collins."

Darcy had no idea what color he had been, for he'd purposely avoided the looking glass. It felt bad enough to be in Collins' body; he'd no desire to see it. But Hill was still in the room, so Darcy decided to smile. Of its own accord his face arranged itself into Mr. Collins' foolish grin.

"That's the spirit!" said Mr. Jones.

Hill went out and Mr. Jones began his examination. He expressed surprise that Darcy was dressed.

Darcy shot him a look. "In a household of females," he said, "I daresay you'd do the same. I'd like to dispense with the bedpan, if you don't mind."

"Certainly, certainly." Mr. Jones' grin became conspiratorial. "Caged among women. They will be ministering angels, eh?"

Angels was not the word Darcy had in mind. Mrs. Bennet and her two youngest daughters were harpies in disguise! Continually they were calling to one another or else laughing and talking with loud voices.

"Since I am able to walk," Darcy said, "I would like to venture out of this room."

"Cabin fever, eh? Very good, very nice. A sign that you are recovering. Have you the head-ache?"

Darcy winced. "Haven't I just?"

"And weakness? Difficulty concentrating? Difficulty remembering things?"

What did Jones mean by that, Darcy wondered.

The man patted Darcy's knee. "These are to be expected," he said soothingly. "Loss of memory and confusion often result from a knock on the head."

Perhaps loss of sanity, too? "I do remember what it is to eat," Darcy said. "If I could manage to gain the dining room and have a meal instead of broth, it would do wonders."

"It certainly would." Mr. Jones eyed Collins' gut. "You've much to keep up, haven't you, my boy? Very well, let's get your coat and shoes on. Down we go for a nice chat with the ladies."

Darcy hesitated. Would Elizabeth be there? "How do I look?" he said, in Collins' anxious squeak. Without thinking he ran his fingers through his hair.

"Ah yes, the hair wants a little work," agreed Mr. Jones. He opened the door and called for Mrs. Hill.

Darcy, who had submitted to the hands of a valet for years, found himself blushing. But what did it matter? It was only Hill, and he was not the master of Pemberley but the bothersome Mr. Collins. And if Elizabeth was there she would see him as such. And she would be, without a doubt, revolted.

The morning room was bright and pleasant, and fortunately the sunlight did not pain Darcy's eyes. Mrs. Bennet and her third daughter were there—Mary, the girl who had made the attempt to play and sing. Yes, Darcy remembered her. She was looking hard at him and smiling. He darted an anxious glance to the pianoforte. Would she attempt to sing today?

"Mr. Collins has the head-ache, as expected," announced Mr. Jones. "But he needs to be up and about. Being a young man, he is making a fine recovery." Mr. Jones turned to Darcy. "You are steady on your feet, very good."

Silently Darcy added the missing very nice. Mr. Jones did not stay, and Darcy sank into an upholstered chair by the fire. The clock on the mantelpiece told him it was well past noon—and he fervently hoped that the Bennets kept country hours for midday dinner.

"You find us quite alone," Mrs. Bennet told him. "Lydia and Kitty have ventured out to Meryton, and Elizabeth and Jane are at morning service."

"To pray for you, Mr. Collins," Mary supplied, "and for Mr. Darcy as well. I would have gone with them, for prayer is an important duty, but Mama wished me to remain." Again Mary smiled at him.

Darcy kept his features under tight rein. Not for anything would he allow Collins' lips to simper!

The door opened and Hill came in with letters, brought by messenger. The first was for Mrs. Bennet, and she pounced on it. "It is just as I predicted, Mary," she crowed. "What fine news! Elizabeth and Jane have been invited to share midday dinner at Netherfield! They will be brought home in Mr. Bingley's chaise."

Darcy stole a look at her. Mrs. Bennet was openly gloating, as if savoring a victory.

She caught his eye. "So you see, Mr. Collins," and she waggled her finger at him. "Our Jane is very much in the way of being engaged. You must set your sights on Lizzy instead."

This was not precisely unpleasant advice! Even so, Darcy squirmed in his chair. A cough in the corner caught his attention. Over the pages of her book, Mary Bennet was gazing at him with rapt attention. He quickly looked away.

The other letter was addressed to Collins, and Mrs. Bennet held it out to him as if it were a treat. Darcy could feel her curiosity.

He turned it over to break the seal and paused. He'd never noticed the state of Collins' hands. They were none too clean (although this might be due to the accident), but Collins had gnawed the nails down to stumps. Here was another habit that would change.

Darcy unfolded the page and glanced at the signature. His brows went up.

Mr. Collins (it began),
I understand from the local apothecary that you are a good deal less injured than my much-loved nephew,

Fitzwilliam Darcy. Therefore, I desire you to wait upon me at Netherfield this afternoon.

My nephew, the sole son of his late and honorable father, is in need of spiritual intercession, and you are uniquely equipped and providentially at hand to provide this. I will send whatever vehicle Mr. Bingley can spare, as I understand that Netherfield is some miles distant. It would be best to arrive after you have had your midday meal, so as not to be an inconvenience.

I shall expect you promptly at two o'clock.

Darcy read the letter through twice. What was his aunt doing at Netherfield Park? Giving Bingley a world of trouble, no doubt. To Netherfield he must certainly go. It seemed that events were deciding themselves.

He folded the letter and slipped it into a pocket. "Lady Catherine summons me to wait upon her at two o'clock today," he said. "She will send, ah, transportation." Knowing his aunt, it could well be a pony-cart!

Mrs. Bennet bounced up in her chair. "What effrontery! She came here earlier today, and Mr. Bennet was summoned—yes, summoned, by her footman, bold as you please! —to speak with her in her coach. Outside, as if he were a common lackey!"

"She is a very important lady, Mama," Mary protested, with an anxious eye on Mr. Collins.

"With no manners whatsoever!"

Darcy decided not to comment. His stomach rumbled, and he glanced at the clock. "Would it be possible," he ventured to ask (in Collins' timid voice), "if I might eat a meal before I go, ma'am?"

Mrs. Bennet turned on him, lips compressed and eyes snapping. "Oh, very well, Mr. Collins. I daresay Hill can scrape together something. Soup or bread or I don't know what."

Darcy, who had been fancying standing rib roast with Yorkshire pudding on the side, humbly expressed his thanks.

Lady Catherine had installed herself in the best sitting room at Netherfield. She sat at an elegant writing desk, frowning over her correspondence, and did not look up when Mr. Collins' name was announced. Darcy shifted from one foot to the other. As a dependent, he must wait for her to break the silence.

It was some minutes before she spoke. "That Dolson person will handle your pastoral duties in Hunsford," she announced, without preamble. "That is the name of your curate, is it not? Dolson?"

Darcy remained silent. He had no idea who Collins' curate was.

"Your duty," Lady Catherine went on, "is here at my nephew's bedside." She glanced at him. "You look well enough."

Well enough? Was she jesting? His face was bruised and scratched, and his left arm was supported in a sling supplied by Hill. So much for an employer's kind consideration!

"Is Mr. Darcy awake?" he said and held his breath.

"From time to time he rouses to swallow beef tea," she said, "but almost at once he resumes sleeping. When he shall gain full consciousness we do not know. I have sent," she added, "for Sir Henry Fleming—not his hasty son; I have no use for medical degrees! —to attend him. My nephew deserves the best of care."

How could Darcy argue with this? "You are kindness itself, milady."

Lady Catherine dabbed at her eyes with her handkerchief. "I loathe the sickroom," she stated, "perhaps because I am never ill. I daresay if I had ever learnt to nurse someone—"

Darcy set his teeth, for he knew where this remark was heading. The audacity of his aunt, to give voice to such an outrageous thought! Was she truly so self-absorbed?

"—I would have been," she continued, "a great proficient."

"Oh, I don't know about that, ma'am," Darcy said, before he could stop himself. "It occurs to me that you have had many opportunities to nurse and encourage your daughter."

Darcy snapped his lips shut. Curse his unruly tongue! He knew that he ought to follow up with one of Collins'

DARCY BY ANY OTHER NAME

babbling compliments, but he could think of nothing to say.

Of their own accord, his lips came to his rescue and formed Collins' simpering smile. "So you see," he heard himself squeak out, "you are proficient at nursing, milady, er, without realizing it."

Lady Catherine stood blinking, trying to determine if this was a compliment.

Darcy hid a grin and added (in his best Collins-like manner), "Such fundamental skills must surely descend from your ancient, noble, and exalted family lineage."

Ha, this was rather fun!

Before Darcy could say more, the butler came in and announced one Dr. Bentley, who was apparently the local rector. He had come at Lady Catherine's request, which was fine with Darcy. If his aunt wished to call for a bigger gun (so to speak), she ought to have a rector who was not a sham!

A small elderly man came in and made a precise and old-fashioned bow. "My dear Lady Catherine," he said, wheezing a little, "I came as soon as your note arrived."

Dr. Bentley turned aside to cough, and then, smiling, added, "Mr. Darcy has been in our prayers, dear lady. How right, how wise you are to come to him."

This, Darcy knew, was how a rector ought to behave, and he drew aside to allow them private consultation. They spoke together for some minutes, their conversation punctuated by Dr. Bentley's rasping cough.

"Mr. Collins," Lady Catherine announced, "we have a Situation."

Darcy sensed trouble was coming. Was there to be another edict from on high?

"Dear Dr. Bentley has contracted a cough," she said, "as you have no doubt noticed."

Of course he had. And how had this kindly old man suddenly become so dear?

"Most irritating, coughs," she went on. "I find them to be both disturbing and noxious, especially during a sermon. They quite destroy the fluidity and lyric beauty of the prose."

Lady Catherine paused, looking at Darcy as one would examine a horse. "You will therefore give Sunday's sermon, Mr. Collins."

Darcy's mouth fell open. Oh he would, would he? She might at least have asked! But no, as always his aunt must be high-handed. What did he know about preaching a sermon? And today was—why, this was already Friday!

Head-ache forgotten, Darcy found himself babbling incoherently like Collins would. No need for pretense here!

Lady Catherine appeared satisfied. "Shall we go up to my nephew now?" She led the way out of the sitting room and made for the wide staircase. Darcy followed, still talking. Indeed he could not help it!

"But my books," he protested. "My, er—" He broke off speaking. What did rectors use to prepare sermons?

Darcy thought fast. "My commentaries! They're in Hunsford." Surely this would get him out of it.

Lady Catherine did not pause in her ascent. "Dr. Bentley, I am sure, will open his library for your use."

Darcy followed after, breathing heavily. With the aid of the banister rail, he hauled himself up the stairs. When they reached the first level, Darcy stole a look at Dr. Bentley. The man smiled kindly at him and coughed.

Blast that cough!

"But Holy Communion," said Darcy. "I should feel most uncomfortable offering that! Ah, in a parish not my own." A sermon was bad enough, but to perform a Sacrament while not being ordained?

At last they reached the level where the bedchambers were located. "I shall be most willing to officiate at Communion," Dr. Bentley assured him. He paused to cough into his handkerchief.

"And your assignment," he continued, whispering, "is not a difficult one. This week's text is from the Old Testament, with several related texts in the New." Dr. Bentley drew a volume from his coat pocket and opened it. "Isaiah 53:6."

Darcy squinted to read the tiny print. Burn it, did Collins need spectacles? *All of us like sheep have gone astray,* he read. *Each of us has turned to his own way.*

Darcy had to work to keep from gaping. He was to preach on the topic of sheep? He loathed sheep! They were not only ugly but stupid! Not all that different from Mr. Collins, now that he thought on it!

Mr. Collins, in whose body he now resided. Darcy drew a long breath. He ought to be more respectful, for the alternative was—

No, he would not think about the alternative. He must live, and Collins must live. There must be some way out of this dilemma, there must!

"I shall be willing to give the sermon, sir," he told Dr. Bentley. He hoped, most devoutly, for an unseasonable down-pouring of sleet, or hail, or a plague of locusts—anything to keep people away from church!

"I look forward to hearing you," Dr. Bentley replied, and he meant it. Darcy had the grace to feel ashamed.

Lady Catherine put her hand on the door latch. "Shall we go in?" she said.

"I shouldn't wish to disturb." Dr. Bentley turned aside to cough.

"Of course you must stay out here. Mr. Collins will do all that is necessary. He knows some beautiful prayers and will recite them at dear Fitzwilliam's bedside."

She paused to smile at both men. "*The efficacious prayer of a righteous man availeth much,*" she recited.

Darcy's eyes narrowed. Somehow that quotation did not seem right. Why was that?

"And while Mr. Collins is not as righteous as he ought to be," Lady Catherine went on, "he is certainly efficacious." Before she opened the door, she hunted up a clean handkerchief. "Poor, dear Fitzwilliam," she said with a tiny sob. "The hope of his family line."

Recalling his uncle's second son, Fitz, and various distant, but hopeful, cousins, Darcy was tempted to laugh. Instead he kept his head down and worked to come up with an appropriate prayer. It would certainly be fervent!

But nothing could have prepared him for the sickroom. The air was slightly sour, and a fire roared on the grate. The bed dominated the room, with massive pillars and heavy curtains. As they entered, a young woman rose to her feet. Darcy assumed she was the nurse.

"He's sleeping yet," said she. "We've been able to get down a bit of broth from time to time, but he remains as you see."

Darcy walked over to the bed. The sight of his own body made his skin crawl. The mouth was slightly open; a trickle of saliva ran down the cheek. And the breathing was uncommonly labored, or so it seemed to Darcy. He reflected now that he had no experience with sickrooms. Even when his dear mother was ill, he took pains to see her only for brief moments.

Not unlike his Aunt Catherine!

His gaze slid to where she stood, grim and resolute. There would be no quick escape this time. "You may now pray, Mr. Collins," she commanded. She dabbed at her eyes with her handkerchief.

This was the very definition of awkward. As Collins, how was he to address the Almighty? With flattery and officiousness, certainly. But he was not merely giving a speech as Collins, he was speaking to Deity. About providing badly needed healing, and not only healing of the body. He, Fitzwilliam Darcy, needed restoration to become once again himself.

Darcy knelt beside the bed. Cautiously he took hold of Mr. Darcy's hand, his own hand, the left one. His fingers closed over the familiar signet right, worn also by his father and grandfather. "Almighty God, Creator of heaven and earth," he intoned, in what he considered a proper pulpit voice. He heard Lady Catherine sigh. "We humbly and sincerely beseech Thee—"

It was a good beginning for Collins, Darcy thought. He was shocked by the next thought that flashed across his mind:

More flattery, more obeisance. Is this what people think I enjoy?

Darcy was stunned to silence. His mind was playing tricks on him, it must be! For these were his words! He'd thought them in the garden in reference to Collins. Why had they surfaced so vividly? It was if a voice had spoken.

Darcy drew a long breath and began again, this time without flattery. "Father God," he said simply. "Please heal Fitzwilliam Darcy, both in body and in spirit. And," he added, "make any changes You feel are needful to set everything right."

His request was anything but eloquent, but it was heartfelt.

Lady Catherine did not share his view, and when they were outside in the corridor she told him so. "What do you mean, heal him in spirit? There is nothing, absolutely nothing, wrong with Mr. Darcy's spirit!" And she said a good deal more, not only about how to address Deity, but also about the impertinence of using her nephew's Christian name.

Darcy listened with head unbowed, another text flashing in his memory. *What I have written, I have written.* Pontius Pilate had said that, hadn't he? How many texts did he know without realizing it? It must have something to do with wearing the clerical garb, he decided. But it gave him the perfect reply to Lady Catherine.

"What I have prayed, I have prayed," Darcy said quietly. "And now if you will excuse me, ma'am, I have a sermon to prepare."

He did not wait to be dismissed but turned on his heel and made for the staircase. He could not miss his aunt's unhappy huff.

It would be a slow, weary walk back to Longbourn.

6 WHIRLIGIG

Darcy descended the staircase as quickly as his legs would allow. Even so, he was plagued with the unfamiliar sensation of self-doubt. Had he said the wrong thing? If Lady Catherine called him back, should he obey? Darcy had never had an employer, but he suspected that he was obliged to offer more than lip-service. He was also acquainted with his aunt's imperious temper. Preferment or no, would she find a way to dismiss him? Collins would thank him for nothing if returned to his body as an out-of-work rector!

When he returns, Darcy reminded himself. Not if but when.

He paused on the landing, debating. Should he turn back and apologize? Collins would undoubtedly take this course. On the other hand, Collins was a mouse and not a man! Why should anyone apologize for the contents of a prayer?

Then too, Collins had had a knock to his head. The symptoms Jones mentioned were formidable and also convenient! He could plead insanity, a pleasant thought. Darcy stood on the landing, biting his lips. Without thinking, he thrust his free hand into a pocket. Lydia Bennet's impertinent question rose in his memory: What has Collins got in his pockets? Here was the chance to find out. A pebble, a piece of thread, and two slim coins.

There on his palm, a meager hoard: tuppence. Yes, Collins had every reason to cower before his aunt.

Darcy resumed his descent. As he neared the ground level, voices, bright and friendly, drifted up from one of the rooms. After the gloom of the sickroom, this refreshing sound pulled Darcy like a magnet. In a flash, the events of the past three days were forgotten.

Sure enough, there were Bingley's cheerful tenor and Caroline's drawl. And there were other voices, female voices, pleasing instead of shrill and demanding. Darcy moved toward the open room door and looked in. The unknown voices belonged to Jane and Elizabeth Bennet.

Without thinking, Darcy reached to straighten his neck cloth, his lips curving into a smile. He moved to a tall pier glass to check the set of his coat. Reflected there was not his trim form, but a bulky black-clad figure, rather like a beetle. Collins!

DARCY BY ANY OTHER NAME

Startled, Darcy turned away. Collins' body was bad enough, but to catch a glimpse of the face? Thank God he'd stopped himself in time! And then he heard a dry cough. Darcy turned to see a footman studying him with a hostile eye.

Darcy lifted his chin and returned the stare. The nerve of the fellow! He was tempted to brazen it out and join the others, but Mrs. Nicholls came sailing into the vestibule. She stopped and stood gazing at him. There was no spark of recognition in her eyes.

"Are you looking for Dr. Bentley?" she said. Her accusation was clear. Why would an unknown rector be wandering the rooms at Netherfield? Not for any honest purpose!

Darcy felt a flush rise to his cheeks. He'd been a guest at Netherfield for nearly a month, yet now he was a stranger to the housekeeper. And to all his friends!

Blast that Collins! Was his body to be a blight forever?

"Ah, no, ah, ma'am," Darcy stammered. "The exit, if you please?"

Wordlessly Mrs. Nicholls pointed to the main door.

Darcy turned and went scuttling out. Gone was his usual confident stride, for he was no longer master of anything. He was nothing more than a second-rate rector in a worn black coat.

Outside the house Darcy found Bingley's chaise at the ready, no doubt to transport the Bennets to Longbourn. He walked past it, and the driver did not bother to look at him.

Darcy skirted the house, retracing his steps on the night of the ball. Here were bare trees and the ornamental gardens. Here Collins had followed him, calling his name in that whining voice—a voice that was now his own.

And if he did not recover? Would Darcy remain as Collins forever? Or would Collins, in a twist of divine comeuppance, return to his own body, leaving Darcy to face eternity?

At last he reached the Folly. As Jones had described, instead of Grecian columns, statues supported the small circular building. According to Jones, these were biblical characters. Darcy studied them. Yes, here was bearded Moses with his tablets, now tilted at a precarious angle. Beside him was John the Baptist, though how Darcy was supposed to recognize him he did not know. By the fur-like garment he wore? And the bearded wild-man look? John stood erect beside the fallen arch.

Darcy circled the Folly. On the other side of Moses he expected to see the usual Adam and Eve. Instead he found a young man with his eyes turned to heaven. Beside him, a glowering man, also young, with his hand lifted threateningly. Darcy studied this pair for some time. Ah yes, here were Cain and Abel, untouched by the lightning.

On the other side of the Folly, completing the circle, were two more: a hearty, bearded fellow, well-muscled but in distress, and a man whose head and shoulders were shrouded with a long cloak. His neatly trimmed beard and a furtive expression were clues, and so was the small bag of coins he carried. Peter, the fisherman, and—Judas! The earnest, but weak disciple, and the betrayer. These too were undamaged.

Cain and Abel. Judas and Peter. Moses and John. What was he to make of it? No, there was nothing here, save for tumbled stones. The fallen keystone, which had supported the arch between Moses and John, had an inscription. Darcy knelt to see. The lettering was worn by the elements, but legible: Mt VI.

Matthew 6? This was the Sermon on the Mount, wasn't it? With all those verses about the poor and the meek and the humble being blessed?

The upshot was clear. He, Fitzwilliam Darcy, was not blessed but cursed. For he was not meek but proud.

Burn it, and so was Collins!

Yes, so was Collins. He was just as pleased with his position in life, both at Rosings and as the future master of Longbourn. For all Collins' cringing ways, didn't he strut about like a cock on a dunghill?

Had pride something to do with the lightning? He and Collins were out here that night, each sneering at the other, each boasting in his own way, each desiring the affection of the same woman. And then the unthinkable happened.

Was this a judgment from heaven? Or a curse from hell? And how would they change back? Should he haul Collins out here and wait for another thunderstorm? How likely was that to happen?

And if this were the judgment of God—an important point to consider—the cure could not be worked out as in magic. There would have to be a heart change.

Darcy set his teeth. He had no desire to make a heart change, not now or ever! And he suspected that Collins wouldn't like it either. Two different men, with different lives and different expectations. It was all so confusing.

So intent was Darcy with his thoughts that he did not hear the voices until they were upon him.

"I do wish you will consider staying to supper," Bingley was saying.

Jane Bennet's gentle voice answered, "I fear not—"

Caroline interrupted. "Nonsense, Charles! Not with poor Mr. Darcy so ill and Lady Catherine at table."

"That's exactly the reason, Caroline. We need someone to lighten the—." Bingley broke off speaking. "Why, Mr. Collins!" Darcy heard him say. "What are you doing out here?"

Darcy raised his eyes and gazed into his friend's face. "I came to see the Folly," he said simply.

"As have we." Elizabeth Bennet came forward. "Did you walk all this way, Mr. Collins?"

Darcy took heart at the concern in her voice. "Lady Catherine had me brought here," he said, smiling a little. "She wished me to pray for her nephew."

"That woman!" cried Caroline. She turned to her brother. "Charles, do you know she had the audacity to accuse us of hiring Netherfield? Simply because I could not give names to those odious portraits?"

Bingley spread his hands. "It's the truth, Caroline." He turned to Darcy. "How are you holding up, old fellow? I must say, you look done-in."

"My head does hurt a little," Darcy admitted.

"And so must your arm," said Jane. "Poor Mr. Collins. You should be in bed. What you need is rest and quiet."

"I fear this evening will be anything but quiet," said Elizabeth. "Mother has invited several of the officers to join us for supper." She turned to Bingley. "Which is why we cannot accept your very kind invitation, Mr. Bingley. Perhaps another time?"

"Officers?" Darcy repeated.

"Colonel Forster and Captain Carter and Mr. Denny. And," said Jane, smiling at her sister in a way Darcy did not like, "Mr. Wickham."

Wickham. In the fuss of becoming Collins he had forgotten about Wickham. The man would not go quietly when his plot had been discovered. No, he must appear at Longbourn.

Wickham's presence decided it. Even if Darcy had to cross Hades itself, he must have a place at that dinner table.

7 Such Amiable Qualities

But being present at dinner was not as easy as it appeared. Darcy must deal with Hill, who made him sit on the bed as she removed both his coat and neck cloth.

"Menfolk," she muttered. "You've no sense, none at all. But it's not my place to say, is it?" She crossed to the wardrobe and removed Mr. Collins' clean nightshirt. "Put this on, and without a lot of talk, if you please."

Darcy could tell she was in no mood for being crossed. He took the garment.

"Remove the shoes and stockings," Hill went on, as if speaking to a little boy. "You had no business going downstairs today, and even less jaunting off to Netherfield."

Darcy was about to blame Jones and his aunt, but the look on Hill's face silenced him. This woman was paid to listen to Mrs. Bennet's excuses, not his.

"And now," said she, putting her hands on her hips, "your head hurts like thunder, doesn't it?"

"Yes, ma'am," said Darcy meekly. He fumbled with the buttons on his waistcoat.

"Here, now," said Hill, and she made a move to assist him.

Darcy pulled away. "I can do this," he grumbled. But his fingers felt thick and awkward.

Hill pushed his hands aside and helped him. She unfastened the top button of his shirt, too. Removing the night shirt from his resistless grasp, she said, "You might as well lie down as you are. It won't make much difference if you sleep in your shirt and breeches."

Darcy was happy to comply. She was right; he was worn to the bone. He lay back against the pillows and closed his eyes.

"There now, Mr. Collins." Hill's voice was soothing instead of scolding. "A bit of sleep will do you good."

He could not sleep! Darcy raised his head to eye the wardrobe. "My evening clothes," he said. "For dinner. Where are they?"

"You will have your dinner brought on a tray, young man, and no mistake." Clucking and fussing, Hill drew the blankets up to Darcy's chin. "You are not well enough to come down tonight. The idea!"

"But," protested Darcy. "Wickham."

DARCY BY ANY OTHER NAME

There was a pause. "What did you say?" demanded Hill.

Darcy lay back against the pillows. "That devil Wickham," he said. "He's coming to dinner tonight."

"Aye, he is. What's it to you?" Her tone accused Darcy of jealousy.

Darcy ignored this. "I must be at table," he said. "Miss Elizabeth does not realize..."

He paused to steal a look at Hill. Her hands were on her hips again. "Miss Elizabeth does not realize what?"

"That Wickham is a scoundrel. She has no way of knowing it."

Hill sat down on the end of the bed, and Darcy heard her give a long sigh.

"Something's not right," she said at last. "I feel it in my bones. The Mistress, bless her, has no notion of what's what, and the Master indulges the girls. Again and again these officers come to the house. They're harmless for the most part, amusing the girls with high spirits and dancing. But that Mr. Wickham? He's not their sort." Frowning, Hill lapsed into silence.

"He speaks well enough," she admitted at last, "but he's not one of them."

Darcy worked his good hand free of the blanket. "I must be at table," he told her.

But Hill did not appear to hear. "Calculating!" she burst out. "That's what he is! A smooth smile and smooth speeches. And up to no good, if you ask me."

"Very much up to no good," said Darcy.

"He's too agreeable! But he watches them, oh he does. And the Bennets know nothing—nothing! —of the ways of conniving men. The Mistress believes any tale told her, and that Mr. Wickham has been telling her plenty. When a man has something to hide," she added, "he talks on and on."

Hill turned a speculative gaze on Darcy. "Perhaps there's more to you than meets the eye, Mr. Collins. But you are not," she added, "up to sitting at table tonight."

Darcy hated to admit that Hill was right, and yet what could he do? He tipped his head to one side, rather like his late father's favorite spaniel. "What do you say to after-dinner coffee, Mrs. Hill?" he offered, smiling appealingly. "In the drawing room? You could put me on the sofa before the others come in."

He paused, studying her expression. "By the fire with a lap blanket," he added. "And with a mug of hot milk."

Mr. Collins was not handsome, but Darcy discovered that he could be charming. Mrs. Hill rose to her feet. "Hot milk!" she scoffed. "As if I do not have enough to do."

But she did not refuse, Darcy noted. And she took with her his spare shirt, frock coat, and breeches to press. When the door closed behind her, Darcy allowed himself to smile. He had made his first ally.

By dinnertime, Darcy was feeling better, and he'd managed to sleep for several hours. Even so, the ordeal of being William Collins was a nuisance. The man might be a guest at Longbourn, but he was the very last to be attended to. Darcy found this new pecking order irksome. There was no hot water sent up, without assistance he had to struggle into his evening clothes (such as they were), and so awkward was he in dressing that he knocked over the night table. Then he noticed that one of his cuff links was missing.

"Botheration!" Darcy muttered, and lowered his bulk to look under the bed.

The match to the lost link was no great loss, being made of tin, and wasn't such parsimony typical of Collins? At Pemberley—no, in his rooms at Netherfield—Darcy had several sets of links, both in silver and in gold, along with a valet to see to his needs. Darcy stifled a sigh and went looking for Hill.

Hill's solution was to sew together two common shell buttons. These held the cuff in place, and Hill was unconcerned that the links did not match. "If a blind man could see," she told him, "he would not notice."

What a blind man would notice, Darcy thought, was that wart on the back of his left hand. It seemed even larger today. How did one remove a wart?

Darcy's dinner tray was brought up almost as an afterthought, and the meal was served all at once instead of in courses. The cover was removed by a kitchen maid, not Hill, and Darcy found himself confronting lukewarm soup and a cold leg of chicken. And what were the pale green globules on the side? Ah, yes. Overcooked Brussels sprouts swimming in butter. In vain he looked for a wine glass. Apparently Hill did not approve of wine for invalids.

She came in later with the coffee pot. "We're serving the dessert now," she said.

Darcy felt his stomach rumble. He was suddenly very interested in dessert.

From her apron pocket Hill produced a cup, and she filled it with coffee. "We've just time to get your hair trussed up and put you in the drawing room before the ladies come in," she said. "Drink the coffee. You could use a bit of vigor."

Whereas earlier Darcy had been treated like a boy, he now felt like an old man. When it was time to descend, Hill offered the support of her arm, and Darcy took it.

And so he waited, seated on the sofa like one of Georgiana's stuffed dolls. No, he amended, squirming to find a more comfortable position, not a doll. What little girl would want a doll whose body resembled a walrus?

Voices drifted in from the dining room and, as at Netherfield that afternoon, Darcy was struck with the isolation of his position. No one knew or cared that he had come.

And then Darcy heard a laugh, Wickham's laugh, light and carefree. The fingers of Darcy's good hand, fat though they were, gripped the arm of the sofa in sudden anger. That man was the devil incarnate, completely and thoroughly without shame! Not seven months had passed since Darcy had foiled Wickham's plan to elope with his sister. It was bad enough to encounter him on the streets of Meryton, but now he must witness the man in action.

Of all the times to be trapped in Collins' bumbling body, this was the worst!

Again Wickham laughed, and the young women laughed with him. Bile rose in Darcy's throat. Wickham, who was everything that was charming, was up to his old tricks.

Darcy heard the sound of chairs being pushed back, accompanied by more happy talk. And what was this? The gentlemen and the ladies were coming together into the drawing room. Apparently Mr. Bennet had no taste for port and cigars.

Darcy thought quickly. On a small table beside the sofa were a number of books and periodicals. Elizabeth Bennet had hidden behind a book at Netherfield, hadn't she, during those evenings while her sister was ill? And from behind the pages she had watched them. Yes, she had watched them closely.

William Collins, Darcy decided, would do the same.

On second thought, a periodical was larger and offered better cover. Darcy chose one at random and opened it.

And none too soon, for Mrs. Bennet came sailing into the drawing room on Colonel Forster's arm. "Why, Mr. Collins," she said, seeing him. "How courageous of you to come down tonight, and so soon after your unfortunate accident."

Out of habit, Darcy rose to his feet, provoking a squeal of protest from Mrs. Bennet. "Good gracious, Mr. Collins, sit down! What nonsense!"

Darcy obeyed and retreated behind his periodical. It seemed that he and Mr. Bennet were the only gentlemen not wearing red coats. Card tables were brought out, and the party began dividing into foursomes.

"Will you not join our table, Mr. Collins?" Elizabeth politely indicated an empty seat, which happened to be very near the sofa.

When Darcy declined, several smiled. No one regretted losing Collins as a partner.

And yet the memory of card playing made Darcy wince. In a similar situation, Caroline Bingley had been pointedly ungracious. 'Miss Eliza Bennet despises cards. She is a great reader and has no pleasure in anything else.'

Over the pages of the periodical, Darcy studied Elizabeth. Would she make a similar remark about his decision? He thought not.

Her partner at whist was Wickham, who sported a bright new uniform, beautifully tailored. The women were not alone in their admiration of it. Darcy caught Wickham casting glances at the pier glass.

Darcy's observations did not escape Lydia Bennet. "Poor Mr. Collins," she crowed. "The red of the army is *much* more becoming than the black of the clergy. Why did you not join the army?"

How would Collins answer this? "I hadn't the aptitude for it," while true, sounded both cowardly and boorish, and Darcy was in no mood to be either.

Fortunately, Lydia did not expect a reply. "Mr. Wickham's red coat looks ever so fine!" she went on, smiling at him. "Don't you think so, Mr. Collins?"

"It sits well across the shoulders," Darcy admitted, before he could stop himself.

And then he realized that all eyes were on him. He must say something else but, please God, not something stupid! "A London tailor?" he squeaked, allowing Collins' lips to form an inane smile. "Cork Street?" And then, because he could not resist, Darcy added, "Or, perhaps, Savile Street?"

Wickham gave a shout of laughter. "Oh, very good!" He turned to Elizabeth. "Your cousin is surprisingly astute. To say truth, Mr. Darcy is fitted out by the very same tailor." He gave another glance to the looking glass.

"Is he indeed?" said Elizabeth. "But you should not make use of the man who has so cruelly wronged you."

Smiling, he spread his hands. "It worked like a charm, I assure you," he said. "No danger there! The slightest mention of the Darcy name—and also that I was old Mr. Darcy's godson—brought splendid results! As you see."

Elizabeth answered Wickham's ingenious smile with a look of reproach. "I cannot believe you mean that."

Wickham became confiding. "In truth, dear lady, I was forced—through circumstances quite outside my control! —to be resourceful. How else could I have my coat made up so quickly? And, might I add, so well?"

Colonel Forster called from the adjacent table, "Wickham outshines us all. That gold braid is especially fine, and I daresay set you back plenty."

"Not at all practical for engaging the enemy, gold," Denny quipped. "Unless your goal is to blind them!"

Laughter followed, with calls for sunny weather, but Darcy did not join in. If Wickham had used the Darcy name, he had surely mentioned Pemberley's steward—who would, no doubt, be receiving the tailoring bill. Such tactics were nothing new for George Wickham.

Darcy watched as he simpered over his cards, laughing at nothing and everything. To see him flirting so openly with Elizabeth made Darcy's blood boil.

It occurred to him that he'd not observed Wickham, *in situ* with the ladies for years. Oh, the man was as handsome as ever and the women admired him, but there was a new, almost reptilian hardness present. The boyish charm Wickham had used to such advantage at Cambridge was not wearing well.

Wickham leaned across the table to tap Elizabeth's wrist. "Yours is the lowest draw," he teased. "You are first dealer."

DARCY BY ANY OTHER NAME

She cast him a laughing look, cut the deck, and passed it to Mr. Denny to shuffle. Soon the cards were in play.

"Speaking of Mr. Darcy," said Wickham, sorting his hand, "does anyone know how he is faring?"

Lydia, who was Denny's partner, spoke up. "Ask Mr. Collins. He called at Netherfield today." She dimpled. "By special order of Lady Catherine de Bourgh."

"Ah, my dear Lady Fault-finder," cried Wickham. "Still alive and kicking, eh?"

Darcy needed no prompting to purse up his lips. "Her ladyship is very well, thank you," he said primly.

"Worried sick about Mr. Darcy, apparently," Lydia supplied. "She came all this way and was very cross about it." She leaned in. "She called here and put Mama into a rage."

Wickham laughed, and the others with him. "Why am I not surprised? Darcy's her nephew," he explained, "as well as her favorite relation. Her darling choice as husband for," he paused to make a face, "her daughter, the wall-eyed Anne."

"Mr. Wickham," protested Elizabeth, laughing. "The poor girl!"

Wickham cast down a card. "There's nothing poor about Anne de Bourgh, Miss Elizabeth. She comes with a wagon-load of ready cash, a mammoth estate, and a sour disposition. I have not seen her for years."

"Then perhaps she has changed."

"I doubt it," said Wickham. "She and Darcy are perfect for one another."

Mr. Denny was in high spirits. "I say, he's not married to her yet! Present me to the maiden! Might as well put the red coat to use, eh?"

"Not a chance," countered Wickham. "Your family's not noble enough, for one thing. And for another, Miss de Bourgh rarely leaves the country."

"So my chance to meet an heiress is practically nil?" Denny grinned and played his card. "Doesn't it figure"?

"You are not to run off and get married, Mr. Denny." Lydia gave his arm a friendly pat. "We need you here to dance with us!"

"A most excellent point, Miss Lydia," he said. "As the saying goes, good friends are better than pocket money."

Wickham glanced in Darcy's direction. "Say, Mr. Collins," he said, very off-hand, "were there other guests at Netherfield? In addition to Lady Catherine?"

Elizabeth played her card. "Should there be?"

"I'm only wondering whether Miss Darcy will be joining her aunt."

"Mr. Darcy's sister?" said Elizabeth. "Has the family been summoned?"

Denny's merry face instantly sobered. "They say he has not improved, poor fellow," he said. "Under the circumstances, I expect they would gather round, yes."

"Aha," crowed Wickham. "Now there's an heiress for you, Denny! And if the brother's out cold, who's to object?"

"But one can't court a girl while her brother's dying," Denny protested. His teasing smile reappeared. "Even if she is ugly," he pointed out, "she'll be in no mood for a flight to Gretna."

"Ah, but Miss Darcy is not ugly. In fact," said Wickham, "I know a little secret about her." He paused, a smile playing on his lips. "Would you like to hear it?"

Darcy lowered his magazine.

Wickham leaned in. "Very few people know this, and I daresay it's a family secret, but—" He looked at each of his listeners in turn. "In truth, Miss Darcy is my namesake."

Darcy gasped aloud. He couldn't help it.

Wickham did not notice. "As a boy," he went on, smiling broadly, "I was Little Georgie, and old Mr. Darcy loved me like a son. And so," he paused to place a sentimental hand on his breast, "when his daughter was born—many years later, this was—he named her Georgiana."

The others at the table burst out laughing. "What will you say next?" cried Denny. "That dear old Prinny was named after you?"

More laughter. Wickham graciously inclined his head. "But of course, old fellow, of course!"

Darcy was fuming. This old taunt, bandied about during their student days at Cambridge, had lost none of its sting. Georgiana was the only near relation Darcy had, and he guarded her with every ounce of his being. And here was Wickham, who had set out to force her into marriage and defraud her of her fortune, strutting and crowing.

It took every bit of willpower to remain seated. Slowly Darcy raised the periodical, his thoughts racing.

At Ramsgate he'd been mindful only of Georgiana's honor, of her reputation and wounded feelings. Instead of enacting revenge against Wickham, he'd quietly removed her and had sent him a scathing letter. What an ill-considered, shortsighted course of action! Obviously words had had no effect on Wickham, he had simply scuttled away.

He ought to have shot the man.

Darcy's eyes narrowed. Yes, that is what he should have done.

And now that he was Collins, perhaps he could! Darcy felt his lips curl into a smile.

Ideas came surging forward, all of them delightful. An unfortunate hunting accident, nicely staged, yes. And Georgiana need know nothing about it, why should she? Better yet, the Darcy name would not be implicated in any way. As for Collins, who doubtless could not shoot any better than he could throw a rock, why, who would believe it? Collins had no motive for murder!

Darcy glanced again at Wickham as he simpered over his cards, darting coy glances at Elizabeth. Was this the reason he'd been put into Collins' body? To enact revenge? A righteous act to rid the earth of a lying menace? It was a pleasant thought.

The memory of the ruined Folly rose in Darcy's mind. Moses, toppled, John the Baptist with his hand outstretched. And on the other side, the statues of Cain and Abel.

Cain and Abel, brothers. Men who were so very different in spirit, with widely divergent destinies. He and George Wickham were raised almost as brothers, in that they'd played together on the estate. Not precisely Cain and Abel, but—

Blast it all, what was he thinking? He, who prided himself on honor and honesty, was now planning to murder a man in cold blood! What was it about being in Collins' body? On every hand it seemed to lend itself to dishonesty and deception!

Or had dishonesty been present within Fitzwilliam Darcy all along?

So occupied was Darcy with this new thought that he did not notice the presence of a seatmate. He glanced up to discover a young woman beside him on the sofa. She looked to be about his age. What was her name?

She leaned in to better see the cover of his periodical. "*Bell's Court and Fashionable Magazine. Addressed Particularly to the Ladies,*" she read aloud, smiling. "Such fascinating reading, Mr. Collins. Are you enjoying it?"

La Belle Assemblée? He'd been reading *La Belle Assemblée?*

Darcy felt a blush rise to his cheeks, and he thought quickly. "Not in my usual line," he admitted. "In fact, nothing female is in my line."

"And now you are surrounded by us. Poor Mr. Collins. Are you a cat among pigeons? Or," she added, "are you rather a pigeon among cats?"

Did Collins have sisters? Given the shabby state of his clothing, probably not. Darcy decided to risk it. "We have precious few girls in my family," he improvised.

"I see." Her smile was kind "So this is the perfect opportunity to investigate feminine reading material."

Though not beautiful, she was most understanding. It seemed she would not make sport of him before the others. They'd been introduced, he knew it. If only he could recall her name!

"If I might make a suggestion?" She took the magazine from him and turned it right-side up. "Elizabeth dislikes being observed so closely."

"I..." he began, and stopped. Had he been so obvious?

"Perhaps we might move to another location?" She indicated a pair of chairs on the other side of the room.

A gust of Wickham's laughter sealed Darcy's choice, and he cast the magazine aside. "That," he said, "is an excellent idea. Conversation is more to my taste, and I have much to learn about Meryton village and its inhabitants. I expect that you," he added, "are an expert."

He rose to his feet and offered his arm. Sudden memory brought a wave of relief. "Lead the way," he said, "my dear Miss Lucas."

8 What I Suffer

The long case clock on the landing struck four. Wincing, Darcy turned over in the bed. His knee ached and so did his shoulder—and his shin and his wrist and his ribs. And for some reason the lump on his forehead was destined to collide with the headboard repeatedly.

To add insult to his injuries, the bedchamber was freezing. Darcy was accustomed to the cold, as was every country gentleman, but this was intolerable. The fire had likely burned to ash, and he was in no mood to get up to remedy it. If there was firewood available, which he knew there was not. Mrs. Bennet might talk a good game, but she was a stingy, tight-fisted hostess. For instance, he could certainly do with another blanket. But to Mrs. Bennet's grasping little mind, guests were a nuisance, or perhaps it was Mr. Collins who was the nuisance. If he froze in his bed and the next day went flouncing off to an inn, so much the better.

Darcy was sorely tempted, until he remembered the state of Collins' purse. Beggars could not be choosers (as the saying went), and William Collins was certainly a beggar. Therefore until Darcy was restored to his proper identity, he must remain as a guest at Longbourn.

Unless, of course, he happened to freeze to death in the night, a happy thought.

What little sleep Darcy snatched was punctuated with memories from the evening before: Miss Lucas, speaking to him with motherly patience. Elizabeth Bennet, her alluring eyes sparkling as she smiled behind her playing cards. Her mother, as noisy as ever, talking to anyone who would listen. And George Wickham, with curled lip and braying laugh, delighting the ladies with his sallies.

Wickham. What was he supposed to do about Wickham?

The man's joining the militia and coming to Meryton had been pure chance, this Darcy knew. But Wickham's pointed interest in the Bennet family was not by chance. Why had he sought out the Bennets again and again? Oh, the company of the daughters was a draw, and Wickham was never one to forgo the society of young women or the offer of a free meal. But hope for financial gain—always Wickham's object—was markedly absent.

For there was simply no money to be had; Mrs. Bennet had made that abundantly clear. In the privacy of the family circle, it was a favorite theme. And there was another like it, though Darcy had pretended not to hear. That he, William Collins, would one day drive the family from their home.

Fortunately for everyone, Mr. Bennet seemed an unusually healthy specimen. Besides, by the time he passed on, Darcy would no longer be trapped in Collins' body. There was a solution, a way to switch back, and he would find it. He had to find it.

The clock struck again, and Darcy made another attempt to find a comfortable position. Naturally, he failed to do so and was left with the cold and his thoughts.

Darcy's eventual decision to get up and dress brought little relief, for Collins' clothes were as thin as they were shabby. As to choice, there was nothing to decide. Other than two white shirts, everything Collins owned was black: black waistcoat, black knee-breeches, black stockings, and black shoes with black laces. Trust Collins to ape a spindle-legged black beetle!

In the bureau Darcy unearthed a wool muffler (also black), wrapped it around his neck, and went hunting for warmer gloves. Small consolation to know that at Netherfield, his physical self would be in much greater comfort!

Darcy crossed the room and drew aside the window curtain. Even if he could see Netherfield (which he knew he could not), the view would be obstructed by hoar frost on the panes. It seemed symbolic somehow: *Through a glass darkly.* Shakespeare, wasn't it? Or was this from the Bible?

And how was he faring at Netherfield? Had his body, with Collins inside, regained consciousness? And if so, what was the man saying or doing?

This situation had all the makings of disaster.

Darcy paced the length of the room, thinking. The night of Bingley's curst assembly—and then the two or three days he had slept away. So this must be Saturday morning. And tomorrow—

Darcy came to a sudden halt. If this was Saturday, tomorrow was Sunday. And on Sunday, confound it, he must give that sermon! There would be no getting out of it, not if he knew his Aunt Catherine.

Darcy resumed his pacing. The sermon would have to be endured. He was not a complete novice, he had given addresses at Cambridge, although not very comfortably. Ah, but here was a thought. As Collins, no one would expect him to be comfortable in his delivery, or brilliant, or even passible. He could probably mumble the entire time!

This might not be so bad.

Ah, but Collins would not mumble. No, the man would be a model of oratorical elocution. Darcy rubbed his hands together to warm them. What he needed was a place to prepare. There would be no quiet in any of the common rooms—no wonder Mr. Bennet kept to his bookroom—so the cold of the bedchamber must be endured.

Darcy lit another candle and went hunting through the bureau. He found Collins' Bible and notebook, and sat down on the bed to work.

And here he paused, arrested by the contents of the notebook. Poor, foolish Collins. His penmanship was uneven, and his spelling choices were laughable. It was unfair, Darcy knew, to judge a man by his jottings, but he could not help himself. Here was a treasure-trove of insight into the workings of Collins' mind. Fascinated, Darcy continued turning pages.

The man had compiled lists on any number of things, each carefully titled: Sermon Topics. Impressive Turns of Phrase. Qualities for a Goodly Wife (no doubt dictated by Lady Catherine). There was also a page titled Qualities Possessed by My Noble Patroness.

This Darcy read with particular interest: Beneficent. Generous. Insightful. Worthy. Noble. Gracious. Unselfish. Forgiving. Merciful.

These were suited not to his opinionated aunt, but to the Almighty! Darcy could make a list of his own in reference to Lady Catherine, oh yes.

On the other hand, what must it be like to have a patroness like Lady Catherine to please?

Burn it, there was no wondering about it. At present he was Collins, and if he could not find a way back to his own body, Collins he would remain.

Darcy pushed this disquieting thought aside. He must make it easy for Collins to resume his identity. Therefore the sermon must be preached in Collins' own style. Now then, what was that text Dr. Bentley had mentioned? Something in Isaiah? Yes, about sheep.

Handel's melody came surging forward: *All we like sheep have gone astray.* Here was an excellent beginning! What else? Psalm 23 and also that text about Jesus the Good Shepherd. And the hireling shepherd who deserted the sheep when danger came.

And then there were the characteristics of sheep themselves. Darcy discovered that he was smiling. Collins the bumbling rector might not know much about sheep, but Darcy the resident landowner did.

The summons from Lady Catherine arrived just as Darcy was finishing the breakfast Hill had brought in.

"Came from Netherfield it did," she said. "And if you are expected, Mr. Collins, to tramp up there in all this cold, why, I have nothing to say except that the woman is plain inhuman."

Darcy looked from the note to Hill's sour face. "I am, after all, a clergyman," he said. "Duty is duty."

"And is it your duty, Mr. Collins, to die of exposure?"

"I'm afraid my aunt—er, patroness, will not take no for an answer." He added, a little wistfully, "Her ladyship did not happen to send a vehicle?"

"That she did not. The poor man who came was near to freezing when he arrived. And so shall you be if you walk all that way, Mr. Collins. You must ask the master for the carriage."

But this Darcy would not do. "The walk will do me good," he said. Hill looked doubtful.

He said the same thing to Mrs. Bennet later, as he fastened the buttons of Collins' overcoat. Fortunately Collins' clothes were no longer so tight, enabling him to wear both sets of breeches and two of Collins' waistcoats. He would have worn two sets of gloves, but Collins' fingers were too fat.

Mrs. Bennet stepped aside as James the footman opened the door for him. "What a pity that you do not ride, Mr. Collins," she said.

And before he had completed the first mile, Darcy found himself in hearty agreement. There was no snow, but his nose and cheeks were stiff with cold, and there was no longer any feeling in his toes. Darcy soldiered on, silently cursing both the perverseness of his aunt and the thinness of Collins' shoes.

Lady Catherine was waiting for him in the green salon, abusing Bingley's generosity by maintaining a roaring fire. Darcy stood before it, hating himself for trembling with cold.

And there was more. Lady Catherine extended her hand to him, palm up. Surely he was not expected to kiss her hand!

"Well?" she demanded. "You have brought it?"

"Brought what?" he shot back. "Er, milady."

The amendment did not appease her. "Your sermon for tomorrow, of course."

Darcy felt his jaw tense, and he willed himself to remain calm. Nothing would be gained by arguing. On the other hand, he was not about to let her order him about. "For what reason?" he inquired.

She gave an impatient sigh. Was this a commentary on his intellect? "I always look over your sermons, Mr. Collins, as well you know. Just because we are in a different parish, do not think you are exempt."

Darcy looked his answer.

Lady Catherine bridled up. "Now see here," she said. "We have been over this before, and you know my position. As I am known to be the sole source of your living—"

Darcy could not let this pass and interrupted. "I should say, ma'am, that God himself occupies that role."

Lady Catherine cast her gaze to the ceiling. She looked so much like Lydia Bennet rolling her eyes that Darcy almost laughed. Some of his amusement must have shown on his face, for his aunt gave him a black look.

"In theory, yes," she snapped. "But in practice it is I who pay out the money. And if you make a misstep, it is I who stand to be embarrassed. Therefore, I reserve the right to read your sermons and offer helpful hints."

Was she serious? Here, Darcy realized, was the reason for Collins' pre-written compliments. In moments like this, when any normal man would be struck speechless, Collins was obliged to reply.

But he was not Collins, was he?

Darcy soon found his voice. "I wonder why I troubled to earn a degree, ma'am," he said. "Since you wish to rewrite my sermons."

"Not rewrite them," she corrected. "I act as your safeguard. And in light of your recent injury," Lady Catherine paused to gather several pages from the desk, "I have taken the judicious step of preparing a draft for you to follow."

In other words, she had written every word of the sermon he would preach. With effort Darcy swallowed his temper and took the papers.

Lady Catherine had more to say. "One must, after all, encourage one's parishioners into proper lines of thought."

"Such as keeping to one's station in life?" Darcy retorted. "With all respect and duty to work? Including," he added, "the timely payment of one's rent?"

Sarcasm was lost on Lady Catherine. "Why, yes," she said. "What a clever young man you are, Mr. Collins." She smiled at him. "Yes, at times you can be very clever."

Darcy folded the sheets and put them in his pocket. "I will see Mr. Darcy now, milady," he said.

She looked startled. "I beg your pardon?"

"To pray for him, pursuant to your request. It is the least I can do. I am, after all, a clergyman." Darcy rocked back on his heels, satisfied. This was just the sort of thing Collins would say.

She opened her mouth to speak and then closed it. At last she said, "Very well," but she was not happy.

Darcy did his best to hide his smile, but apparently his control of Collins' face was not yet perfect. Lady Catherine's expression became unusually sour.

The sickroom was much as before, but this time there was no hanging back. Darcy walked directly to the bed and took Collins' hand in both his own. "Hello, William," he said softly.

Again he was struck with the curious sensation of gazing into his own face. Dark circles underlined the closed eyes, the expression was drawn and gaunt. He had not been shaved, Darcy noted. Given the sharpness of the blade, this was probably just as well.

Lady Catherine came rustling forward. "Fitzwilliam," she called.

Darcy looked up. "Softly, milady, if you please."

Naturally, this did not please Lady Catherine. "I know my way about a sickroom, Mr. Collins. One must speak distinctly in order to make oneself heard."

She would also scare poor Collins half to death! "How are you, William?" Darcy murmured.

At the mention of his name, the lids fluttered. Slowly the eyes came open.

"Fitzwilliam!" Lady Catherine cried. "Dear Fitzwilliam, I am come to take you home! All shall be well!"

Darcy saw the lips move, as if to form words. The face took on a peevish, Collins-like expression, and yet there was honest distress as well.

"William, lad," said Darcy gently, and he pressed the hand.

"Fitz-william," corrected Lady Catherine. "His name is Fitzwilliam, Mr. Collins. And you will kindly refer to him as Mr. Darcy."

Darcy closed his eyes and counted. He must not allow his temper free reign!

Presently he said, with marked patience, "He is not himself, milady, surely you see that. In such cases, it is wise to treat the sufferer as a child." His gaze returned to Collins. "A confused and bewildered child."

For Collins' eyes were open and he was studying Darcy's face, that is to say, his own face.

"You," he rasped. "You! But—!"

"Calm yourself, William," said Darcy, with quiet authority. "You were injured when you fell. In time, all will come right."

Collins drew a shuddering breath.

"You ought to sleep now," said Darcy. "Sleep and rest. All will be well."

The eyelids closed; Collins let out a whimper.

So did Lady Catherine, and she wrung her hands. "He does not know me! His own beloved aunt!"

Again Darcy kept irritation in check. "I wonder at him knowing anyone at all, milady," he said mildly.

She began to pace about the room. "This is dreadful, dreadful! Has he lost the use of his rational mind?"

"Of course not. Only consider," said Darcy, "that the poor fellow is not in his usual bedchamber here. No wonder he is confused. And I daresay his head hurts like fire. Mine did when I came to myself."

Lady Catherine swung round. "Your sufferings are of no interest to me, Mr. Collins."

At the mention of his name, Collins stirred.

"Furthermore," continued Lady Catherine, "although you are ignorant of the ways of the gentry, it is most unmannerly to refer to such a personal matter in my presence."

Darcy returned his attention to Collins. If this was how she spoke to the man, no wonder he cringed! "Perhaps," he said slowly, "I ought to bear him company for a bit." He looked to the woman seated in the corner.

What he wanted was a chance to speak to Collins privately. "I am not unfamiliar with the sickroom," Darcy said smoothly—as Collins the clergyman, this was not precisely a lie— "and I daresay both you and his nurse would like a respite."

Lady Catherine considered this. Then she nodded and went out of the room.

DARCY BY ANY OTHER NAME

The nurse gave Darcy a grateful look. "Be sure to ring, sir, if I am needed." She indicated the bell pull. "I shall not be away long."

Darcy answered with a smile. "It makes no difference." A sudden thought occurred. "And what is your name?"

"Rosie, sir."

"God bless you, Rosie," Darcy said. This was the sort of thing a clergyman was supposed to say, but Darcy meant it. Caring for an invalid and having to put up with his aunt's officiousness were wearing tasks for anyone.

And so Darcy kept vigil, and he was mindful to recite several prayers. Presently his attention began to wander, and the door of the wardrobe caught his eye. Darcy had never cared much about clothing—a respectable appearance, with garments of the best workmanship, had been enough to satisfy. But now—

He glanced at Collins. The man was sleeping deeply; there would be no opportunity for conversation today.

Ah, but his fingers itched to open the door of that wardrobe, to gain access to what his valet had brought for his months in the country. After all, they were his clothes, purchased with his money. What would it matter if he wore them?

This appealing thought grew and took shape. The waistcoats were useless, thanks to Collins' oversized stomach, but the cravats? And the stockings? The gloves? The beautiful hats?

Then Darcy's plan suffered a check. His garments would not be in this room, but in his original bedchamber. And although he paid little attention to what he wore, others did. Caroline Bingley was always complimenting this or that, much to his annoyance. And wouldn't dear Miss Bingley be shocked to see one of his silk cravats around the lowly Reverend Collins' neck?

It would be almost worth it to hear her screech. But the cravat would likely not fit Collins' stocky neck, nor could Darcy manage the intricate knots his valet delighted in making.

So he would have to purchase what he needed in Meryton. That meant money.

This he could remedy. With a look to the closed door, Darcy rose to his feet. The wardrobe door creaked when he opened it, but Collins slept on. The shelves were empty, but hanging there was the coat he'd worn to the assembly. At last, a miracle! For in the pockets were coins, at the ready in case he needed to tip the footmen. Best of all, no one else knew the coins were there.

Ha, look at that. Among the shillings, a half-crown! No, two! And several sovereigns. No wonder the servants were always so attentive. He'd never given it much thought, but he knew now. Mr. Darcy was a very generous tipper.

Darcy pocketed the coins along with the nagging voice of his conscience. It wasn't as if he were a thief. He was Darcy, he just happened to be in the wrong body.

"But not for long," Darcy said aloud, with another look to Collins.

Presently he resumed his seat to wait for Rosie's return. And sometime later, as he left the sickroom, Darcy pressed one of the half-crowns into her hand.

Here was something else he was learning. It was the poor, not the rich, who knew how to be generous.

9 Petticoat Wag

After Rosie returned, Darcy did not depart for Longbourn but went searching for a quiet nook. He found a chair under a window at the end of the upstairs corridor, the perfect spot to study his aunt's sermon. And what a sermon it was.

 Lady Catherine began well enough, with the Light shining into the darkness (for this was the first Sunday of Advent), and she transitioned to the shepherds watching over lambkins on the verdant fields of Bethlehem. But the mention of shepherds launched her into the true purpose of her sermon: moralizing. Here were all her favorite themes: contentment with one's occupation (no matter how lowly), duty to one's superiors, and working hard to earn salvation in the afterlife.

Darcy was no theologian, but he knew that salvation was by grace through faith. And wasn't she a fine one to talk? How would Aunt Catherine measure up against the Almighty's holy standard?

And the sermon fairly dripped condescension. As a listener, Darcy would be angered and offended to hear someone like Collins prose on in this superior way. There was no encouragement here, only pious talk and patronizing. Was this what Collins' congregation had to endure?

Not this Sunday! Darcy was still Darcy, and there was no way on earth he would preach this sermon.

He rose to his feet, stuffed the pages into a pocket, and made for the stairs. Not that he looked forward to the tramp back to Longbourn, but if the weather worsened he would be stranded here, and even Mrs. Bennet was preferable to his aunt.

Nor did he wish to encounter Charles Bingley. His friend would never guess the truth of his situation, but it was awkward to act the part of Collins in his presence.

And of course, whom should Darcy meet as he reached the main floor but Bingley coming up. Darcy felt a stab of isolation, and just as quickly cast it aside. He must behave as Collins, the odious rector. Indeed, the man's inane grin was now forming on his lips. Darcy quelled it, removed his ugly hat, and made a polite bow.

Bingley came to a halt, what else could he do? "Hallo, Collins," he said. The pause became awkward.

DARCY BY ANY OTHER NAME

Darcy understood what his friend was thinking. *What the devil is that bounder Collins doing here? How can I get rid of him?*

But Bingley was a kindly soul; he would be polite to any guest, no matter how unwelcome. Smiling a little, he said, "I daresay you've been up to see poor, er—" Flustered, Bingley broke off speaking and coughed.

"Good morning, sir," Darcy murmured. "I have been to see Mr. Darcy, yes."

"I-I've never been one for the sickroom," Bingley confessed. "And to see poor Darcy like that."

Fortunately, Bingley did not require a response.

"But Jones says Darcy's improving," he continued. "Don't you agree?"

Darcy's answer was guardedly optimistic, and he was rewarded with a wave of disjointed talk.

"His color is better, at least I think it is. A very good sign, I must say. The girl attending him says so too, and so does Caroline."

There was more in this line, and Darcy did his best to listen. But it was difficult to keep his face from mirroring his thoughts. Phrases like "struck down" and "looking as weak as a fish" and "a shadow of his former self" did not go down well.

Bingley kept talking, and Darcy realized with a start that he'd been invited for luncheon. Darcy was touched. Who else but Charles Bingley would invite Collins to share a meal? Darcy certainly would not!

Collins-like, Darcy stammered his acceptance, and soon he was following Bingley through the rooms of the house as he searched for Caroline. Wouldn't she be pleased at the news? Darcy steeled himself for a snub.

"My sister is desolated by Darcy's injury, but she isn't much for nursing," Bingley said over his shoulder. "No experience, for one thing. We Bingleys are a healthy lot."

"Your hardy Northern forebears," said Darcy, "likely had a hand in that." And then he gave himself a mental kick, for Collins would know nothing of Bingley's family.

Charles did not notice the slip. "And that aunt of Darcy's—what a tartar!" He opened the drawing room door and glanced inside. The room was empty. "Can't seem to keep her from twitting him. A rum business, that, for she won't be stopped." Bingley shut the door and moved on.

Darcy chose his words carefully. "Lady Catherine," he said, "is a very determined woman."

"Darcy's described her, oh, in roundabout terms. Not often a fellow can pry information out of Darcy. But he did mention that his aunt wants to marry him off to her daughter." Bingley gave him a look. "Any possibility of that?"

Darcy did not hesitate. "None whatsoever."

Now why was Bingley looking amused? "I daresay Darcy feels the same," he added.

After a look in one of the smaller parlors, Bingley was off again, leaving Darcy struggling to keep up with his long strides. "I believe there's a nice fire here," said Bingley, opening a door. He motioned Darcy inside. "I'll just have a look round for my sister."

The Netherfield library was large and comfortably furnished, with windows overlooking the park. Darcy crossed to the mantelpiece and, as was his habit, stood frowning into the flames. His negligent stance was not as easily accomplished, for Collins was not only wider but less dexterous.

It was bad enough to be fat, but to be clumsy and fat?

And stupid? Ah, but was Collins as unintelligent as he appeared? Darcy thought over what he had observed at Bingley's ball. Yes, he decided. Most unfortunately, Collins was thoroughly stupid.

The library had two doors; the one on the far side now came open. "Charles, you didn't," he heard. It was Caroline Bingley, and if she meant to keep her voice low, she failed. This was no surprise to Darcy. Neither Miss Bingley nor her sister knew how to whisper.

Bingley murmured something in reply; whatever it was did not please her. "As if we have not had enough of provincial society—"she began.

"Not provincial," Bingley protested.

"And now," Caroline continued, as if he had not spoken, "you must thrust this—this person on me. Honestly, Charles, what *will* you do next?"

"Should I let the fellow starve? He has been very good to Darcy, calling every day."

Miss Bingley gave an unhappy huff. "I daresay I shall yawn myself to death."

"Would you rather hear Lady Catherine gabble on? I thought Mr. Collins would be an improvement."

"It is most unfair, Charles! *You* needn't sit at the table looking at him."

"Caro, do understand."

Darcy could hear the pout in her voice. "It isn't as if he's anyone important. How I am to converse with him I do not know."

"Fine," Darcy heard Bingley say. "We'll go up to the billiard room until luncheon is ready."

Miss Bingley gave an audible sigh. "I suppose I must now greet the creature."

Darcy heard her footfalls trip across the parquet floor until she reached the carpet. He did not turn to look at her.

"My brother tells me that you are to join us for luncheon, Mr. Collins," she said. "What a pleasant surprise."

From beneath his brows Darcy gave her a quelling look.

He heard her gasp; her hand crept to her throat. "Why, my gracious," she said in an altered tone. "Oh, my gracious. For a moment, Mr. Collins, standing as you are, I could have sworn that you were—"

Darcy raised an eyebrow, but did not smile.

"But no, that is silly," she went on unsteadily. "How could you be anyone but Mr. Collins?"

"How could I indeed," he said drily.

"I fear it will be some time until luncheon is served." She gave a brittle laugh. "We do not keep country hours among ourselves, Mr. Collins. And why should we? As soon as Mr. Darcy is able to travel, we shall return to London."

Thus Miss Bingley made her recovery. Bumbling Collins, her disdainful gaze said. What care I for you?

Darcy had seen this expression in Elizabeth Bennet's eyes. But then Darcy remembered Collins' behavior at ball; perhaps Elizabeth had reason. But what had Collins ever done to Miss Bingley?

No, her contempt was solely because Collins was beneath her. She could claw higher on the social dung hill by putting someone like Collins beneath her feet.

Conversation lagged. Darcy was of no mind to break the silence.

At last Bingley came to the rescue. "Do you play billiards, Mr. Collins?" he chirped.

William Collins was probably as ignorant about billiards as he was about everything else. It would never do to show skill, or even aptitude. While the lamps were lit and a second footman ironed the green baize table, Darcy selected his cue stick. He made an awkward business of it, first gaping at the rack like a yokel and then taking down one stick after another. He asked a greenhorn's questions, too—about the cue ball, the spot, the red ball, and the rules by which they would play. Bingley showed remarkable restraint, answering each of his questions with kindness. At last Darcy became ashamed of himself.

Collins' hands were not as large as Darcy's, so he chose a stick with a smaller shaft. And he made sure to hit Bingley's ball during the lag, giving his friend the advantage. Darcy hesitated and chewed on his lower lip; he moved around the table and sighed like an old woman.

But once the game was in play, long years of habit and competitive spirit took precedence. Without thought, Darcy assumed the correct striking stance; his follow through was straight and relaxed and therefore all wrong. He felt Bingley's eyes on him as he moved round the table. Blast!

And so before he took the next shot, Darcy chalked up with vigor, twisting the chalk on top of the cue stick like a rustic. He then studied the position of the balls from multiple angles, leaning over the table and waggling his hind end to and fro.

He heard Bingley choke back laughter, disguised as a cough.

When Darcy finally took his shot, he struck the ball with an abrupt hit so that it bounced. A foul! Fortunately his stick did not damage Bingley's baize-covered table.

DARCY BY ANY OTHER NAME

Charles took his shot and then set aside his cue stick. He said, with studied nonchalance, "Bye the bye, how is Miss Bennet?"

Darcy's stick went clattering to the floor. So the wind was still in this quarter, was it? "Miss Bennet?" he repeated, with Collins' goggling stare.

"Yes, Miss Jane Bennet. I trust there has been no relapse of her sickness?"

Darcy's eyes narrowed. Hadn't Charles seen Jane at the ball? On the other hand, perhaps as Collins he could learn the extent of Bingley's infatuation. "Her sickness?" he repeated.

The story of Jane's stay at Netherfield was related, with Jane as the central emphasis. Her sister Elizabeth, who had so captured Darcy's attention, was not mentioned by name. Indeed, to hear Bingley's version, Elizabeth had been as a passing shadow.

"And how does Miss Bennet spend her time?" Bingley went on. "Does she sew or paint? Or play the pianoforte?"

How should Darcy answer? He was not about to encourage Bingley's interest in Jane!

Bingley was smiling, his cheeks were flushed. "You cannot tell me that she does not sing. She has, I am sure, the voice of an angel."

And the devil of a harpy for a mother!

"She, ah, helps her mother with the management of the house," said Darcy. "And she oversees her sisters."

"Charming!" cried Bingley.

Darcy knelt to retrieve his cue stick from the floor. He did not call keeping Lydia from pulling Kitty's bonnet to bits—and intervening in the resulting cat fight—charming. Mrs. Bennet had taken Lydia's side! What a household! What a family!

While Bingley was blissfully gazing out the window—no doubt daydreaming of Jane—Darcy made sure to take a solid swing shot.

By the time luncheon was served, Darcy was exhausted. A look out the windows brought more bad news: it had begun to snow.

And of course, as soon as the meal was served Lady Catherine began to complain. Here was one benefit to being Collins, Darcy realized. He was no longer related to Lady Catherine!

"A French-trained chef, my dear," she said, with a look to Caroline Bingley, "is worth the expense. There is far less waste. To illustrate, this soup is quite inedible. Although," she added, "you might find it acceptable. I have no idea what people from the North prefer."

"Potatoes and savory puddings, perhaps?" muttered Darcy.

Lady Catherine glared a rebuke. Collins-like, Darcy became occupied with his soup.

Since they could not speak of the convalescing Mr. Darcy (for fear of upsetting the ladies), topics for conversation were limited. "Looks like sleet tonight,"

Bingley remarked, "or so the servants say. Not good if that physician of yours is traveling over the road, ma'am."

"Sir Henry Fleming knows what I am due," was Lady Catherine's reply. "I have every expectation of seeing him." She continued to eat the inedible soup.

"For my part," said Miss Bingley, "I long to return to London, most especially the theater." She smiled condescendingly at Darcy. "Such an enchanting diversion. I hear that *Artaxerxes* will soon be presented at Covent Garden." She gave a sigh. "How vexing that I must only read of it."

"I believe," said Darcy, "that Madame Catalani was considered for the role of—"

Conversation at the table stopped.

Caroline Bingley lowered her spoon. "Good gracious! Do you follow the theater, Mr. Collins?"

"Mr. Collins," corrected Lady Catherine, "did not understand you properly. He never goes to London, much less to the theater."

Darcy thought quickly. "Er, during my school days, milady. Before coming to Hunsford." He felt a blush mount to his cheeks. What an idiot he was for mentioning school! Where the devil had Collins studied? Not Cambridge or Eaton or Harrow. His aunt certainly knew. Darcy braced himself for a round of awkward questions.

Ever the host, Bingley came to the rescue. "There's nothing I enjoy more than a night at the theater," he said, and he forced a laugh. "Pantomimes are my favorite. You know, *Harlequin, Colombine, Pantaloon*..."

"Afterpieces," said Lady Catherine, "are contemptible. And the theaters themselves? Death traps."

"Oh, surely not, milady." This was from Caroline.

Lady Catherine rounded on Miss Bingley. "The Theater Royal, Drury Lane? And your precious Covent Garden? I remember those fires, if you do not, Miss Bingley. Burnt. Such tragic loss of life."

Poor Bingley was now pink in the face. "Eh, Mr. Collins," he chirped. "How is the family at Longbourn? They are all well?"

"We are all rather cold, what with the weather," Darcy replied.

"As are we."

"Charles!" Caroline objected.

"Well, we are. We might burn a forest of logs, and still we freeze."

"It's this house," said Caroline. "Which is why we must go to London. If not for poor Mr. Darcy, we would be there now." Her voice caught. "Poor Mr. Darcy. Poor, *dear* Mr. Darcy." She dabbed at her eyes with the napkin.

There was a pause, during which Lady Catherine gazed at her. "Mr. Darcy is dear," she said slowly, "to me, but not at all to *you*. I wonder, Miss Bingley, that you would use so personal an appellation."

"Oh, but milady," Caroline protested, blushing furiously. Darcy had never seen her so out of countenance.

DARCY BY ANY OTHER NAME

Lady Catherine studied her. At last she said, "If you have designs on becoming mistress of Pemberley, I advise you to banish them."

During this awkward pause the soup plates were taken away. Darcy had the misfortune to break out coughing.

"And it is not necessary," Lady Catherine went on, "to invite Mr. Collins to every meal. I certainly do not."

Charles Bingley looked pained.

"I am not about to do so," Caroline retorted. She transferred her gaze to Mr. Collins. "He is, after all, a man of no relations, other than the Bennets. And who are they?"

"You are a fine one to talk," said Lady Catherine. "Mr. Bennet, who is Mr. Collins' cousin, is a gentleman, in both birth and behavior. You will recall that was he, and not your brother, who informed me about my nephew."

Caroline Bingley was struck speechless. Darcy sat silent, as Collins would no doubt do, taking in every morsel of the exchange. The butler and footman moved with noiseless precision. They were obviously drinking in every word.

"You," continued Lady Catherine, "are a new creation from the North, according to my nephew. In other words, you are no one."

Caroline found her voice. "I beg to differ!"

"Whom do you know, apart from my nephew?" said Lady Catherine. "No one."

Miss Bingley put up her chin. "Our circle of acquaintance is most extensive, ma'am!"

"I see. That explains why you have taken this desolate house in humbug country. And have invited no one besides my nephew (and your drunken relations) to stay."

Caroline's eyes were bright with anger. "Upon my word!"

Lady Catherine cast her napkin upon the table. "So we come to it with the gloves off, as the gentlemen say. You are no doubt thinking that I, as your guest, have no right to say such things." She narrowed her eyes and went on.

"As if I did not know that you have written to everyone in your circle that Lady Catherine de Bourgh of Rosings Park is staying at your country house."

Caroline had the misfortune to wince.

Lady Catherine smiled at her discomfort. "Ah, but you see, I saw the stack of letters on the hallway table.

"And you will be polite and take your medicine, Missy," she went on. "Or I shall write to the friends of *my* circle—who are considerably better-placed than yours—and tell them exactly what I think of you. And of your unseemly matrimonial ambitions."

"Oh, but I haven't—" Miss Bingley's words caught in her throat.

"Yes, I thought so," said Lady Catherine. She rose to her feet; Bingley and Darcy did the same. "And now," she announced, "I am *quite* exhausted. You will therefore please excuse me."

The remainder of the luncheon was consumed in silence. And as soon as he could manage it, Darcy made a hasty exit.

10 STEP STATELY!

The Netherfield butler had Collins' ugly overcoat and hat at the ready; Darcy could guess what he thought of them. As the man opened the main door, Darcy wound Collins' black muffler around his neck and settled his hat. Outside it was snowing furiously, with flakes the size of shillings, a good four inches blanketing the ground. A gust of cold air pushed at Darcy, sending snowflakes swirling about his shoulders. He hesitated. Perhaps this was unwise. Bingley would put him up for the night.

And then a sharp voice came travelling down the stairway, and it echoed through the vestibule. "Is Mr.

Collins still here? Bring him up at once. I have something more to say to him." It was his aunt, and she did not sound pleased.

That settled it. Turning his collar against the cold, Darcy lowered his head and set out.

Before he reached the gates and the lodge, he was again wishing he'd borrowed that horse. The animal would know its way home, for one thing. Darcy marched through the snow on what he hoped was the road to Longbourn. There were no birds to break the silence, only the whisper of falling snow and his own footfalls. Gusts of wind made visibility difficult; snowflakes stung his cheeks and eyes. At length he wearied of brushing snow from his coat and simply let it remain.

His trek took almost two hours. Clucking and fussing, Hill drew him inside, helped him remove his overcoat and then took it away to dry. He stood in the vestibule, blinking and stunned with cold. The under-maid came in carrying a broom, and she gave him a dark look. This was rather startling.

"Might as well dump a bucket a snow right there on the floor," she grumbled, and she began to sweep. "If that ain't a man all over."

What was this? A maid-of-all-work, who should have been glad of employment, had no business giving him a scold. Was Collins such a worm that even servants felt free to berate him?

He attempted a rebuke, but his face was still stiff with cold; he could not speak. And then he glanced down at his feet.

He felt a little ashamed then, for he had brought in rather a lot of snow. He felt a sudden stab of pity, not for the maid but for Mrs. Hill. It was a struggle to keep this house clean and in order, a thing Darcy had never considered. At Pemberley, mud and dirt simply happened and were dealt with.

Hill returned, but not before the maid-of-all work had given Darcy another look. The snow on Collins' muffler had thawed and was now dripping freely. She went out and came back with a towel.

And of course, being inhabited by Bennets, the house was anything but quiet. "I do not see why James must be out in the barns with Ned," he heard someone say above stairs. It was Lydia Bennet.

She descended to the landing. "Do help us, Hill," she called down. "We must have James come back. He cannot help with the livestock all day."

"After all," said Kitty, hard on Lydia's heels, "he is an inside servant. He belongs here."

"Except when there's a bitter storm, Miss," said Hill mildly, "as there will be tonight."

Lydia gave a huff of disappointment. "But we need that trunk, Hill."

"We must have a proper game tonight," added Kitty. "Cards simply won't do!"

Lydia turned to look at Kitty. "Won't Denny find it amusing? And Wickham?" She made a face. Both sisters dissolved into giggling.

Wickham again. Wordlessly Darcy stripped off Collins' muffler and passed it to Hill.

Lydia came down to the vestibule. "Oh, look," she called to her sister. "It's Mr. Collins."

"What luck," said Kitty, smiling at him. "You are just the person to help us."

"Now Miss Kitty," said Hill, "don't you be bothering Mr. Collins. He ought to be in bed with a hot brick and a glass of milk."

Darcy was nettled. So he was to be wrapped up and tucked in like an old woman? Was this the sort of thing Collins preferred? Not on his watch, Darcy decided. After all, his arm was out of the sling. He looked inquiringly at Kitty.

Lydia caught the meaning in his look. "It's a crisis, Mr. Collins, that's what it is. We're simply perishing with disappointment. And here you are, a gentleman, ready to be of service. Famous, I call it."

"Miss Lydia," Hill protested.

"I daresay," Lydia went on, "that *any* man can help us. Save for Papa, as he is rather old." Two pairs of eyes surveyed Darcy. "You are not too old, are you, Mr. Collins?"

"Miss Kitty, your cousin is in no condition to be hauling down a trunk."

DARCY BY ANY OTHER NAME

Lydia eyed Darcy appraisingly. "He looks fit enough to me. He looks stronger than James, who is so skinny."

"Come now, Mr. Collins, you cannot refuse," said Kitty. "For we're to play Shadows after dinner, once the officers come. And we need costumes for disguise!"

Speaking was still difficult due to the cold. "S-shadows?" Darcy managed to say. Gad, he sounded like a half-wit.

Lydia frowned at him. "Surely you know how to play Shadows," she said. "We disguise ourselves and parade before a branch of candles, making shadows on a sheet. And the person on the stool has to guess who it is. Hill," she added, "do give us one of the big white tablecloths. It needn't be the best."

"*Not* the one with stains!" said a voice.

Mrs. Bennet came rustling into the vestibule with all flags flying, like a ship of the line.

"The largest, nicest cloth has *gravy stains*," Mrs. Bennet announced. "Such a shame. What *does* that girl do for her wages, Hill? It cannot be so very difficult to remove a common gravy stain. Even if it is particularly large."

From the dark look Mrs. Bennet gave him, Darcy realized that Collins was probably to blame. What had he done, upset the gravy boat?

"Very well, Mama," said Lydia, "we'll use a bedsheet. Hill can choose which one, won't you, Hill?"

Meanwhile Darcy felt Kitty's appraising gaze. "Mr. Collins is tall enough to help us hang it."

"Gracious me, not now, Kitty," protested Mrs. Bennet. "If you must hang a sheet in the drawing room, hang it after dinner."

"I daresay we could cast shadows on one of the walls instead," Lydia said. "Mr. Collins can take down all the pictures."

"No, that he cannot," said Mrs. Bennet. "You girls will turn this house topsy-turvy. My poor nerves." And she gave a shudder.

Not that either of her daughters noticed. "We must collect all the lamps and the stool from the kitchen. And the hall table, too, the narrow one."

Hill returned Darcy's wet gloves. "You'll be needing these when you lift the trunk," she said quietly. "Once these girls have their minds set on a thing, they don't relent."

"So I understand," Darcy said. He turned. "Where is this trunk to be found?"

"In the attic," said Lydia. "Which is at the very top of the house, above even the servants' rooms."

Mrs. Bennet gave a great sigh. "You might as well take him," she said. "Look over all the house while you are at it, Mr. Collins, as it will be yours one day when Mr. Bennet is dead."

Darcy scarcely heard this last. Three flights of stairs, or four? Collins' spongy body was in for punishment. And how unfair that Darcy should be the one to feel the pain.

Lydia and Kitty had him by the elbows and pulled him toward the stairs.

"I'll thank you not to scratch the walls, Mr. Collins," Mrs. Bennet called after. "And don't put the trunk in the drawing room."

"But Mama," the girls protested.

"I will not have that horrid old thing where it can be seen. Put it in the back parlor."

Darcy began to climb. Sure enough, by the time they reached the landing, he was gasping for breath.

A small window lit the attic, brightened by reflected light from the snow outside. It was not only dirty here but also freezing. It took the girls some time to locate the trunk they wanted.

Amid the detritus of generations, Darcy stood frowning through the dust. There was no order here! When an item was unwanted, it was brought up and dropped in any empty spot. And that would be the last anyone thought about it.

Presently Kitty gave a crow of victory, and Darcy picked his way over to her. The trunk she indicated was uncommonly large and made of heavy oak, with corners reinforced by iron brackets. The lock was unfastened; heavy iron latches held it closed. He could in no way carry such a monster down even one flight of stairs.

"No," he said. "I am sorry to disappoint you, dear cousins. But to carry that behemoth would require an army of men."

"Oh, Mr. Collins! How can you be so disobliging?"

Darcy raised an eyebrow. "When was the last time this, ah, colossus was carried down?"

"Oh, never," said Kitty. "We take what we need and go down."

"But we were so hoping that you could help us," said Lydia. "Are you quite certain you are not strong enough?"

The attic door opened, and someone holding a candle came in. "Who is not strong enough?" she said.

Darcy swung round to see Elizabeth.

"Mr. Collins isn't," said Lydia, with a pout. "He promised to take the trunk down to the parlor for us, and now he refuses."

"He says it is too heavy," added Kitty.

"I daresay he is right," said Elizabeth. "Gracious, it is freezing here."

"Have a care, Miss Elizabeth," Darcy said. "It is quite dirty and there are any number of spiders' webs."

"Spiders!" cried Lydia and Kitty.

Elizabeth put down the candlestick. "Mr. Collins," she said, giving him a look, "is only funning. At this time of year the spiders are dead."

Darcy was stung by this rebuke. "Not necessarily," he countered. "Their egg sacs are everywhere. See here, there is one attached to the hem of your gown."

Lydia and Kitty screamed, and Elizabeth looked annoyed. She brushed at her skirt.

Darcy turned to the younger girls. "Let me see if I can get the trunk open."

"It would be warmer to open it downstairs," Kitty pointed out.

Darcy brushed dust from it using Collins' handkerchief, and then knelt and tried the latches.

"Do hurry, Mr. Collins," Lydia complained. "It is beastly cold."

"Don't I know it," he retorted, working at the latch. "But it's a long shot better than being outside."

At last he was able to pry each one open. Grasping the leather straps of the lid lift, he opened the trunk. It was lined with cedar. The scent transported Darcy to his dressing room at Pemberley.

Straightway the girls began pulling out garments and hats, crowing over their finds. Elizabeth located a large basket for their use.

"I fear I have destroyed your sisters' confidence in me," Darcy remarked to Elizabeth, aside.

Elizabeth's eyes flashed, and Darcy smiled. "You are perfectly right, Miss Elizabeth. I never had it in the first place."

"I did not say so, Mr. Collins."

"And," he continued, "while I am prepared to sacrifice a great deal for my fair relatives—"

"Such as," she retorted, "entering into matrimony?"

Darcy's brows went up. Had Collins hinted at marriage to Elizabeth? No wonder she hated him.

"While I am perfectly willing to do even that," he admitted, smiling a little, "I draw the line at injuring my back."

"You are not very gallant, Mr. Collins," she said.

"I have long been a selfish creature." He took from the trunk an old-fashioned tricorn hat and clapped it on his head. "Shall we go down?"

The younger girls trooped down the stairs, whooping and giggling in a most unladylike manner, leaving Darcy to manage the unwieldy basket.

Lydia opened the door of the back parlor and went in. "How jolly it will be."

It was all Darcy could do not to roll his eyes. She'd been saying this again and again. Talkative young ladies, he decided, made his head ache.

And yet there was one fact he wanted to have clear. "I take it," Darcy said innocently, "that the officers will be coming? In spite of the storm?"

"Oh, yes," said Kitty. "Of course."

"And why not?" said Lydia. "Why should they be cooped up in their quarters, or wherever they stay, when they can be here, amusing us?"

Officers did not sit around in their sleeping quarters, they lounged in taverns. But Darcy did not say so to

Lydia. "Will, er, Mr. Wickham be of their number?" he said.

"Oh, I hope so," said Kitty.

"If he is not, I shall have words with Colonel Forster," added Lydia, laughingly. "And so will Lizzy." She twinkled at her sister.

"Lydia, really!"

Darcy found a spot for the basket and set it down.

"Why so glum, Mr. Collins?" said Lydia. "Oh, wait. Is it because Wickham beat you handily at loo?"

More giggles.

"I did not play cards with Mr. Wickham," said Darcy frostily. "Or with anyone."

"Oh but you did. Don't you recall? At Aunt Phillips' soiree."

Darcy grimaced at the slip. But no one noticed; they thought him that stupid.

"Poor Mr. Collins," said Elizabeth. "I'm afraid you were not a very good loser."

In reply Darcy made a small, tight bow. He might have lost to Wickham once, but that would not happen again.

Accompanied by the music of their laughter, Darcy left the parlor. A warm brick and a glass of milk were sounding better and better.

11 Rose is Red, Rose is White

To Elizabeth's surprise, several of the officers braved the snowstorm for after-dinner coffee. She came into the drawing room shortly after they arrived and found a seat on the sofa beside Jane.

"Poor Lydia," she said to Jane. "This isn't quite the evening she had planned."

For Sir William had come, though Elizabeth could not guess why. Mr. Bennet remained in the drawing room to speak with him, forestalling Lydia's game of Shadows.

Even so, it was an amusing evening. Scorning *Vingt-et-un* and Loo, Lydia and Kitty convinced Mr. Wickham and Mr. Denny to build a house of cards. A lesson was now in progress, with dubious results.

"The slightest nudge, the lightest breath," Mr. Denny was saying. "Disaster!"

Mr. Wickham took the lead. "Now then, Miss Kitty," he encouraged. "You must have a steady hand. Place the card you're holding—yes, that's the one—atop the box Denny has made."

Kitty sounded uncertain. "Do you mean as a roof?"

"Exactly," said Mr. Denny.

"But—" Kitty hesitated, looking from him to the card. "It's the queen of hearts. Does that matter?"

"Not a bit," said Mr. Denny.

"And hideously ugly she is," agreed Mr. Wickham. "Place her face-down if you prefer."

"Off you go," said Mr. Denny. "Take no prisoners!"

Mr. Pratt drew up a chair and put his oar in. "Faint heart never won fair lady!"

And yet still Kitty hesitated.

"Oh, lord," said Lydia. "What a goose you are, Kitty. Place the card!"

"I shall call for reinforcements," Mr. Wickham told her. "Miss Elizabeth," he called.

Elizabeth gave a start; George Wickham was smiling broadly. "Do step in for your poor sister," he said. "Your nerves are steady enough!"

Kitty protested, and the others laughed.

Elizabeth returned the smile, but remained where she was. She would rather converse with him apart from the noise of her younger sisters.

The banter around the card table resumed. "Nerves?" Lydia crowed. "What a very good joke. Just like poor Mama. Plagued by nerves."

"Do you mind?" Kitty said. "This is not as easy as it looks." She stretched out her hand and immediately drew it back.

"She cannot do it, Wickham," Lydia pointed out. "What did I tell you?"

Elizabeth's gaze wandered to her cousin, Mr. Collins. There he sat, solemn and silent. He held a periodical, but he did not read. Where was his insincere smile? His desperate attempts to insinuate himself into every conversation? It seemed to Elizabeth that Mr. Collins' attention was fixed on the group at the card table, and his eyes held an unfriendly glint. What in her sisters' behavior could have offended him?

Mr. Pratt cleared his throat. "My dear Miss Kitty," he said, and he took hold of a leg of the card table, as if to steady it. "Try not to *breathe* on the cards."

Lydia gave an unladylike snort.

Poor Kitty sucked in her breath, steadied her hand, and broke out giggling. The would-be house of cards collapsed.

Wickham laughed at her discomposure, and the others laughed with him. Elizabeth glanced again at her cousin. His brows had descended into a thundering frown.

"How stern he looks," she whispered to Jane.

"Mr. Wickham? Oh, surely not."

"No, Mr. Collins. He is so grim and disapproving."

Jane's gaze traveled to where Mr. Collins sat. "He is probably in pain, Lizzy. Perhaps his head aches."

"I think he dislikes Mr. Wickham," Elizabeth said. "Do you suppose he is jealous?"

Jane considered. "Of what would he be jealous?" she said at last. "Of Mr. Wickham's red coat?"

Elizabeth had to smile. "I had in mind his easy manners or his conversation. Our cousin has neither."

"Mr. Wickham is a pleasing companion," Jane agreed. "And yet we know so little about him." She paused. "We know so little about any of these officers."

Elizabeth would not be drawn in. Their new friends were exactly as they should be, amusing and well-mannered. Her gaze returned to her cousin. "Mr. Collins," she said to Jane, "has no business to be so morose. He quite spoils the evening."

"He isn't spoiling my evening, Lizzy. He's in no one's way where he is. And he isn't pushing to be the center of attention, as he did when he first came."

"Before his injury, do you mean? I suppose it has taught him a sense of proportion."

Which was nonsense. Mr. Collins knew nothing of proportion or subtlety or nuance. A thing had to be strikingly obvious for him to even notice. And yet now he was all subtlety. That answer he had given about marriage, for instance. There had been a look in his eye, a flicker of comprehension.

Elizabeth's lips compressed. No, it was quite impossible. William Collins was what he always had been, a fool.

And there he sat, quietly turning the pages of one of her mother's magazines. It wasn't as if he were looking at the pictures. In fact—

Elizabeth excused herself and rose to her feet. Mr. Collins, intent on the party at the card table, did not see her until she stepped into his line of vision. He gave a start and dropped the magazine. Immediately he rose to his feet, but not without wincing.

"I did not mean to disturb you, Mr. Collins," Elizabeth said sweetly, and she sat in the chair opposite his. "Please continue with your reading." She gave him a pointed smile, and was rewarded with a wary look.

"A fashion periodical, is it not? Miss Lucas has told me of your interest."

He grimaced, and Elizabeth fought to conceal a surge of triumph. So the man could be embarrassed after all! She reached for the magazine. "May I?"

With reluctance Mr. Collins surrendered it.

"What lovely pictures." Elizabeth did not bother to conceal her sarcasm.

He raised an eyebrow. "They look better upside down, you know."

She blinked. "I beg your pardon?"

Mr. Collins took back the periodical and turned it. "Like this," he said. "Or did Miss Lucas not tell you?"

Charlotte had, and how Elizabeth had laughed. Was Mr. Collins now laughing at himself? Her eyes narrowed. "How do you mean?"

Mr. Collins stretched his feet toward the fire and gave her a sidelong look. "By viewing from a different angle, one's observation is enhanced."

She knew he was lying, but she decided to play along. "By looking at these upside down? I rather doubt it."

He did not hesitate. "Certainly. As a printer reads the text of a book in reverse to spot errors." He paused. "Now that I think on it, the print itself is set backward, so perhaps it isn't so unusual a practice. But I find it helps me notice memorable features."

"Of gowns?" she scoffed. "Mr. Collins, you quite surprise me. Why would memorable features be important?"

"Why, for compliments." Mr. Collins' lips twisted into a half-smile. "Ladies are always hanging out for compliments."

"Oh, certainly," said Elizabeth. "And you are happy to oblige."

Mr. Collins spread his hands. "Why, of course."

"Very well." Elizabeth indicated the page. "How would you compliment this woman?"

"The one in pink?" He studied the illustration. "On a night like this, I would think she'd be half frozen, as well as exposing an unflattering expanse of gooseflesh."

Elizabeth choked back a laugh. Had Mr. Collins made a joke? When she stole a look at him, his eyes held a twinkle.

"I daresay the designers of gowns are heartless fellows," he continued. "Observe the caption: Costumes for February."

"Perhaps," Elizabeth said unsteadily, "it is a dress for dancing."

"In that case, she would jolly well be more comfortable than I, not having to wear a coat and be half-choked by a neck cloth. By the end of the evening, a crowded ballroom is stifling; the gentlemen are sweating like pigs. Which is one of the reasons I dislike dancing."

Now she knew he was lying. "You, dislike dancing?"

He made a little bow. "Present company aside, of course."

"The Netherfield ballroom," Elizabeth pointed out, "was not at all stifling."

"On that occasion, no. But there are times, such as at Almack's—"

"Mr. Collins, really. When were you at Almack's?"

He looked rather taken aback, and Elizabeth rejoiced. She had caught him.

But he made a quick recovery. "In my younger days," he said, with an elaborate shrug. "When I was a student I, ah, attended in the company of friends."

"Who, most conveniently, provided vouchers," she countered. "And who were, most fortunately, acquainted with the patronesses."

"Well, yes," he admitted. "Something like that. It was a most uncomfortable evening."

This Elizabeth did not doubt. With his finesse at dancing, he would have been roundly drummed out of this exclusive club! But of course, he was lying.

"Now, to return to your original question," he said, "I would tell this woman that she looks lovely. And if pressed for details—"

"Yes?" said Elizabeth. "Although I must point out that it is most ill-mannered to demand specifics."

He leaned forward. "My noble employer is keen on the specifics, Miss Elizabeth."

"And to oblige her, you concoct compliments beforehand? Ah, you see, we know about that. Don't you recall? Papa taxed you with it on your first day here."

Elizabeth's intent was embarrassment, but Mr. Collins actually smiled. "A survival tactic that has proven helpful," he said, "for Lady Catherine has peculiar tastes in clothing. Extemporaneous compliments are, shall we say, a challenge. I daresay you would do the same."

"I? Never!"

He raised an eyebrow. "No doubt you have thought out what to say," he continued, "when Miss Mary asks your opinion of the yellow gown she wears. Which, though new, is an unflattering shade and with sleeves three years behind the current trend."

Elizabeth was struck speechless.

"As to this lady," he continued, indicating the illustration, "I would begin by mentioning that the drape of the fabric calls to mind the Elgin marbles."

"The Elgin marbles?" scoffed Elizabeth. When had he seen the Elgin marbles?

Mr. Collins had the grace to look sheepish. "A difficult comparison, that," he confessed. "For most of them are missing their heads, are they not? As well as their hands and feet."

"Why let that stop you?" said Elizabeth. "You might as well say that she is Venus de Milo, of whom we have heard so much."

Mr. Collins made a strangled sound. "I fear not," he said unsteadily. "For she is missing most of her clothes."

Lydia's shrill voice interrupted, which was a very good thing because Elizabeth nearly laughed. And it would never do to laugh with Mr. Collins!

"Lizzy," Lydia called across the drawing room. "Do come. For Denny says he and the officers cannot stay. And it is far too early, for we have not played Shadows."

"Miss Lydia, please understand," Mr. Denny pleaded. "The snowstorm."

Elizabeth rose to her feet and, without a word, abandoned Mr. Collins.

"If Sir William had not come when he did," Lydia complained to her, "and if Papa had not remained in the drawing room forever, we would have had our game!"

"Another time, Miss Lydia?" Mr. Pratt said.

Lydia was now pulling at Elizabeth's arm. "Convince Wickham to stay, Lizzy. They'll listen to Wickham. And Wickham will listen to you."

Mr. Wickham made a charming bow. "I am yours to command, Miss Elizabeth. What care we for snow and ice?"

"For ice, a great deal," said Mr. Denny. He walked away to make his farewells to Mrs. Bennet.

"I am sorry my comrades are such cowards," Mr. Wickham told Elizabeth, smiling. "For we've scarcely spoken all evening."

Elizabeth felt a flush mount to her cheeks. "I was taken up with entertaining my cousin."

"As I saw," said Mr. Wickham. "The next time I come, he will be deprived of your company."

"Wickham!" Mr. Pratt's voice was urgent.

Elizabeth and Mr. Wickham went out into the vestibule with the others. Hill and James were assisting the officers with their overcoats.

"Listen," said Lydia. "The snow is noisy. Like pebbles hitting a windowpane."

They all fell silent and James opened the door. Pellets struck against the windows of the house and the snowy drive.

"Sleet, that's what this is," said Mr. Denny, grim-faced. "It's time we were off, lads."

Lydia and Kitty said all that was proper, but after the officers had gone, they flounced back into the drawing room. "All our fine plans, spoiled," said Kitty, casting herself onto one of the sofas.

"It was good of them to come at all," Elizabeth pointed out.

"It was remarkably foolish," said Mr. Collins. He resumed his seat by the fire. He did not, Elizabeth noticed, take up the fashion periodical.

"A pity about the weather," said Mrs. Bennet. "You'll have an empty church for your sermon tomorrow."

Elizabeth whirled to face him. "You are giving the sermon?"

Mr. Collins' reluctant look returned.

"Girls," chirped her mother, "your cousin is preaching in Dr. Bentley's stead tomorrow. Won't that be a fine thing?"

Only Mary looked hopeful. "Would you care to practice it, Mr. Collins?" she said.

Mr. Collins looked stricken. "That," he said, "will not be necessary."

"Thank goodness!" Lydia said, and threw herself onto the other sofa. She began picking at the fringe of a cushion. "And we were to have such a splendid time tonight. Now what is there to do? Since we are not," she added, "listening to sermons."

"Mr. Collins could read one," said Mary helpfully.

"I thank you, Miss Mary, but I ought to rest my voice," he said.

Mrs. Bennet was also looking unhappy. She sighed and found a seat. "You can ring for Hill," she said, "to clear away those playing cards."

"I'll do it, Mama," said Elizabeth. Mr. Collins was looking her way, and she did not wish to resume her conversation with him.

Lydia gave another sigh. "Only ten o'clock. I'll die from boredom."

"Would you care to read?" William Collins held out his magazine.

"O, lord, I've seen that one a hundred times. And if you mean books—" Lydia made a face.

Silence descended. Mr. Collins got up to add more wood to the fire. Jane and Mary took out their embroidery.

Presently Kitty wandered to one of the windows and pulled the drapery aside. The click of sleet against the glass was still audible. She stood there a long while, gazing out at the snow.

At length she wiped at the glass with her hand. "Mama," she said. "I do believe there's someone outside on the drive."

"In all this snow and ice?" said Mrs. Bennet. "Nonsense. Who would travel on a night like this?"

"Only idiotic officers," Elizabeth heard someone mutter. She could have sworn that it was Mr. Collins, but he was occupied with a book. She joined Kitty at the window. "It looks like a traveling coach," she said.

"And the horses," added Kitty, "See how they are sliding on the snow?"

"But we aren't expecting anyone," cried Mrs. Bennet.

Lydia jumped up for a look. "Is that James? No, it can't be, can it? But there's a man out there with the horses. Dear me, he's fallen. How exciting!"

Jane came to stand beside Kitty. "Travelers stranded by the storm," she said. "Surely we must help them, Mama."

"Help them?" Mrs. Bennet rose to her feet and came to the window. "But," she said. "But—"

"Oh, famous!" said Lydia. "I wonder who they are."

"Ruffians and highwaymen," said Mrs. Bennet. "Come to rob us and drive us from our home!"

The tap of the door knocker sounded.

"Lizzy, fetch your father!" Mrs. Bennet cried. "Hill, do not open that door!"

But Hill could not hear her. Above the tattoo of the sleet came the grind of the bolt being pulled back. The main door whined as it opened.

"Girls," cried Mrs. Bennet, "you will remain here. Girls!"

But Kitty and Lydia had already made a dash for the drawing room door, and they collided with Hill as she came in. A liveried servant, red-faced and powdered with snow, followed.

"Ma'am," said Hill to Mrs. Bennet. "A young lady and her companion are seeking shelter."

The liveried servant murmured something to Hill.

"And the lady's physician," Hill added. "They are bound for Netherfield Park, ma'am, but the distance is too great. The roads are coated with ice." She presented a calling card.

"Take it, Lizzy," Mrs. Bennet said, gasping. "I am too agitated to read."

The card was of excellent quality. "The Honorable Miss Anne de Bourgh," Elizabeth read aloud. She glanced wonderingly at Mr. Collins.

The liveried servant stepped forward. "Of Rosings Park, ma'am," he added. "A right venerable family."

All eyes were fixed on Mr. Collins, who was now on his feet. "Anne de Bourgh, here?" he sputtered. "But that's impossible."

"It is all too possible," said Mrs. Bennet.

"But why would Ann—er, Miss de Bourgh come to Netherfield?" he said.

"Why, to see Mr. Darcy, of course," said Mrs. Bennet. "She is, after all, his cousin, is she not? I daresay the family expects the worst." She turned to the liveried servant. "Please tell Miss de Bourgh that we will be delighted to offer shelter."

And as soon as Hill had gone out, Mrs. Bennet gave a withering look to Mr. Collins, who was plainly flummoxed. "Mr. Collins, please," she hissed. "Do mind your manners."

12 No Humor at Present

From habit Darcy rose to his feet, his eyes fastened on his cousin's wan face. There was no mistake, this was Anne. Jaunting about the countryside on such a night, with no one but that fool of a companion for protection!

Mrs. Jenkinson was her usual mousy self, Darcy noted, if mice could be meek and stooped. Her tentative smile never seemed to reach her eyes. But there was nothing new in that.

And the person with them? A so-called physician, though Darcy had his doubts. The man was sandy-haired and thin. Mr. Bennet came into the drawing room; Darcy's eyes narrowed as he listened to the introductions. Fleming was his name. The question was, how well did Fleming know Collins?

Darcy knew the best thing to do would be to scuttle off to bed. But he had become accustomed to remaining unseen, and besides, observation was useful. Ten to one Anne would not notice him.

Collins himself would have come surging forward to greet Anne and gabble compliments. Darcy remained by the fire. If Anne looked his way, he would bow and then wash his hands. But she did not.

"My dear," said Mrs. Bennet, taking possession of Anne's arm. "What a night to be out! Do come and sit by the fire. Mr. Collins," she called, "you must surrender your seat."

So much for remaining inconspicuous!

"Miss de Bourgh," he said quietly. He unfolded the lap robe he had earlier cast aside and held it at the ready.

Mrs. Bennet led Anne to the fire, clucking and fluttering. "A frightful night, unfit, as they say, for man or beast. Never fear, you are among friends, Miss de Bourgh. Mr. Collins, whom I daresay you know very well, is our relation."

The look Anne gave him was not encouraging.

Darcy knew he ought to smile and say something. A single nod was all he could manage.

Though travel-worn, Anne's hair was crimped and braided elaborately. Mrs. Bennet's sign of admiration was audible.

And of course, Mrs. Bennet must fuss. "What were you thinking, to be out in such a storm?" she said, bringing a cushion for Anne's feet. "For you have been traveling some little distance, if you've come all the way from Hunsford."

Anne stretched her hands toward the fire. "Coachman John said it was fifty miles," she said. "And Mr. D-Darcy—" She broke off speaking; her face puckered. Darcy wondered whether Mrs. Bennet would interrupt.

Anne drew a long breath and rallied. "And Mr. Darcy," she said at last, "thinks nothing of fifty miles of good road. In fact, he, he—" She broke off speaking and burst into tears.

At once Mrs. Bennet surrendered her guest to Mrs. Jenkinson and went to Jane's side. "Oh dear," Darcy heard her whisper. "What are we to do?"

"Poor Miss de Bourgh," was what Jane said. "She feels Mr. Darcy's injury deeply."

Mrs. Bennet blinked. "Er, yes, of course. But what I mean, Jane, is that Mr. Collins has the guest room." Mrs. Bennet gave Darcy a look.

"And what is to be done?" she continued. "Where shall we put Miss de Bourgh? And that other gentleman? Gracious, and the companion? Although," Mrs. Bennet went on, "she can share with Hill easily enough."

Darcy felt a stab of compassion for Mrs. Hill. Apparently she had no say in the matter.

"Miss de Bourgh may have my room, Mama," said Jane. "I'll share with Lizzy."

Mrs. Bennet accepted this as a matter of course. "I suppose that Miss de Bourgh's physician can share with Mr. Collins."

This was most unwelcome, but what could Darcy do? He could only hope that Fleming despised Collins as much as he did. Given Collins' character, it seemed a reasonable assumption.

Meanwhile, Anne sat sniffing into her handkerchief. Elizabeth drew forward a chair. "Mr. Darcy is your relation, I understand," she said kindly.

Miss de Bourgh nodded but continued to weep.

Elizabeth cast a look in Jane's direction, and she came over at once. Darcy supposed that Kitty and Lydia would come as well, but they remained on the far side of the drawing room, whispering together.

"We have heard nothing from Netherfield," said Jane. "So we are encouraged to think that Mr. Darcy is improving, as surely he shall."

Elizabeth lifted her head and looked at Darcy. "Mr. Collins," she said quietly. It was a summons.

"Have you any news regarding Mr. Darcy's condition?" In Elizabeth's eyes was a mute appeal to be tactful.

Anne lowered her handkerchief. This meant that there were three pairs of eyes fastened on Darcy—three opportunities to betray himself.

"Well now," said Darcy, in his best Collins-like manner, and he twiddled his fingers. He could not help it,

Anne was staring so. Too late he recalled his bruised and battered face. No wonder she looked surprised.

There was nothing for it; having begun Darcy must continue. He puffed out his chest as Collins would do. "He did seem improved this morning, Miss de Bourgh. Mind you," he added, as Anne gave a gasp, "he is a long way from being his usual self."

"For that matter," murmured Elizabeth, "so are you, Mr. Collins." But her tone was kind.

"Er, yes," Darcy admitted. He turned to Anne. "We were both injured during the same incident."

Lydia spoke up. "Mr. Collins and Mr. Darcy were hit by lightning," she said with relish.

"Lydia," said Elizabeth.

"Well, they *were*," Lydia protested.

"It was not as bad as it sounds," Darcy told Anne. "Your cousin was able to speak a little this morning."

Hope surged into Anne's eyes and her pinched expression softened. "Did he ask for me?"

Darcy was taken aback. Not once—no, not ever! — would he think to ask for his cousin. He never thought of Anne at all.

"I believe not," he said gently. "In all fairness, he did not ask after anyone."

"And did he know you, Mr. Collins?"

How should Darcy answer? Collins had known him all right, but not in the way Anne supposed.

"He did," said Darcy. "But he has been sleeping much of the time. Your, ah, mother was distressed because he did not respond to her."

"Oh, Mother," said Anne. "She always twits at one. I often pretend." She paused to sniff. "Mr. Darcy is nobody's fool. I daresay he did the same."

Darcy felt his eyes narrow. This sharp observation was not what he expected from timid, badgered Anne.

"So Mr. Darcy is your cousin," gushed Lydia. "Just as Mr. Collins is ours." She giggled a little.

Anne's chin came up. "Mr. Darcy," she said, "is rather more than just a cousin."

There was a short silence, and Darcy felt a prickle of discomfort.

A thin smile appeared on Anne's lips. "Mr. Darcy," she said distinctly, "is also my affianced husband."

There was a collective gasp, which Anne apparently enjoyed, for she colored up. It was all Darcy could do to keep from gaping. Of all the bald-faced lies! For this was a lie, it had to be.

Immediately Lydia and Kitty began gabbling nonsense about romance. Lydia came nearer and knelt before Anne's chair. "Is he in love with you?" she wanted to know.

"Lydia," cautioned Jane.

"Of course he is," said Kitty. "Else why would he propose?"

"Do tell us all about it," said Lydia, and she took hold of Anne's hand. "We," she added, "are the soul of discretion."

Darcy snapped his lips shut. Another lie from Lydia. Why was he not surprised?

He expected Anne to recoil, but she did not. Apparently the attention was too tempting. "Our engagement has been of a long duration," she confessed.

Oh, certainly! A passing remark between their mothers as they hung over a cradle! Remembered by his scheming aunt and passed on to her daughter!

"And also," Anne went on, "Mr. Darcy is such a kind and thoughtful gentleman."

Oh he was, was he? Darcy set is teeth. At the moment he was feeling anything but kind.

"As well as rather handsome," added Lydia.

"I'll say," said Kitty.

Anne's blush intensified. "The Pemberley estate," she continued, "is lovely."

Darcy folded his arms across his chest. What did Anne know of Pemberley? Perhaps she had visited as a girl, although he did not recall it. Hadn't she been too sickly to travel? No, Anne's information came from artists' renderings of the grounds and her mother's descriptions.

"To be mistress of so fine a house is something," said Elizabeth. She sounded sincere, but Darcy detected an ironic twinkle.

He repressed a grimace. His sickly, timid cousin mistress of Pemberley? Not in his lifetime!

"Your mama must be so pleased," Jane said politely.

"And so are we," interrupted Kitty. "For the militia is quartered nearby, and the officers come to call quite often. And if you are safely engaged, why then—" Kitty hesitated. "That is to say—"

Lydia jumped into the gap. "We greatly admire red coats, Miss de Bourgh," she confided. "Officers are vastly amusing, don't you agree?"

Anne was blushing again. "Another of my cousins," she offered, "is a colonel."

"Famous!" cried Lydia. "You admire red coats too! You'll adore Denny and Pratt and Captain Carter. And Wickham. He is such a fine dancer." Kitty and Lydia shared a look, and then burst out giggling.

Darcy pressed a hand to his temple. The thought of Anne in the company of officers made his head ache.

Hill brought tea, which only served to enhance the growing intimacy. Kitty and Lydia were now in full swing, battering Anne's chilly shyness with whispered confidences and laughter. Within the family circle girls were talkative, Darcy was learning, and talk meant friendship. How long would it be before Anne was chattering and laughing with them? He studied Anne's thin face. She was looking rather taken aback, but not at all displeased.

Lydia slipped into the seat Elizabeth had vacated. "Do tell us about Pemberley," she said. "We want to hear everything."

"Oh, yes," urged Kitty. "Is it a grand house? Is the park immense? Are there gardens and walks?"

Even Mary came near to listen. "Is there a music room? And a private chapel?"

As Anne launched into her description, Darcy suppressed a sigh. He had had enough of lies and half-truths. He rose to his feet and excused himself.

But Darcy had forgotten about Mr. Fleming. He found the man in his bedchamber sorting through a small traveling trunk that had been brought in. Indeed, the wardrobe was more than half filled with Fleming's clothing.

"Collins!" he cried and came forward. "Never did I think to meet you here!" He gripped Darcy's hand and shook it warmly. "So these are your cousins, eh? And this is the house?"

The smile transformed Fleming's face. He did not appear unhealthy, but his clothes hung on him. He needed a tailor almost as much as Collins did.

But Fleming's smile was short-lived. "I say, you have been knocked about!" His long fingers stretched toward Darcy's swollen forehead. "Nasty-looking knot you've got there."

Darcy pulled away. "Isn't it just?" he muttered.

Fleming did not press the point. "You cannot imagine my relief," he said, "to see you here, old boy. Nothing like the face of a friend to put heart in one. I am not cast adrift among strangers."

So Fleming was a friend. "It has been quite a night," said Darcy cautiously.

"Isn't that the truth? I thought my number was up back there at the bend," Fleming said. "We nearly overturned, not once but several times. Old John's a marvel, for we were sliding all over the road. All praise and credit due him."

Darcy pursed up his lips without realizing it.

"Er, sorry," said Fleming. "Praise to God as well. A pleasure to be where it's warm."

Darcy's gaze shifted to the smoking fireplace. "You are jesting, surely," he said.

Fleming was not at all stupid, and he took Darcy's meaning at once. With long strides he crossed the bedchamber and added several logs to the fire. The blaze caught, and Fleming stretched his hands to the warmth.

"Compared to spending the night in the Lady Catherine's barouche," he said, "or more probably, leaving it to the ladies and sleeping underneath, this is a maharajah's palace." His grin widened. "Mighty fine set up if you ask me."

Darcy hid a grimace. "It isn't mine yet."

"Ah yes, the death of the resident landholder. That would be the gray-haired fellow."

"A long life to him," Darcy said. "Inheriting a house," he added, "that is half falling down and in need of modernization is hardly a boon."

"Hardly a boon?" Fleming gave Darcy a long look and rubbed his chin. "You've changed your tune, Collins," he said. "Although I must say the selection of marriageable females isn't half bad. Now then, let me have a look at your head."

Darcy set his teeth, but Fleming's fingers were surprisingly gentle as he probed the bruised area. "A fine gash here," he remarked, "and another over here. Healing nicely, though. What caused them?"

"I fell to the pavement," Darcy said. "With, ah, Mr. Darcy—" the name sounded foreign on his lips "—beneath me."

"Poor devil," said Fleming.

This expression summed up the situation nicely. There was only one bed in this room, with nowhere else to sleep but the floor. Darcy had never in his life shared a bed. But his stint as Collins was teaching him that there was a first time for everything.

"Fleming," he said grimly," I couldn't agree more."

13 To Crown the Whole

The silence in the bedchamber had nothing to do with quiet. Like the ocean it roared and growled and hissed. This noise was constant, like the pain behind his eyes and in his ribs. Try as he might, twitch and turn and twist, everything hurt. It was painful even to breathe. Such suffering was grossly unfair, and he felt this deeply.

Fever had come in waves. Swash and backwash, heat followed by bone-shaking chills, leaving him trembling and weak. There was a fire burning on the grate; he could hear its snap and crackle. A wood fire, yes, with the hiss of pine sap. Every pop was like a slap.

There were voices, too. Almost an assault, words came at him and he was powerless to resist. Whispers were as loud as shouts, paining his ears. Oh, his head ached worse than anything!

It hurt like Hades, to be precise, though it was beneath his dignity to say so. But would anyone care if he did? What would happen if he thrashed and cursed like a sailor? At the moment, however, he could call no curses to mind.

That girl, whose name he did not know, was supposed to be of assistance. Did she soothe his fevered brow and offer comfort? Not a bit! She sat in the overstuffed chair—for he'd glimpsed her there—napping for most of the time. A jovial fellow came from time to time, to prod and poke and ask questions. Was he a physician? If so, he was certainly a charlatan, for none of his cures had worked.

Occasionally a sharp-voiced woman fretted over him, mispronouncing his Christian name and fussing with the bedclothes. She reminded him of Lady Catherine, though this could not be right. His noble patroness, who was charity itself, would never condescend to linger in his bedchamber. Which meant that he was delusional, seeing and hearing things.

He knew this was so because he'd seen his own face, hovering over the pillow, leering. Easier to surrender to the chills and fever, yes. Still, that ghastly face haunted him.

He was now damp with sweat and thirsty, too, fair dying of it. His mind formed the word Water, but he could not speak it. He attempted to moan, but no sound came.

He cracked open a cautious eye to search for the errant girl and gasped in shock. One of the draperies was open! What treachery was this? For he'd heard the jolly-voiced man say that light was harmful. Even the glow from the fire was dangerous, and he'd been carefully shielded.

The voices started again. Babbling sounds, punctuated by words. He ventured another look at the window. Yes, there was the girl looking out and beside her stood someone in livery. A footman? He had no business to slouch like that!

Unaccountably, their words formed into sentences that he could understand.

"Would you look at the snow," the fellow was saying. "A fair blizzard, I call that. No sign of letting up."

"It's at least waist-deep," the girl said. "I was below-stairs when Charley came in with the milk and eggs. Covered from head to foot he was."

Eggs. A memory stirred. *Charley Barley, butter and eggs. Sold his wife for three duck eggs.*

"A point in our favor, being in service," said the footman. "I feel for Mum and Dad, though. Can't be easy working the farm in all this, what with the livestock to see to."

Livestock. Horses. *A farmer went trotting upon his grey mare, bumpety, bumpety, bump.*

"And the farm is where I'd be, sure enough," continued the footman, "had Netherfield been left empty."

"Thank heaven for Mr. Bingley and his sister," the girl said.

Netherfield. He turned the word over in his mind. He'd heard the name Bingley, too. These should mean something, but what? He closed his eyes and gave himself to the chore of thinking.

"Even so," the girl went on, "it's a bit rough for you, having to stand about and take orders all day."

"From the old lady, do you mean? Huh, when it comes to ranting, Mum outranks her any day. And clonks me with the broom for good measure!"

The girl broke out laughing.

"Below the lady's dignity to do that," he continued cheerfully, "though it's well no brooms is handy. She's in fine form this morning, I must say. The church bells not ringing set her off something awful."

Ding, dong, bell. Someone in the well. But who was in the well he could not say.

Morning bells are ringing, ding, dang, dong.

"I doubt there'd be Sunday service," the girl said, "what with the snowstorm and all."

At this his eyes blinked open. Was this Sunday? Why, he must lead the Hunsford congregation through the liturgy and officiate the communion. And preach the sermon, receiving afterward, with gracious humility, his parishioners' thanks and praise.

There was a disturbance, and he heard the door come open. Someone came or went, but he could not see who. Oh, the wretchedness of his helpless state!

And so the Hunsford service must be left to his scraggy curate, Doleman, and he knew how the man would muck it up. He had neither dignity nor pulpit presence; Lady Catherine would be seriously displeased. He could hear her now, berating him for being weak and neglecting his pastoral duties.

Are you sleeping, are you sleeping?

Of course he was! What else could he do?

Mercifully, the pair at the window had stopped talking. He next heard a rustling of skirts.

"What business," said a new voice, "have you to be loitering at the window, my girl? My poor nephew might be in desperate straits, struggling for his very life, and yet here you are, lollygagging."

The girl began to protest, saying that he was sleeping peacefully. Which showed how much she knew!

"The draperies are to remain closed! Stupid girl, did you not attend to Mr. Jones' instructions? Not that he knows how to care for an invalid, but that is not for you to decide. Shut them at once!"

"Yes, milady."

"At once, do you hear? Country servants," the voice added, "are so unbearably slow!"

Unbearably slow. *Snail, snail, put out your horns, I'll give you bread and barley corns.*

He had no business with nursery rhymes, but it was useless to resist. Here was more proof that he was going mad. He gave a shuddering sigh and surrendered to the embrace of the pillows.

Quick footsteps crossed the room—did they belong to the sharp-voiced lady? He could sense someone standing beside his bed.

"See here," shrilled that same voice, "he's awake. His eyes are closed, but no matter. Beneath the lids I see movement. You will bring beef tea and a fresh mustard poultice. After that, he will need a wash and a shave."

A wash? Had the girl been attending to so personal a matter? The thought that she might wield a razor made him nervous. Still, a shave would relieve the itch of stubble. Yes, now that he thought on it, the itch was uncommonly irksome. Slowly and with much effort he brought his fingers to feel his chin to find whiskers, sharp and stiff. Yes, stiff.

"Good gracious, look at that! Fitzwilliam, you can move!"

"Thanks be to God," said a softer voice—the girl's?

Hands gripped his shoulders and gave him a shake. "Say something!" the shrill voice commanded. "Speak to me!"

Her tone was such that, painful or not, he dare not disobey. Words bubbled up and he said them.

"*Four stiff standers, four dilly-danders.*"

"What did you say?" the woman cried.

He labored to continue. "*Two lookers, two crookers.*" He paused, working to remember the rest.

The hands gave his shoulders another painful shake. "Fitzwilliam, you are speaking nonsense! Dilly-danders, indeed. Pull yourself together."

There was a pause, followed by the sound of the bell pull being yanked repeatedly. "Send for Mr. Jones," the woman said to whoever came in. "At once, do you hear? Never mind the snowstorm, never mind the Sabbath—no one here appears to observe it! He must come without delay. We have reached another crisis!"

She returned to the bedside. "Say something, Fitzwilliam, I beg you!"

William, he longed to say. My name is William. But the words would not come out.

"You must rally," she ordered. "Do exert yourself and try."

Yes, he must try, or else this woman would give him no peace. Summoning his strength, he managed to open one eye and then the other. Slowly the face of his interrogator came into focus. It was strange that someone so ugly and wrinkled would look so familiar. Did he know her?

Her features were as pinched and sharp as her voice. She wore a dark velvet hat with a large tassel. He watched it swing to and fro.

"Speak!" she commanded. "Speak to me!"

To and fro, to and fro. The remainder of the rhyme fell into place. His dry lips formed a grin of triumph.

"*Two lookers,*" he recited solemnly. "*Two crookers. And a wig-wag!*"

The expression on the old lady's face was so comical that William Collins began to giggle. "A wig-wag," he chortled. "A waggy-wig. Bumpety-bumpety-bump."

"Madness," she gasped out. "Heaven help the Family!"

"Snow, snow, beautiful snow." Kitty's singsong chant gave a cheerful air to breakfast. Except that the snow was banked halfway up the windows. And Mr. Collins had chosen this morning to come down.

Elizabeth stifled a sigh. He would come to breakfast. Of course he would, as would any guest, what did she expect? It was just that since the accident he'd taken his meals in his bedchamber, which was excellent in every way. If only he would only stay there until he was well enough to travel!

For as his health improved, she knew that his fondness for oratory would revive. Mr. Collins did not converse like other men, he pontificated. If there was a gap in the conversation, Mr. Collins was sure to fill it. Unasked-for advice seemed to be his special delight. By comparison, the silent brooding of Mr. Darcy was not such a bad thing.

Mr. Darcy? What was she about, to be thinking of Mr. Darcy? Elizabeth became occupied with buttering a piece of toast. Mr. Collins had been more subdued for the past several days. She devoutly hoped this new mood would continue.

Mr. Collins brought his plate to the table and chose a seat opposite Elizabeth's. Quickly she averted her gaze. No doubt he wished to begin speaking with her, and he must not be given an opening.

But after murmuring a polite good morning, he became busy with his fork and knife. Apparently hunger had overcome his appetite for talk.

From beneath her lashes Elizabeth studied him. Mr. Collins was using his flatware with surprising grace this morning, a welcome change from his usual awkwardness. She watched him cut a single slice from a sausage before spearing it with his fork. He chewed thoughtfully, without attempting to converse, and then sliced off another.

Where had these table manners come from? Never would she forget Mr. Collins' first breakfast with the family. She'd seen him fumble with his knife, vigorously sawing all of his sausages into a pile of pieces. He conversed while chewing, too, to the amusement of Elizabeth's father. According to him, Mr. Collins had boardinghouse manners. Her father's seat at the far end of the table, out of direct sight of Mr. Collins' mouth, was a distinct advantage. Elizabeth had been anything but amused at her cousin's boorish behavior.

And now? Was Mr. Collins truly changed? Had his injury caused him to forget all his bad habits?

But that could not be right. A savage, for instance, could not abandon his uncouth ways. Not knowing better, he wouldn't know how. Mr. Collins was certainly uncouth, but not this morning.

Mary came into the dining room and took a plate from the sideboard. She hesitated, studying Mr. Collins with an appraising eye. Mary, Elizabeth knew, was keen to engage their cousin in conversation whenever she could. This morning she did not disappoint.

"What a pity, Mr. Collins," Mary said, "that you will not be able to preach this morning."

Elizabeth saw him put down his fork, and she braced herself. Now the flood of words would come, for surely he must answer.

But it was her mother who spoke up. "Not able to preach?" she said. "Nonsense! Who minds a little snow?"

From the far end of the table, Elizabeth's father gave a slight cough. "Have you looked outside lately, Mrs. Bennet?" he inquired politely. "Two feet on the ground at the very least, with more to come."

She waved this aside. "Of course we shall have church," she said. "What is more, I shall wear my new bonnet in honor of the occasion." She gave a very pretty smile to Mr. Collins.

He flushed and looked uncomfortable.

Mr. Bennet coughed again. "My dear, have you heard the church bells this morning?"

There was a pause.

"No, you have not," he continued, "for they will not be rung. Dr. Bentley is no fool. No one should venture out in this storm." Mr. Bennet turned a page in his book and marked the place with his finger. "I believe you may count yourself excused, Cousin Collins," he said. "It must relieve your mind of a weight."

It most certainly was a relief, thought Elizabeth. Mr. Collins merely gave her father a nod and resumed eating.

Had he nothing to say? Not one word about the duty of a rector to instruct those under his care and protection? No lament that his scholarly efforts would be wasted or that his eloquent admonitions would remain unspoken?

Elizabeth could not allow this to pass. She leaned forward. "Confess the truth, Cousin," she said. "You are disappointed to postpone your sermon."

His eyes met hers. "I have no intention of postponing it, Miss Elizabeth" he said.

"Of course you do not," cried Mrs. Bennet. "Lizzy, what an excellent idea. At eleven, we'll arrange our chairs in rows like pews so that you may preach to us, Mr. Collins."

"Oh, but Mama," Elizabeth said.

Mr. Bennet looked down the table. "There you are, Mr. Collins. A captive audience—or shall I say congregation? —who will doubtless admire your grandiloquence."

Her father's tone held gentle sarcasm, but Mr. Collins did not appear to notice. "I thank you, sir, for the suggestion," he said, "but I think not."

Mary brought her plate to the table. "We will never believe that you are not a skilled speaker, Mr. Collins," she said. "After all, we were present to hear you at the assembly. You do recall," she added helpfully, "the admonitions that you gave us in the Music Room?"

Mr. Collins did remember, for Elizabeth saw him flinch. Could it be that he was embarrassed by how he had behaved? Surely not! He was too self-absorbed and stupid.

She watched him blot his lips with the napkin. "My, ah, humble efforts, Miss Mary, are most unworthy. And when one considers the extent of the snowstorm, apparently the Almighty agrees." He flashed a look to Elizabeth. "My poor sermon has been effectively silenced from on high."

Elizabeth nearly laughed. Hastily she composed her features. "We shall all be disappointed, nonetheless," she said politely.

Just then the dining room door opened and Lydia came in, arm and arm with Miss de Bourgh. "Who will be disappointed?" she demanded cheerfully.

"We shall," said Mary. "For because of the snow there will be no service, and Mr. Collins refuses to preach his sermon to us."

"Is that all?" Lydia shared an amused look with Anne de Bourgh. "I daresay you have heard him preach often enough, Anne. Is he *very* dull?"

Miss de Bourgh dimpled but said nothing.

Lydia led her to the sideboard, where together they began to fill their plates. Suddenly Lydia turned round. "Mama," she said, "do you know where our copy of *The Castle of Ontranto* is? Anne has never read it. She has never read any novels, can you imagine? We'll soon fix that!"

Mr. Collins made a strangled sound. Elizabeth eyed him carefully. Of course he would disapprove.

"Who am I to look after your books?" Mrs. Bennet said. "Perhaps Hill knows."

Lydia giggled. "Imagine Hill, reading! You needn't look so disapproving, Mr. Collins. *Ontranto* is quite acceptable, something a grandmother would read."

"If that is the case," he countered, "I am surprised that you would recommend it."

"Never mind Mr. Collins," Lydia said to Miss de Bourgh. "It's tremendously exciting and you'll love it. One has to say something to the elderly naysayers." She gave a slanting look to Mr. Collins.

Miss de Bourgh merely giggled, and Lydia joined her.

Kitty spoke up. "Just because it is a novel does not mean it is wicked, Mr. Collins."

Mr. Collins spread his hands. "Did I say anything?"

"No, but you would like to. I can see it in your face," said Lydia. "Any lady would enjoy *Ontranto*."

"If she has a great deal of time to waste, yes," said Mr. Collins.

Lydia and Kitty rolled their eyes at him and began talking of something else. Elizabeth said, "I imagine your noble patroness would not approve."

"Perhaps not," he agreed. "It stretches credulity too far for my taste: mysterious voices, doors opening of their own accord, a helmet that launches itself from the wall." His lips twitched into a smile. "Poor Conrad. Crushed by an enormous helmet."

"You have read it?" said Elizabeth, smiling in spite of herself.

"Ah, but the question is, did I finish?" Mr. Collins raised an eyebrow. "Do you suppose that I read only theological works?"

Before Elizabeth could reply he turned to Hill, who refilled his cup with fresh coffee. He thanked her and took a tentative sip.

Elizabeth could not contain her surprise. "Without cream or sugar?"

He lowered the cup, his eyes suddenly intent. "Is that so unusual?"

"When first you came, you astonished us by taking five lumps of sugar."

"Five?" There was no mistaking the loathing in his voice. He took another sip of the black coffee.

"Lizzy," called Lydia from the other end of the table, "after breakfast you must fetch your pencils and drawing paper. Dear Anne needs a sketch of each of the officers. How else will she recognize them when they come?"

The last thing Elizabeth wished to do was sketch. Somehow she did not wish to expose her drawing ability to Mr. Collins. For he'd then pronounce her drawings to be charming and would prose on with compliments.

But it was Mr. Collins who answered Lydia. "Judging by the weather," he said, "we could be snowbound for several days. I doubt anyone will call."

"Surely the officers will," said Kitty.

"Lizzy, please?" pleaded Lydia.

"I'd rather not," she said. "You can describe them well enough."

"Of course we can," Kitty cried. "We'll begin with Mr. Denny, Anne. He's the one with sandy hair. And in the front, his hair curls backward. What do they call that?"

"A cowlick," said Lydia. "He's fond of dancing, and playing cards, and he laughs with the funniest sound, like this." She demonstrated.

"You'll love Mr. Wickham, too," added Kitty. "We all do. He is tall and dark and so very amusing."

"And he's even better at cards."

"I daresay he is," Elizabeth heard Mr. Collins mutter. "He's had rather a lot of practice."

His jaw was set; his eyes held an angry flash. Here was more evidence of his dislike for Mr. Wickham. But he'd scarcely met the man!

Elizabeth was about to ask why when her mother came rushing over. "What a very promising thing this new friendship is!" she confided.

Although her mother meant to whisper, delight overcame good judgment. Her voice carried, and Elizabeth could tell that Mr. Collins was taking in every word.

"For Miss de Bourgh will bring them into company with other rich young women," her mother went on, twinkling. "And you know what that means!"

Again Mr. Collins surprised Elizabeth. "But you are assuming, ma'am," he said quietly, "that Miss de Bourgh has an extensive circle of friends. I can assure you that this is not so. Aside from the charm of her company, your daughters will gain very little."

"Oh, Mr. Collins," cried Mrs. Bennet. "How would you know?" And she moved away.

But he would be in a position to know, Elizabeth realized, perhaps better than anyone.

Mr. Collins finished his coffee, pushed back his chair, and excused himself from the table.

Elizabeth watched him go, feeling more perplexed than ever.

14 A Fine Thing

Darcy came into the bedchamber to find Fleming sorting through garments. He looked up with a grin. "One benefit of traveling under threat of a storm," he said, "is that one packs extra sets of clothes! I'm hoping there are enough dry stockings to see me through."

Darcy digested this statement. "An extended stay," he said carefully, "does appear likely."

"Ah, but the snow has stopped, have you noticed?" said Fleming. "That fellow Ned put me on to the farm manager, or whoever he is. From him I have borrowed snowshoes. So I'm off to Netherfield to attend to my patient."

Snowshoes! Was it too much to hope for a second pair? One way or another, Darcy must get to Netherfield. God only knew what Collins was up to.

Then too, every minute spent here, especially in Elizabeth's presence, was disaster. This morning was no exception. Elizabeth was annoyed with him, though he could not guess why.

A half-empty breakfast plate was on the dressing table, and Fleming leaned over to snatch a bite.

Darcy chose his words carefully. "In a hurry to be off, then?"

Fleming made a face. "Unfortunately, yes. All in my line of work," he said, around another bite. "Yours too, come to think on it. Though you are usually summoned later, eh?"

No doubt if Collins-as-Darcy expired—a disaster Darcy did not wish to contemplate—he would be called to officiate at the funeral. But he had no time to be annoyed with Fleming, for the man had given him the perfect opening.

"There wouldn't be a second pair of snowshoes available?" Darcy said off-hand.

"I don't see why not—" Fleming broke off speaking. "Hang on," he said, suddenly serious. "You aren't thinking of coming with me."

Darcy shrugged. "As you say, the sickroom is rather in my line. And you need a guide to direct you to Netherfield."

Fleming's expression was not encouraging, but Darcy would not be put off. He went directly to the wardrobe and took out Collins' overcoat and muffler.

"Collins," said Fleming. "You are in no condition to walk that far."

Darcy pulled open a drawer and removed Collins' stockings and breeches. From under the bed he unearthed what he guessed was Collins' valise. "It's only two or three miles," he said. "And you forget, this will not be the first time I've walked it."

"In several feet of snow?" Fleming said. "Seriously, old fellow, you shouldn't risk it."

Darcy raised an eyebrow. "And leave you to face her ladyship alone?"

Fleming hesitated.

"She won't like seeing you in place of your father," Darcy pointed out. "And she will like your news about her daughter even less. You, ah, are planning to tell her about Miss Anne?"

Fleming sat down on the bed. "I'm still thinking that one out," he confessed. "Theorizing, you know. Plotting the best strategy for breaking the news."

"And what have you concluded?"

Fleming's ready smile reappeared. "Ha," he said. "That it is most expedient to blame poor Jenkinson!"

Darcy had to laugh. "Much better to blame me," he said. "It'll come down to that in the end." This might not be true, but he knew his aunt's nature. Collins practically begged to be kicked, and she was certain to oblige.

"Collins," began Fleming.

"It is the truth. In the eyes of my exalted patroness, I am the perfect scapegoat." He leaned forward. "Do take me with you, Fleming. If only to spare yourself—and Jenkinson—a nasty scold. I've broad shoulders."

Fleming grimaced. "I'll get a scolding, sure enough. But Jenkinson?" he said. "The poor woman has no spine."

"And neither have I," said Darcy cheerfully.

"You don't understand the difficulty I was under, Collins," Fleming said earnestly. "Miss Anne would not be refused; I was forced to comply. I had no idea that we would run into a storm."

"Don't I know it? Let's hunt up that other set of snowshoes before it starts to snow again."

Fleming rose to his feet. "Better to die in the wilderness than to be slain by the dragon, eh?" But Fleming was also smiling.

Downstairs in the drawing room a debate was in progress. The younger girls were campaigning to have Ned shovel out the main entrance, which was no small amount of work. Hill stood by, supported by Mr. Bennet, who agreed that under the circumstances the service entrance was sufficient access to the house.

DARCY BY ANY OTHER NAME

"What else has Ned to do?" said Mrs. Bennet. "If any of our friends should call, we must be prepared, Mr. Bennet. How would it look to have the front entrance blocked up with snow?"

"It would look," replied Mr. Bennet, "as if we, along with all our neighbors, have experienced the largest snowstorm Hertfordshire has seen for years."

"But the officers!" cried Kitty. "Surely they will call." She and Lydia put up such a fuss that to have peace Mr. Bennet relented.

He caught sight of Darcy standing there. "I cede to you, Mr. Collins," he said formally, "the enviable position of Man About The House." Mr. Bennet then retired to his bookroom and closed the door.

Lydia exchanged looks with Kitty and Anne de Bourgh. "Only imagine," she said saucily. "Mr. Collins as the man about anything!" And they dissolved into giggles.

Mrs. Bennet regarded Darcy with narrowed eyes. "Do not take too much upon yourself, Cousin Collins," she said.

Darcy was only too glad to follow Hill into the kitchen.

What he did not expect was a fight over his intent to leave Longbourn.

Fleming came in from the yard with the news that he'd procured a second pair of snowshoes. They were old, he said, but looked serviceable. Darcy buttoned Collins' coat to the throat and wrapped his muffler securely.

Hill put her hands on her hips. "And where do you think you are going?"

Fortunately, Fleming had sense to remain silent. "To Netherfield," said Darcy, drawing on Collins' gloves.

"Walking there in all this snow? And you, with arms and legs as weak as a chicken's!"

This caught Darcy by surprise. What did Hill know about Collins' legs?

"I'm strong enough," he protested. "More so, in fact, than when I made the trek yesterday."

"Trek!" said Hill. "Isn't that the truth? That woman," she added wrathfully, "to be ordering you about as if you were her slave! It's unchristian!" But there were tears in Mrs. Hill's eyes.

Darcy wanted to reach for a handkerchief, and if he'd been himself he would have several ready in a pocket. But he was Collins, and had nothing to offer but a square of rough linen, none too clean.

Hill pulled hers from her sleeve and blew her nose.

"My dear Mrs. Hill," said Darcy. He placed his gloved hands on each of Hill's shoulders, as he would in making a point to Pemberley's Mrs. Reynolds. "I am strong enough," he said gently. "And should anything go wrong, I have Mr. Fleming with me, a physician."

"You'll fall and break a bone," Hill faltered. "And then where will you be?"

"Fleming will set it. Won't you, Fleming?"

DARCY BY ANY OTHER NAME

Fleming began to answer, but Darcy cut him off. "Even you must admit," he said to Hill, "that if I become stranded, I won't starve." Smiling, he patted his protruding stomach.

She gave an unhappy sniff. "I don't like it," she said.

"And neither do I," said another voice.

Elizabeth Bennet stepped forward, and Darcy felt a flush rise to his cheeks. What was she doing in the kitchen? And how much had she heard?

Her arguments, like Hill's, held weight, and he listened while she said her piece. But while it was one thing to be scolded by a worried servant, it was quite another to be ordered about by a pert young woman.

Darcy drew himself to his full height and faced Elizabeth. He saw her chin come up, a martial light sparkled in her eyes.

"As I have explained to Mrs. Hill," he said crisply, "which no doubt you overheard, it is imperative that I reach Netherfield. My position as Lady Catherine's rector demands it."

"It most certainly does not," she countered. "The risk is far too great. You are a fool to consider such a thing."

The word fool rankled and Darcy felt his lip curl. "I appreciate your heartfelt concern."

"Concern has nothing to do with it," she flashed. "You are the hope of the family."

Her sarcasm hit a nerve. He was no weakling!

• 189 •

He put on his hat, took up his satchel, and faced Fleming. "We'd best be going before conditions deteriorate. Good-bye, Mrs. Hill, Miss Elizabeth."

"But Mr. Collins," protested Elizabeth. "This is madness."

Again he met her gaze. "I prefer to think of it," he said, "as a calculated risk. I should be back in time for supper." He tipped the brim of Collins' parson's hat, pulled open the door, and went out into a world of white.

The snowshoes were cumbersome to affix to his shoes—curse Collins for choosing inadequate footwear! Surprisingly, it was warmer out than he'd expected, for there was no wind. Darcy raised his eyes and took in the trackless expanse of snow.

"She is right, you know," said Fleming, speaking through his muffler. "This is madness. But no one lives forever. Best to be off."

"We'll follow the road," said Darcy.

Fortunately the wall around Longbourn's park was high enough to be visible, so he was able to get his bearings. Darcy set out with striding steps in what he hoped was the right direction.

All too soon he was sweating. Why hadn't he thought to carry a walking stick? There was no hope of finding one along the way, as everything was so deeply buried.

Fleming marched alongside, swinging his physician's satchel. Collins' valise, which contained their extra clothes, became heavier and heavier. To spare his shoulder, Darcy switched hands.

"I suppose," said Fleming sometime later, "that when we arrive, exhausted and half-frozen to death, her ladyship's anger will be somewhat mollified."

Darcy had been Collins long enough to know better. "By all means think so, if it gives you comfort."

This was something Collins would never say, but Darcy was too weary to care. What was usually a pleasant one-hour stroll now required all his strength and concentration. Were they traveling in the right direction? Were they following the road? Casting his doubts behind him, Darcy soldiered ahead.

Presently above the trees he noticed a line of smoke. On a day like this every chimney at Netherfield would be belching smoke, or so he hoped. God be praised for his aunt's aversion to the cold!

He and Fleming trudged in silence for a good half hour. Then Fleming took up the conversation. His breathing was only slightly labored, Darcy noted, whereas he himself was gasping for air like a fish.

"Will she have my head on a platter, do you think?" Fleming said cheerfully. "Like John the Baptist's?"

"You won't suffer alone," Darcy managed to reply. "She already blames me for taking a holiday."

"Ah yes," Fleming said. "To find that all-important wife."

To do what? It took Darcy a few minutes to find his voice. "Is this common knowledge?"

"It's hardly a secret. A child could see through her ladyship's intent."

So he was not imagining it—all the more reason for Elizabeth to take him in dislike! Then again, he did not wish Elizabeth to like him. Not as Collins!

"It's not like you have cause to complain," Fleming went on. "Five unmarried sisters, most of whom are quite pretty." He came to a halt and looked around. "How much farther do we have?"

"A mile, if my bearings are right." Darcy's calves and thighs were burning. Collins' roly-poly body was good for nothing! He could not ride, he could not shoot, and he could not dance. Even walking a country mile was too much!

Patches of blue had broken through the gray above, and they gave the snowy landscape a hopeful aspect. "Best to be moving on," Darcy said presently. "If we halt too long, I'll keel over for good."

As before, within ten minutes Fleming resumed talking. "There must be plenty of unmarried ladies in the countryside round about," he remarked. "There always are in places like this, according to Lady Cat."

"According to whom?" demanded Darcy.

"Lady Cat. You remember, my little name for her ladyship?"

Darcy did not know how to answer this, so he marched on in silence. Besides, his nagging aunt was not a cat. Lady Fox Terrier was more her style.

At length Fleming spoke again. "I pity the woman, whoever she is."

"What woman?" Darcy wanted to know.

Fleming gave a shout of laughter. "Why, your wife!"

"Not precisely complimentary this morning, are you?" grumbled Darcy. "I pity her myself. I am not the easiest of men to live with."

"No, no, old man," cried Fleming. "What I meant is, The Cat needs occupation. Wants to add your wife to her list of dependents. She'll manage her half to death and in every detail. Aha!" Fleming added, pointing. "Look there."

They came to a halt. Darcy's instincts had been correct. In the distance was the Netherfield mansion, dark against the spotless snow.

"In every detail, you say?" Darcy set down the valise and massaged his aching shoulder. "If dear Lady Cat intends to manage even my marriage bed, I'll—"

Fleming gave a snort of derision. "I daresay she would if she could. Instructs me on the contents of my satchel, the shining of my boots, the books I read, any number of medical procedures she's read about in the London papers. She ought to have married an innkeeper, with a score of servants and guests to manage."

Then Fleming clapped Darcy on the shoulder. "So which of the sisters is it to be? The golden-haired beauty? Or the darker girl with the lovely eyes?"

Darcy could not answer in kind, how could he? The truth was that neither of them would have him. He'd fallen from being a matrimonial prize to a leper-like outcast. He was, in fact, attractive to no one. His companion's laughing face did nothing to help.

"Fleming," snapped Darcy, "kindly have the goodness to shut up."

And of course, being Fleming, he did nothing of the sort. He teased Darcy about wife-hunting all the way along the road to Netherfield.

15 PICKING OF STICKS

As Darcy dragged himself across the final snowy mile, images swarmed in his mind: bright fires and tasty food, warmth and safety and cheer. Well, perhaps not cheer, for at journey's end was Aunt Catherine. Why had he and Fleming come on this trek? Ah, yes, because of Collins. Asinine, chuckle-headed Collins, trapped in Darcy's own body.

Darcy was now so cold and so weary that coming to Netherfield no longer seemed worth the effort. His respect for Fleming, who had no personal stake in the matter, increased tenfold.

At last they gained the yard, and Netherfield's shoveled-out service entrance came into view. And if Darcy had not been so weary, he would have shouted along with Fleming. As it was, they had to pound on the kitchen door repeatedly before it was opened.

Their snowshoes were a source of wonder to Mrs. Nicholls.

"Just this morning," she said, relieving Darcy of his coat, "Hobbes set off for Meryton, as her ladyship felt the need was urgent, but the snow was too deep. Before he'd even reached the lodge he had to turn back. In the process he sprained an ankle."

Mrs. Nicholls handed off Darcy's coat and signed for someone else to assist Fleming with his. Then she paused. "Knowing her ladyship as you do," she said, "what is to be done?"

Darcy had stripped off Collins' gloves and was rubbing feeling back into his hands. The cold had made him stupid. Was Mrs. Nicholls asking his advice?

"If you will kindly permit us to borrow the snowshoes," she went on, "one of the footmen can be sent. I daresay the return trip will be difficult for Mr. Jones. You gentlemen are much younger than he."

This got Darcy's attention. Had something happened to Collins? "Do you mean Jones, the apothecary?" he said.

Fleming, who was warming himself at the kitchen fire, glanced in their direction.

"It's Mr. Darcy, sir," said Nicholls. "According to her ladyship, he is saying nonsense words."

Fleming came over. "This is the other man who was injured?" he said to Darcy. "Confusion after a head injury is not uncommon."

Nicholls pursed up her lips. Her reaction was hardly surprising, for Darcy had omitted the introduction. "This is Mr. Fleming, physician to Lady Catherine," he said.

Her reserve vanished. "A physician?" she repeated. "Lady Catherine's physician? Why, this is remarkable. We needn't send for Mr. Jones after all." She brought a hand to her breast. "Her ladyship will be so pleased."

"We'll just put on dry stockings," said Darcy, "and you can take us up."

"If you please, sir," said a small voice at Darcy's elbow. "It's Hobbes, sir. If you wouldn't mind saying a prayer for him?"

It took Darcy a moment to remember that he was a clergyman.

She was a slip of a girl, perhaps the scullery or maid-of-all-work. "He's just there," she said, and pointed to a chair where a boy sat huddled under blankets.

Were there tears in her eyes? He was forcibly reminded of Georgiana.

"Not now, Kate," said Mrs. Nicholls. "The rector has more important matters to attend to."

And so he had. Still Darcy hesitated. The girl was trembling. She was quite young, perhaps eleven or twelve. The work apron she wore hung on her thin frame.

"I apologize for her manners," Mrs. Nicholls said briskly. "Kate and her brother are new to us. If you will just follow me, please?"

"Just a moment," said Darcy. He bent to address Kate. "Hobbes is your brother?" She nodded. "We'll have a little word, then."

Collins' shoes were wet; as he walked the leather made spongy sounds. And no wonder, for his stockings were soaked through.

"If you please," chided Mrs. Nicholls. "We should not keep Mr. Darcy waiting."

Did everyone feel free to order Collins about? "In a moment," Darcy told her. He turned to Kate.

"As you see," he confided, "I am in need of dry stockings. Fortunately, Mr. Fleming has thought ahead." He retrieved a pair from the valise and returned to the fireplace. Hobbes was a year or two older than his sister and was also quite thin.

"Hello, Hobbes," said Darcy, finding a seat near the hearth. "Hats off for braving the snow and without snowshoes too. A courageous feat, to soldier on so far. No wonder you're worn to the bone."

"T'ain't nothing, sir," said Hobbes. His eyes found the floor.

"Having walked those miles myself, I cannot agree. And now you are injured."

"Not much, sir."

"Fleming?" Darcy said over his shoulder. "Have a look?"

While Fleming examined Hobbes' foot, Darcy removed Collins' shoes and stripped off the socks. The dry pair felt heaven-sent.

"Not a bad sprain," Fleming remarked. "Mind that you keep off your feet for several days."

At this Hobbes looked truly frightened, and Darcy understood it. Employment at Netherfield meant a great deal to this family.

"I'll speak to Mr. Bingley on your behalf," Darcy promised. "And in the meanwhile, while you are off your feet..." He dug in Collins' pocket and pulled out several coins. "This is for your trouble," he said. "A brave deed deserves a reward."

Color came into Hobbes' thin cheeks. "Thank you, sir."

"Not at all. Now then, your sister wishes us to say a little prayer."

"Mr. Collins?" called Mrs. Nicholls from across the kitchen.

Darcy gave her a quelling look. "Shall we pray?" he said crisply. At once she bowed her head and shushed the others in the kitchen.

Collins would have had a prayer book to read from, but Darcy was not so equipped. He would have to improvise.

"Father in heaven," he said, scorning to use Collins' unctuous tone, "I thank You that You are..."

He opened one eye. It occurred to him that Hobbes and his sister were country people.

"...that you are the Good Shepherd," Darcy went on, "and that You watch over your sheep. You saw Hobbes, here, when he was struggling alone in the snow, and You brought him safely back. We pray for his healing, and for the health of his family, and we thank You for his sister's loving care.

"Thank you, too, for bringing a physician for the, ah, gentleman above-stairs. And that no one else need venture out on his behalf. In the name of our Savior."

The others echoed his Amen. Darcy tied Collins' shoes and rose to his feet. The eyes of Hobbes and his sister were shining. "And now I must obey Mrs. Nicholls," he whispered, "or face a scold."

He was answered with a pair of shy smiles.

At Darcy's request Nicholls took them up the back stairs. "Who would have guessed it?" said Fleming, speaking low. "The mercies of Providence, if you will. I am cast, not as a villain, but as a savior. Perhaps our Lady Cat will be mollified."

Darcy did not answer. His aunt's true nature did his family no credit.

Once inside the sickroom, Fleming took the lead. He was gentle with his patient and spoke soothingly.

Darcy's valet was in attendance; apparently he had just finished shaving Collins—or rather, Mr. Darcy. The mental correction made Darcy wince, for he was losing track of who was whom. He introduced Fleming to his valet, Holdsworth, and stepped away.

"An apoplexy is what we think, sir," said Holdsworth, in answer to Fleming's questions. "As he is not speaking like himself. Meaning no disrespect," he added, "but her ladyship thinks he's gone mad."

Her ladyship, thought Darcy ruefully, had no idea how true this was!

Fleming returned to his examination, and delivered his verdict. Collins' responses were merely childlike. He was not mad, and his incapacitated state would not last. When he'd spoken with Collins there had been comprehension. He would be up and talking soon enough.

Before returning to Longbourn, Darcy decided to engage in bit of subterfuge.

He studied Fleming and Holdsworth. They would be occupied for some time.

Darcy slipped from the sickroom and headed down the hall. The door to his former bedchamber was closed. There was no need to have the room looked after, so until Holdsworth returned he would be unobserved.

He opened the top drawer of the dressing table; his keys were where he had left them. From the wardrobe he brought his writing desk and unlocked it.

Out came paper, pen and ink, and sealing wax. His signet ring was still on Collins' finger—that could not be helped. But Darcy had to risk writing.

The date would present a problem, or would it? Darcy counted back to the day of his accident, yes, that would do nicely. He would slip the letter into a pocket, produce it in Holdsworth's presence, and request that it be posted on Mr. Darcy's behalf.

He sat thinking for a minute, and then set to the task of writing to his steward.

Bellowes,

A circumstance has arisen that requires your immediate action.

My aunt, Lady Catherine de Bourgh, has lately retained a rector for the Hunsford parish.

Not that Bellowes would care, but some explanation seemed in order.

While in Hertfordshire, he and I have had the occasion to become acquainted. I have reason to suspect that my aunt has not provided for him as she ought. Therefore I would like to establish an annuity, effective immediately, of one thousand pounds per annum, to be paid quarterly to Rev. William Collins of Hunsford parish, Kent. Additionally, he is to receive by return, a letter of credit in the amount of one hundred pounds.

Darcy gave the direction for Longbourn House and brought his letter to a conclusion.

Please understand that I do not wish my name to be mentioned in connection with this matter. Mr. Collins, ever a grateful recipient, tends toward volubility in his praise.

As always, I rely on your discretion.

Darcy signed his name and waited for the ink to dry. Carefully he folded the sheet, sealed it, and wrote the address.

Ten to one Bellowes would not check the seal. And if he did, Darcy's own signature, so familiar, would clinch the matter.

So that would take care of money for the time being. His next worry was Georgiana. The best course of action would be to write to Fitz—and say what?

Precious minutes ticked by as Darcy considered what could be done. None of his ideas were sound. In the end, he wrote and requested that his cousin call on Mr. Collins at soon as possible. Somehow he would make Fitz understand. And if Collins-as-Darcy was declared insane? Fitz would take sole guardianship over Georgiana.

He closed and locked the writing desk, and replaced it and the keys. As there was no sign of Holdsworth, Darcy allowed himself one last look at the bedchamber he'd occupied. It was nothing special, or so he'd thought at the time. Now he wondered if he would ever again have a room so nicely appointed.

Of course he would! There had to be a way back.

Collins was still awake when Darcy returned, though he appeared vexed and muddleheaded. Fleming seemed to regard this as a good sign.

Darcy drew nearer and studied his own face. He'd never realized that his features could assume so petulant an expression. Collins had complaints about everything, from careless attention he'd received from the girl to the bedding.

"Try sleeping in that lumpy bed at Longbourn," Darcy muttered. And then he realized that Collins had slept there. There was no satisfying some people. Apparently the man was born to complain.

Holdsworth's ability with the razor came under fire next, and Darcy's hand stole to finger his chin. He had been shaving himself of late, with dubious results. What he wouldn't give to enjoy the services of a valet!

And then it happened, Lady Catherine came in marching in. "Why, Mr. Collins!" she remarked. "Nicholls said that you had come."

Was she pleased to see him?

"I told her that someone could get through, snow or no snow. And I was right." Her eyes narrowed. "The trouble with servants, Mr. Collins, is that you must do all the thinking for them. What was called for was a little effort."

Holdsworth was no fool. Darcy noticed him rapidly packing his gear. A hasty retreat was certainly in his best interest!

"And it is the same with my nephew." Lady Catherine indicated the bed. "If Fitzwilliam bothers to exert himself, he will overcome whatever madness has seized him. Wig-wag, indeed."

Darcy stole a look at Collins; his lower lip was protruding. Was the man pouting?

And how long would it be before his aunt noticed Fleming? The first to strike in battle gained the advantage, so Darcy decided to take the lead. "Mr. Fleming has been telling us about jolts to the brain," he said, "and—"

"Mr. Fleming?" Lady Catherine interrupted. "No, as usual you are wrong, Mr. Collins. Sir Henry is the man you mean, and I must say, he has kept me waiting long enough!"

And then she caught sight of Fleming sitting beside the bed. "What *is* the meaning of this?" she demanded of Fleming. "I sent for your father, not you."

Fleming's hand slipped into a pocket. "He has been ill, ma'am. I have here his letter for you, explaining it."

Lady Catherine tore it open.

"We did the best we could," Fleming explained, as she read. "Mr. Darcy is progressing nicely. He is a bit confused, but that is usual for the nature of his injuries. I suggest he be given something to eat."

"Not Darcy," said the man in the bed. "Collins."

"Mr. Collins!" called Lady Catherine. "Come here. My nephew is asking for you!"

She came nearer and took hold of his hand. "Fitzwilliam, can you hear me? We are here. Even Mr. Collins."

"Softly, milady," said Fleming. "Mr. Darcy is sensitive to sounds."

"Perhaps it is better if I am left alone with him?" Darcy suggested. "If you do not mind, Fleming?"

"Indeed, I have a great many things to say to this man," said Lady Catherine, "so it is just as well."

"I shall join you presently," said Darcy. "And together we'll share with Lady Catherine the news—all the news—of Longbourn."

"I have not the least interest in Longbourn or its inhabitants."

"But you will," Darcy murmured, as the pair left the room.

He turned to the figure on the bed, who was gaping at him. "All right, Collins," Darcy said sternly.

The man on the bed twitched. "Yes, I know who you are. And you know who I am."

"But—" said Collins.

"You are not going mad, nor am I. I have become you, and you have become me. I do not know who is to blame for this mishap. Until we can manage to switch back, let's get a few things straight."

"I am Darcy?"

"In name only, Collins. As far as I can tell, none of my skills devolve on you. So if you cherish ideas of spending my fortune, banish them. Indeed, you cannot even sign my name."

"I am Darcy," Collins repeated. In his rasping voice was a note of wonder.

"And you will keep your mouth shut, do you understand?" continued Darcy. "You will say nothing about what has happened. The risk of being locked up as a lunatic is very real."

"I am not mad. I am Darcy," Collins whispered.

"And for the present time, I am Collins," said Darcy. "And let me tell you, what I have had to put up from Aunt Catherine would try the patience of a saint!"

Collins smiled a little.

"I am doing my level best not to ruin your life or call attention to the problem. I almost had to preach a sermon this morning, crafted by my officious aunt. What right has she to dictate what you preach?"

Collins' mouth was working.

Darcy leaned in. "You must not make a misstep, Collins. We must make it easy for the other to resume his rightful place, once this situation is remedied. And there will be a remedy, Collins.

"I am Darcy." The pleasure in Collins' voice was disquieting.

"Kindly recall that I can muck up your life quite thoroughly if I wish. What would happen if I were to tell my supercilious aunt exactly what I think of her? Never mind the preferment, she would toss me out. You would have no income."

"Inherit Longbourn," Collins rasped.

"Not if you are declared mad," said Darcy. "It will devolve on some other sorry relative."

"Elizabeth," Collins whispered.

Darcy thought back to Bingley's assembly. He'd seen the man's infatuation with his own eyes.

"Luckily for you," Darcy said drily, "Miss Elizabeth loathes Fitzwilliam Darcy. You have a better chance with her as yourself, old fellow."

He heard sounds in outside the door. His opportunity was almost over.

"When Lady Catherine returns, I will not be able to speak freely," Darcy said. "Keep your mouth shut and do your best to act like me. Grow a backbone, man. And for heaven's sake, stop complaining. It is undignified."

"But—"

Darcy leaned in. "It will do neither of us any good to be shut up in Bedlam," he said darkly, "so guard your tongue."

He heard the door open. "And now, my dear Mr. Darcy," he said in his most unctuous tones (and he had the satisfaction of seeing Collins recoil), "let us pray together, shall we?"

16 DRIVE THE COLD WINTER AWAY

Kitty and Lydia burst into another gale of laughter. Apparently Anne de Bourgh had never played Spillikins, and they were determined to rectify the omission.

Elizabeth's gaze drifted from the pages of her book to the clock. Six hours. That was not so long a time, was it?

"Mother attempted to teach me loo," she heard Anne confess. "But I took an instant aversion to it."

"Why?" said Kitty. "We love loo, even if Lydia cheats."

Lydia bounced up in her seat. "I do not cheat," she cried. "Or if I do, I take care not to get caught. Every woman for herself is what I say, especially when playing for penny points."

"But loo," said Anne, "is a game of strategy." And she sighed and looked away.

Anne had spent much of the day resting, Elizabeth knew. Would she again retreat from the drawing room? It certainly looked that way.

"Spillikins involves strategy of a different sort," said Kitty. She successfully extracted a stick and added it to her pile. "There, you see? I have six and this is the seventh." She hung over the table and hunted for another.

"I am so easily muddled and mixed up," Anne confessed. "And whenever I make an unwise move, Mother rants at me."

"I say," cried Kitty. "I would be rattled too, if someone did that to me." She selected a stick and began to work it loose from the pile. The girls fell silent, for it was a difficult maneuver.

"Oh!" they cried together when Kitty failed.

"Your turn, Anne," said Kitty cheerfully. "And look there, I've made the job easier for you. I dislodged that bit in the center."

Anne reached out a tentative hand. "I shall try for the green one, just there."

"Off you go, then," said Lydia. "And be thankful that you don't have Denny or Pratt breathing down your neck and laughing. This game is a favorite of theirs."

Elizabeth closed her book and set it aside. She watched as Anne drew out the green stick successfully.

It was a simple accomplishment, but it made all the difference to Anne. Her face was immediately less ashen.

Kitty was all encouragement. "Now try for another," she said. "Remember, the one who prises out the most sticks wins the game. You already have five."

"The red one, I think," said Anne, reaching for it. "I do like this game after all. My mother," she added, "insists that I be first in everything I do. To be a credit to the family, she says."

"First?" said Kitty. "How do you mean?"

"When I play a game," Anne explained, "I must win. And so often I do not!"

"I must win any game I play," said Lydia, "but only when there is money in the pot."

Jane, who shared the sofa with Elizabeth, gave a sigh of sympathy. "No wonder Miss de Bourgh is often ill," she whispered. "In her place, I would be very discouraged. You know how stupid I am at loo. Lydia can best me every time."

Elizabeth smiled. "Lydia would make a good tradeswoman, I think. She has the bargainer's eye."

Jane selected a length of silk and threaded her needle. "Mr. Mitchell must be on his toes when she comes into his shop. Mama ought to remind Lydia that haggling over price is unladylike."

"Not in Mama's eyes. How else would she be able to dress us as well as she does?" Elizabeth's gaze strayed once more to the window.

Apparently Jane noticed. "What a very good thing that the snow has not resumed," she said, echoing Elizabeth's thoughts. "I daresay Mr. Fleming and Mr. Collins should not have gone to Netherfield."

Elizabeth found her book and opened it. "Attendance on the sick," she said, "is in Mr. Fleming's line." She turned a page.

"But surely not in Mr. Collins,'" said Jane. "He had no business at Netherfield."

"I think perhaps he did," said Elizabeth. "Although Mr. Fleming should have found someone else to show him the way. Mr. Collins knows nothing of our countryside. He is sure to get lost."

To conceal her concern, Elizabeth added, "And we know how stupid Mr. Collins is."

"Do we?" said Jane. She fell silent and then said, "I wonder if we have been mistaken, Lizzy. When first he came, he seemed very foolish indeed. But later—"

Elizabeth interrupted. "He was a good deal more than foolish! That letter he wrote to Father," she said. "A pompous, condescending piece of nonsense. Designed to put himself forward in the most disagreeable way."

"But the man himself is quite unlike that letter."

"He seems so now," scoffed Elizabeth. "But not when he first arrived."

"I wonder," said Jane. "Perhaps he thought it was the sort of letter he ought to write? Being accustomed, as he is, to producing sermons."

"Odious and condescending sermons," put in Elizabeth. "I pity his parishioners."

"The tone of his letter might also have been influenced by the woman who provides his living."

This point Elizabeth was unwilling to concede. "You cannot forget how he behaved at the Netherfield ball. And that dreadful speech in the Music Room. How I longed to sink into the floor!"

"I, ah, was not attending to Mr. Collins just then," Jane admitted, smiling.

"You had much better company. You also did not dance with our dear cousin. My toes have been aching ever since, not to mention my pride."

Jane set aside her embroidery frame. "If Mr. Collins disgraced himself," she said seriously, "perhaps the punch was to blame."

Elizabeth's book slid to the floor; she did not bother to retrieve it. "Jane," she whispered severely, "you are much too kind. Of course it was not the punch."

"If it was especially delicious," Jane pointed out, "I daresay Mr. Collins had too much."

"In other words, he was drunk," said Elizabeth. That would explain quite a bit, but she was not convinced.

"You know as well as I," continued Jane, "that gentlemen sometimes drink too much when they feel uncomfortable."

"Mr. Collins was fortifying himself?"

"It was in bad taste, certainly, but think, Lizzy. Every one of the guests was a stranger to him."

Elizabeth gave another glance at the windows. "But we were not."

"Yes we were," insisted Jane. "When he arrived he knew none of us, not even Father. Consider how uncomfortable that must have been."

"He set about to get on familiar terms soon enough," said Elizabeth. "And he ate as though he were starving."

"Perhaps he thought it was a compliment to Mama. She prides herself on setting a good table."

Elizabeth gave Jane a look. "So if we were foreign, Mr. Collins would have belched?"

Jane laughed. "No, Lizzy, of course not. No one is that ill-mannered."

But Elizabeth did not laugh with her. "Mr. Collins does not have the sense to feel discomfort or shame. He simply blunders ahead."

"But the punch would explain his dancing."

"Jane," said Elizabeth, "he did not know the steps. The man was floundering about, spinning where he should not spin, skipping down the line like a numbskull, blundering into couples. And then smiling and bowing and apologizing!"

"As would any gentleman who had had too much to drink."

"He made me look a fool," said Elizabeth. "And our family as well, since he announced to the world that we are related."

Jane took up her embroidery frame. "I daresay it would be well for a rector to avoid liquor or sweets," she said, "if he has so little self-control."

Elizabeth leaned in. "It's funny that you should mention sweets. Do you know, Mr. Collins now prefers black coffee? I suppose the injury took away his aversion for it."

"Adversity," said Jane, taking a stitch and pulling the silk through, "causes a person to think more seriously about life. Perhaps Mr. Collins has taken himself in hand."

"Meaning that he has reformed? Turned over a new leaf?" Elizabeth gave a huff of disbelief. But she looked again to the window. Was it her imagination or was it darker out?

"Other men have done so," said Jane serenely. "Why not Mr. Collins?"

Jane's smile made Elizabeth uneasy. She reached down and retrieved her book from the floor. But though she bent her eyes to the pages, she did not read a word.

Sometime later Hill came in and went directly to Mrs. Bennet. The younger girls, having abandoned Spillikins, were now clustered near one of the windows. Lydia had coaxed Anne de Bourgh to try her hand at drawing Kitty.

Whatever Hill was saying must have been of interest, for Elizabeth saw her mother sit up and listen. Then she gave an unhappy sniff.

"What care I? If he dies in the snowstorm, so much the better!"

Elizabeth rose to her feet and went over.

"Hill thinks we should mount a search for Mr. Collins. Apparently—and we do not know this for a fact—Mr. Fleming intended to stay over at Netherfield."

Elizabeth felt a tendril of fear curl around her heart. Mr. Collins would be walking those miles alone?

"As if we can spare any of our menservants," her mother went on. "Mr. Collins may fend for himself, I say."

"Perhaps he will also remain," Jane suggested. "As I did when I became ill."

Lydia leaned back in her chair. "You've missed your chance with him, Lizzy," she called. "I daresay Mr. Collins has designs on Miss Bingley."

"Do be quiet, Lydia," said Mrs. Bennet. "He has nothing of the sort. Lizzy is still first with him. I have eyes."

"Mama, really," said Elizabeth. She turned to Hill. "I daresay that is the explanation."

"Mr. Collins is as stubborn as they come, Miss," said Hill. "He promised to return the snowshoes, as they're needed tonight. He swore to keep his promise. On pain of death, he said."

Trust Mr. Collins to make maudlin promises he could not keep! And yet—

Elizabeth studied Hill's face. This woman was not easily taken in by flattery. How had William Collins won her confidence?

Meanwhile, Lydia and Kitty had taken up the amusing subject of Mr. Collins' success with Miss Bingley. Had her sisters been gentlemen, they would probably be placing bets!

"Oh, oh!" cried Anne, laughing and gasping for breath. "Poor Miss Bingley, to be saddled with *such* a husband!"

"You needn't feel sorry for her," said Kitty. "She lords her precedence over us something awful."

"Not precedence, Kitty, riches," said Lydia. "Her fine clothing and jewels. I daresay *you* could put her nose out of joint, Anne," she added.

"But her brother," Kitty hurried to say, "is not stuffy at all. He is very nice. And so good looking."

Anne was then treated to more detailed descriptions. Jane, Elizabeth noted, became intent on her embroidery frame. Elizabeth took another look at the clock. It would be time for dinner soon.

"But the names combine so perfectly," Lydia was saying. "Caroline Collins. Poor Mama. To be replaced as mistress by someone like that."

Mrs. Bennet clucked and fluttered and trembled.

Elizabeth spoke up. "Mama, surely you would remain in residence," she said. "Mrs. Collins could afford a magnificent London house, which would suit her very well."

"You cannot pull the wool over *my* eyes," fretted Mrs. Bennet. "I know how the world turns. And the lure of becoming a resident landowner is strong, Lizzy. Of course they will want Longbourn, if only to lord it over—"

"Mama," Elizabeth broke in. "We are only funning. Mr. Collins and Miss Bingley would never wish to marry."

"Oh," her mother cried, still in a flutter. "Play something, Mary. Something cheerful."

Mary went to the instrument and opened it. "Mr. Collins," she said, "has been in my prayers all this day. And Mr. Fleming, of course. And Mr. Darcy."

Elizabeth had forgotten all about Mr. Darcy.

Hill came in with candles and the hanging lamp was lit. Elizabeth did not need to look to the windows to know that it was dark.

Mary launched into a *fantasie* of Mozart's, playing the triplets and arpeggios badly. This proved the perfect complement to Elizabeth's state of mind.

Presently they sat down to dinner, with William Collins' place conspicuously empty. Elizabeth unfolded her napkin and smoothed it. The soup was served.

"Now don't you worry about Mr. Collins," her father said. "It's early in the season; the solstice is several weeks away."

There were smiles all around the table.

"And besides," her father added, "any animals that might be roaming about will present no danger. At this time of year they are not as hungry as they will be in, say, late January."

Elizabeth choked on her soup.

"Now, now," said her mother. "You should not tease poor Lizzy. She is quite right to fret over Mr. Collins."

Elizabeth could not meet her mother's saucy look. Fortunately her mother was soon distracted by the talk of the younger girls. Elizabeth lifted her spoon and then set it down again.

He was lost in the snow, she knew it. And he hadn't the sense to follow his own tracks back to Longbourn. His presence was not necessary at Netherfield, but would he listen?

Surely he was the most stubborn of men! Determined, too, for that light had been in his eyes—that steely glint. He'd gone ahead, and this was the result.

The soup was taken away and the main course served. Elizabeth toyed with her fork and took several bites for the sake of eating. The members of her family were giving her sidelong looks, as if her behavior was out of the ordinary. Even Anne de Bourgh looked inquisitive.

It was all Elizabeth could do to conceal her irritation.

"Consumed with worry," her mother remarked, "A very good sign."

Elizabeth laid down her fork. "Our cousin," she said, "is quite capable of taking care of himself."

Lydia gave a snort.

Elizabeth put up her chin. "I would be concerned about a dog left out in such weather."

Her mother lifted her glass. "And if Mr. Collins does happen to perish in the snow," she said hopefully.

"Another would take his place, my dear," said Mr. Bennet. "A man who is, perhaps, not quite so easily managed. Nor possessed of so pliable a nature."

Which showed how much her father knew about William Collins. He was anything but pliable! Intractable, obstinate, pigheaded—

At last Elizabeth excused herself from the table.

It was half-past six and fully dark, with only moonlight to show the way. Elizabeth pictured a ship at sea, navigating through crashing waves toward an inhospitable coastline.

A ship.

And an idea.

Elizabeth snatched up a candlestick and returned to the window. Could it be seen from outside? No, this was too low. It must be high, like a lighthouse.

Out of the drawing room she went—quickly, before any of her family came in—and up a flight of stairs to the bedchambers.

It so happened that Elizabeth's own room faced the front of the house. She drew the draperies aside, pulled up a small table, and set the candle before the window glass.

Was it enough? Frowning, she studied the effect. No. She brought her own candlestick from the bedside table and lit it. Two lights. Should there be three?

Elizabeth went directly to Mary's bedchamber and found Mary's candlestick. Three lights. Perhaps he (or some other weary traveler) would see it and be directed to safety?

The candles were new and could burn unattended for hours. Somewhat comforted, Elizabeth closed the door and descended to the drawing room.

Perhaps an hour later, or what seemed like an hour, there came banging on the main door. Elizabeth heard cries of "Hurry!" and the bolt being drawn back. She was on her feet in an instant, as were the other members of her family. Into the vestibule they spilled in time to see William Collins stagger across the threshold. He was red in the face, with crystals of ice on his coat. And he held the extra pair of snowshoes.

Hill surged forward, drawing him in, fussing all the while. Crying a little too, if that could be believed.

Mr. Collins laid aside the snowshoes and took her hand in both of his. "God bless you, Mrs. Hill," he said, "for the light in the window. A beacon of hope it was, found in my darkest hour. You have saved my life."

Elizabeth looked away from her cousin's face, afraid to confront the honest sincerity written there. Hill sent Sarah running for a change of clothes and took Mr. Collins to the kitchen to be warmed.

Suddenly shy, Elizabeth returned with the others to the drawing room. Her mind, however, was taken up with the candles. She must extinguish them before anyone noticed. Let Mr. Collins think them a figment of his imagination!

Conversation resumed, and Elizabeth took up her book. As soon as she could manage it, she slipped out and hurried up the stairs. At once she blew out two of the candles and waited for the wax to cool—why must it take so long? But the wax must not splash onto the floor, so she had no choice. And why must there be such a fog of smoke?

Her own candle she replaced on the bedside table. Mary's candle must likewise be returned, but there was the matter of the smoke that could drift out. Why would it not dissipate? She heard various sounds. Was someone climbing the stairs? She waited, praying that no one would come in.

At last she decided that it was quiet enough. Everyone should be below in the drawing room. Cautiously Elizabeth opened the door and waited. She then took up Mary's candlestick, stepped out into the corridor—and collided with William Collins!

His bulk blocked the passage; his hair was ruffled and wild. He looked from the candle to her face.

Elizabeth could feel blushes rising to her cheeks—oh, that the dimness would hide them from his notice! But he did notice. His eyes were intelligent and comprehending.

What could she say? Nothing! And so she waited, counting her heartbeats. Why would he not move out of the way?

He just stood there, gazing down at her as the minutes passed.

At last he said, gruffly, "Good night, Cousin," and stood aside to let her pass.

17 Cheerily and Merrily

On the following morning, Collins discovered that his head did not ache nearly so much. In fact, he felt more like himself than ever. Except that he was not himself, he was Darcy.

Sometime later a gentleman and lady came to visit. They seemed familiar to Collins, especially the man, but he could not place their names. Were they husband and wife?

"Hello, Darcy," the man said cheerfully. "We heard you are better and have come to see for ourselves."

Collins attempted to rise to the occasion by smiling. It took effort to twitch his lips into the proper shape.

"You look to be on the mend." The man gave an awkward laugh.

"Do be quiet," the woman said. "Poor Mr. Darcy. He has been very brave."

She came forward and sat in the chair beside the bed.

At last, sympathy! Not that Collins was feeling brave, but if this fine lady said so, who was he to disagree?

These strangers were obviously his friends. How disquieting it was to have everything turned upside down! Collins fingered Darcy's gold signet ring, heavy and solid and real.

On the other hand, he must keep in mind that there were benefits to this new identity. Yes, he must rise to the occasion.

"Soon enough, Darcy, we'll be riding again," said the man. "A gallop to Longbourn will do you good, put heart into you."

"Gallop?" repeated Collins. Did he mean they would ride at breakneck speed on horses? The thought made him shiver.

The lady must have noticed because she said, "Charles, stop. You are scaring him. Indeed," she added, bending nearer, "you shall not go anywhere until you are ready, Mr. Darcy. You are welcome to remain with us until you are completely well."

"Not—Longbourn," Collins managed to bleat. He could not face his cousins, not yet.

"Oh no," she said, smiling. "Certainly not Longbourn. There is nothing of interest there."

"Actually—" the man called Charles said.

The woman gave him a look. She turned to Collins with a smile. "You have everything you need right here with us," she said.

By Jove, it paid to be Darcy! No one—with the possible exception of his long-deceased mother—had ever smiled at him like this lady did.

She was expensively dressed and wore an amber necklace, which complimented her gown. "Beautiful," Collins said, gazing at her, and he brought his fingers to his neck. "Amber?"

She understood! He saw her finger the beads.

"Your gown, exqui—" It took several tries to work out the pronunciation, but he managed it.

"Exquisite?" she cried, and turned to the man. "Charles, he said exquisite! This shows great improvement. Indeed, his aunt's fears are quite unfounded."

"No harm to his intelligence, eh?" Charles said. He gave another awkward laugh.

There was a look exchanged between them that Collins did not understand. He returned his attention to her.

"Set a fashion," he said, indicating her gown. "In London. Among the Nobs." And because she smiled, Collins smiled too.

"Oh, Mr. Darcy," she said. "This dress is nothing special." But Collins could see that she blushed.

He fastened his gaze onto her face. "You are," he said solemnly, "Diana. No, not Diana, the other one. Venus. Beautiful like Venus."

He saw her eyes widen. Not in revulsion like his younger cousins, not in amused skepticism like Elizabeth, but in wonder. Such a simple compliment, too. Of course she did not look like Venus, but he knew ladies liked hearing that they did.

And Collins couldn't help but laugh in delight at her response. Except it came out as a giggle. But she did not seem to mind.

Yes, being Darcy certainly paid.

Mary slid into the seat beside Elizabeth. "Really," she said. "Miss de Bourgh has better uses for her time than reading novels."

Elizabeth had to agree, for Anne had done nothing but lie on the sofa all morning. Apparently she was reading a romance, for her sighs were audible.

"To be fair, there is little else to do," said Elizabeth. "A walk to Meryton is out of the question."

"There are other pursuits in life besides shopping," said Mary.

Elizabeth turned a page. "Not according to Kitty and Lydia."

Mary gave a sniff and returned to her book, their father's well-worn collection of Shakespeare's poetry.

Mr. Collins got up and added several logs to the fire. Mary's eyes followed him. "Perhaps you ought to read to us, Mr. Collins," she said.

He just stood there, blinking. If Elizabeth did not know better, she would say he was reluctant. "Very well," he said slowly. "What do you suggest?"

"A selection from Fordyce's sermons would be most welcome. I forget where you left off."

"Where I left off," he echoed. "Better yet, what are you reading, Miss Mary?"

"Shakespeare's sonnets."

"Ooh, sonnets!" called Mrs. Bennet from the other side of the room. "Just the thing. Read us a sonnet, Mr. Collins." She brought a hand to her breast. "*Let me not to the marriage of true minds admit impediments,*" she quoted.

This was the only line of Shakespeare that her mother knew. Elizabeth tried to ignore her emphasis on the word marriage.

But surely Mr. Collins wished to read sermons and was waiting to be urged. She was determined to be disobliging.

"Do you mean to imply, Mr. Collins," said Elizabeth, "that you actually read poetry?"

He gave her a look. "Of course I do. I'll go one better. As a boy, I was made to memorize several of Shakespeare's sonnets."

Elizabeth felt her lip curl. "I daresay you were. Very well, we are listening." He looked surprised, and she bit back a smile.

"Which one?" Mary wanted to know, her book at the ready.

"The 73rd," said Mr. Collins. He came and stood before Elizabeth, his expression faintly mocking. He paused, as if to collect his thoughts, and then began.

> *That time of year thou mayst in me behold*
> *When yellow leaves, or none, or few, do hang*
> *Upon those boughs which shake against the cold,*
> *Bare ruin'd choirs, where late the sweet birds sang.*
> *In me thou seest the twilight of such day*
> *As after sunset fadeth in the west,*
> *Which by and by black night doth take away,*
> *Death's second self, that seals up all in rest.*
> *In me thou see'st the glowing of such fire*
> *That on the ashes of his youth doth lie,*
> *As the death-bed whereon it must expire*
> *Consumed with that which it was nourish'd by.*
>
> *This thou perceivest, which makes thy love more strong,*
> *To love that well which thou must leave ere long.*

"An unusual choice for a schoolboy," was Elizabeth's only comment. He had recited well, handling the cadence easily and with feeling.

"Lizzy," whispered Mary. "He was word-perfect."

Elizabeth sought refuge in her book.

Lady Catherine came to see Collins after dinner. Tonight her smile was more unattractive than usual, and it put him on his guard. Her next words clinched matters.

"I believe it is time that we had a little talk, Fitzwilliam."

"Oh?" said he, with sinking heart. These little talks never turned out well.

"You are much recovered, and the situation is so perfectly arranged that I believe it is time to move forward," she said. "You cannot be in the dark as to my meaning."

Of course he was in the dark! Darcy had told him not to be an idiot, and he was trying. But Lady Catherine's specialty was being incomprehensible.

"As you know, Anne—your cousin—has come into Hertfordshire."

Collins managed a polite nod. He did not know this, and he did not see how Anne's coming involved him. Apparently it did.

"When Anne heard the news of your accident," Lady Catherine went on, "she was so *overcome* with worry that she *forced* Mr. Fleming to bring her here. Along with Mrs. Jenkinson, of course."

She looked closely at him.

Was he supposed to respond? Several phrases extolling Anne's virtue leapt to Collins' mind, but Darcy had warned him not to flatter. It was just as well that words were still so difficult to pronounce.

"Of course," he said.

Her expression told him that this response was not precisely right. "I would not wish you to have the wrong idea," said Lady Catherine crisply. "Anne was properly chaperoned at all times."

Collins murmured assent. How else could he reply?

"I find your attitude remarkably blasé," snapped Lady Catherine, "considering that Anne is your fiancée."

Collins' mouth fell open. "My what?" he said.

"Mr. Fleming tells me," said Lady Catherine, taking a seat beside the bed, "that my Anne has been telling everyone that you are her fiancé, Fitzwilliam."

Darcy had said nothing about being betrothed, nothing! Collins' lower lip pushed out. This was most unfair. Darcy ought to have given him warning.

"Therefore, I assume that you and Anne have settled it between yourselves, without consulting me."

Collins attempted to object, but without success.

"I beg your pardon?" she demanded.

Anger stirred in Collins' breast. He was not a child! Thunder and turf, he was Darcy of Pemberley! Not some down-at-the-heel rector, hat in hand, hanging on her every word! Who was she to govern his life?

He put up his chin and returned Lady Catherine's glare. "Her consent—is what matters," he blurted out. "Not yours."

Lady Catherine's eyes narrowed. In spite of being Darcy, Collins' knees began to shake.

"Very well, have it your way," she snapped. "The point is, you have come to your senses at last and have acceded to your mother's wishes and to mine."

Did Darcy not wish to marry Anne de Bourgh? Collins could certainly see why, for Anne was sickly and cross.

"And so I have been thinking," continued Lady Catherine, and she fastened her gaze upon him.

Collins felt himself cringe. What scheme had she hatched? In truth, he had no need for this alliance. He was Darcy of Pemberley!

A vision of his lovely cousin Elizabeth flooded his mind, and Collins' heart nearly leapt from his chest. Why, now that he was Fitzwilliam Darcy, Elizabeth would welcome his attentions! He would have to get out of marrying Anne.

Lady Catherine's eyes narrowed still more. "Fitzwilliam, are you listening?"

"No-oh," he said, but it came out as a moan.

At once Lady Catherine's expression changed. He saw a stab of fear cross her features, and he knew precisely what to do.

Collins had sometimes wondered whether Anne took refuge in illness. He now knew that she did. He allowed himself to breathe heavily and moaned again, this time quite distinctly. "My head," he rasped. "Pain in my head. No-oh."

Lady Catherine fled the room, and he heard bells ringing to summon help. Collins settled back on the pillows, congratulating himself for being so clever.

No longer would he be a lowly rector, begging for crumbs and favors as if he were a dog. Darcy he was, and Darcy he would be!

In the candlelight, the gold of the signet ring gave an answering twinkle.

By nine o'clock that evening, Darcy was thoroughly tired of his book and of listening to the foolish gabble of the younger girls. They had been talking all afternoon, throughout dinner, and most of tonight on the same subjects. Even the presence of the loathsome officers would be a welcome relief.

It was up to him, apparently, to introduce variety. Darcy rose to his feet and strolled to where Elizabeth sat. She did not seem to be engrossed in reading any more than he.

"Time to pay the piper, Miss Elizabeth," he said, looking down at her. "I recited that sonnet. Now you must play the pianoforte." He saw her lips part to object, but he held up a silencing hand. "I know that you play, for your mother told me."

"I cannot deny it," she said. "I fear, however, that you will be disappointed. I am sadly out of practice."

"Not at all," he said politely.

As she opened the instrument, she threw him a look. Open speculation was there, along with a challenge.

"What?" he whispered suspiciously.

"To cover my deficiencies, Mr. Collins," she said, smiling archly, "I would like you to sing as I play."

There were groans all round. Mr. Collins, sing?

Darcy groaned as well. But since Elizabeth had acquiesced to his request so gracefully, he could not squirm out of it.

Besides, who knew if Collins could sing? The man had been trained in oration, and he was accustomed to speaking. His body might be flabby with disuse, but perhaps not his voice?

And wasn't Elizabeth a minx to taunt him? Darcy decided to risk it. "I am not afraid of you," he said, returning the smile. "I would be happy to sing."

"A Christmas carol, perhaps?" suggested Mary quickly. "It would be easier for you, Mr. Collins," she added. Obviously she expected him to make a fool of himself.

Darcy glanced at Elizabeth. She was now looking uncomfortable. Apparently she had expected him to refuse.

But what was there to lose? Not dignity, not respect—Collins had neither. Once again Darcy was struck with how freeing it was to be ordinary and obscure. If he made a fool of himself, who would care?

Darcy lifted the music books from the rack and paged through them. What would Elizabeth know how to play?

He paused at Purcell's *If music be the food of love*. He'd heard Georgiana sing this one often enough. The melody line was challenging. Still, he might try a bit of it.

"*If music be the food of love*," Darcy sang under his breath, "s*ing on, sing on, sing on, sing on. Till I am filled, am fill'd with joy.*"

Collins' voice held! Up and over the high notes it sailed.

Elizabeth turned to him with a started expression. "You know this song?"

"Too well to inflict it upon an audience."

"But this is a family party," she pointed out.

He gave her a look. "Even family members have ears. And they deserve to have their hearing remain intact. See here." He set the score on the music rack and pointed. "Those high notes are murder."

Open challenge was in her eyes.

"Very well then," he said, "allow me to demonstrate. *Your eyes, your mien, your tongue declare, that you are music—ev'rywhere.*"

Sure enough, on the word *music* his voice cracked.

"Enough of that," said Darcy, smiling. He continued turning pages. "This one is rather good. I've heard it done in school." He threw her a laughing look. "Quite appropriate under the circumstances, wouldn't you say?"

Elizabeth looked as if she did not know how to respond. "I-I've never learned the accompaniment for any of these," she confessed.

"Nor have I," he said. "If you will kindly make room for me to sit—" Darcy broke off speaking. Collins would never fit on the bench beside Elizabeth. He procured a straight-backed chair and brought it close beside her.

"Now then, we'll both be readers, shall we?" he said. "And see here, the wonder of the Baroque. Your part is *basso continuo*, that is to say figured bass. Meaning you play only chords, Miss Elizabeth. As soloist I do all the heavy lifting. Most unfortunately."

He reached across and placed his right hand on the keys. "I'll just run through my part," he said, "before I make a complete fool of myself."

He worked through the melody line. Yes, it was as he remembered it. "I will probably slide over these sixteenth notes," he admitted.

She listened with obvious astonishment. "You play the pianoforte, Mr. Collins?"

"Only one note at a time," he said, twinkling. "Much to the disappointment of my sainted mother. She was most insistent about lessons."

"But your mother died when you were very young," she protested, "or so Father was given to understand."

Darcy refused to be deterred by this slip. "Ah, but one is never too young to begin learning to play," he quipped. "And how clever of you to guess her last words to me. 'William,' she said, 'you must practice!'"

Elizabeth broke out laughing. "How wretched you are! To jest about your poor mother!"

"Thus I am saved from weeping. Dear Mother. I hated practicing and would much rather ride my pony. Shall we begin?"

"Your pony?" Elizabeth sounded astonished. "But I thought—no, Mr. Collins, you told us that you do not ride."

"A mere conversational gambit, that. To, er, save myself from embarrassment."

Elizabeth was openly doubtful. "What embarrassment?"

He spread his hands. "How was I to know that you would not make me mount a raging stallion and go galloping across fields?"

"As if we had such an animal!" she said, laughing. "Even our carriage horses are used on the farm."

"Ah, but I did not know then what lived in your stables. If you have a pony, Miss Elizabeth, I will gladly ride him. Although," he paused to pat his abdomen, "it would be rather a kick in the teeth for the pony."

Elizabeth continued to laugh, and he joined her.

"Now then," he said at last, "shall we begin? Miss Lydia is looking impatient." Actually, it was Anne de Bourgh who was staring at him. Obviously Collins had never been pressed to sing at Rosings Park.

He pointed to the page. "Here we are."

DARCY BY ANY OTHER NAME

She leaned in to read the words. "*I resolve against cringing and whining.*" Again Elizabeth broke out laughing. "Very well, Mr. Collins." She struck the first chord and shot him a challenging look.

"*I resolve against cringing and whining,*" Darcy sang. He broke off to point at the score. "You have a chord just there," he whispered.

"I—was taken up with the excellence of your singing," she whispered back, and spread her fingers over the keys.

"You should know better than to lie to a clergyman," he countered. "Shall we begin again? And go straight through?"

"*I resolve against cringing and whining,
In a lover's intrigue so unfit.
'Tis like saying grace without dining,
And betrays more affection than wit.
To kneel and adore, to sigh and protest
And there to give o'er, whereabout lies the jest?*"

Again Darcy stopped. "It is bad enough that I must carry the melody, dear Cousin. But if I am left to sing *a cappella* because you cannot stop giggling long enough to play..."

"I do apologize," she gasped, still laughing. "But these words!"

He pulled a mournful face. "The story of my life." He pointed. "Here is your next chord."

Obediently she played it.

> "*Dearest mistress, I prithee be wiser,*
> *Recant your platonic opinion,*
> *Whilst you hoard up your love, like a miser,*
> *You starve all within your dominion,*
> *And when the dread foe is vanquish'd by you,*
> *I'll kiss the boy's bow, and forever be true.*"

His performance was greeted with enthusiasm, but all that mattered to Darcy was the warmth that shone in Elizabeth's eyes. Could it be that disdain had given way to admiration? And why did this now mean everything to him?

18 A Parson's Farewell

Was it the snow, that vast expanse of white that kept them imprisoned in the house? Was it having to crouch before the fire to feel warm? Was it Lydia's giggle and Kitty's shrill laugh, as they vied to entertain Anne de Bourgh? Whatever the cause, Elizabeth's nerves were frayed to the breaking point.

And of course, whom should she find at breakfast but Mr. Collins? What mood had seized her last night? According to Jane, she had flirted shamelessly with the man.

Of course she had not flirted. Laughing and talking were not flirting! And if they were, why, she had done the same with Mr. Wickham often enough and no one said a word. Nor would they, for George Wickham was harmless, the sort of man one did not take seriously. He was amusing, and Elizabeth enjoyed being amused.

Even so, it was troubling to encounter Mr. Collins. How could she have forgotten herself so completely in his company? Elizabeth would chart a very different course today. Let William Collins so much as smile at her, and he would learn his mistake!

Tea and toast were all Elizabeth was feeling up to. It was otherwise with her mother, who launched into a lament over the choices on the sideboard.

"Ham," she said wrathfully. "And more of the same for luncheon and for dinner. I daresay we'll have ham soup as well."

There was no dealing with her mother in this mood. Elizabeth applied herself to buttering a piece of toast. William Collins she ignored.

"I do not see why we cannot have poultry tonight," her mother went on. "Chickens are as plentiful in winter as they are the rest of the year." She lifted one of the covers and peered beneath. "Bacon," she said wrathfully.

Elizabeth noticed a movement and looked up. William Collins was attempting to hide a smile and no wonder. His plate was loaded with bacon. He caught her gaze; his eyes twinkled.

She quickly looked away.

"No Englishman will find fault with bacon," he said to no one in particular. "I daresay we could eat it for every meal."

"Speak for yourself, Mr. Collins," said Mrs. Bennet, lifting another of the covers. "And why in the world are there no eggs?"

"I suppose the hens will not lay," Elizabeth offered.

"Most distressing. I shall speak to Hill about it. This cannot be allowed to continue."

Elizabeth bit her lips to keep from smiling. "One cannot force hens to lay, Mama."

"I do not see why not. We give them a warm coop in which to live and we feed them. It isn't like we just *toss* them into the paddock and expect them to fend for themselves! And this is the thanks we get?"

Mr. Collins rose to his feet and politely held the chair for Mrs. Bennet. "I believe it has something to do with the dark and the cold, if that is any consolation, ma'am," he said. "Or so I have been told."

Elizabeth looked away. Now it would come, an homily on the raising of poultry, as if William Collins knew anything about a farmyard. She had been waiting for the sermonizing side of his personality to emerge.

From beneath her lashes she watched him resume his seat and apply himself to his precious bacon. If only the snow would melt so that he could take himself back to Hunsford!

"How I despise this season," said Mrs. Bennet, and she shook out her napkin. "The days are short and the meals are uninteresting. And it isn't even Christmas. And here I was hoping for a nice brace of partridges from Mr. Bingley."

"Mama," Elizabeth protested. Mr. Bingley had promised no such gift. How embarrassing that her mother would expose her assumptions before Mr. Collins!

"And of course, no one can hunt in all this snow," continued Mrs. Bennet. "Not that anyone will bestir himself to *try*." Her gaze slanted down the table toward Mr. Collins.

"What a pity that you do not indulge in shooting," she told him. "I suppose we must have sermons preached, but I do wish that you could do more than lounge about and eat."

This remark was hardly fair, but it was all Elizabeth could do not to laugh. From the corner of her eye she saw William Collins put down his knife and fork.

"As a matter of fact," he said quietly, "I do know a little something about guns. And if your husband has a firearm in his possession, I would be happy to oblige."

He hesitated and a grin appeared. "At any rate," he added, "it can do no harm to try my hand at—how do the sportsmen say it? Bagging some game?"

"By all means, Mr. Collins," said Mrs. Bennet. "Do make yourself useful."

Elizabeth became occupied with the contents of her teacup. How like him to pretend a skill in order to puff off his consequence! Fortunately none of their neighbors would be present to see the spectacle. Mr. Collins, shoot? What would George Wickham say? Elizabeth could almost hear his mocking laughter.

Mr. Collins pushed back his chair. "If you do not mind, I shall ask him about it directly."

"Mind your manners when you do," said Mrs. Bennet. "His cold has not improved—I daresay he caught it from Dr. Bentley—but will Mr. Bennet remain in his bed? Foolish man, he insists on keeping to his chair in the library. Mind his fire when you go in. So often he allows it to burn to nothing."

Mr. Collins excused himself and went out.

"Just look at that," her mother said. "How quickly we go through wood. Ring for someone to build up the fire, Lizzy. I am fatigued to death with snow and cold."

Weren't they all!

Elizabeth obeyed her mother's request and then left the dining room. Would her father agree to loan one of his guns? He had not taken a gun out for years. He gave various reasons, but Elizabeth suspected his eyesight was to blame.

And yet, in a sardonic mood she knew that he would give the gun to William Collins and then amuse himself by watching from the window.

The door to his library adjoined the drawing room and was closed. Was Mr. Collins within? Elizabeth settled into an overstuffed chair and took up a book.

Her instincts were correct. Soon Mr. Collins emerged with a rifle, the long black one with the brass filigree on the stock. He also had a leather pouch. A powder horn was slung over his shoulder.

She peeked at him over the pages of her book. Why was he not holding the gun at arm's length? She'd pictured Mr. Collins taking squeamish, mincing steps to avoid setting it off. Which was ridiculous, for none of her father's guns were loaded.

William Collins crossed to one of the windows, apparently to better examine it. His fingers moved over the length of the barrel, and he drew out the ramrod. His gaze was intent. It seemed that her prosy cousin knew something about firearms after all.

"This is somewhat of a surprise," he remarked. "Not a fowling piece, but it will do."

Was he speaking to her?

"An Austrian military rifle," he went on, "no doubt built for an officer perhaps twenty years ago."

Did he expect her to say something? He was smiling at her in an expectant way.

"Austrian riflemen have fought on both sides of the war," he went on, "not that Napoleon cares. He should, though."

Were Mr. Collins' eyes twinkling? "Everyone hates mercenaries," he added. "They're like gossips, loyal only to what's best for themselves."

Did he think she cared about mercenaries? And why did she continue to study him? Her dreary book was surely to blame!

"The barrel looks to be in good shape," he said, "and so does the front sight."

Some answer was required, so Elizabeth said, "Oh."

"Now to see if it will shoot. But first, a thorough cleaning is in order."

"Do you know how to clean a gun?" Elizabeth was betrayed into saying.

"What an incompetent you must think me," he said. He hitched the powder horn's strap higher on his shoulder and took up the leather pouch. "Come and see."

He walked away from the window, leaving Elizabeth with her book. Come and see? Was this an invitation? Or was it a challenge?

Voices in the vestibule told her that her sisters would soon be coming in.

"Very well," said Elizabeth, and she put the book aside. "I believe I shall."

Mr. Fleming had told Collins that his improvement, once begun, would progress rapidly, and he was perfectly right. Collins was feeling and looking much better. The swelling of his face had gone down, and his lip looked almost normal. Speaking would be easier.

Today he occupied a sofa, fully clothed, since Mr. Fleming insisted that he take a turn about the room from time to time.

In other words, he must walk. Fleming could call it walking if he liked, but it was more like being dragged about by Holdsworth.

But Darcy's body was lean and muscular, and it responded to exercise. Even after a small amount of movement, Collins could feel strength returning. From somewhere Fleming had unearthed a cane, and Collins made grateful use of it.

It was well that Holdsworth had the care of his clothing, for when Collins came into Darcy's bedchamber and saw the amount of it, he was staggered. How could one decide among so many fabulous choices?

Just now, for instance, he wore a snow-white shirt, nicely starched, of such fine quality that it almost made him swoon. Returning to his own scratchy linen would be difficult, if not impossible. And the fine lawn did not wrinkle like his linen shirts had. By mid-morning, Collins usually looked as if he had slept in his shirt.

And then there was the glorious silk neck cloth and striped waistcoat. The dark blue coat—not black! —was tailored to perfection, as were the fawn breeches. Indeed, it was worth taking short walks just to gaze into the looking glass.

Because Holdsworth was not present, Collins did so now. He stood for a long, delightful interval before his reflection, turning this way and that and sighing. By Jove, his physique was a marvel! His shoulders needed no padding, his waist was slim, his thighs firm. And his calves were beautifully muscular.

Collins turned, made a leg, and chortled for joy at his reflection. This was beyond his wildest dreams! And with Holdsworth to instruct him on what to wear and when, he would always look right, from the top of his head—with hair that was perfectly styled—to the tips of his shining Hessian boots.

He was not wearing Hessians now, of course, but he'd caught a glimpse of the boots in the dressing room. And then there was the delight of his face, with its decisive jaw, well-shaped nose, and cleft chin—so handsomely noble!

Collins was just admiring the way the blue coat covered his backside when there came a soft knocking at the door.

He heard the door swing open a crack. "Holdsworth?" said a woman's voice. "Mr. Darcy?"

"Yes?" said Collins. His voice was crisp and clear. Wonderful!

"It is I, Caroline Bingley. May I come in?"

This would be Miss Bingley, the mistress of the house, sister to Charles. In addition to his skills as valet, Holdsworth was an excellent source of useful information.

Collins turned away from the looking glass and took hold of his cane. "Please do," he called.

For it occurred to him that Caroline Bingley was also a source of useful information.

Finding space in the crowded kitchen was a challenge, but Elizabeth had not reckoned with Hill. Anything dear Mr. Collins needed was no trouble at all. She set a kettle to boil, one with a narrow spout to accommodate pouring water into the barrel of the gun, and she herself cleared a work area.

And Hill provided aprons. It was great fun to see a big man like Mr. Collins solemnly struggle to tie the sash. Elizabeth decided to help him. She could not help but notice how his clothes hung on him, and she studied his profile. What had become of his double chins? And his hair was so much more attractive now that it was not slicked down flat.

"So in a bit," he was explaining, "we'll pour the hot water into the barrel." He passed her a towel.

Somehow she had become Mr. Collins' assistant. As he seemed to expect her help, she complied. He emptied her father's leather pouch and sorted through its contents, naming them for her benefit: vent pick, shot, priming powder, cloth for the patch, and extra flints.

Hill produced a flat-headed tool, and Mr. Collins removed and disassembled the firing mechanism for cleaning. He was, she realized, a thorough workman.

When the water was hot enough, he drew out the ramrod. "The trick here," he said, "is to tie the cloth securely. There's a world of trouble if it becomes stuck in the barrel."

He competently tore a strip of Hill's cheesecloth and began wrapping it around the end of the ramrod. "So," he said, twinkling, "we shall see how well I can accomplish this."

He poured water into the barrel, changing it and the cloth several times. At length what he poured into the bucket came clean. He reassembled the gun with similar thoroughness. He proceeded to shine the stock with wax.

And then Mr. Collins tidied their work area instead of leaving it for Sarah or Hill to clear away.

Hill produced surprises: a thick brown overcoat, a woolen flat cap, gloves, and a pair of boots, all of which fit Mr. Collins very well.

"Will you go out to hunt now?" Elizabeth said.

"In a bit," he said. "First, I must learn how this fires. And also, I must obtain bait for the birds, since I won't have beaters and a gamekeeper to flush them out for me."

"Ah, the gentlemen's hunt," Elizabeth said, smiling.

"Not terribly sporting, is it?" he agreed. "But convenient for large parties, which are more about eating and drinking than shooting."

She dimpled. "What do you know about gentlemen's hunts, Mr. Collins?"

He lowered the gun and returned the smile, a rather bashful one. "Not as much as I'd like. If I am waiting for an invitation from Rosings, I'll be waiting for rather a long while."

"Perhaps you'll be invited once Anne marries Mr. Darcy?" she said. "Although, I suppose they will live at his estate, not hers."

He looked rather taken aback. "I wouldn't count on that blessed event."

"But Miss de Bourgh said—"

"Anne is acting on information from her mother. I doubt her intended bridegroom will have the banns read any time soon, if at all."

"You are very confident, Mr. Collins."

He shrugged into the brown overcoat and began buttoning it. "That, my dear Elizabeth, is because I am."

"But how do you—"

He interrupted. "I'll just load this outside, shall I?" he said. His tone was rather sharp, which surprised her. "I see your father does not have a cow's knee," he added, "so it is well that it is not snowing."

"A what?" said Elizabeth.

"A cow's knee. To shield the firepan from rain or snow. It guards against misfires."

Elizabeth just looked at him.

"And now, if you will excuse me," he said, "I have some shooting to do."

And giving her a bow, he collected his supplies and pulled the door open.

"But Mr. Collins," she called. "You've forgotten your—"

The service door was pulled firmly to.

"He's forgotten the cap, Hill," said Elizabeth. "And the gloves."

Hill shook her head. "That's way of young gentlemen and guns, Miss Elizabeth," she said. "When they are upset or put out, they shoot."

Was William Collins put out?

DARCY BY ANY OTHER NAME

"Never you fear," Hill went on. "Mr. Collins knows what he's about, doesn't he, Ned?"

Because James had a cold, Ned had come in from the barn to assume his duties. "That's the trouble," he said, "with old guns that are left to sit. Rab Miller learned the hard way. Whole side of his face, burnt to a crisp."

"Do you mean," said Elizabeth, "that Father's gun could explode?"

"Not explode, Miss, but near enough. Stay clear of the lock-side, that's what I say."

Elizabeth snatched up Mr. Collins' cap and gloves and went stumbling after him, out the door and into the snow. She found him in a shoveled-out area of the paddock, engaged in loading the gun.

"Mr. Collins!" she called. "Stay clear of the lock-side!"

Miss Bingley had ordered tea brought in, and together she and Collins enjoyed a cozy *tête-à-tête*.

"Ah, Pemberley," she was saying. "A fine house, richly furnished, truly impressive. For situation, unparalleled."

He sat back and, over the rim of his teacup, smiled at her. "I so enjoy hearing your impressions and memories, Miss Bingley. Please continue."

She colored and looked pleased. "The grounds and gardens are delightful. I am told," she said, "that you have some of the finest woods in the country. I must confess, I care more for the elegant gardens than for wilderness. My brother will say that the fishing is very fine." She gave a tittering laugh. "As you know, you are by far the better fisherman."

Collins repressed a shudder. He disliked everything about fishing.

"The river and the trees and the winding valley—surely you remember them, Mr. Darcy."

"I do, in bits and pieces. But it pleases me to hear you describe them."

"I am happy to do anything I can for you."

Collins helped himself to another biscuit and hazarded a guess. After all, ladies fancied flowers. "My mother had a special garden, did she not? Roses?"

"Yes, and a very fine one. Georgiana must have its oversight by now, along with your army of gardeners." She paused. "You do remember Georgiana?"

Collins hazarded a guess. Darcy was not married. "My sister," he said.

Miss Bingley clapped her hands in delight. "Yes, yes, you do recall. She is so lovely and plays the pianoforte with exceptional artistry." She paused. "Our dearest wish is that she will come to see Charles as more than your friend."

Did Miss Bingley wink? Collins was not sure. At any rate, hearing about Darcy's sister made him nervous. He devoutly hoped that she would remain at Pemberley, or London, or wherever it was she lived and not come here.

"How does the interior of the house strike you?" he inquired.

"As large and spacious and very fine," said Miss Bingley. Here she hesitated. "The interior is, shall we say, reflective of the taste and style of previous generations? It would be improved, in my opinion, with a bit of modernizing.

"You will forgive my saying so, Mr. Darcy," she added quickly. "I have long lived in London and am accustomed to everything in the first style."

"But of course," said Collins. "I appreciate your candor. What do you mean by of the first style, precisely?"

"I mean, since you ask, the addition of furnishings that strike a note of true opulence, as is suitable for your family's wealth and prominence. I've long thought that the vestibule cries out for a larger chandelier. Cut crystals, as you know, fairly dance with light and are so elegant. Also, the draperies are not quite rich enough."

"For myself," said Collins, "I favor the style of Rosings Park. There is a carved chimney mantelpiece in one of the parlors that is very fine."

Again Miss Bingley gave her tittering laugh. "Rosings Park," she echoed. "I have not had the privilege of seeing that estate. Nor am I like to, unless..."

She gave him a sidelong look. But even that was gratifying, for she smiled so warmly.

Collins crossed one shapely calf over the other and returned Miss Bingley's smile.

"Do go on," he invited. "What else would you modernize?"

As she spoke, Collins' gaze came to rest on the humidor on one of the bureaus. Darcy smoked cigars, fragrant and costly. Here was a habit Collins had longed to indulge, even since university days. And now he could. Cigars and elegant clothing and fine wines. And beautiful women as well?

Miss Bingley was not precisely beautiful, but she was well-dressed in every detail. No one could find fault with the costliness of her lustrous pearls, and she seemed to be well-connected socially.

This brought to mind something else. "Tell me something about my house in town," he said, for surely Darcy had one. "And if you wouldn't mind just refreshing my tea?"

The eagerness with which she took his cup and saucer was entirely gratifying.

Mr. Collins gazed at her, wide-eyed and solemn. Clad in that sturdy overcoat he looked like a large brown bear.

"Our neighbor's stable boy, Robert Miller," Elizabeth gasped out, "had his face burned by an exploding gun! Do have a care!"

To cover her embarrassment, Elizabeth added, "Here are your gloves and cap." She placed them on the piled-up snow.

DARCY BY ANY OTHER NAME

"Thank you," he said quietly. "I'll know more after I've fired several shots. Often a gun throws to one side or the other."

How should she answer? For he obviously was not deterred by possible danger. "Practice makes perfect," she said lamely.

"That it does," he agreed. He just stood there, looking at her.

"And you will avoid the lock-side?" she added, hoping he knew what that meant. Why did he not put on the cap and gloves? Why did he just stand there?

She searched in vain for something else to say. "I have not seen many birds. You might not have success. But it does not matter," she added quickly. "Mama can do without pheasants."

"Or else Mr. Bingley will send them."

So he'd caught that remark. She was afraid that he had.

"Ah, but this is survival," he confided, smiling. "Therefore I will not take a sporting approach. I will broadcast oats and barley, which I'll borrow from the stable, onto the snow. Then I will hide until the birds come."

Elizabeth returned the smile. "Very pretty. So long as the birds are not intelligent."

His eyes twinkled. "What a bumbling incompetent you think me."

"Not incompetent," she protested.

"According to you, I am incapable of doing even one thing. I shall prove you wrong."

She spread her hands. "Aside from dabbling in music, I have not seen you do anything. Not even preach a sermon."

"You have seen me clean a gun," he suggested.

"I daresay I could do the same, given rudimentary instruction."

He laughed and slung the powder horn from his shoulder. "What a skeptic you are, Elizabeth," he said. "My harshest critic. My most severe censor."

"I speak only of what I see."

"In your eyes, I have no skills." But his eyes were laughing.

"No masculine skills," she corrected. "Singing and playing one note at a time do not count."

"Not one ability," he said, moving nearer. "Aside from potentially causing an explosion."

"Or being struck by lightning."

He laughed. "There is always that."

He looked more like a bear than ever. A smiling bear.

"The only ability I can see, and it might not be always beneficial," she said, dimpling, "is stubbornness, Cousin William. There seems to be little that deters you from something you want."

"I thank you for the vote of confidence." She felt his fingers brush her chin. His eyes were warm. "Not one manly skill?"

"Alas, no," she said softly.

"Skeptic!" he said. And then he bent and kissed her.

His lips were on hers, warm and soft and surprisingly tender. He did not immediately pull away, nor did she.

"Forgive me," he whispered. "I am not in the habit of kissing."

She ought to have pushed him away. She ought to have run into the house. Instead she just stood there, her fingers stroking the lapel of his bearlike overcoat.

The second kiss was tenderer, less tentative, and longer lasting.

She was kissing Mr. Collins, a man she loathed!

Those lips of his were on hers, and she did not mind. No she did not mind at all. That she hated him only added to the thrill.

He was solid and warm and—passionate? Was this passion?

His arms came round her, pressing her against his chest. Was Mr. Collins, by turns foolish and reserved, also seriously earnest? Elizabeth abandoned trying to decide and surrendered to the kiss.

And after he had seen her to the door and gone his way, Elizabeth was left to blush and scold herself. What had she done?

She had kissed William Collins. Not once—that was forgivable, since she was taken unawares. But twice?

Had anyone seen, or was she hidden by piled-up snow? Would anyone suspect? Kissing Mr. Collins! Her mother would be thrilled.

And yet Elizabeth was the one to be thrilled. A staid and steady rector, so buttoned up and solemn. And yet he had kissed her like that!

At one time she had wondered whether George Wickham might kiss her—he had looked as if he wanted to. And a kiss from him would be a light, flirtatious gesture, nothing more.

There was nothing flirtatious about William Collins' kiss.

Elizabeth pressed her hands to her flaming cheeks. Such a thing could never be repeated. "I shall take this," she vowed, "to my grave."

19 THE JOVIAL BEGGARS

What began as light drizzle quickly changed to sheeting rain, hissing as it struck the snow. Darcy took aim and fired, but this time nothing happened. The firepan and the flint were soaked, and the pheasants lived on to finish their meal. With a sigh, Darcy lowered Mr. Bennet's rifle.

Returning to the house was out of the question, for he could not face Elizabeth. Why had he kissed her? He'd asked this question countless times, and the answer was always the same. Weak, he was weak—and thoroughly stupid as well. If he ever had a hope of winning Elizabeth as himself, that hope was gone. For it was Collins she had kissed.

Collins, the man who would inherit her family's home. Collins, who would provide an income and stability. It was a prudent move on her part, but there was more to it than that. Elizabeth had loathed Collins and had spurned him without a second thought. But not anymore. Those kisses told Darcy everything.

Meanwhile the rain continued to fall, soaking his coat and cap, running down his face and neck, pooling beneath his collar. Held prisoner by self-accusation, Darcy scarcely noticed.

For who was responsible for Elizabeth's beguiling change of heart? No one but himself. For some perverse reason he was unable to resist the delight of her company. Like a fool, he'd abandoned all sense and rushed headlong into love.

For love this was, it could have no other name. To see Elizabeth smile, to join with her in laughing, to spar with her and share confidences—what happiness! And in the end, she preferred him above all men, even George Wickham.

Like a madman, Darcy stood smiling in the rain. Yes, she preferred him to Wickham.

By the time he had slogged to the service door, he was in a pitiable state. He was confronted by Hill, who stripped him of his sodden coat and cap and the birds he had managed to shoot. The loaded rifle he delivered carefully to Ned.

"The Master's cold worsening by the hour," said Hill. "And I daresay your fate will be the same."

DARCY BY ANY OTHER NAME

Darcy began to protest, but Hill interrupted. "And for what have you caught your death?"

"Five pheasants?" Darcy offered.

Hill was not impressed. "I trust the Mistress will be satisfied with her meal. Come along, Ned." And, taking up a stack of towels, Hill shooed Darcy from the kitchen.

"We have meat aplenty," she scolded, following close on his heels, "without you being soaked to the skin to shoot birds. Why did you not come in at once?"

How could Darcy tell her his reasons?

Up the back stairs they went, with Ned trailing behind. "It's been scarcely a week since you were struck down," continued Hill, "and what must you do but walk for miles in all weather!"

Yes, he'd been a fool, and Hill's accusations stung. "But Lady Catherine," he protested.

"*And* Mrs. Bennet," said Hill. "*And* that physician. It isn't right, being at everyone's beck and call the way you are."

Darcy had to smile. "Including yours?"

Hill was not amused. She followed him into the bedchamber, looked around with distaste, and put down the towels.

"When you are finished with Mr. Collins, Ned, you will bring more wood. The future Master of Longbourn should not be made to freeze in his bed."

Ned went to work building up the fire.

Darcy stood there, making a puddle on the floor. What did Hill expect him to do? He could hardly remove his waistcoat and breeches while she was present. He then noticed that she had the wardrobe open and was removing his garments.

"Ned will take away your wet things and help you into a dry nightshirt," she said. "And then, Mr. Collins, you will remain in this bed, with a hot brick, until morning." She folded his spare coat, breeches, and waistcoat and piled them on the chair.

"But my clothes," protested Darcy.

"They are sadly in need of taking in," said Hill. "Which I shall do while you are in bed."

"I cannot lie about all afternoon."

"You most certainly can." Hill put her hands on her hips. "I have trouble enough with one sick gentleman, and I do not wish for two."

"But I am not ill."

"You had no business allowing yourself to be out in that icy rain. You are not trustworthy, Mr. Collins. You are too obliging. I daresay you will dress yourself and sidle into the drawing room to keep the young ladies from feeling lonely."

This drew a reluctant laugh. "I am incapable of sidling anywhere, Mrs. Hill," said Darcy. "Or haven't you noticed?"

"You are a shadow of your former self," said Hill. "And I daresay Miss Elizabeth has noticed the improvement. She can do without your company for one day."

Darcy's eyes found the floor. Shame was present—for how much had Hill seen? —along with relief. As Hill's prisoner, he would not have to face Elizabeth.

Hill crossed to the door. "I'll not worry the family with melodrama, if that's your concern," she said. "It does no harm to be cautious. Sarah will bring soup and a hot brick presently."

Soon Darcy was alone, dry and warm and bundled into bed, with the snap of the wood fire and the drumming rain to bear him company.

How thin were Longbourn's walls! For he heard voices in the corridor, Hill's and Elizabeth's, and his cousin's concern was palpable.

Darcy's heart warmed. How he longed to reassure her!

Ah, but Hill would give no quarter. Mr. Collins must be allowed to rest.

"Which is a very good thing, Lizzy, you know it is," said another voice. "For when the roads are clear he will be well enough to go back to Hunsford where he belongs."

Sadly, Darcy realized that this solution might be the very one he would have to take.

It was becoming a habit of Miss Bingley's to visit Mr. Darcy after every meal. Collins knew that Lady Catherine would not condone this practice, but Miss Bingley was an evasive creature. Besides, there was nothing improper, since Holdsworth was usually at work in the dressing room.

That was the thing about Netherfield, there was always someone lurking about. Collins supposed that this was only to be expected, since Netherfield required an army of servants to function. He was coming to realize that the size and style of Longbourn House, though not as impressive, was more to his taste.

That evening Miss Bingley was jubilant about the rain. "For once the snow is washed away," she said, "we shall travel to London, as we were planning to do."

His confusion must have been evident, for she added, "Surely you recall that Charles has business there. Something about his properties and investments. He is keen to have your advice."

"My—advice?" stammered Collins.

"But of course. You are such a competent adviser."

She went on talking, but Collins did not listen. He knew nothing about business, save for the general wisdom about investing in the four-percents, whatever those were. Having no fortune of his own, he'd never paid attention. Now that he was Darcy, the troubling world of finance must be dealt with.

The thought made his head hurt.

"We were supposed to depart for London immediately after the ball, you know," she added.

No, Collins did not know. He sighed heavily.

Caroline Bingley's face grew solemn, and she laid a sympathetic hand on his arm. "Please do not think it was any trouble for us to remain, Mr. Darcy. We could not leave you to suffer alone."

Of course Collins thanked her. What else could he do?

"As soon as you are well enough to travel, we shall return to London. And after that?" She paused to give him a sidelong look. "I daresay you will wish to spend Christmas at Pemberley."

Her hand remained on his sleeve, and her smile was coy. Was she angling for an invitation?

As for Pemberley, Collins could only imagine what horrors awaited him. His sister would be there and his business manager and his housekeeper. And a fleet of servants and tenants and God only knew who else, all of whom he was supposed to know by sight.

Collins closed his eyes and drew a long breath. There was only one way to manage this sort of trouble, and it was beautifully effective.

"If you will excuse me, Miss Bingley," he said. "My head has begun to ache again. Would you mind summoning Mr. Fleming to administer another dose of medication?"

Caroline Bingley looked crestfallen, and Collins breathed a sigh of relief.

It rained steadily all night. On the following morning the view from Darcy's window showed that the blanket of white had subsided. Longbourn's paddock was threatening to become a pond.

Hill advised breakfast in bed, and Darcy gratefully accepted. He would encounter Elizabeth later in the morning, safely in the company of others. Should he come upon her at the breakfast table, alone, there was no telling what his weakness might allow.

But his time was not wasted. Darcy studied Collins' little notebook and, with paper unearthed in a drawer, practiced copying the man's handwriting. Fortunately the foolish fellow had signed the flyleaf.

Presently Ned came up with hot water for shaving and Collins' clothes. Hill had done an admirable job with the alterations. It was wonderful to have clothes that fit. Aside from having to wear black, Darcy was feeling more like himself.

The bedchamber door swung open with a clatter. Fleming stood on the threshold, red-faced and wet, his physician's satchel in hand.

Darcy came out of his chair. "Upon my word! Have you come all the way from Netherfield?"

Fleming gave him a wan smile. "Haven't I just? On horseback, no less."

Ned came in with towels and stood at the ready. Darcy was unsure about what to do. As himself, he would have retired to a discreet corner. But as Collins he held the wet clothing that Fleming struggled to remove.

"I never arrive at this house but what I am grateful," said Fleming, after Ned went out "As if the rain were not enough, we must have mud and standing water. It's a wonder that the horse did not fall and break a leg." He grimaced. "The gamekeeper's most reliable mount."

"It's a wonder that you ventured out at all."

Fleming spread his hands to the fire. "Her ladyship gave me no alternative. I bring letters for her daughter and the unhappy Jenkinson."

"One can guess the contents," said Darcy.

"A sound scolding to be had by all." Fleming straightened. "And now that I am dry and somewhat warmed, I am duty-bound to deliver them."

"You'll find everyone in the drawing room, save for Mr. Bennet."

"Hiding in his library?" Fleming remarked, as he went out. "Wise fellow."

Darcy followed. "He's confined to bed with a cold."

Fleming glanced back. "Is it serious?"

"According to Mrs. Bennet, yes," replied Darcy. "If the man so much as sneezes, he's at death's door. But Mrs. Hill is concerned, and that worries me."

As soon as he came into the drawing room, Darcy's eyes found Elizabeth. How should he behave? A dignified silence would never do, but neither would urbane insouciance. He quietly found a seat on one of the sofas.

To his credit, Fleming delivered the letters without a fuss. Mrs. Jenkinson received hers with such obvious dismay that Darcy struggled not to laugh. She thrust it, unopened, under her knitting basket. Her shaking hands could no longer hold the needles, so she did nothing but sit and look miserable.

Anne's color came and went, but like Jenkinson, she put her letter aside. This Darcy could not understand. Why not open it and face the worst?

His expression must have mirrored his thoughts, for he felt Elizabeth's ironic gaze. But there was warmth in her eyes, not coldness. And when she exchanged her seat to share the sofa with him, he blushed and smiled like a schoolboy.

Of course he must speak with her. For some reason he said the first thing that came into his head. "Is it a habit among women," he whispered, "to avoid bad news?"

"How do you mean?"

"Miss de Bourgh knows that she has a scold coming from her mother," he murmured. "And yet she waits to read it, thus becoming a victim to her fears. Why not face the worst and be done with it?"

Elizabeth's chin came up. "And why is it," she countered, "that men always assume the worst? Her letter might be from her fiancé."

Darcy felt his lip curl. "My dear girl," he murmured.

Lydia interrupted. "Do open your letter, Anne," she called. "For of course it is from Mr. Darcy. And of course it is romantic."

Darcy felt Elizabeth's elbow dig into his ribs.

Anne did not inquire after Mr. Darcy's health—so much for the object of her devotion! Elizabeth did not ask after him either, so it was left for Darcy to do.

"He is up and about," Fleming answered. "I daresay he's on his way to becoming his usual self."

Darcy thought he heard a sharp intake of breath. Was it Anne's?

"All things considered, he is making splendid progress." Fleming lowered his voice. "Do you know Mr. Darcy well, Collins?"

Darcy's answer was guarded. "No more than usual."

"Rather a dressy gentleman, I must say. Fond of his reflection."

Darcy caught Elizabeth's suppressed laugh. Blast that Collins! Parading in front of the mirror, no doubt. What would Holdsworth think?

"Fond of the ladies, too," Fleming went on. "He has your gift for compliments."

There was no one at Netherfield to compliment, save for—

Darcy swallowed a groan. Was Collins flirting with Caroline Bingley?

"All praise and credit to Lady Catherine," said Darcy grimly. "Under her tutelage I perfected the art."

Fleming laughed and so did Elizabeth.

Meanwhile Anne had her letter open and was scowling at it. "It is not from Mr. Darcy," she said. "It is from Mother. And she is most unfair. Can you imagine? She demands an apology."

"Oh," cried Kitty, ever loyal. "As if you did anything wrong."

"Furthermore," Anne went on, "she insists that I return home at once. I am not an infant! I refuse to be ordered about!"

"Hear, hear," said Lydia.

Anne gave her a gratified look. "She also accuses me of ruining my health."

"Which is completely untrue," said Kitty. "You have been ever so well since you arrived."

"And also," Anne went on, "of accepting the hospitality of inferior persons."

Kitty and Lydia protested loudly. Darcy glanced at Mrs. Bennet. It was well that she had not caught this remark.

"I do hope," said Kitty, "that the roads remain absolutely impassable, dear Anne, so that you must stay with us all winter."

"Save for the roads to and from Meryton," amended Lydia. "For we do want the officers to come."

"Oh yes," said Kitty. "We must have them. Games and dancing and everything amusing."

"We ought to dance *now*," cried Lydia, and she jumped to her feet. "Dancing is the cure for everything," she said to Anne. "Whenever Mama gives me a scold, or when I am told to moderate my behavior, a little dance takes the sting away."

"But we cannot dance," said Kitty. "Which is too bad, for I daresay we could use the practice."

Anne put her letter aside. "We have Mr. Collins and Mr. Fleming."

Lydia and Kitty broke into laughter. "Mr. Collins?" scoffed Kitty.

"Do not look at me like that, Mr. Collins," said Lydia. "You are shockingly bad at dancing."

Darcy heard Elizabeth chuckle, and this stung. "And you, Miss Lydia," he retorted, "cannot dance without laughing and shrieking."

"Oh," Lydia cried. "Shall we punish him? Shall we make him dance with us?"

Kitty was on her feet and joined Lydia in pushing back chairs.

"Come along, Mr. Fleming," Lydia called cheerfully. "Dancing is the cure for sore feet. Who will you have for your first partner?"

Darcy saw Fleming draw a reluctant breath. Ever the diplomat, he said, "Choose for me, Miss Lydia."

"Why, Anne, of course!"

Fleming crossed to where she sat and made a bow. "If Miss de Bourgh will consent."

She colored and looked confused. Darcy understood it. Ought Anne to dance with the son of her mother's physician? Another thought occurred: did she know how to dance?

"I daresay she is wishing for one of the officers," said Lydia. She twinkled at Fleming. "You lack a red coat, sir, but I shall dance with you if you'll have me. And you, Mr. Collins?"

Darcy needed no urging. With a smile playing about his lips, he held out a hand to Elizabeth. "Will you do me the honor?" he said. "I have much to account for, given the debacle at Netherfield."

She hesitated.

"Come, Cousin. Allow me to make right a debt. I promise not to tread on your toes."

"Or collide with other couples?"

"Even that."

She placed her hand in his, which fortunately was not sweaty or damp, as he wore no gloves. Elizabeth's hand was soft and warm. Darcy led her to the cleared area of the drawing room. Someone had rolled back the rug.

"Shall we dance a reel?" said Lydia. "Play *The Jovial Beggars*, Mary. I daresay that is easy enough, even for Mr. Collins."

"Do you know this dance?" Elizabeth whispered urgently.

"Fairly well," he whispered back.

It was obvious that she did not believe him. Was she worried that he might make a fool of himself?

"Do call the figures as we dance them, Lydia," Elizabeth suggested. "For Mr. Collins' sake."

Darcy had a sudden idea, and he released Elizabeth's hand. "Come now, Miss de Bourgh, we cannot have you sitting on the side. Miss Bennet will dance with you, will you not, Miss Bennet? And Miss Kitty, you must dance with your mama."

"Posh," said Mrs. Bennet, but Darcy noticed that she looked pleased.

"You cannot convince us that you do not love to dance, ma'am," he said to her. "Up with you." Darcy handed Mrs. Bennet to Kitty and went directly to Anne.

She shrank back against the cushions. "No shirking, Miss de Bourgh," he said. "Up you come."

But it was Jane who coaxed Anne into the set. "It's only a family party," she said, smiling. "We often dance together for practice."

Meanwhile Fleming and Lydia were clearing more space. Elizabeth's eyes were on Darcy and when he joined her, she whispered, "What an excellent idea."

"Eight dancers are better than four," he said, "and your sister is right, Miss de Bourgh must dance." He glanced in her direction. Anne's nervousness had not abated, but the thundercloud of anger toward her mother had passed.

Elizabeth must have guessed his thoughts. "Jane will guide Anne through the steps. She is the most patient of teachers."

"And will you tutor me, a poor stumbler?" he said.

But Darcy would not stumble. *The Jovial Beggars* was as old as time; he could dance it in his sleep. Given his current mood (for Elizabeth was smiling) he would gleefully add Collins' twirls and flourishes.

The dancers formed two lines and the music began. At once it was clear that Anne was struggling. Darcy called out, "Best to slow down, Miss Mary."

Mary stopped playing and turned round.

She was not the only one to feel surprised. What was he doing? He had never stopped a dance in his life!

Lydia gave an unhappy huff. "Oh, lord."

"Play it slowly, if you please." Darcy clapped the tempo at half speed. "La-DA-da-DA-da-DA-DA. Have pity on me, your sad cousin."

They began again, at the Grandmother's Tempo (according to Lydia).

"Gypsy Half!" Lydia called. Jane guided Anne through the figure.

"First couple, lead down!"

This meant Darcy and Elizabeth would join hands and walk down the line. "One-two-three-four!" Darcy counted for Anne's benefit. "And back two-three-four."

"And Gate!" called Lydia, oblivious to Anne's distress.

Again Darcy stopped the dance. Again he produced Collins' foolish grin. "Could we go through what Gate means?" To say that he had forgotten was a lie, for he had walked through *The Jovial Beggars* with Georgiana when he was last in London.

Step by step Anne was taken through the dance.

"Now we'll do it again right through," said Darcy, as soon as the song finished. "I'm beginning to get the feel for this."

"But I am tired," Anne complained.

"You cannot quit now," said Darcy, "or you risk forgetting what you've learned. Let's take our positions, everyone.

"But I wish to stop," said Anne.

Darcy ignored her. "Begin again, Miss Mary."

Mary began playing, and Anne threw Darcy a dark look. But she performed her part of the Gypsy Half perfectly, and when she and Jane were first couple, they led up and back without mishap.

"You see?" he said. "You are doing splendidly, Miss de Bourgh."

Eyes on Anne, he put out his hand and smoothly led Elizabeth through a turn.

"And so are you, Mr. Collins," said Elizabeth. "You know this dance very well."

He could hear the admiration in her voice. "As a matter of fact, I do," he confessed. "Not too long ago I taught it to Georg—" He stopped himself just in time.

"To George?" cried Fleming, who had caught this remark. "You taught it to George who?"

"Ah," said Darcy. "You might not know—him."

When the dance brought Fleming near again, he said, "I know everyone around Hunsford. I cannot think who you mean. Unless—"

Fleming gave a shout and led Kitty through a turn. "Is George Doleman's Christian name?"

"Doleman?" said Elizabeth to Darcy.

He had no idea how to reply. Who the devil was Doleman?

"His curate," called Fleming. "Who is blessed with an apt surname. He's the most mournful fellow imaginable."

"First couple, lead down," called Lydia.

Darcy took Elizabeth's hand, and down the line they went.

"You taught your curate to dance?" said Elizabeth. "Did the organist play? Did you dance up and down the center aisle?"

Darcy laughed. "Clergyman," he confessed, "sometimes need watching."

"The sooner Collins returns to Hunsford," called Fleming, "the better his parishioners will like it. For Doleman's preaching is worse than his dancing."

"Unfortunately for them," said Elizabeth, smiling, "the roads will not allow travel. But perhaps," she added, "not so unfortunately for us?"

Did she give his hand a gentle squeeze before she released it?

It was all Darcy could do not to skip and cavort. For he was limed, a ready prisoner to Elizabeth's blushing admiration. And glory be, the roads were yet impassible.

20 New, New Nothing

Later that evening, amid jesting about the rain, Mr. Denny, Captain Carter, and Mr. Wickham were brought into the drawing room.

Mr. Wickham went directly to Mrs. Bennet and kissed her hand. "Bad weather," he declared, "could never keep us away."

Darcy refrained from rolling his eyes. Where had Wickham been for the past three days? Holed up in a tavern or wherever it was that officers lived.

He glanced at Elizabeth, who sat beside him on the sofa. She continued to ply her needle. Could it be that she was unimpressed by Wickham's arrival? Darcy felt his lips curve into a foolish smile. Hastily he quelled it and turned another page in his book.

"Your standing invitation, Mrs. Bennet, is most welcome," said Captain Carter. "We could no longer tolerate staring at one another, so the rain and the roads must be braved."

Lydia tugged at Wickham's arm. "Come and meet our new friend," she said. "We have been telling her all about you."

"Lord, I am shaking in my boots," said Wickham, laughing. "I daresay you have given her an earful."

"Nonsense," said Lydia. "We've told her nothing that isn't true." She led him to where Anne sat before the fire. "Anne, this is Mr. Wickham, who has lately joined the militia. Isn't that jolly? Mr. Wickham, this is Miss Anne de Bourgh."

"Lydia," protested Kitty, "she is the right honorable Miss Anne de Bourgh of Rosings Park."

Darcy's gaze never wavered from Wickham's face. Sure enough, at the mention of Anne's name his eyes brightened, and he swept a graceful bow. The uniform gave an air of distinction, and this was not lost on Anne.

"Miss de Bourgh," said Wickham smoothly, "although you know me not, I feel as though we are friends already. From childhood your cousin Fitzwilliam Darcy and I were the best of friends."

"Whichever way the wind blows," said Darcy under his breath.

Elizabeth leaned nearer. "What do you mean?" she whispered.

"That fellow," he muttered, "is a perfect chameleon. It suited you to see Mr. Darcy as Wickham's enemy. And it suits Anne to see Mr. Darcy as Wickham's friend."

Elizabeth tied a knot in her embroidery silk. "What a suspicious mind you have."

"Then prove me wrong. You'll not see him leave her side all evening."

Elizabeth pursed up her lips and said nothing more.

"Dear Anne tells us," announced Lydia, "that she is Mr. Darcy's fiancée. Is it not a small world?"

"Well," said Wickham, placing a chair for Lydia. "This *is* a piece of news."

Elizabeth made a movement, and Darcy turned to her. She was frowning. "What is it?" he whispered.

"It was Mr. Wickham who told me of their engagement. And yet now he seems surprised."

Had she found a chink in Wickham's armor? "Did your mother never tell you to beware of men with smooth speech?"

Elizabeth gave an unhappy huff. "Why should she, when you are here to perform that office?"

Meanwhile, Collins was intent on mastering a skill. The cigar, along with the after-dinner glass of port, was considered *de rigueur* among gentlemen of Bingley's set. And since Collins would be dining with the family tomorrow night, he must learn how to smoke. Darcy would never hack and cough, doubled over and wiping streaming eyes. Nor would he fail to keep the blasted thing lit.

Collins struggled with all of these. But he also knew that Lady Catherine abominated smoking, and this added much to its appeal.

Thus he gathered his courage and removed a second cigar from the humidor. He propped a looking glass on the desk (for he must handle the cigar with nonchalance), cut the end, and strolled to the hearth to light up.

Eventually the looking glass showed a more debonair reflection. By this time the room was well-fogged, but what of it? Collins lounged in his chair, puffing lightly without inhaling the smoke, balancing the line of ash at the cigar's end. He was, in fact, quite the man about town.

There came a sharp knock at the door, and Miss Bingley walked in. "My gracious, Mr. Darcy!" she cried. "What is wrong with the flue?" She broke out coughing and waved the smoke away.

Collins hurried to remove his feet from the desk.

When Miss Bingley realized the cause of the smoke, her expression changed. "Must you smoke indoors?" she said wrathfully.

Collins recoiled, for he had never heard her speak with such sharpness. At once he took the cigar from his lips.

"What a vile and poisonous habit!"

A stream of apologies came ready to his lips, and then he recalled his identity. Who was she to order Darcy of Pemberley about?

He met her glare with narrowed eyes. "I beg your pardon," he said. "I meant no offense. After all, this is not one of the public rooms of the house."

Miss Bingley looked unhappy but said nothing more.

He then noticed that she held a bundle of papers. "What have you there?"

She brightened. "Newspapers from Charles' library, such as they are. The news is old, of course. What else can one expect, buried as we are in the country?" She gave a brittle laugh. "But I thought you might like to be informed of what has been going forward in the civilized world."

Collins now realized that he had remained seated, a breach of manners. On the other hand, was he not an invalid? "Do sit down," he invited. She did so.

To oblige her Collins flipped through the papers: *The Morning Post and Gazetteer. Baldwin's Journal. The London Gazette. The County Herald.*

Such stuff! He could make neither heads nor tails of any of the headlines. Military battles and court trials and gossip about the London social set. What use had he for these?

"The financial section," she said helpfully, "was of particular interest to my late father."

Collins continued to turn pages. Here were rows of numbers and symbols that to him meant nothing. He sighed heavily.

"You might also enjoy the political articles," she suggested, "with all the doings of Parliament."

"In session now, is it not?" Collins remarked. He had to say something.

Caroline Bingley hesitated. "Surely you are interested in Parliament, Mr. Darcy?"

Not if he could help it! Then again, as Darcy he would have to be interested. He turned another page.

Apparently Miss Bingley had more to say. "We, that is, your sister and I, have been hoping that you would one day sit in the House of Lords."

Collins was thunderstruck. "The House of Lords?" he said. "Me?" He had ambitions to become a bishop, certainly, or better yet an archdeacon. But a Member of Parliament?

"I daresay your uncle, the earl, could help arrange it," she added helpfully.

There was steel behind that smile of hers, and Collins felt himself cringe. Why, this Miss Bingley was made of the same stuff as Lady Catherine!

Just to annoy her, he took another puff on his cigar. "You are very kind," he said. "At the present time, however, I prefer to remain a private gentleman."

Anger snapped in Miss Bingley's eyes, and her smile became forced. Had they been on more intimate terms, would she have contradicted him?

"I have all I can do to manage my own estate," he explained.

"But you are capable of so much more, Mr. Darcy," she cried. "Elevation to the peerage would add such distinction."

What an ambitious creature Miss Bingley was! "Why not encourage your brother?" he said.

"Charles?" she scoffed. "He has neither the capacity nor the proper sponsorship, whereas you—"

Miss Bingley continued to talk. Women, Collins decided, were a nagging lot. And since all husbands seemed destined to be hen-pecked, he would much rather suffer at the hands of lovely Elizabeth.

"Permit me to tell you, Miss de Bourgh," said Wickham, "that you have beautiful eyes."

It was such an obvious compliment, but Anne blushed and smiled.

"To say truth," he went on, "they remind me very much of Lady Anne's."

Darcy became aware of Elizabeth's gaze. "Lady Anne," he explained, "is Mr. Darcy's late mother, Anne's aunt. The nerve of the man is astounding."

And there was more. "That particular shade is so pleasing, like the beauty of a summer's day."

Lydia looked over her shoulder. "Wickham is storing up memories of England while he can," she said. "Before he is sent to France or Spain or some other foreign place."

Wickham laughed. "Be not alarmed, Miss de Bourgh," he said. "The militia will remain right here on English soil. Then too, I have much to learn before I am fit for service, as any of my brother officers will tell you."

There was general laughter and Anne smiled, while Darcy ground his teeth. Wickham, fit for service? Only as a paltry militiaman. Whose duties, it seemed, included little more than making the social rounds.

Darcy met Elizabeth's eye. "I would have thought," he muttered, "that he could do better than that."

"Would you rather he quoted poetry?" she whispered.

"*Shall I compare thee to a summer's day?* I think not. He was never one for memorization."

She smiled. "How do you know?"

Wickham was still speaking. "One becomes so weary of white. Always the ladies wear white. The color of extreme youth, I say."

"Oh!" cried Lydia, who was guilty on both counts.

"Present company excluded, of course," amended Wickham.

More compliments, more flattery.

"What fine eyes you have. What fine teeth," Darcy murmured in Elizabeth's ear.

"Cousin William," Elizabeth protested, laughing. "Really."

"It's like hearing Riding Hood question the wolf, save that the positions are reversed."

Elizabeth put aside her embroidery frame. "What a dreadful person you are. Has no one ever told you that it is rude to eavesdrop?"

Darcy turned a page. "I am not eavesdropping," he said. "As you see, I am reading."

"Reading human nature," she said, "instead of the text."

Darcy had to laugh. "Rather more engrossing, yes."

"Wickham," cried Lydia, "you are not to monopolize Anne. She would like to converse with the other officers."

"I monopolize nothing," protested Wickham. "Behold, here I am, Miss de Bourgh, entirely at your service." He paused to smile. "Now then, what are your other two wishes?"

Again there was general laughter. Elizabeth looked annoyed.

Hill came in with a tray of glasses. "At last," said Mrs. Bennet. "Gentlemen, here is fortification from the cold."

Darcy began to rise. "Oh, no, you don't," said Elizabeth, and she took hold of his arm. "No sherry for you."

He sat down again.

"I have seen what happens when you have too much to drink. The punch, remember? At the Netherfield ball?"

Darcy studied her eyes, so earnest in their appeal.

"You know perfectly well how to dance, William Collins. And I refuse to allow you to indulge a weakness."

Dearest, loveliest Elizabeth. Had she explained away every one of Collins' idiocies?

Her hand was resting on his arm, and Darcy allowed himself the luxury of covering it with his own.

"*How poor are they that have not patience,*" he said softly. "*What wound did ever heal but by degrees?* I shall therefore content myself with coffee."

"Black coffee," she added, twinkling.

He gave her hand a squeeze. "*Poor and content is rich, and rich enough.*"

Shakespeare, Darcy realized, was quite a wise fellow.

21 Very Lively Hopes

"Mr. Wickham has the happiest manners," said Anne, around a sigh. "He is quite head and shoulders above the others. So handsome and distinguished."

Elizabeth glanced down the table at the laughing trio. Must they gossip even at breakfast? Her mother did nothing to discourage them.

Anne kept talking. "He is the most agreeable man I have ever seen. So amiable and pleasing."

Naturally Lydia and Kitty agreed. More giggles, more laughter and talk.

Elizabeth stirred her tea in silence. She saw William Collins come in and busy himself at the sideboard. Her father's place at the foot of the table remained empty.

She could not recall when he'd been so hobbled by a cold. Was he truly ill?

"And which of the officers," said Anne, "do you wish to marry, Kitty?"

A movement caught Elizabeth's eye. William Collins had pulled out the chair opposite hers, his gaze intent on Anne.

"None of them, alas," said Kitty. "I would dearly love to follow my heart, but my circumstances are such that I—"

Kitty broke off speaking, for Anne de Bourgh was staring. Obviously she was surprised.

Mary filled the silence. "You see, Miss de Bourgh," she explained, "my sisters and I have only a very small fortune."

"At present we have plenty of money," Lydia was quick to add, "but Mr. Collins will one day take it away." She threw a look in his direction.

And then no one said anything at all.

"Fortunately for us," Kitty said, "our father is ever so healthy."

"He most certainly is *not*," cried Mrs. Bennet. "He has the most shocking cold, with great circles under his eyes and a sore throat. Mark my words, he could soon be at death's door."

"Mama," explained Elizabeth, "is overly concerned, Miss de Bourgh. He is planning to walk with me to Clarke's to exchange books."

"Not today," cried her mother.

"No, Mama," said Elizabeth. "Not today."

Lydia soon returned to their favorite topic. "The officers," she told Anne, "haven't any more money than we do. You can imagine how tragic it is. We are such good friends, but that is all we can ever be. For they must marry well."

"And so must we," said Kitty.

"But you, my dear Anne, may marry whomever you wish," said Lydia. "La, what am I saying? You have a fiancé already."

Anne did not answer right away. "I do not know," she said slowly, "whether Mr. Darcy is my choice or Mother's. He is nothing like Mr. Wickham."

"Gracious, no," said Lydia. "He is so reserved and disapproving. But not around you, surely."

"He speaks with me, of course. And I believe he pities me. But Mr. Wickham is kinder in his attentions than ever Mr. Darcy was."

"What a heartless brute!" cried Lydia. "You will excuse me for saying so, Anne, but when I think that you may have any man in England simply for the asking!"

Anne gazed at Lydia with wonder. "Any man?"

Elizabeth was now alarmed. "My sisters are fond of exaggeration," she said. "Of course you cannot marry any man. He must be a gentleman."

"The officers are gentlemen," said Anne slowly. "Are they not?"

"Well, yes," admitted Kitty. "Certainly they are."

Elizabeth knew that Kitty's answer was somewhat forced. Were the officers gentlemen? She became aware of Mr. Collins' gaze. That disquieting glitter was again in his eyes.

That same morning Collins made an unhappy discovery: namely, that when two ladies, each strong-minded and stubborn, were together at table, breakfast would be anything but tranquil.

For whenever Miss Bingley made a comment (and she made several) Lady Catherine was quick to contradict. Thus, although it was damp and muddy out, it was a lovely day. No, Mr. Darcy was not looking well, he was haggard—quite understandable since the beds here were typical of a hired house. And no, the roads were most unsuitable for travel, even a simpleton could see that.

Collins avoided these conversational powder kegs by lingering at the sideboard. The selection offered was superior to the fare at Longbourn House, including a delicacy he'd only read about, *apfelstrudel*, enticingly dusted with confectioner's sugar. When Miss Bingley and the footmen were looking the other way, Collins quickly helped himself to two.

"I shall be calling at Longbourn House this afternoon," announced Lady Catherine, "and in my own barouche, Miss Bingley, so you needn't offer yours."

"I was not about—" Miss Bingley began, and then stopped. "I thought, milady, that the roads were bad."

"Driving to Longbourn House, a mere two or three miles, has nothing to do with the roads."

Collins slid into a chair and gazed at his *apfelstrudel*. There were three more on the sideboard.

"My nephew," said Lady Catherine, looking down the table at Collins, "shall accompany me, of course."

Collins was caught with a mouthful of strudel. At the very least she might have asked him! He looked from one woman to the other. Fortunately he was not obliged to answer, which was just as well, for how could he pacify both? He took a sip of coffee, shuddered, and reached for the sugar bowl.

"The fresh air will do you good, Fitzwilliam," said Lady Catherine. "And our hostess has better uses for her time than to lounge about and converse with you."

Caroline Bingley was now red in the face. "Upon my word," she said.

"Speaking of conversation, Fitzwilliam," and Lady Catherine paused to smile, "there will be opportunity for you to converse privately with your beloved Anne."

Collins kept chewing and gave a reluctant nod. He glanced at Miss Bingley. Her pinched expression reminded him of sour lemons.

"She has journeyed all this way to be with you." Lady Catherine wagged a playful finger. "And you know what they say about absence."

To keep from answering, Collins took another bite of strudel.

"*No matter where a man may wander, absence makes the heart grow fonder.*"

Collins figured that Lady Catherine had come up with this ditty herself, as it was anything but true. Anne was sickly, irritable, and silent. Absence from her brought relief.

On the other hand, he was rather missing Elizabeth Bennet. He speared a bite and chewed thoughtfully.

"As well," continued Lady Catherine, "I shall be bringing Anne to stay at Netherfield until we are able to travel."

"Oh," said Miss Bingley, "but ma'am!"

Darcy had a habit of delivering snubbing looks, and Collins was beginning to understand why. He directed one at Lady Catherine.

"Would you have her remain with these Bennets?" she protested. "People about whom we know nothing? I daresay Anne is ill and miserable."

Collins blotted his lips with a napkin. "There are five daughters in the family," he offered. "Perhaps Anne enjoys being with women of similar age."

Lady Catherine gave him a look. "But are they gentlewomen? I think not."

"I quite agree with you on that point, ma'am," said Caroline Bingley.

Lady Catherine's eyes narrowed. "Then again," she said, "who are you?"

Collins felt his lips twist into a smirk. He knew better than to comment, so he took a sip of coffee.

"However," continued Lady Catherine, "the Bennets are related to Mr. Collins. And he, being a knave, is certainly no gentleman."

Collins sent his cup crashing into its saucer.

It was well that he would not be returning to Hunsford as a rector. For he was coming to despise Lady Catherine.

The sound of wheels pulled Kitty and Lydia to the windows. "A traveling coach," cried Kitty. "And look there, a crest on the door."

Lydia pressed her face to the glass. "Can you see whose it is?"

Elizabeth shared a look with Jane. Could this be Charles Bingley?

Mr. Collins joined the younger girls at the window. "That," he said quietly, "is the de Bourgh crest."

"Are you certain?" cried Kitty.

"Quick, everyone!" said their mother.

Elizabeth did what she could to straighten the cushions and magazines. Mrs. Jenkinson fussed over Anne's hair and gown. Elizabeth glanced at Anne's expression. If her mother was expecting submission and repentance, she would be disappointed.

Kitty took hold of Anne's hand. "I shall not leave you," she declared, "though she rant and order me away. A mother's tirades do not last forever."

Presently the drawing room door came open. "Lady Catherine de Bourgh," announced Hill. She paused to consult the cards. "Mr. Fitzwilliam Darcy and Mr. Charles Bingley."

Elizabeth heard Jane draw a sharp breath. "You must find a way to speak with him," Elizabeth whispered. "Depend upon it; this is why he has come."

"How can I, amidst all this crowd?" said Jane.

"You managed it at the ball."

"But Lizzy!"

With a rustle of skirts, Lady Catherine swept into the drawing room. Elizabeth knew her at once—she was the woman from the barouche—and she was looking every bit as dictatorial and insolent as Mr. Wickham described.

Mr. Bingley and Mr. Darcy remained in her shadow, which was either very cowardly or very wise. After the briefest of greetings, Lady Catherine addressed her daughter.

"Why, may I ask, are you in the drawing room? It is far too early, as well Jenkinson knows. A lady must reserve her strength."

"There, you see, Anne?" said Lydia. "That's very sensible advice. A lady must save her strength for dancing."

Lady Catherine wheeled. "And who might you be?"

Mrs. Bennet came forward. "She is my youngest daughter, your ladyship. Lydia is her name. And may I say that it has been a pleasure to have your charming girl among us."

"She is hardly a girl," said Lady Catherine.

"Yes she is," said Kitty loyally. And she is also charming. She dances beautifully."

Lady Catherine's brows descended. "With whom has my daughter been dancing?"

"Only Mr. Collins and Mr. Fleming, ma'am," Mrs. Bennet hastened to say. "Most unexceptional partners."

"It was not my fault," Anne protested. "Mr. Collins insisted that I take part."

Lady Catherine rounded on him. "What have you to say for yourself, Mr. Collins?" she demanded.

Elizabeth steeled herself to bear whatever excuses he would make. After all, her ladyship was a formidable opponent. He looked rather pale.

"Dancing is beneficial," he said slowly. "Especially as we were house-bound by the snow. You needn't picture a late and tiring evening, ma'am. We danced in the afternoon— for practice, as it were."

"For practice!" scoffed Lady Catherine.

Mr. Collins had more to say. "Mrs. Jenkinson is an excellent teacher, but there is a limit to what she can do. Dancing practice is important for any lady."

"What do you know about it, Mr. Collins?"

"I daresay your niece practices her dancing."

"Georgiana Darcy? As if you knew anything about her." She turned to Mr. Darcy. "What say you, Fitzwilliam? Does your sister waste her time with such foolishness?"

Mr. Darcy was looking rather panicked. His gaze traveled to Mr. Collins, as if seeking strength and reassurance. What changes the accident had wrought!

"O-of course she does," he stammered. "All young ladies must dance and gentlemen too. Consider how awkward dancing is for those who are unschooled."

Lady Catherine looked even more annoyed. She turned to Elizabeth's mother. "I would like to speak with my daughter privately, if you please. Perhaps in the dining room? You do have such a place?"

"Why, yes," said Mrs. Bennet. "Of course we—"

Lady Catherine interrupted. "After I have had my say, Anne, you will be at liberty to speak with your fiancé, for whom you have traveled these many miles."

Anne's face was flushed. It seemed to Elizabeth that she was looking rather worried.

"You," said Lady Catherine to Jenkinson, "may wait in the vestibule. Or better yet, you will pack Anne's things. She is returning with me to Netherfield."

"No," cried Anne, and she put up her chin. Kitty did the same. "That I shall never do."

"No, never," echoed Kitty.

Mrs. Jenkinson rose to her feet, knocking her knitting basket to the floor. A ball of wool went rolling and lodged behind one of the sofas. Mr. Collins went after it.

The disturbance grew, Kitty declaring that she would not leave Anne's side, and Lady Catherine ordering her to stand down. She seized Anne's shoulder, pulled her to her feet, and propelled her out of the drawing room.

Elizabeth's mother and her younger sisters followed. She and Jane were left with Charles Bingley and Mr. Darcy, and also with Mr. Collins, who was behind the sofa.

Lydia came back inside. "Jane, Mama needs the sal volatile, but Hill cannot find any of her bottles; you know how Mama leaves them everywhere. She says you have one."

"In the back parlor," said Jane. "But it's on one of the high shelves." She glanced to Mr. Bingley. "I'll gladly fetch it, although I fear I am not tall enough to reach."

"Allow me," said Bingley, and they went out together. Elizabeth concealed her smile.

By this time Mr. Collins must have located the wool, but he remained behind the sofa. Elizabeth could see him there, kneeling. She frowned at him, but he did not move.

The drawing room door closed with a click, and Elizabeth was left to confront Mr. Darcy.

With dawning wonder Collins took in his surroundings. Was he alone with her? And where was Darcy? Out in the vestibule with the others, probably. He'd never realized what a poor figure he cut, dressed so shabbily in black. Ah, but all that was changed now.

And here was Elizabeth, as lovely as ever. By Jove, she was a beauty! Miss Bingley could not hold a candle to her.

"Miss Elizabeth." He made a formal bow.

"Mr. Darcy. Won't you sit down?"

Her eyes, as she gazed at him, were more beautiful than he remembered. Indeed, Collins' felt his knees turn to jelly, and he grasped the mantelpiece for support.

"I daresay Jane and Mr. Bingley shall return shortly," she added.

They would, and his opportunity would be gone. Here, as if heaven sent, was his chance to fix her affection. That was what he'd heard it called, the all-important prelude to declaring love for a lady.

"You seem to have recovered from your injuries," she said.

His heart warmed to see her concern. Drawing a long breath, he moistened his lips. "We seldom have the opportunity to be alone, you and I."

"Actually," said Elizabeth, with a look toward the corner of the drawing room, "we are not precisely al—"

She broke off speaking. Collins glanced toward the corner. There was nothing there.

"I suppose we are," she said slowly. "For the moment."

Her eyes were now upon him. Collins was all too aware of the intelligence in that gaze. What was she thinking? Admiring thoughts, he hoped. He had chosen his waistcoat today with particular care.

Aware that sweat was beading on his forehead, Collins began to pace back and forth. Declaring one's affection was anything but easy! He found Darcy's handkerchief and mopped his face.

Voices sounded from the vestibule—was someone about to come in? Collins came to a halt and stood before Elizabeth, rocking on his heels. This was it, now or never. He must speak.

How his heart was pounding! How difficult it was to breathe! His fingers began to twist together in the hand-washing habit Darcy had warned him about. Collins thrust his hands behind his back.

But he had nothing to fear, nothing. He was Darcy of Pemberley!

"Mr. Darcy," said Elizabeth, frowning. "Are you quite well?"

Collins found his voice. "In vain have I struggled," he declared. It was a good beginning, for he had her full attention. Indeed, those lovely eyes were narrowed with concern.

"Are your injuries painful?"

Injuries to his heart, yes! An upwelling of affection threatened to overtake Collins' senses. "My feelings," he stammered out, "will not be repressed."

"Your feelings?" she repeated.

Why was Elizabeth frowning? Why did she glance to the drawing room door? Collins understood it. Joy of joys, she did not wish to be interrupted by her family!

"Please do not stand upon ceremony, sir," she said. "If your stomach is troubling you, why—"

His stomach? He was declaring love and all she thought about was his stomach? But that could not be right, for Darcy's stomach was perfectly flat!

"It will not do," Collins burst out. "You must allow me to tell you how ardently I admire and love you."

And then he waited, scarcely daring to breathe.

Elizabeth was staring. "Mr. Darcy," she said and rose to her feet.

Did she wish to be embraced? Collins took a step toward her, but Elizabeth shrank back. "Allow me to call Mr. Fleming, sir," she said.

Fleming? What need had he for Fleming?

"For truly, sir," she continued, "you are not—"

He cut her off. "You are doubtless overcome by the honor—the very great honor—of being the recipient of my heartfelt affection."

"But," she said, "what of Anne de Bourgh?"

Here, Collins decided, was evidence of Elizabeth's maidenly reserve. Perhaps he ought to smile a little? Yes, that was it. He'd been too solemn. No lady wished for a solemn suitor.

"My regard for you," he said, "although undeserved, cannot be unwelcome."

Elizabeth's chin came up. "Undeserved?"

Her tone made him jump. Did she not comprehend the extent of his admiration? He spread his hands. "For aside for your beauty and vivacious wit," he explained, "what is there to recommend you? A share of your mother's four thousand pounds?"

Elizabeth's eyes narrowed. "How do you know about—?"

"Perhaps," interrupted Collins, smiling more widely, "I know more than you think. But I have chosen to disregard our disparate social and financial positions, dearest, loveliest—ouch!"

For from behind someone had pinned Collins' arms in an iron grip. A voice said in his ear, "You have said quite enough."

Collins swung round, but his assailant was heavier and stronger.

"Please excuse Mr. Darcy," Collins heard the man say—in his own voice! Blast that Darcy! Where had he come from? Collins fought to free himself.

"I suspect, Miss Elizabeth," said Darcy, "that our friend has had Too Much Laudanum."

"What?" cried Collins. "I have not!"

"One spoonful in a glass of water is sufficient," said Darcy. "Not half the bottle." And he gave a cruel twist to Collins' arm.

"Ouch!" cried Collins. "Confound it, that hurts!"

"If you must knock back laudanum like gin, sir—"

"But I haven't!" squealed Collins.

Darcy ignored this and spoke to Elizabeth. "If you wouldn't mind asking Mr. Bingley to step inside?"

Trust Darcy to humiliate him in Elizabeth's presence! But two could play at this game. Collins kicked savagely at Darcy's shins.

Darcy's hold tightened. "We must get him back to Netherfield," he said, panting a little, "and soon. His aunt must not see him like this."

Collins was betrayed into a groan.

"I believe his stomach pains him," said Elizabeth.

Collins watched her walk to the door and open it. Was she leaving? And without giving him an answer?

"Elizabeth," he whimpered.

"Stomach, eh?" growled Darcy in his ear. "Getting a bit tubby, aren't we, Collins?"

"How dare you!" Collins spat.

"The next time you intend to propose, kindly wait until you are sober."

"I am sober!" cried Collins. "Moreover, I am Darcy of Pemberley! Any woman would be grateful to receive my addresses. Grateful, do you hear?"

Darcy tightened his hold. "As we have seen."

Collins tried to ignore the smile in Darcy's voice and gave him another kick.

22 OF MEAN UNDERSTANDING

Only a madman would interfere between Lady Catherine and her daughter, Darcy knew. But peacemaking was a clergyman's lot, so it fell to Darcy to negotiate a truce. It took some time to reach an accord.

"Understand this, Miss de Bourgh," Darcy summarized. "In twenty-four hours—barring unforeseen changes in the weather—your mother's barouche will arrive to take you to Netherfield. And you will go willingly."

Anne kept her face averted. Darcy ignored Lady Catherine's disapproving sniff.

"That," he said, "is your part of the bargain. Your mother's part," and it was all Darcy could do to keep from glaring at Lady Catherine, "is to allow you to remain at Longbourn House, with your friends, until that time."

He paused. "Are we in agreement?"

Anne's expression remained mutinous, but she nodded. Lady Catherine opened her mouth to speak, but apparently thought better of it. She also nodded.

"Then I believe we are finished here." Darcy rose to his feet and stood ready to assist Lady Catherine.

"Indeed we are *not*, Mr. Collins." She stood and shook out her skirts.

Her tone did not bode well for Collins, but Darcy was past caring. "Milady," he said, "Charles Bingley is waiting to take you to Netherfield."

"I am going nowhere until Anne has spoken with my nephew. He has come expressly to see her."

Darcy gave a dry cough. "Mr. Darcy was not feeling well, ma'am. He has already returned to Netherfield, and Mr. Bingley has come back for you." He crossed the dining room and opened the door.

"Without informing me?"

"Your ladyship was, shall we say, occupied."

"Nonsense!" Lady Catherine gave another sniff. "You have not heard the last from me on this matter," she said, and went sailing out of the dining room. Her daughter did likewise.

Darcy set his teeth. What a pleasure it would be to resign his post!

Instead of returning to the drawing room, Darcy made for the staircase.

It was his confrontation with Collins that had been the most troubling. How unnerving it was to see his own face, twisted by Collins' indecision as he swung between pride and folly. Moreover, Collins' declaration—"I am Darcy of Pemberley!"—had shaken him to the core.

At the landing Darcy paused and hung over the bannister rail, lost in thought. If Collins could never be Fitzwilliam Darcy, then he could never be William Collins.

That snowstorm was to blame, isolating him and muddling his thinking—and keeping beloved Elizabeth so close at hand. But Darcy now knew that he could no longer shrug off the painful truth. He should not live as if he were William Collins.

And if he could not soon find a way to become himself again, he must return to Hunsford. The longer he remained at Longbourn, the more his heart blended with Elizabeth's. Like a fool he'd allowed himself the luxury of loving her, and that was utterly unfair.

Was Elizabeth in love with him? It was hard to say. Fascinated, perhaps. Infatuated, certainly. But genuinely in love?

No, he decided. There was too much of Collins' physical presence for that to happen. How could he have guessed that Collins' ugly face would be a benefit? In time Elizabeth would forget their kisses in the snow. Perhaps she would even laugh about them.

Was he in love with her? There was no need to answer. He loved her too well to ruin her future. No, the only right course of action was to fade out of Elizabeth's life altogether.

A slam of the main door told him that Lady Catherine had departed. With a sigh, Darcy resumed his climb. Upstairs he encountered Fleming emerging from Mr. Bennet's bedchamber.

"How is he?" There was no need to whisper, but that is what one did outside sickrooms.

"As well as can be expected," Fleming replied. "He coughs constantly, which is most unfortunate. No fever as yet, which eliminates several troublesome illnesses." Fleming listed the options on his fingers. "Pneumonia, influenza, scarlet fever, to name a few."

"Troublesome indeed."

"You might like to know that the post has come," Fleming added, as he went by. "And with it, contact with the outside world."

The outside world. That meant his steward, his cousin Fitz, and Georgiana. Darcy pulled up short. He'd written to his sister last week and was expecting a reply. If Collins were to receive it—

He turned and followed Fleming down the stairs. "Have you a reason to return to Netherfield?" he called.

Fleming paused at the landing. "Confound it, that curst horse! I promised to take it back. I'd best do that now."

"Half a minute," said Darcy. "I have an idea."

The letter on the butler's silver salver was addressed to Darcy, and Collins thought it beautiful. Indeed, it was the one bright spot in an otherwise wrenching day.

Miss Bingley had been all sympathy when he returned and provided every comfort. But her ministrations were small consolation. Like a fool he'd declared his love before Elizabeth, and she spurned him—or near enough. He expected her to fall into his arms. How could she confuse passion with stomach pains?

Yet Collins was grateful for Darcy's excuse, feigning headache and fatigue to Miss Bingley. A few heartfelt moans were enough to convince her that there should be no traveling to London tomorrow.

For this Collins was devoutly grateful. And if he'd had his prayer book on hand, he would have read to the Almighty a proper expression of his thanks. As it was, he mounted the stairs wondering if it was too early for a cigar.

Once in his suite of rooms, Collins shrugged out of his coat and rolled up his sleeves. A look at his upper arms showed bruising. All the more reason to get even with Darcy!

Casting himself into a chair, Collins took out his letter and opened it. It was from Georgiana Darcy. The flawless copperplate, flowing in orderly paragraphs across expensive paper, was impressive. Then too, this Georgiana wrote with perfect grammar and spelling.

The scholar in Collins sighed. A young woman of quality.

Elizabeth Bennet would also write letters like this one. Collins sighed some more. To think of her brought a pang. Collins knew that he should put today's debacle out of mind, but his thoughts would not let go.

Elizabeth thought him ill and therefore insincere. He'd put a foot wrong somehow.

Halfway through his cigar Collins discovered the reason. He'd spoken extemporaneously, hadn't he? That was always a disaster, both in sermons and in private conversation. If he'd taken the time to prepare his speech instead of babbling like a fool, Elizabeth would have understood.

Besides, he'd heard that at a first proposal young women often affected disinterest. The next time he had opportunity to speak with Elizabeth, he would be fully prepared.

Or perhaps he ought to speak with her parents first? Mrs. Bennet would welcome his suit with open arms, and so would Elizabeth's father.

Collins rubbed his hands together. Even now compliments were bubbling up, and he meant to capture them. Where did Darcy keep his writing paper?

Darcy descended the stairs and in the vestibule encountered Hill. "There you are, Mr. Collins" she said, and held out a letter. "This has come for you."

DARCY BY ANY OTHER NAME

Darcy took it as a treasure hunter unearthing an artifact. Here was a mystery, a glimpse into Collins' world. The paper was inferior, the handwriting crabbed and poorly-formed. It was sealed with dark wax, ill stamped. What were the odds?

Sure enough, the writer was Doleman, the melancholy curate, and he asked a number of specific questions. All the more reason to consult Collins. All the more reason to take that horse back to Netherfield.

And yet it seemed wise to go around Hill, for she would certainly oppose him. Darcy arranged with Ned to have the horse saddled and brought round to the front of the house.

And wasn't Darcy every bit the bumpkin? Never in his life had he ridden without the proper clothing. And no one, not even a rustic, would wear stockings and shoes instead of riding boots.

He stepped up to the horse and stroked its shoulder, allowing the animal to nose his collar. Wise to the ways of horses, Darcy brought out the sugar lumps he'd pocketed from the sideboard.

Even so, he could feel the stable boy watching him. Apparently he had seen Collins in action and was expecting disaster. Darcy hid a smile as he took the reins and competently swung into the saddle. He took a moment to adjust the stirrups.

And then he heard a knocking on the window glass. Sure enough, Lydia's merry face appeared. She said something over her shoulder and soon there were other faces at the window: Mary's, Kitty's, and Elizabeth's.

Darcy's heart sank, for Elizabeth's concern was evident. He tipped his cap and wheeled the horse. And then he heard the door open.

"Cousin William," called Elizabeth. "Where are you going?"

Darcy's heart sank. He ought to ignore her and ride off. He ought to distance himself from her in every way. Instead, caught by the worry in her voice, Darcy turned back.

"I'm returning this horse to Netherfield."

"But," she said, "you are riding."

What else could he do but reassure her? There could be nothing lover-like in that. "This poor slug is not so different from a pony," he said. "A safe, reliable mount, according to Fleming. Even for a fellow like me."

Now would be the time for one of Collins' repellant mannerisms to show itself: a smirk or a grimace or a tic. Darcy kept his face blank and waited hopefully, but nothing happened. Elizabeth stood gazing at him.

Dearest, loveliest Elizabeth.

The horse stepped to the side, and Darcy settled her. Too late he realized that a show of uncertainty would have been more Collins-like. "I plan to return in an hour or two," he said lamely.

She drew nearer. "Will you walk? All that way?"

Were there tears in her eyes? "Elizabeth," he said, leaning down. "It's less than three miles, my love. A distance you yourself said was insignificant."

"But it is not insignificant!" she protested. "Look there, the drive is flooded with muddy water. And the road could well be worse."

"What care you and I for mud?" he said, before he could stop himself, and his mutinous lips curved into a smile. "As I recall, you thought only of Jane, not your gown. And I," he added, "must mend fences with Mr. Darcy. I was rather too stern with him, you know."

Here he hesitated. "I wouldn't take anything he said to heart," he added. "If you can believe it, the man meant to pay you a compliment."

"Mr. Darcy despises me and meant to insult me. I assure you, the feeling is entirely mutual."

Darcy sat silent, wondering how much to say. "Can you understand," he said at last, "that in all his experience, you are entirely unique? Have you any idea how rare it is for him to meet with an honest rebuff?"

"His arrogance deserves it."

Yes, Collins was arrogant, and Darcy himself had been arrogant. She had him there. Still, he had to try.

"How often do you think Mr. Darcy encounters a lovely and intelligent young woman who is not eager to become his wife?"

"Not often enough," said Elizabeth promptly. "He informed me, as you recall, that I was undeserving of his attentions."

Darcy had to smile. "A facer, that."

"My poor pride may never recover," she agreed, dimpling. "If Mr. Darcy did not hate me before, he surely hates me now."

"I rather doubt that," Darcy said. "I am the one he now hates."

"I fear so," she admitted. "Lady Catherine is not pleased with you either."

"Will wonders never cease?"

"Have a care, William. As your patroness she provides your living."

"My patroness from Hades, you mean. Once she opens that mouth of hers, bats fly out."

Elizabeth gave a delicious gurgle. "You are incorrigible! But you will be careful?"

"I shall be careful," he said. "And for your sake, I will refrain from enraging Lady Catherine."

He took in Elizabeth's upturned face and the loving light in her eyes. She was thinking of his future—of their future. How easy it would be to lean down and kiss her!

But the spell was broken by knocking on the window panes. He waved at his cousins—no, they were Collins' cousins, not his—and tipped his cap jauntily to Elizabeth.

If only he could wheel and take the lane at a hand gallop! Instead, reason prevailed. Darcy urged the horse into a sedate walk.

It was not until he reached the main road that he realized he'd called Elizabeth his love. Did that explain the light in her eyes?

"Confound it!" he burst out. Even his own heart was against him.

What care you and I for mud? Elizabeth turned this over in her mind. She'd related to Mr. Wickham how she'd arrived at Netherfield, muddy and disheveled, and they had laughed over Miss Bingley's reaction.

But she could not recall telling William Collins of it.

What she wished to do now was visit her father. Mr. Fleming had assured her that he was in no danger, but she was not so sure. He usually shrugged off a cold.

This time he was content to remain in bed. He lay back against the pillows, a book and his spectacles at hand. The room smelled like mustard.

"Your mother," he said, smiling wanly, "may get her dearest wish after all. Here is the chance to indulge all her favorite fears." He broke out coughing.

"Father," Elizabeth protested. "Surely you aren't as ill as that."

"Perhaps not," he admitted, with another smile. "But a winter cold is misery."

She made an attempt to cheer him. "At least you have peace and quiet."

"Rather too much quiet," he said.

"Join us in the drawing room for a bit."

He hesitated. "I do not trust myself to navigate the staircase, my dear. By the time I dressed myself, I would be longing for bed. Sitting in a chair involves a great deal of effort. For as you know, one must appear cheerful."

Elizabeth did know it, and she now suspected that it cost him to speak with her. "You might lie on the sofa," she suggested.

"And displace Miss de Bourgh?" His chuckle turned into coughing. It was some minutes before he got hold of himself.

"Would you like to play backgammon?"

"It is enough to see your smiling face, my dear. My eyes are sore from reading, and my chest aches."

"Shall I read to you?"

"Bless you, sweet girl, no. I am unable to concentrate." He turned aside to cough.

"I am ever so glad that Mr. Fleming is here to attend you."

"He seems a sensible man." He cocked an eyebrow in his usual manner. "Is Mr. Fleming possessed of a fortune? Your mother must be pleased to have another unmarried gentleman underfoot."

"I think not." Elizabeth hesitated. "Has—Cousin William been to see you?"

"Oho, Cousin William is it now? No, he has not. Should I expect him?"

"I—do not know. He—I thought he had something he wished to ask you."

"Aha. Will he be seeking permission to address Mary?" Her father's eyes were alight with amusement. "She is the only one among you able to tolerate his prosing," he added. "Tell him to take her and with my blessing."

Elizabeth's throat constricted. "Not Mary," she whispered, but her father never heard. His laughter had turned into coughing.

Her eyes found the floor. William Collins had become so different, so decisive. And yet why had he said nothing to her father?

23 A Fine Companion

If Darcy had intended to apologize, that desire vanished as soon as he entered Collins' rooms. Mrs. Nicholls' disapproval was palpable, but she said nothing. Darcy was under no obligation to remain silent.

"Confound it, Collins," he said, as soon as the door closed behind her. "Must you smoke like a curst chimney? Take your feet off the sofa. And for heaven's sake, put on a coat. You look like a tradesman on holiday."

Collins blew a stream of smoke. "What care I for what anyone thinks?"

"You ought to care. Where is your sense of dignity?"

Collins pulled himself into a sitting position. "Speaking of that," he said, "I do not wish to figure as one who had been swilling laudanum. It was no such thing, as well you know."

"If you are telling me that you were sane when you made that proposal," said Darcy, "then Bedlam is too good for you. Get up. We are going out."

Collins' lower lip protruded. "I do not wish to go out."

Darcy ignored this and stalked into the dressing room. He came out with a pair of riding boots, a hat, and an overcoat. "Here," he said, tossing the boots at Collins' feet. "Take off the Hessians and put on these."

"But I like the Hessians. They're my boots. And my feet."

"That," said Darcy, "is entirely temporary. It is muddy out, and I won't have you ruining the leather. You have no idea how exacting Holdsworth can be about maintaining the mirror finish."

Collins sucked his teeth. "What is the point of having stylish boots if I cannot wear them?"

"Indoors, Collins, and around town. Not in the stables. Learn not to punish your clothing."

"It isn't as if I cannot afford more." Collins put down the cigar and began to pull on the boots. "And I do not see why I must go out."

"Because this curst charade has gone on long enough. We must affect a change. Therefore, I intend to examine the scene of the lightning strike, and you are coming with me." Darcy held out the overcoat. "Put this on."

"But I want the other one. The one with the brass buttons."

"For heaven's sake, there will be no one to see you. Save the fine feathers for when you have an audience."

Collins gave Darcy a sidelong look. "Miss Bingley might see me. She says that I am the most handsomely dressed gentleman of her acquaintance."

"She would," said Darcy. "But she will skin you alive if she finds you've burned holes in the rug."

Collins grimaced and tamped out the cigar. And then, after another sigh, he stood and shrugged into the overcoat. He then took up the hat and followed Darcy down the staircase and out of the house, complaining all the way. Even the pale sunshine did not alter his mood.

But there was nothing remarkable about the Folly. There it stood, surrounded by withered leaves and patches of snow. Collins picked his way along the flagstones, unhappy with the damp and cold. Darcy, who wore Collins' shabby shoes and threadbare stockings, made no comment.

"Well?" said Collins at last. "It's the same Folly, with the same decrepit statues marching round in a circle. What of it?"

"There have got to be clues. Look around."

Collins followed Darcy. "For what are we looking? Evidence of witchcraft? A pentagram? A circle of stones?"

"Anything out of the ordinary. Although with Moses and John the Baptist, I think witchcraft is out of the question. Let me know if you find something."

Collins gazed up at the sky. "That lightning was out of the ordinary," he said. "But I daresay it will not strike today."

Darcy was now running his gloved hands along the Folly's columns. "Obviously not. But there could be some irregularity, an abnormality or a so-called anomaly."

"Anomaly-homily," scoffed Collins. "What I would like is a tasty morsel and something to wet my whistle."

Darcy turned round. "Something to do what?"

Collins shrugged. "It's just an expression."

"It's a vulgar one, which you will kindly refrain from using until you are yourself again."

There was a pause. "As to that," said Collins, "I am not certain that I wish to become myself. In fact, I know I don't. I rather like being you."

"That's because all you've done is sleep and eat. And smoke," said Darcy. "But whenever you open your mouth to speak, you find yourself in deep sludge—as we saw this morning."

"I'll have you know," said Collins primly, "that I am recovering from an injury to my brainpan."

Darcy resumed his examination of the statues. "To the extent that you cannot ride or shoot? Or converse on any intelligent subject?"

Collins kicked at a pile of leaves. "Of course I can converse."

"You'll have ample opportunity in London. As I recall, Caroline Bingley is keen to leave Netherfield."

"I am not such a simpleton as you think. So long as I avoid Westminster and anything to do with Parliament, all will be well."

"Parliament? Why Parliament?"

"Because Miss Bingley wants your uncle to sponsor me for the House of Lords."

Darcy gave a snort. "I would like to see him try! Speaking of relations, you'll have another thing coming when my cousin Fitz arrives. He'll roast you on a spit."

Collins had the sense to look worried.

"Don't stand there gaping," said Darcy. "We'll soon run out of daylight. Keep searching."

"I do wish," said Lydia to the drawing room at large, "that we could get a message to the officers. How will they know that this is Anne's last evening with us?"

"I daresay one of the stable boys could take a note," Kitty offered. "If only we knew where to direct him."

Elizabeth had had to listen to various versions of this lament. "If only we had not been introduced to the officers in the street," she said tartly. This was not precisely true, but she was weary of hearing her sisters complain.

"It was no such thing," cried Kitty. "You might have met Mr. Wickham in the street, but we were introduced to Colonel Forster and the others at—whose party was it? Aunt Phillips'?"

Lydia could not remember. "And what is wrong with meeting people in the street?" she wanted to know. "One does so every day. We met your precious Mr. Collins in the front drive."

"It was no such thing and you know it," said Elizabeth. "And," she added, "he is not my Mr. Collins."

"Isn't he? Then why do you keep looking out the window? If he means to be here before dark, he ought to hurry."

"Are you certain that you can't exchange Father's books today, Lizzy?" said Kitty. "After all, it was dry enough for Mr. Collins to venture out."

"Mr. Collins," said Elizabeth, "is stubborn and foolish."

"But if you did go, you might encounter one of our friends," lamented Kitty. "And we do so want them to come tonight."

"Trust Mr. Wickham to find a way," said Lydia. "Of all of them he is the cleverest. And," she added, "the handsomest."

Darcy bent to brush withered leaves from the pavement. "There must be something."

Collins gave a snort of derision. "The long and short of it, Darcy, is that you are stuck being me."

"Then may God help the Hunsford congregation. What do I know about being a rector?"

"But there you are mistaken," said Collins. "It is not at all difficult, I assure you. The forms of service are nicely written out. I daresay you are already familiar with the responsive readings, only you will be leading out instead of following."

Darcy continued his examination of the paving stones. What was he looking for? A mark left by lightning? Something in addition to Mt. V? There had to be a way to undo their wretched exchange! There had to be a clue.

"As a matter of fact, I very nearly had to give a sermon," Darcy remarked. "My busy aunt volunteered my services while Dr. Bentley was ill."

Collins was suddenly anxious. "I trust you did a credible job," he said. "Filling in for a fellow rector is useful, so far as advancement is concerned. These little connections help one become noticed. Pulpiteering," he added, "is a serious business."

Was pulpiteering a word?

"Fortunately for everyone," said Darcy, "the heavy snow prevented the service from taking place. Nevertheless, in preparation I read many texts about shepherds. To have charge of a congregation is no small undertaking."

"But you have reckoned without the traditions of the church," Collins protested, "which make everything easy!"

"Easy?" said Darcy. "Never mind the sermons, what about the rest? Visiting the sick or attending a deathbed?"

"But it's all in the book," cried Collins. "There are prayers for every situation. You need only read the appropriate one, nicely and with modulation so that everyone may hear you, and be done with it."

"Sounds curst sanctimonious to me."

"My dear sir, you completely misunderstand your role. Are you thinking that you must *personally* offer comfort? There is nothing personal about it! Your presence is what offers comfort, and the liturgy does the rest. It is, after all, what people expect."

"You," said Darcy, "are the quintessential churchman, Collins."

Was the man blushing? "Why, thank you," he said.

"You mistake my meaning," said Darcy. "You are the sort of fellow that the Scripture refers to as an hireling."

Collins heaved a sigh. "This," he said, "is what comes from reading the Bible for oneself. So many mistaken ideas."

"Surely God has given me the right to make up my own mind."

"Providence, my dear sir," Collins almost wailed. "We refer to Him as Providence. Or, better yet, as the

Almighty." He wrinkled his nose. "To say 'God' is so common, so low."

Darcy could only stare. How incredible that his own face could so closely resemble a rabbit's! And what had happened to his voice? Why was it now so shrill?

"And I will have you know," continued Collins, "that I *am* an hireling—or rather, you are—for you are *paid* for the services you render."

But Darcy was no longer attending. How could he have been so blind? For on the other side of Folly, just visible in the failing light, were more inscriptions.

"The church," Collins went on, "is a noble career for gentlemen of nice habits, most especially those with a scholarly turn of—ouch!"

Darcy's fingers dug into Collins' arm, and he swung him round. "Look there," he cried. "Carved into the keystones. Do you see? Scriptural texts."

"How can those be clues?" scoffed Collins. "They were put there ages ago. Do you think them miraculous? I would put more faith in a heathen pictogram."

Darcy let go of Collins and hunted for a notebook and pencil.

"Do you honestly believe in miracles?" said Collins. "That the head of an ax could float or a donkey speak? Or a chariot of fire descend from the heavens? Nonsense. Stories for infants. We," he added, "live in the age of reason."

"O ye of little faith," muttered Darcy, and he continued copying. He moved to the far side of the folly.

Collins followed. "My good man, the Almighty is no longer in the business of performing miracles. Or didn't you know?"

Darcy glanced up. "And you and I," he said, "caught in our very awkward exchange, are living proof that miracles *never* happen."

He snapped the notebook shut. "I'm off to look these up," he said.

And leaving Collins standing in the garden, Darcy stalked off in the direction of Longbourn.

24 More Secrets Than One

William Collins arrived just as Elizabeth and her family went in to supper. Lydia made a quip about how he had been so thoughtful to change into his better clothes (which he had not), but he never cracked a smile. Indeed, throughout the meal he was subdued and solemn. Elizabeth did not badger him with questions. Apparently his conversation with Mr. Darcy had not gone well.

Shortly after supper the officers arrived. Of course her younger sisters were jubilant, Anne most especially. Elizabeth's gaze traveled to the far corner of the drawing room. William Collins was sitting close beside a branch of candles with a notebook and a Bible. What had he found that was so absorbing?

A short time later the door came open again, and Mr. Bingley was announced. At once Elizabeth rose to her feet. "Do take my seat, Mr. Bingley," she said. "I have forgotten my workbox in the other room." He seemed happy to comply.

"Where is your sister?" she heard Jane ask.

"Caroline prefers Mr. Darcy's company this evening," said Mr. Bingley. "If you can believe it, they have embarked on a fierce backgammon competition. Quite unlike Darcy. But then again he has not been his usual self since the accident. And so," he added, smiling, "I rode over alone."

Mr. Wickham, meanwhile, had not been idle. He was seated beside Anne, talking and laughing, much to the amusement of the others. Elizabeth wandered over and took a seat near Mr. Collins. He was muttering to himself.

"P 16:18," she heard him say, and he scowled at his notebook. "Must be Proverbs, not Psalms, it has to be. But why isn't there an R?" His fingers turned pages. When he came to the place he was looking for, he sat staring.

"What have you found that is so absorbing?" Elizabeth said, smiling.

He glanced up, surprised. Was it her imagination, or did he seem pleased that she had come? "A—text," he said. "Inscribed on the Folly at Netherfield."

"A text on the Folly? I had no idea there were any. Should I know it?"

"I believe everyone knows this one," he said. "*Pride goeth before destruction, and an haughty spirit before a fall.*"

"Sounds ominous."

"It is ominous," said Mr. Collins, "for pride is common to us all."

"Most especially to Mr. Darcy," said Elizabeth. "He is an expert when it comes to being haughty. Indeed," she added, "I do not believe the poor man can help it."

William Collins looked worried. "Do you think so?"

"Mr. Darcy is both stubborn and fond of holding a grudge. I take it your apology did not go well?"

"Apology? Ah, no." He smiled a little. "Our conversation was, shall I say, disappointing. I only wish—"

Elizabeth leaned forward. "What do you wish?"

"It's this text. Inscribed right above the statues of Cain and Abel. It's got to be the cause. But how to affect a solution?"

"Is that where the storm damaged the Folly? Mr. Bingley should see to the repairs. Shall we ask him?"

Mr. Collins looked worried again. "No, not just yet," he said. "He—seems to be enjoying your sister's company. We won't disturb him."

"He is not the only one enjoying himself," Elizabeth pointed out. "Mr. Wickham is once again monopolizing Anne de Bourgh's company."

William Collins gave a sigh. "Wickham. I had forgotten him."

"You were right, Cousin William, about his preference. But must he be so obvious in his pursuit?"

"George Wickham overrates his abilities. It does not occur to him that he will fail."

"He shall if I can help it," Elizabeth said. "I believe they have sat together long enough."

But William Collins was not listening. His fingers were busy turning pages.

"Who was the fellow who lived like an ox?" he said. "You know, eating grass for seven years and living in that paddock?"

"No one I know."

He looked up and smiled. "I mean in Bible times. A Persian king. No, it would have to be earlier, a Babylonian. Strutting on the parapet of his castle, proud as a peacock. And in a flash, humbled by the Almi—by God."

"Do you mean Nebuchadnezzar?" said Elizabeth.

"That's the one. Humbled because of his haughty spirit."

"Perhaps Mr. Darcy should be on his guard," she said, smiling. "As for Mr. Wickham, what do you say about putting an end to his *tête-à-tête* with Miss de Bourgh?"

"By all means. What to you propose?"

Elizabeth rose to her feet and faced the others. "What about dancing?" she announced. "I believe there are gentlemen enough for all."

A joyful chorus agreed, and soon furniture was being pushed back and rugs rolled.

"Five gentlemen!" counted Lydia. "Where is Mr. Fleming?"

"Five? No, there are six," called Wickham. "Mr. Fleming had better stay where he is, for he would be very much in the way. As it is, poor Pratt will have to sit out." Laughter accompanied this announcement.

Soon Mary was playing the introductory chords. Elizabeth went directly to her cousin and claimed his hand. "Your studies will have to wait, sir," she announced. "For tonight it is your duty to dance."

Would he refuse her? Would he be put off by her bold invitation? William Collins gazed solemnly into Elizabeth's eyes for a long moment, and then he smiled. "I am delighted to oblige."

An hour later refreshments were brought in and the dancing concluded. The dancers sat about on disarranged chairs, enjoying cake and talking.

"A happy end to a most pleasant evening," said Mr. Denny, and Elizabeth agreed. The dark cloud that had hung over William Collins had fled away.

"Not an ending! It's far too early," cried Lydia. "I know, let's play Shadows. Who will fetch the costumes?"

Lydia's suggestion was met with delight, most especially from the officers. Hill brought in fresh coffee and the decanter of sherry was passed round. Captain Carter, Mr. Pratt, and Mr. Denny proposed various toasts.

Elizabeth discovered that the chair beside hers was empty, and warmth rose to her cheeks. Obviously the others left it vacant for William Collins. She also noticed something else. Mr. Wickham was nowhere to be seen—and neither was Anne. Elizabeth stiffened. She now knew that time alone with a man meant kissing!

"Is something wrong?" Mr. Collins was now seated in his chair.

"It's Anne," whispered Elizabeth. "She is no longer here, and neither is Mr. Wickham."

He reacted at once. "Where would they go?"

"Perhaps to fetch the costumes for Shadows. You remember, from the trunk you carried down from the attic?"

"I believe Ned and James did that," he said. "Is it in the back parlor?" He rose to his feet.

So did Elizabeth. "Do you mind if I accompany you? Being confronted by the rector is bad enough. Anne deserves some dignity."

He did not answer. Indeed, he must have been feeling quite crabby, for when he arrived at the parlor door he pushed it open without knocking.

The room was lit by a single candlestick. Sitting on the trunk was Anne, with George Wickham bending over her. He held her hands in his.

"What is all this?" demanded Mr. Collins.

A most unnecessary statement, for obviously they had been kissing. Mr. Wickham was not even flustered. Without turning a hair, he said, "Just the man we need,

Collins. I find I am unable to carry this trunk without help. Do lend a hand."

Here Elizabeth was surprised. For instead of reading Mr. Wickham a lecture, Mr. Collins took hold of the trunk. He and Mr. Wickham went out with it, leaving Elizabeth to face Anne. She was blushing rosily.

Elizabeth could guess how Anne was feeling, but had little compassion. After all, Mr. Wickham was not William Collins. "I would not put much confidence in Mr. Wickham if I were you," she said lightly. "He is an outrageous flirt."

Anne said nothing and flounced out of the parlor.

Back in the drawing room Elizabeth poured herself a cup of coffee. Jane came over. "Lizzy," she said. "What has happened? What is wrong?"

Was her irritation so obvious? "We caught them kissing," she whispered.

"Who?"

"Anne and Mr. Wickham."

"Lizzy, no! Where?"

"In the back parlor. They were supposedly fetching costumes from the trunk."

"Oh, dear," said Jane.

"I no longer trust Mr. Wickham's intentions. He is obviously after her money. What else is there to attract him?"

"Poor Anne."

"She, of course, suspects nothing," Elizabeth went on. "I daresay she has been warned about fortune hunters for years."

"This must be the first time she has met one," said Jane. "He appears so charming and handsome."

"Charm and looks are not as important as I once thought. Intelligence and honor count for much more. Your Mr. Bingley is all of these, and in the best way."

"He is not my Mr. Bingley, Lizzy," said Jane softly.

"The hats," cried Kitty to the room at large. "Where are the hats?"

"Oh, those." Lydia was busy sorting the costumes, helped by a rosy-faced Anne. "They must be in that basket in the parlor, do you remember? I believe it's in one of the corners."

"I shall fetch them," Jane offered, and she rose to her feet.

The drawing room was now a tumult of activity. Furniture was again being moved, a sheet was fetched and hung up. All was laughter and merriment. Hill brought in more cakes.

Elizabeth felt a touch on her arm. "No doubt you will say that Wickham has given me a suspicious mind," William Collins murmured. "But does it occur to you that your sister has vanished?"

"Lydia is over there, and so are Kitty and Mary and—" Jane was no longer in the drawing room.

"And where is Charles Bingley?"

Elizabeth looked round and caught her breath. Had Jane taken him to the back parlor? *Jane?*

"What ought we to do? If they are in the parlor together, I do not wish to—"

William Collins drew out his timepiece. "They have three minutes by the clock to return. At the end of that time, I go in."

Elizabeth grasped his arm. "William," she whispered urgently. "You will knock this time, won't you? After all, Mr. Bingley is not Mr. Wickham. And they deserve a quiet moment to—"

What was she saying? This was the man who had himself stolen kisses! Those eyes of his were too intelligent and much too comprehending. He knew exactly what she meant.

He had the audaciousness to lift an eyebrow. Any hint of solemnity was gone. Indeed, those eyes of his were smiling.

"To—express their affection," Elizabeth said in a rush. "She loves him dearly, you know."

"Does she? I see no evidence of it."

"Jane is reticent to display her feelings before others, the very opposite of our youngest sisters, who at the slightest disturbance must howl at the moon."

He laughed.

"Jane is a dear," Elizabeth went on. "And she has been pining dreadfully for Mr. Bingley. Have you not seen this?"

It appeared that he had not. He stood gazing at her, holding his timepiece. And she was clutching his arm—she had forgotten this until his free hand covered hers. His fingers were warm and comfortable.

"As you wish," he said quietly. "Three additional minutes. We'll allow them a proper kiss."

Elizabeth's eyes found the floor. By proper he did not mean polite, but thorough.

The lights were extinguished, save for a branch of candles behind the sheet. "Come along, then," called Lydia. "Let's line up and disguise ourselves. Who shall be first to guess? Denny? Excellent. You'll find a chair just there, ready and waiting."

Elizabeth now discovered that she was holding William Collins' hand, very quietly and without fuss. How had this come about? He was not even looking in her direction. To the casual observer, there was nothing amiss. This man was not only thorough, but also intensely private.

With some noise the drawing room door came open. Jane sailed in, carrying hats. Mr. Bingley followed with a large basket. Though the darkness concealed much, Elizabeth could see that Jane was smiling and her cheeks were flushed. Mr. Bingley seemed unusually cheerful.

"So," rumbled William Collins in her ear, "it appears that our assumption was correct."

Elizabeth turned and met his gaze. Even in the dark she could see that his eyes were dancing.

"What?" Elizabeth demanded, even though she knew the answer. "What are you thinking?"

He bit his bottom lip, probably to keep from laughing. "I was merely wondering," he whispered back, "whether they brought in all of the hats. Perhaps several were left behind?"

Her eyes narrowed. "They brought in every one," she said evenly.

"Are you quite certain? Shouldn't we check?"

"Only," she whispered back, "if Mr. Bingley is willing to time our absence. And I daresay you would require more than three minutes."

His laugh rang out, and heads turned in their direction.

He released her hand. "*Touché*, Elizabeth," he said and smiling, he moved away.

She rather wished he hadn't.

25 A Matter of Pride

The trouble with being alone was that he was prey to his thoughts—and what a fine feast was to be had! That remark he'd made yesterday, for instance, about stealing a kiss from Elizabeth. What was he thinking? He hadn't been thinking. And wasn't this an apt illustration of the root of his struggles? The absence of rational thought. It was as if being Collins gave him an excuse not to think, and his heart had taken full advantage. Emotions were untrustworthy, he knew this now, both his own feelings and hers. For she would have welcomed that kiss—

No! At all costs he must avoid Elizabeth's adorable presence. This morning the cost was breakfast.

And so instead of loading his plate at the sideboard, he wandered the fogged streets of Meryton, feeling cold and rather hungry. The baker's shop was open for business and deliciously warm, so Darcy parted with a few pennies for muffins and a pot of tea. There he sat at a tiny table with an out-of-date London newspaper.

Steam from his cup curled invitingly, and Darcy bit back a sigh. In Elizabeth's presence he must laugh and jest and flirt. Yes, flirt—he, Fitzwilliam Darcy! As William Collins he was outrageous! Collins had none of Darcy's dignity, and wasn't this a cruel twist of fate? The real Collins craved dignity. Darcy, who had always had it, found that he no longer cared.

And didn't Meryton present a different face to the Reverend Collins? Among the gentry Collins was ignored, but here in the village he was avoided. Oh, respect was given—Darcy had been greeted numerous times in the street (for his parson's hat was unmistakable, even in the mist)—but it was politely done. Too politely and therefore forced.

Darcy removed Collins' threadbare gloves in order to consume one of the muffins. He ought to have asked for a fork—and if he were himself, one certainly would have been offered. But apparently Collins was the sort of man who must eat with his fingers. And be satisfied with a paper that was over a week old.

The door's bell tinkled as customers came and went, each bringing in a wave of cold air. Darcy rested his fingers on the warm teapot.

"Morning, Parson."

Darcy looked up and acknowledged the greeting, wondering who the fellow was. Too well-dressed for a laborer, too worn around the edges for a servant. And with a hint of insolence in the tone. A tavern keeper, perhaps?

"Doing the Lord's work, are you?" the man said with a wink. The implication was clear: that he did no work at all.

Which, knowing Collins, was probably very true.

What else could Darcy do but smile? The man paid for his purchase and went out. Darcy refilled his teacup and, sighing, applied himself to the newspaper. Was there anything as dull as old news? At length he put it aside and with one of Collins' gloves dried a pane of the window glass. Through the fog various figures appeared, including one fellow who was obviously newly-sober and heading home.

Could this be Wickham?

Darcy wiped the pane for another look. No, the man was too stocky. But the thought opened a new line of thinking. After he left Longbourn's drawing room, where did Wickham go? Surely not home to bed.

The thought of Wickham made Darcy tired.

And wasn't the man leveling at the moon by flirting with Anne de Bourgh? He would never succeed in winning her. Today Anne would return to her mother's watchful care—sooner rather than later, if Darcy knew his officious aunt—and heaven help Wickham's plans then. The moment he showed himself at Netherfield, Lady Catherine would send him packing.

A smile tugged at Darcy's lips as he pictured her scorn. If his aunt recognized Wickham as the son of Pemberley's late steward, so much the better. Such a thing, however, was too rich to hope for.

Was Anne in danger from Wickham? Not in the way Georgiana had been. There simply was no way to—what was the term? Cut her out of the herd? Darcy also drew comfort from Wickham's indolent cowardice. If exertion was required—storming the battlements to seize fair maiden—Wickham would shy off. He was after the low-hanging fruit, the easy conquest. Anne's lonely heart would likely be bruised, but not her virtue.

By now the tea in the pot was tepid. Darcy finished the last muffin, drained his cup, and left the bakery. The cold struck him like a slap, prickling through Collins' coat and shoes and thin gloves.

Less than three weeks until Christmas. Would he face the New Year as Collins? Darcy sighed heavily, and his breath hung in the air. Very probably. It had been almost that long already. He could well be Collins until his dying day. Darcy wound the muffler more securely around his neck, thrust his hands in his pockets, and went trudging along the misty street.

Collins crept down the staircase toward the breakfast room, but did not go in right away. Darcy was a careful, cautious fellow, and Collins was beginning to understand why. His main concern this morning was to avoid Lady Catherine. Through the door he could hear Caroline Bingley complaining to someone, perhaps her brother? Collins put his ear nearer to the opening.

"Her ladyship will be bringing her daughter *here*," said Miss Bingley, "and without as much as a by your leave. If they were not so intimately connected with the Darcy family, I would turn them out, Charles. You know I would."

"There's no sense in making a mountain out of a molehill," Collins heard Charles Bingley say. He sounded unhappy.

"I tolerate them for dear Mr. Darcy's sake. As well as for dear Georgiana's," she added.

There was something about the way she said Georgiana that Collins did not understand, but no matter.

"And for mine as well, I hope," said Bingley. "There is little I would not do for Darcy."

There was a pause, during which Collins strained to hear. The chime of silverware against china, the rattle of a newspaper.

"I simply cannot believe the reports about the roads and flooding," Miss Bingley said at last. "Mr. Darcy is improving by the hour. I do not see why we cannot leave for London today."

"He is not fit for travel. And, more importantly, he is not fit for polite company. If you had seen how he behaved yesterday at Longbourn!"

Collins felt a flush mount to his cheeks.

Miss Bingley said nothing more, and Bingley pressed his point. "Yesterday evening," he said, "how was he at backgammon?"

There was a pause. "Passable, Charles," she said slowly. "His play was passable, but not brilliant. Does it seem to you that poor Mr. Darcy is rather…?" Caroline Bingley hesitated. "Oh dear, how shall I put this? Rather less intelligent?"

"If you ask me, he is a great deal stupider."

Collins had been taught as a child not to eavesdrop; he now knew why. Miss Bingley was a fine one to call him stupid!

"Everyone has noticed the change," Bingley went on. "I fear the poor fellow may never recover."

"Of course he shall recover," Miss Bingley said stoutly. "I shall make certain of that."

"Caro," her brother said more seriously, "given Darcy's present state, Lady Catherine intends to take him with her to Rosings."

Collins gasped. He would rather face prison than Rosings!

For there would be no rest, none at all. At every meal he would endure the company of Anne and Lady Catherine. And he would spend each evening with them in the drawing room, a boredom so complete that even visits from Darcy would be welcome.

Again came that stabbing thought, which extinguished his delicious dreams: *Might you not be better off as yourself?*

But an exchange was clearly impossible! What if he were stuck being Fitzwilliam Darcy forever?

Caroline Bingley interrupted his thoughts. "Mr. Darcy will be far happier with us than with his aunt, Charles. I think we ought to leave at once."

"Abscond with him, do you mean? It is not easily done, not to mention being in rather bad form. You have been reading too many romances."

"As to romances," she replied, and the archness in her tone was unmistakable, "I think that you wish to remain for another reason. Jane Bennet is a sweet girl, Charles, but I hardly think she is worth losing your heart to. I daresay you will survive without her. Mr. Darcy," she added, "seems to have recovered from his preference for Elizabeth Bennet."

Collins' head came up.

"Shall we consign Miss Elizabeth Bennet to her bumbling cousin?" Miss Bingley gave her trilling laugh. "Yes, we shall trust Mr. Collins to be taken captive by her fine eyes," she said.

"Caroline, really."

"But they shall do very well together, Charles! A match made, dare we say, in heaven? She, a fishwife in the making and he, a paltry rector without two shillings to rub together."

She laughed again. This time Charles Bingley reluctantly joined in.

The conversation turned to more conventional topics—what was to be served for dinner and should they invite Dr. and Mrs. Bentley—but Collins did not go in. He had never thought of himself as having a pugnacious temper or vengeful ambitions, but this much was clear: he would exact payment from Caroline Bingley for those words. Paltry rector indeed!

Through the mist rose the form of Meryton's parish church, and on a whim Darcy tried the door. It was open, so he went in. There was not much warmth here, but it was someplace to be other than Longbourn.

The church was built in the traditional cruciform shape. Darcy wandered down the center aisle and slipped into a pew. At once he removed Collins' hat. It would surely keep him warmer, but if Dr. Bentley (or anyone else) happened by he did not wish to be recognized. Much better to remain anonymous.

Behind the altar was an arched glass window, and Darcy sat gazing at it. The church was solemn and silent, unlike the baker's shop or any of the rooms at Longbourn, leaving Darcy alone with his thoughts. Oddly enough, in this setting he did not mind.

He checked his timepiece. Morning vespers were at, what, eleven? Until then he would be undisturbed.

He cast his thoughts back to the Folly, intent on reasoning out what he'd discovered. But the text he'd found yesterday did not leap to mind. Instead, another crowded forward: *Not my will but Thine be done.*

The Savior's prayer at Gethsemane: Thy will be done.

Darcy sat for some time, listening to the sound of his own breathing. Thy will. Was he meant to be Collins, then? Was he meant to be humbled to this extent?

Before extinguishing his candle last night, Darcy had located the story of King Nebuchadnezzar and found in it much food for thought. The man lived in a paddock eating grass, thoroughly mad. His sanity was eventually restored, but not until seven years had passed. Wouldn't seven days have been sufficient?

When God did a thing, Darcy realized, He was frighteningly thorough. And if Collins must likewise be humbled, it would take not seven years but seventy!

Darcy gave a sharp sigh, and his breath rose in a cloud. He could not solve Collins' part of this puzzle, but he ought to be responsible for his. Did this mean willingly embracing life as Collins? Not only as pertaining to Elizabeth (the sole benefit!), but in every area of life?

An accompanying thought was just as bad: Should he prepare Collins to do the same?

Never! Let the man fall on his face.

The silence swallowed this waspish thought. Too late he realized his own latent arrogance. Again Darcy sighed.

It had been a long time since he had knelt down to pray of his own accord, especially in a public spot like church. Apparently it had been too long.

26   Rag, Tag, and Bobtail

The insistent rapping at the main door took everyone by surprise.

"Dear heaven, it's Mother," cried Anne de Bourgh.

"But it can't be; it's too early," protested Lydia. "And besides, we would have heard her barouche in the drive."

"Your mother would never walk all this way," said Kitty.

"Or ride a horse," added Lydia.

Even Elizabeth listened for the scrape of the main door as it opened. There were voices in the vestibule and then a hearty, "Thank God." It was a distinctly male voice.

Elizabeth laid aside her book. This was not William Collins. Could it be—?

Lydia bounced up. "It's Wickham! Anne, he has come. And from the sound of it he is not alone."

With him was Denny, and when Hill brought them into the drawing room Kitty and Lydia cheered.

"We are in time," said Mr. Wickham, smiling. "Never was I so relieved to see trunks stacked in a vestibule." He crossed the room, took Anne's hand, and kissed it soundly. "We are not too late to say good-bye."

"It is no such thing," said Mrs. Bennet. "Dear Miss de Bourgh goes only to Netherfield."

There was a small silence, and Mr. Denny filled it. "I say, let's play cards, shall we? Better than sitting about waiting for the other shoe to fall. Miss Lydia and Miss Kitty, do help me clear a space. Miss Mary, you must sit down with us."

Elizabeth remained with her book. Very nimbly did Mr. Denny keep the others occupied while Anne and Mr. Wickham sat together on the sofa, whispering. Miss Jenkinson sniffed and looked disapproving. Anne not only ignored this but turned her back to the woman.

Over the pages of her book Elizabeth covertly studied the pair. He was talking, while she blushed and hung upon every word. Then from the corner of her eye Elizabeth saw a movement. Mr. Wickham was looking at each of the others in turn. At once Elizabeth lowered her gaze, every sense on the alert.

She turned a page and raised her eyes in time to see a folded paper pass from his hand to Anne's. This disappeared beneath the folds of Anne's gown.

Thanks to Mr. Denny's antics, no one else had seen the exchange. Elizabeth sat and considered what to do. Was this a love note?

Presently she closed her book and rose to her feet. "What a surprise it is to see you up and about so early, Mr. Wickham," she said pleasantly.

He gave his easy laugh and spread his hands. "In truth, a miracle. A pity your cousin is not here to appreciate it."

"And here I thought you never rose before noon."

"An exercise in efficiency, Miss Elizabeth. Breakfast and luncheon rolled into one meal. Old habits," he added, "die hard."

He turned his smile on Anne. "I have yet to learn country habits and hours."

"That or return to London," said Elizabeth flatly. "Miss de Bourgh, might I impose upon you to—"

But Elizabeth never finished her sentence, being interrupted by the sound of an arriving coach. At once Lydia and Kitty threw down their cards and rushed to the windows. "Oh, no!" cried Kitty. "So soon?"

Anne was on her feet at once. "I must introduce you to Mother," Elizabeth heard her say to Mr. Wickham.

"Perhaps—another time," he said. "If she has not been happy to have you here, she will not be pleased to meet me."

"Of course she shall," protested Anne. "For you are Cousin Fitzwilliam's very good friend. Promise, please promise, to call on Mr. Darcy soon."

Wickham looked uncomfortable. "I—do not wish to intrude."

"It would be no intrusion, believe me," said Anne. "After spending so much time with Mother, Cousin Fitzwilliam will welcome a friendly face. And," she added, "so will I."

Mr. Wickham gallantly kissed both of Anne's hands before surrendering her to Lydia and Kitty. Hill came in to say that Miss de Bourgh's trunks were being loaded, and that her mother was waiting in the coach.

This struck Elizabeth as a cowardly maneuver. But as tears were flowing freely, perhaps it was for the best. But what had become of Wickham's letter?

There was the usual commotion involved with saying farewell. When it was over, the younger girls stood at the windows and waved the coach down the drive.

"And that, my dears," said their mother, "is that. I daresay you will write to dear Miss de Bourgh."

"Oh, certainly," said Kitty. "I shall write at once. And Mr. Collins will take my letter for me, since he goes to Netherfield every day."

Elizabeth was careful to keep her tone light. "Is that where he is? I thought he was keeping to his room."

"He came in, oh, perhaps an hour ago," said her mother. "He said something about riding with Mr. Darcy, and off he went."

"Riding with Mr. Darcy," echoed Mr. Wickham, sliding into a chair near Elizabeth's. "It seems that my old friend is recovering. But I thought your cousin does not ride."

"Of course Mr. Collins rides," Kitty interrupted, "for we have seen him. Now then, I must begin my letter."

Lydia cast herself onto one of the sofas. "You may write, if you wish. I do not find letters amusing, unless they are written to me. And most especially," she added, "if they are love notes."

"What do you know of love notes?" scoffed Kitty.

"Girls!" cried Mrs. Bennet.

Elizabeth studied the floor. Was what Mr. Wickham had given a love note? Surely not.

It was only to avoid Caroline Bingley that Collins had agreed to Darcy's scheme. He now stood in the paddock, looking from Darcy to the saddled horse. "But I do not wish to ride," he protested.

Darcy had the bad taste to ignore him and took the horse's bridle from the groom. "Come and stroke the horse," he said.

"Do what?" Collins was not about to come any nearer to such an enormous beast. He could see it twitch and move its eyes. "Why should I?"

"Because she is an animal, not a piece of furniture. She needs to know you, to trust you."

"I have no desire to trust her. And I daresay the feeling is mutual."

"My dear fellow, you are forced to trust her."

"Not if I do not ride," Collins pointed out. "I'll drive about in a chaise-and-four. I do own a chaise?"

"Several," said Darcy. "Put out your hand and stroke her shoulder. Like this."

Inside his fine leather gloves Collins could feel his palms sweating.

"Come along," said Darcy, more softly. "Must I hold your hand?"

Collins consented to touch the horse, but with shrinking fingers.

"There. Is that so bad? Bingley says she is an excellent mount for a lady. Meaning that she is very gentle. Just the thing for you until you recover."

"Not very clean, is she?" murmured Collins, examining his gloves.

"Nonsense," said Darcy. "She has been well-brushed and is in perfect form."

This was a complete lie, for there were hairs on his glove! Then Collins remembered that the stable boys were watching, so of course Darcy had to say this.

Darcy led the horse to the mounting block. "Up you go," he said to Collins. "Always mount on the left side, if possible."

Collins reluctantly obeyed. From the corners of his eyes he could see the stable boys grinning at one another.

"Place your left hand on the mane, while your other hand holds the front of the saddle."

Was Darcy serious? He must do both at the same time?

"Your left boot goes into the stirrup, there. Then swing your right foot over."

"Swing my right foot over," Collins repeated.

"As you do," continued Darcy, "make sure not to kick the horse."

Collins placed his hands where Darcy indicated. His knees were knocking together. "I—do not think I can do this," he confessed.

Darcy gave a long sigh. "If things remain the way they are, this is a skill you will be expected to have mastered. We'll get you settled in the saddle first, to give you the feel of keeping your seat."

"Keeping my seat?" said Collins. "At the moment I'm working on keeping my breakfast."

Somebody coughed to disguise a laugh. Gathering his courage, Collins took hold of the mane and somehow managed to struggle into the saddle.

"It's so high," he said, gasping. He could feel the horse moving beneath him. He was going to faint, he knew it, or slide off and be trampled to death. Why had he allowed Darcy to persuade him? And what had happened to his hat?

"Your injuries," said Darcy distinctly, "have increased your awareness, that is all."

Collins could feel his knees trembling, and he wondered if the horse could feel it too. How he hated his own cowardice!

"I'll walk the horse around the paddock for a bit," said Darcy. "Later we'll move on to the trot."

"Later," faltered Collins. He devoutly hoped that later would never come.

After spending what felt like hours in the paddock, Collins was cold and worn to the bone. He did not see how Darcy's suggestion of a bath would cure any of these, and he had said so to anyone who would listen, most notably his valet.

Oddly enough, Darcy was right. Collins was restored to his rooms clean, dry, and feeling remarkably well. The exertion of the ride, while nerve-wracking, must have been beneficial. Even so, he hoped that Darcy would forget his promise to return tomorrow for another lesson.

The fire was crackling merrily when Collins drifted off to sleep. When the knocking at his door woke him, the fire was a bed of bright embers.

Collins rubbed his eyes. Was this a dream, or was Lady Catherine standing there? He scrambled to his feet. "Yes?" he said politely.

But Lady Catherine had turned back to the doorway. "Of course you will speak with your cousin," she said to someone Collins could not see. "Why are you so reluctant? And for goodness' sake, close the door."

Whoever it was made a reply that Collins did not hear. And then he realized that Lady Catherine was addressing her daughter. He knew that Anne was due to arrive today, but he did not figure it would be so soon.

"If a gently-bred girl," he heard Lady Catherine say, "makes a perilous journey to see her fiancé…"

"He is not my fiancé!"

"Hear, hear," said Collins. Not softly enough! Lady Catherine turned and gave him a dark look.

She rounded on Anne. "Then why did you tell the Bennets that he was?"

"To explain my journey, of course." There was insolence in Anne's tone, something Collins had never heard. He angled his position to get a better look.

"You felt the need to rush to Fitzwilliam's side?"

"Yes, but…"

"Why?" demanded Lady Catherine.

Anne put up her chin. "A week ago I was a very different girl."

Lady Catherine's fingers fastened on Anne's arm. "How do you mean?"

"I was desperate to leave Rosings! I was desperate to see something of the world! So when Mr. Fleming told me where he was going, I made him take me with him."

"Foolish girl! You are too ill for travel."

"I am not too ill. For the past days I have danced and played games and laughed and—"

"And what else?" Lady Catherine said waspishly.

"Nothing," said Anne. Her eyes studied the rug.

"You have been in the company of men!"

"No men worth mentioning. Only Mr. Collins and Mr. Fleming."

Collins set his teeth. A fine tribute to his manhood!

"Did you dance with Mr. Collins and Mr. Fleming?"

"In a large company, yes," said Anne. "What of it?" But there was something evasive about her manner.

"The fact remains, my girl, that you left your home to rush to the bedside of a man. Therefore, to prevent a scandal, you will return to Rosings as a married woman."

"That I shall not!" cried Anne.

"Lady Catherine," Collins protested.

She silenced him with a glance. "You will marry Fitzwilliam," she said to her daughter. "If the roads were better I would already have sent for a special license."

"Mother, no! Fitzwilliam dislikes me as much as I dislike him!"

Lady Catherine was not deterred. "You will find him sadly changed," she admitted. "But perhaps that is for the best. You and he can be ill together."

"But—I do not love him!"

"Since when is love important in marriage? Scores of married couples do not get on in private. This is why a large estate is beneficial."

"Mother!" pleaded Anne.

"Leaving each of you free to pursue your own interests. Fortunately," added Lady Catherine, "Fitzwilliam's interests will not bring shame on the family."

Anne flashed him a dark look.

"Come, take his hand," Lady Catherine coaxed. "Let us make a beginning."

Anne recoiled. "No! He will only look at me in that cold way of his. I marvel that I ever thought him attractive."

It was all Collins could do to keep from sneering. Darcy, unattractive? Anne was hardly a prize!

"Fitzwilliam is not amusing, Mother," Anne pleaded. "When he comes he scarcely speaks. Does he entertain us with games or stories or dancing?"

"Is it necessary," Collins broke in, "to speak of me as if I were not present?"

This Lady Catherine ignored. "Of course he does not dance at Rosings. Even if he wished to, there would be no one to play. And with only one couple..."

"Mrs. Jenkinson can play. As to couples, there is Mr. Collins."

"Please," said Lady Catherine. "How on earth would you make a proper set? Enlist the housekeeper? The footman? You are being nonsensical. Come here and speak with Mr. Darcy. His thinking may be muddled," she added, "but he knows his duty."

"Would you marry me to a half-wit, Mother?" Anne wailed.

"No one of our ancestry," said Lady Catherine, "can ever be a half-wit." She gave Collins a look.

It was well that Collins was skilled in acting dumb, or he would have replied in kind. Anne turned on her heel and went storming out.

27 If All The World Were Paper

No hot bath awaited Darcy when he returned, and as usual Longbourn was calamitous. This time it was Mrs. Bennet, fussing in the vestibule with Hill. Or rather fussing at her. Mrs. Hill, who valued her position, would not dare to argue back. It took Darcy a full minute to realize that Mrs. Bennet was almost enjoying herself.

"I do not see," she was now saying, "why we cannot have chicken."

Chickens again! If he was ever restored to his proper identity, Darcy vowed to send Mrs. Bennet a wagonload of chickens.

"And yet," she went on, "I learn that you have cooked several."

Hill took Darcy's hat and coat. It seemed to him that she was looking unusually distraught. "For the Master, ma'am," she protested. "It was Mr. Fleming who ordered it and rightly so. My old grandmother swore by chicken broth."

"I care this little—" Mrs. Bennet snapped her fingers, "—for what your ancestors thought. Sarah," she called, hailing the girl as she passed by. "Fetch Mr. Fleming, I would like a word with him. At once, do you understand?"

"Mr. Fleming is with the Master, ma'am," said Hill, "and shouldn't be disturbed."

Mrs. Bennet's response was to flounce into the drawing room. Darcy followed, but at a distance.

It seemed to him that Fleming was looking drawn when he came in and stood before Mrs. Bennet. There were dark circles under his eyes. He suggested a private conversation, but she would have none of it. Her grievance about the chickens must be heard by all.

"I fail to see," she began, "why our hens must be fed solely to Mr. Bennet. Eggs are difficult to come by at this time of year, and yet you must have laying hens slain to gratify him."

"Your husband's appetite has fallen off," said Fleming, "and yet he willingly takes the soup."

"Thus we are deprived to gratify his whims?"

Fleming did not return her smile. "If Longbourn is unable to provide the chickens for his broth, then we must purchase them elsewhere."

"Spend good money when we have chickens here? Nonsense."

"You fail to understand, ma'am, that your husband's health has taken a turn for the worse, which is why I suggested a private conversation. But as everyone is here, it is perhaps best to state the case plainly."

"A turn for the worse?" faltered Mrs. Bennet.

"Please understand," said Fleming, "that there is no cause for alarm. Mrs. Hill and I are managing his care nicely. But in all honesty I must inform you that your husband is not out of the woods."

"Not out of the woods?" echoed Mary.

There was silence in the drawing room as the gravity of those words came home. And then Mrs. Bennet began to wail.

"First Miss de Bourgh is taken away," Mrs. Bennet said, mopping her eyes. "Such an opportunity for my girls, and to what end? Then Hill must rage at me over chickens. And now Mr. Bennet is dying!"

"Mama." Elizabeth sat down beside her mother and took her hand. "That is not what Mr. Fleming said."

"It is what he meant! Not out of the woods, he said. Not out of the woods!"

Darcy did not have to guess what would come next.

"At any moment Mr. Bennet could be gone, and what will become of us? We shall be put into the street, that's what. Cast from hearth and home."

Darcy's eyes met Elizabeth's. "Please do not distress yourself, ma'am," he told Mrs. Bennet.

Mrs. Bennet lowered her handkerchief. "Oh, Mr. Collins," she said. And she made a play with her wet lashes.

That soulful look! She was waiting, Darcy knew, for his assurance that Longbourn House would always be her home. This he could not (and would not) promise, for it was unfair to commit Collins to such a course. When the time came—many years from now—he would make provision for Mrs. Bennet.

"Have faith, Mama," said Elizabeth. "Father needs rest and quiet and Hill's wonderful broth."

This opinion was soundly seconded by a gentleman's voice: Wickham's!

Darcy swung round. Had Wickham been here all along? There he sat at a card table with Denny and the younger girls, taking in every morsel of information. Darcy turned his gaze elsewhere.

There came the sound of chairs scraping against the floor. In a rare display of tact, Wickham and Denny were leaving. Darcy watched them approach Mrs. Bennet. "Your husband is in need of quiet, and I daresay you are wishing us at Jericho," said Wickham smoothly. "Please accept our best wishes for his speedy recovery."

"But you cannot go," protested Lydia. "Otherwise we'll sit staring at one another. And nothing is as dull as that."

"Lydia, really," said Mary.

"Father has a cold, that is all," said Lydia. "Please tell them to stay, Mama. At least until we have finished our game."

But Lydia's protests fell on deaf ears. The officers took their leave, and Mrs. Bennet sat twisting her handkerchief.

"We shall be forced to live on my money," she lamented, "which amounts to almost nothing. Barely enough for a set of rooms in Meryton, Mr. Collins. After the comforts of Longbourn, it will be insupportable!"

Darcy shifted in his chair. Accommodations in town, or a cottage on the Longbourn estate, were precisely the style of provision he would offer.

"And what a thing for my girls," Mrs. Bennet went on. "To have to wear the same gowns year after year, with no money for hats or dancing shoes or anything fine. Not even books, Lizzy."

"Mama," said Elizabeth, "Mr. Fleming said nothing about—"

"Don't you tell me," Mrs. Bennet flashed. "Mr. Fleming was being polite, not wishing to upset me. All is certainly *not* well. I have a sense about these things." She took refuge in a fresh onslaught of sniffing.

"Oh dear," Elizabeth whispered to Darcy. "I'm afraid there is no dealing with her in this state."

"Perhaps," he suggested, "she should see for herself how your father is faring." Darcy turned to Mrs. Bennet. "Once he awakens, ma'am," he said, "you might like to sit with him."

Mrs. Bennet's head came up. "Me, enter the sickroom?" she cried. "Witness poor Mr. Bennet's sufferings as he thrashes about and struggles to breathe?" She paused to blow her nose. "Certainly I would *like* to be of comfort to him," she added, "as it is a wifely duty. But my nerves will not allow it."

An awkward silence descended on the drawing room, broken only by Mary's dry cough. Presently Elizabeth rose to her feet, and Darcy did the same. Jane approached, embroidery frame in hand.

"Dearest Mama," Jane said, taking Elizabeth's empty seat. "Might I have your advice?" She indicated several skeins of silk.

Mrs. Bennet waved her away. "What have I to do with fripperies? Soon enough every pretty trifle will be banished. Or, more likely," she added, with a look to Darcy, "sold to pay for food."

But Jane persevered in her gentle way. "Which shade of pink would be best? The lighter or the darker?"

Mrs. Bennet pinched up her lips, but her gaze was drawn to Jane's embroidery. "Primrose and violet?" she protested. "Why did you choose such colors?"

"Because of the flowers themselves. But as for the rose blossom, Mama, what do you think of..."

Jane continued speaking, and Darcy followed Elizabeth to the windows. "I'll have a word with Fleming," he told her quietly. "I doubt that your father is in serious danger."

"No, of course he is not, but—" She caught hold of his arm. "He gave her a letter," she whispered. "I saw it."

Darcy was at a loss. "Fleming?"

"No, Mr. Wickham. He gave a letter to Anne this morning, just as Lady Catherine came to take her away."

Darcy felt his lips compress. He could guess what the letter contained. "As usual, Wickham's timing was perfect."

"As usual? What do you mean?"

It was no good talking here. "Come into the dining room," he said. "I'll go first, and after a bit you follow."

She gave him an exasperated look.

"Listening ears," he whispered. He then raised his voice and said, "I'll have a word with Fleming about your father, then."

"Oh," cried Mary, bouncing up. "Please do."

Darcy heard Elizabeth give a sharp sigh. "As you wish," he heard her whisper.

She saw him place a chair for her and draw another forward for himself. There was a short silence. "I daresay the note is harmless," Elizabeth said. "Nothing more than an expression of regard. But I thought you would like to know."

He shifted in his chair. It now occurred to her that William Collins was looking both tired and unhappy.

"And if it is more than that," she added, "why, Anne de Bourgh is an heiress. She must be accustomed to receiving notes from admirers."

"I doubt whether she has encountered a man of Wickham's ilk."

Jane had said the same, and to hear it repeated irked her.

"For that matter," he continued, "I doubt whether you—" He broke off speaking.

Elizabeth's chin came up. "Whether I what?"

He did not answer but instead studied the floor.

"I know you think him a fortune hunter. Do you blame him for being tempted by her wealth? Any gentleman would be."

He gave her a look. "Any gentleman?"

"Just because the man is a flirt does not mean he is a reprobate!"

"This rug," he remarked, "has a rather unfortunate stain."

"Stop trying to change the subject." She leaned in. "You have always disliked Mr. Wickham, even from the first."

"The word *mistrusted* would be more accurate."

Elizabeth gave a huff of frustration. "Just now you remind me very much of Mr. Darcy."

William Collins looked thunderstruck.

"He has always hated George Wickham," Elizabeth added.

"Mr. Darcy," he said grimly, "has his reasons."

"How decided you are in your opinion! On the face of it, one would suppose that both you and Mr. Darcy are envious."

"Envious?" he broke in. "Of Wickham?"

"Disliking him for his looks," said Elizabeth, "or his accomplishments—"

"What accomplishments? He has none!"

"—or his manners or his easy address or his skill at cards."

"You must be joking."

"Or," Elizabeth added, smiling a little, "because he is attractive to women."

"He most certainly is that, and for reasons I cannot fathom."

But he was looking so unhappy that Elizabeth's irritation vanished. She reached for his hands and took them in her own. "But your objection runs deeper than envy. Do tell me, William. Why do you dislike him so?"

Again he fell silent. "The answer to your question," he said at last, "involves information that is not mine to share."

"Your position as a clergyman compels you to silence?"

"Something like that."

She drew a long breath and let it out. "George Wickham is an incorrigible flirt, and he is wrong to encourage Anne's affections. But her mother will put a stop to it."

William did not look convinced. "Anne is both foolish and persuadable." He hesitated. "I fear he will persuade her into an elopement."

"That is an unfair assumption. Always you assume the worst."

"With George Wickham, yes."

"Then we must read that letter, if only to clear Mr. Wickham of suspicion."

William Collins made a sound that was very like a snort.

Elizabeth put up her chin. "It is only right to know the truth. The question is, how do we obtain it?"

"How indeed?"

Elizabeth lapsed into thinking. "If what you suspect is true, Anne will guard it carefully. We must therefore obtain the sequel. For surely she will reply, and then we shall know."

"And how do you suggest we do that?"

"You will become Anne's courier, of course."

He looked astonished. "Me?"

"Who else will Anne find to deliver her letter? None of the Netherfield servants; the risk of discovery is too great. Unless Anne is able to pay."

"I doubt she has access to money," he said. "You are suggesting that I present myself at Netherfield and offer my services? Rather an aggressive strategy."

"Won't it be Anne's part to enlist your help? You will simply show up and—what is the word? Ah yes, hobnob."

His scowl dissolved into a grin. "You do realize that Anne loathes me," he said. "She thinks I am the greatest bore in nature. Not that I blame her."

"You are nothing of the sort," said Elizabeth.

"But I am! Rational conversation is impossible, for anything I say Lady Catherine pounces on and adds to her armory. Thus I take refuge in flattery."

Elizabeth had to laugh. "Do be serious. Tomorrow you must find a reason to go to Netherfield and spend time in the drawing room. Overstay your welcome. Force Miss Bingley to invite you for a meal."

"In other words," he said, smiling, "I will make a nuisance of myself. That should not be difficult."

"Your fulsome compliments will be put to good use."

"Must I compliment Miss Bingley?" he wanted to know. "I will have to begin thinking now, for an extemporaneous remark will be hopelessly bad. And then there is Anne, who never looks well. Along with Lady Catherine's questionable taste."

"Your skills will be sorely tested," Elizabeth admitted. "If only I could be in the drawing room to watch you work your magic. But alas..."

The dining room door came open. "Lizzy!" someone hissed.

Too late Elizabeth realized that she and William were sitting with their heads together. At once she drew back and released his hands.

The messenger was Kitty. "Mama wants to know what has become of Mr. Fleming. Lady Catherine's coach has come to take him to Netherfield."

"In other words," Mr. Collins murmured, "our dear Anne has suddenly become ill."

But Darcy could not find Fleming anywhere, until he entered the bedchamber they shared. There he lay, fully clothed, stretched out on the bed. He was fast asleep and no wonder. How long had it been since he had slept?

Darcy found a blanket to cover Fleming, and then went out. He found Hill standing in the vestibule. "Mr. Fleming is asleep," he told her, "and I am not about to wake him. Lady Catherine can wait."

"But if the need is urgent," Hill protested.

"I rather doubt that it is," said Darcy. "Anne was perfectly well when she left us this morning. Ten to one she has shut herself in her bedchamber and is feigning illness. Either for attention or to avoid her mother.

"And under ordinary circumstances," he continued, "I would not object. If Lady Catherine wishes to pay Fleming to dance attendance, so be it. However, Fleming's expertise is needed here."

"We are able to care for the Master in his absence," said Hill. "There is no crisis, sir."

Darcy smiled a little. It had been like an eternity since anyone had called him sir. "But it will worry Mrs.

Bennet, and her anxiety will impact everyone in the house."

Hill's expression confirmed the truth of this.

"Invite her ladyship's coachman in for a hot drink and some of your pie, Mrs. Hill. Lady Catherine can wait. An hour or two will make little difference to Anne de Bourgh."

Supper that evening was somber. According to Hill, Mr. Bennet was sleeping soundly. But Mr. Fleming was now at Netherfield, and Mrs. Bennet felt his absence keenly.

"Never again," she lamented, "shall I look at a chicken without thinking of this tragic night."

Darcy and Elizabeth shared a look, and he said, "I am ready to ride to Netherfield at a moment's notice."

This did nothing to mollify Mrs. Bennet. And so the family ate their soup in silence. Even Kitty and Lydia had the sense to refrain from talking. Darcy had to wonder whether George Wickham would continue to visit Longbourn. With Anne's fortune within his grasp, playing cards for half-penny points might be too tame.

Georgiana and now her cousin Anne. A wretched farce driven by Wickham's insatiable greed.

Darcy paused, his spoon in midair. Was there more to this that met the eye? Did Wickham deliberately choose Anne, not only because of her tempting wealth, but also to exact revenge against Darcy's family?

"Might we venture out to Clarke's tomorrow?" he heard Mary say.

"Books!" Mrs. Bennet said. "How can you think of books at a time like this? If you go to Meryton at all," Mrs. Bennet continued, "it will be to visit your Aunt Phillips. Yes, and you will bring her here. She will keep vigil with me and also help with arrangements that must be made."

Dear Mrs. Bennet, already fretting about her husband's funeral.

Darcy's thoughts returned to Wickham. But the mention of Meryton gave him an idea. Given Collins' fondness for black, if he went into town wearing different clothes would he be recognized?

Not for nothing had Darcy attended Cambridge with Wickham. Even though his objective then had been to avoid the fellow, he had grown to know his habits.

How would he procure clothing for a disguise? He meant to go tonight, for if elopement was Wickham's plan, time was of the essence. There were coats and hats of Mr. Bennet's in the house.

These Darcy immediately rejected. It was bad enough that Mrs. Bennet was cringing over ordering the man's coffin. To borrow his clothes would be like stealing from a corpse.

"It was kind of Wickham and Denny to call this morning," Kitty said.

Lydia gave a heavy sigh. "If they come tonight," Darcy heard her whisper, "Mama will send them away.

Which is tragic, for I was hoping that we might play Shadows."

Shadows! And that trunk filled with clothing! Never mind that he was sore from walking and riding. Never mind that in the process he had ruined a pair of Collins' shoes. Tonight Darcy would venture out in search of George Wickham. And he had a good idea about where to find him.

28 Faults on All Sides

Of all the ill-considered things that Darcy had ever attempted, tonight's plan to spy on George Wickham would top the list. He cared little for his cousin, save that she was an innocent, and even less for his aunt. So why was he stumping along a dark country lane toward Meryton? Simply for the pleasure of foiling Wickham.

A reconnaissance mission his cousin Fitz would call this, to determine which of the public houses Wickham preferred. The man would be found in the gentlemen's parlor, set apart from the laboring class. To this private enclave Darcy would be excluded, no thanks to the contents of that trunk. He'd avoided the ancient skirted coats and tricorn hats, but he consented to wear a dark cloak, the lining of which had faded to an unfortunate shade of pink. At best he would be thought an eccentric and at worst, a laughingstock.

Darcy set his teeth. To think that he used to pride himself on his clothing! Beneath the cloak he wore a borrowed frock coat and beneath that, a brown waistcoat of boiled wool—heaven help the buttons! The most shudder-worthy item was the plaid neck cloth. Never had Darcy worn anything other than white in the evening. This might be only Meryton, but a man had his standards. He'd wrapped Collins' muffler high around his throat and hoped for the best.

The moon was hidden by clouds. The temperature was falling, with waist-high fog drifting across the lane. Darcy knew that he ought to have begged a lantern from Mrs. Hill. But then he must confess to her his errand, and he knew where that would lead. Mrs. Hill would raise a ruckus, and in the end he would look even more a fool.

And wasn't it too bad that his letter to Fitz had gone awry. Ten to one his cousin had been sent off somewhere—with Fitz one never knew—but how he would enjoy himself tonight. Unlike Darcy, Fitz was fond of larks and pranks.

Darcy turned his mind toward his destination. There was a name; Denny had said it or perhaps Captain Carter. About how the officers' usual game could set a fellow back at— Darcy paused to think. Yes, that was it—at the Rose and Crown.

The Rose and Crown was located on the main road, attached to a coaching inn. There was a yard and stabling area for horses, convenient for an elopement. Darcy must study the network of coaching inns, especially those leading to the north.

The taproom, warm with conversation and laughter, was a welcome change from the cold silence outside. This was the domain of laborers and farmers. Darcy nodded pleasantly to the barkeep, a man he'd seen in the bakery. There was no glint of recognition in the fellow's answering nod. Directed by the scent of quality tobacco, Darcy located a curtained door, the entrance to the gentlemen's parlor.

He hesitated, then tossed his gloves on a table nearby and stepped up to the bar. A few of Collins' coins were exchanged for a pint of brew.

With an eye on the curtain, Darcy settled in at the table with an old London newspaper of Mr. Bennet's he'd brought for this purpose. Presently the curtain parted and a young women came through, along with the sound of laughter. Darcy thought he heard Wickham's voice. He glanced again to the bar, but no one was looking his way.

Soon Darcy was settled at a corner table, but this time on the other side of the curtain. At another table sat Wickham, intent on a game of whist.

After a time Darcy laid aside the newspaper to watch the game. Wickham's partner passed at four, not an encouraging sign. Would Wickham proceed? Without a strong hand he would be done for. But did Wickham care? He played his hand and lost with the merriest of groans.

Darcy did not know whether to laugh or sigh as another game was begun. For a man who lived by his wits, Wickham's skills at cards ought to be better. He laughed too much and interrupted the play with sallies and asides. Distractions were the domain of the cheater, but sleight of hand was not Wickham's strong suit. Still laughing, he ordered a round of drinks for all at the table. Darcy shook his head. Too much *bonhomie*.

His fellow officers did not seem to mind Wickham's antics. Why should they, when he was losing? Like everyone else, they were taken in by his easy ways and fine clothing. Obviously they thought there was money to be won.

Had Wickham succeeded in marrying Georgiana, her share of the Darcy fortune would be gambled away just like this. Was Anne to be sacrificed to fund Wickham's greed?

But money was not enough for Wickham, was it? The pretty barmaid had not escaped his notice, and with her Wickham was at his charming best. Very adroitly did he play the role of the gentleman-officer. In both looks and manners, he could be the son of an earl. Wickham was certainly more handsome than Fitz. And that was saying something, for Fitz was no slouch.

Darcy drained his glass, in part to see what would happen. Sure enough, his empty glass remained unnoticed. Wickham's smiles and jesting laughter claimed all the barmaid's attention.

Good looks, an easy laugh, delicious conversation, and—Darcy hated to admit it—Wickham's skills as a listener drew women. Even shy Georgiana and painfully reticent Anne—even Elizabeth Bennet! —had been taken in by this man. The worldly-wise barmaid was no exception. Darcy noted how she touched Wickham's shoulder. And when she brought his pint, Wickham smilingly took it from her with both hands, his fingers brushing against hers on the glass.

It was the same old story. Darcy opened the newspaper and turned a page.

Presently there came a scraping of chairs and more laughter. Darcy lowered a corner of the newspaper. Wickham, in his role as prince among men, was gaily writing out IOUs.

When Darcy glanced up again, Wickham was gone and so was the dimpled barmaid.

There was no reason to remain, but Darcy sat with his empty glass. Never had he felt more powerless.

If Wickham intended to elope with Anne, Darcy could do little to stop it. He simply hadn't the funds to pursue them. If he involved Lady Catherine, Collins would certainly lose his position.

And then what would Darcy do? He would be cast into the wide world to earn his living.

It was with a heavy heart that Darcy returned to Longbourn. The fog was now thick, promising heavy frost before dawn. A thunderstorm—his only hope for transformation—did not appear likely.

He found the kitchen door unbarred and a lit candle on the table. Had Mrs. Hill left this for him? On second thought, the candle was for Fleming. Darcy paused, listening. There were no sounds of movement in the house. Apparently Mr. Bennet was sleeping soundly.

He lit another candle and crept toward the back parlor. A creak here, a misplaced step there—who would be awake to hear? And yet he took pains to be quiet.

Once inside the parlor, off came the cloak, the borrowed neck cloth and waistcoat. Into the trunk they went. Carefully, dreading a squeak of hinges, he pulled shut the lid. The cloak and hat, damp from the fog, he set aside to dry.

Darcy did not hear the door come open or see the light from her candle until he heard her voice.

"William Collins!"

Elizabeth's gaze swept him from head to foot. "Where have you been? Your shoes are damp," she observed.

Even if he could speak to answer, Darcy could not tear his gaze away. She was wearing a dressing gown—sturdy and serviceable, but definitely a dressing gown, with her nightdress underneath. Her hair was tumbling out of its long braid.

"William, it is the middle of the night."

"I know," he said lamely. Too late he realized that he wore no waistcoat, only a shirt.

He shrugged into Collins' black frock coat. "I have been—out."

"To the stable to check on the horses?" To his chagrin, her fingers found the cloak. "And why have you been wearing Sir Magico's cloak?"

He had to smile. "Sir Magico?"

"Our dress-up name for that particular garment."

There was nothing for it. He must tell her the truth. "I—needed a disguise," he said. "I gambled that this cloak had not been seen by those frequenting a particular public house in Meryton."

"You went to a public house?"

"To the Rose and Crown, yes."

Her eyes narrowed. "William Collins," she said. "Have you been drinking?"

"Only a pint. But George Wickham had rather more."

"George Wickham!"

"Elizabeth, please," he said. "Keep your voice down."

"How do you know—that—about Mr. Wickham?"

Darcy sat on the lid of the trunk. Fatigue was now catching up with him. He glanced at her, and his gaze lingered. "Have you been awake all this time?"

"Waiting for Mr. Fleming, yes."

Darcy's head came up. "Your father has taken a turn for the worse?"

"No, he is sleeping. Mrs. Hill is with him and so is Jane. I could not sleep."

"Mrs. Hill has sent for Fleming?"

"Before she went to bed, Mama sent a note to Netherfield, informing Mr. Fleming that if he could be spared, the kitchen door would be left open. But you have not answered my question about Mr. Wickham."

"I—acted on my suspicions," he said. "From what I know of Wickham, I figured he was low on funds. Gaming is his method of generating income, and I found him at the card table. The trouble is, Wickham doesn't have sense enough to live by his wits."

"Isn't that the pot calling the kettle black?"

Darcy gave her a measured look. "What I mean is that Wickham is not smart enough to hedge his bets. He is hasty. He wants to rake in the earnings quickly—and that is not the way to win at cards. He was losing fairly heavily tonight."

Elizabeth's color came and went. "Gaming!"

"He is in the habit of running up debts, yes."

"How do you know this?"

"I've had to settle—" Darcy stopped himself in time. "I have had past dealings with him. Acting in another's stead, of course."

"And yet when he met you, he never said a word."

"He wouldn't."

"I cannot understand it," she said. "He behaved as though you were a complete stranger."

"For a man of my profession, it's nothing new," he said. "George Wickham's memory is adaptable. I am someone who was, shall we say, convenient to forget. This explains why he did not recognize me tonight, sitting in the corner with my pint."

"You were involved in spying?"

"It was the work of a coward; do not praise me. I needed to see with my own eyes the lay of the land. That letter he wrote to Anne—"

"You know that he was merely flirting. He—" Elizabeth hesitated. "He enjoys flirting."

Darcy's temper flashed. "And he enjoys taking a tumble in the hay when he can get it," he said. "He disappeared tonight, and so did the unfortunate barmaid."

"W-what?"

"George Wickham is a practiced seducer, Elizabeth. And one way or another I must part him from Anne."

"Surely he would not trifle with Anne," she cried. "He would not dare—"

"He has attempted this sort of thing before."

"I cannot believe he would be so foul. Anne sees him as Mr. Darcy's friend."

Darcy leaned in. "He has been very free with his opinion of Mr. Darcy, has he not? It was Darcy's own sister who was his intended victim. They were discovered in time."

Elizabeth's eyes were wide. "So this is why Mr. Darcy hates him."

"I should have shot Wickham when I had the chance."

"W-were you involved, William?"

Darcy got hold of himself. "In a manner of speaking," he said, more mildly. "The best policy has been not to mention it. Or to acknowledge that we have had dealings together."

"Then at the Netherfield ball—" said Elizabeth slowly. "You were acting a part, were you not?"

What could Darcy say? He watched the play of emotions cross her lovely face. Her hair was dark against the gray of her wool dressing gown. He now realized that the fabric clung to her figure alluringly. He quickly looked away.

"How long ago was this?" she demanded.

"Just this past spring."

"And to show his gratitude, Mr. Darcy recommended you to Lady Catherine?"

"Not at all," he said quickly.

She smiled. "Not that either of you will admit. This explains everything—your flattery and sycophant adoration."

"Not adoration," he protested. Still, he had to smile. She was so adorably pleased with herself. And this explanation was rather brilliant.

She rose to her feet and came nearer to where he sat. "You are a puzzling sort of person," she said. "You have done a great deal of good for the Darcy family, and yet you desire no praise. You make yourself a laughingstock to spare Mr. Darcy's pride, and you conceal your role in what can only be a grievous blow to his sister."

Her fingers caressed the lapel of his coat.

Darcy steeled himself and rose to his feet. It was time he was gone.

"It is like something from a novel," she said. "You play the part of the fool to conceal the serious man beneath. But you are no fool, William Collins."

How he wished she had said Fitzwilliam instead! But he could not allow her to continue. "Elizabeth," he said, "I am not the man you think me."

"Of course you are, William," she whispered. "You are everything and more. You, my dear, are a hero!"

29 Topsy-Turvy

The warmth in Elizabeth's eyes banished regret. Even so, Darcy must try to make her understand.

"During the ball at Netherfield," he began, "I went into the garden after supper. I, ah, followed Mr. Darcy."

"To speak to him, yes," she said, smiling. "And I was vexed that you were so forward. I had no idea that you and he were acquainted. But of course you were, because of his sister."

So much for his solemn confession! It was all Darcy could do not to return her smile. "The storm blew up while he and I were arguing."

"Were you arguing? Why?"

"Then the lightning struck," he said, plunging ahead. "When I came to myself, everything was—changed. I was another person altogether. You will think this strange, but it was as if I had left behind my very identity."

"But there is nothing unique in that," she said. "Mr. Fleming told us that those who suffer serious injury are often changed."

Blast! Could he not explain the simplest thing? Darcy made another attempt. "When I woke up," he said, "I was in the wrong house. You see, I expected to be at Netherfield."

"Of course you did. Because that is where you were struck down."

Did she have an explanation for everything? "But surely you noticed how my behavior was changed."

"Of course I noticed," she said, with another smile. "Everyone did, even Anne de Bourgh."

"Did this never trouble you? That I was so unlike myself?"

"Should improvement be troubling? The only thing that troubles me is..." She hesitated. "William," she said at last. "Why have you not spoken with Father?"

In other words, why hadn't he proposed?

"Your father has been ill," Darcy heard his voice bleat. "Furthermore, I—did not wish to force myself upon you."

"Force yourself?"

"By obliging you to accept what your family—and most especially your mother—is so eager to have transpire. A match between us," he added, "is greatly to their advantage."

"I would never accept you for that reason."

"Elizabeth," he said, gazing into her eyes. "I have nothing to offer you, truly."

"Longbourn is hardly nothing," she said. "In spite of its shortcomings, I love it dearly. And it is the other way round, William. I am the one who has nothing to offer."

"Nonsense," he said warmly.

"A wife should bring some benefit to her husband. My portion of Mama's fortune is small, and I've so many sisters who need—"

"Do you mean money?" he interrupted. "As if I cared for that."

"You ought to care. It is only prudent."

"A paltry consideration," Darcy scoffed. "If it mattered," he added, "why, I would be chasing after Caroline Bingley's twenty thousand."

She laughed, just as he hoped she would.

"And how dearly I would pay," he added. "Miss Bingley behaves well enough in public, but her private manners are execrable."

Elizabeth dimpled. "What do you know about Miss Bingley's private manners?"

Another slip! Darcy thought quickly. "I may be unnoticed as I tread the corridors of Netherfield, but I have eyes. And ears. What a harpy!"

Elizabeth's eyes were sparkling.

"Surely you recall from your stay at Netherfield," he added. Before he could stop himself, Darcy leaned in to kiss Elizabeth's cheek. "As you might imagine, she and Lady Catherine have got on splendidly."

Another gurgle of delicious laughter. "Oh, dear."

"The principal consideration when choosing a wife," Darcy said, "and I remind myself whenever the beauties and their mamas promenade—is what sort of mother she will be. I had an excellent mother. But to be saddled with sons and daughters who take after Caroline Bingley would be intolerable!"

"Beauties and their mothers," echoed Elizabeth. "You are much sought after in Hunsford, sir?"

Darcy felt himself blush. "Somewhat," he confessed. "But I am immune to feminine lures."

"Save for mine," she whispered.

"Yes," he admitted, fingering a tendril of her hair. "Save for yours."

"A country miss without connections or advantages," she went on. "I cannot further your career in any way, save for after you inherit Longbourn."

How could he not put his arms round her? And kiss her cheek tenderly? "Dear heart," he murmured, "your father is a robust fellow who will live for many years."

"But oh, William," she faltered, "he has never been so ill."

"And he shall recover."

"If the worst should happen…"

"We will face whatever comes, for good or for ill," he promised. "You shall not face this alone."

"And when Father recovers?" she whispered. "Will you speak with him?"

"And what am I to say to him, dearest? 'Mr. Bennet, do me the honor of giving me the hand of your favorite daughter (for you are his favorite). And I will take her miles away to a hovel of a parsonage, where she shall live with an inadequate income, under the heel of a tyrannical despot.'"

"William," she said, smiling into the lapel of his coat, "you are no despot."

"I meant Lady Catherine."

She continued to smile, but he heard her sigh. He had a point and she knew it.

"And now to list for your father the benefits of the match," Darcy continued. "'Of an evening, sir, when your lovely daughter is not bringing soup to impoverished families of the parish, she will be invited to Rosings Park, a true treat, where she shall sit in Lady Catherine's draughty drawing room, making polite conversation with her ladyship and the silent Miss de Bourgh.'"

"You mean Mrs. Wickham and her husband," Elizabeth put in. "Should the so-called elopement take place."

Darcy gave a snort. "Wickham will be well entertained. One of my unc—I mean, her ladyship's husband's forebears—had the ceiling painted in the style of the Sistine Chapel. Greek gods and goddesses, showing more flesh than is tasteful."

"Oh—dear."

"One learns to keep one's eyes on the rug because most of the women are built along Raphaelesque proportions."

"William!"

"*Wherewithal shall a young man cleanse his way?*" said Darcy, quoting the familiar psalm. "By keeping out of Lady Catherine's drawing room. My mother was—ah, would be—rather scandalized. But," he added, "I will not have you living under Lady Catherine's heel. It would be nothing but misery."

"Do you think me weak?"

"I think myself weak. I would be in danger of slapping Lady Catherine, were she to abuse you. Which she certainly shall, as she prides herself on speaking her mind."

"My knight errant," Elizabeth murmured.

What else could he do but kiss her cheek? How far he had wandered from his confession! He must tell her about the switch with Collins, and he would. Of course he would.

"Why," she added, touching his cheek with her fingers, "you have whiskers."

Darcy's felt his insides turn to jelly. She was taking liberties with his person—as well she might, for it appeared that she was now his fiancée. And did not a fiancée deserve a kiss?

"William," she said presently, "I can manage Lady Catherine; I have managed Mama's interference all my life. And her ladyship cannot be with us every moment of the day."

"Or night," he murmured, remembering the kiss.

Her fingers moved to his chin. "You ought to have a dimple just here," she said. "Odd that I should think so, is it not?"

Darcy did have a cleft in his chin, just not as Collins! God help him if this should continue. And why must he smile like an idiot?

"You will speak to Father?"

"Yes," he said slowly. "But..."

"We ought to meet with Dr. Bentley as well, or whatever is done in these circumstances—you know best, of course. Do you think the banns should be read on Sunday?"

"So soon?" But he was smiling.

"What a pity that you are not a titled gentleman, even an impoverished one," she said teasingly. "For a special license would answer nicely."

"It takes time to send to Doctor's Commons, love," he said. "And you wouldn't wish to be married immediately. Where would we stay?"

"Why, in my bedchamber, of course," she countered.

"Not the most private of situations," he said. "I doubt your bed will hold my weight."

She had to laugh. They both laughed.

"If all goes well, I shall return with you to Kent," she said, resting against his shoulder. "Is the parsonage large?"

God help him, he was a hopeless weakling. He had kissed her, and now they were making plans to keep house together. He ought to say: My love, I cannot marry you. Indeed, all that was needed was to form the words: I am not William Collins. I am Fitzwilliam Darcy, a man you loathe.

And yet his lips would not obey. "The parsonage is adequate," he heard himself say. "Not in the style of Longbourn, but I believe you will be comfortable there."

Idiot! What was he saying?

"Then I am content." She nestled her cheek against his.

Elizabeth was content. To marry him as Collins, without Pemberley or even an adequate income.

"Whatever comes, for good or ill," she added, "we shall face it together."

Weary though he was, Darcy could have sat with her for hours. But every man's honor had limits, and Darcy knew he was well past his. He rose to his feet, gave Elizabeth her candle and a chaste kiss on the forehead.

"Back to your room," he said. "It is well that Jane is your bedfellow and Fleming is mine."

Darcy could have bit out his tongue; what a thing to say! Elizabeth ought to be scandalized. Instead she drew away from him with something like regret.

"The situation is rather compromising," she admitted, "as we are alone and I am in my nightdress. Fortunately you are—almost fully clothed."

A condition that could be remedied in less than a minute! Darcy looked away, afraid that he had said as much with his eyes.

"Here is proof that you are an honorable man," she said admiringly. And she lifted her chin.

"Off you go," he said, kissing her lightly. And then, because he was Collins and could say outrageous things, he added, "I forgot to inquire, do you snore?"

She gave a gurgle of laughter. "Of course I do not snore!"

He opened the door and stood aside for her to pass. "That," he said, "is what everyone says, even Fleming. It is an absolute lie."

He heard her laughing all the way along the corridor.

Darcy returned to the trunk and opened it. Sir Magico's cape was put to rest. A world of trouble this garment had caused, but did he regret anything that transpired between himself and Elizabeth? No, he decided. After all, Mr. Bennet could refuse consent.

There were footfalls in the corridor and the door came abruptly open. He heard his name and looked round. Behind Elizabeth was Mrs. Hill, and the expression on her face said it all.

"Thank God, sir, that you are awake."

"Mr. Bennet?"

"There is no crisis," Mrs. Hill assured him. "But his breathing is labored in a way I cannot like, and the fever has returned and is rising."

Darcy pushed aside his weariness. "I'll fetch Fleming at once. If I might borrow the brown overcoat and a lantern?"

Elizabeth came nearer. "You must ride one of our horses to save time," she said. "Do you know how to saddle a horse, or shall we wake Ned? I would help you, if I knew how."

Darcy put his arms round Elizabeth and kissed her cheek, heedless of Mrs. Hill's watching eyes. "I know how to saddle a horse, dearest," he said. "Fleming will return directly, never you fear."

But would Fleming be in time? God forbid that Mr. Bennet would pass on, leaving Darcy to inherit Longbourn!

Then again, was this what was meant to be?

30 Decked in the Garb of Fancy

The evening ground on. It was Miss Bingley's stated intent to accustom him to fashionable hours, such as he would find in London. What brutes Londoners were! Supper had been abominably late—even Mr. Bingley had complained—and then they must play cards and converse and listen as Miss Bingley played the pianoforte until the small hours.

But Collins' tedious evening was brightened by the contents of Netherfield's wine cellar, in particular a decanter of beautifully-aged cognac. Such a lovely, golden amber it was, served in special glasses to warm it. Bingley sipped his. Collins, who had never before tasted brandy, tried to follow suit but could not. It was simply too delicious. Mellowed and warmed, he found himself humming a tune as he refilled his glass.

Not that he'd had the funds in those pinched university days for as much as a pint of beer. But from the mists of memory an old drinking song bubbled up.

"*With women and wine I defy ev'ry care,*" Collins sang. "*For life without these is a bubble of air.*"

He drained the glass, marveling at the delicate flavor of the brandy. He stole a glance at Miss Bingley. She was looking both surprised and disgusted. Wonderful! Smiling, he continued humming. "*A bubble of air.*"

Charles Bingley began to laugh. "Upon my word, Darcy," he said.

Again Collins reached for the decanter. Wasn't it odd that a song he'd never sung came so easily to his lips? This time Charles Bingley sang with him.

"*Each helping the other in pleasure I roll,*

And a new flow of spirits enlivens my soul—"

"Really, Charles," said Caroline Bingley, "you shouldn't encourage him. We have enough to put up with in Mr. Hurst." And she tugged on the bell pull.

Collins shared a grin with Charles Bingley.

Sometime later Holdsworth appeared, as neat as a pin, wearing his usual wooden expression. Apparently the man's intention was to escort him to his bedchamber.

"Good night, Miss Bingley," Collins called, as he was led from the drawing room. He was soon grateful for

Holdsworth's arm, for he staggered as they climbed the staircase together. Bingley followed.

"*For life without—cognac—is a bubble of air,*" Collins sang. "*A bubble of air.*"

Yes, a merry song. For some reason Holdsworth did not enjoy it.

In the upstairs corridor they encountered the physician Fleming and, of all people, Darcy.

"Oh, look," Collins told Charles Bingley. "It's Darcy. Confound the fellow, he's always turning up. And in such clothes."

"Good evening, Mr. Collins," said Charles Bingley politely.

"What are you doing here?" Collins said to Darcy. "Another riding lesson? Torture disguised as exercise? I won't have it."

Darcy was speaking apart to Fleming, who was drawing on his gloves. "Take the horse. It is cold, but there is no ice in the lane, thank God."

"I am sorry that you had to venture out," Collins heard Fleming reply. "But I've slept, and a bit of that works wonders."

The two of them looked so long-faced that Collins broke out giggling. "*Defy every care,*" he sang.

"Chin up, my friend," said Fleming to Darcy. "You'll do no good by assuming the worst."

"Is something wrong?" Bingley said quietly.

Darcy turned. "It's Mr. Bennet. We fear he has taken a turn for the worse."

"At his age," added Fleming, "one cannot rule out pneumonia, especially at this time of year."

Collins watched him go. "Time for the old fellow to cash in his chips, eh?" he said. "Fine news for you, Darcy." He gave another giggle. "I mean, Collins. Always getting the names wrong. I am him, and he is me. Fiddle-de-dee."

"I apologize for my friend," Charles Bingley said to Darcy. "Brandy has loosened his tongue."

"Cognac," Collins corrected. "The most delicious cognac. Only good thing to come out of France." Collins clapped Darcy on the shoulder. "Best to pop over and speak with Papa Bennet while you can. Seal up a pretty future for yourself."

"Darcy," said Bingley warningly.

But Collins saw no reason to keep quiet. "Longbourn and the lovely Elizabeth," he added, giggling.

The irritation on Darcy's face was wonderful to behold, and it spurred Collins on. "Mind, it will do you no good," he said, "as the lady is fond of saying no. You are, after all, only a paltry rector."

"Stow it, Darcy," said Bingley. He turned to Darcy. "Is Jane's father truly in danger?"

"Jane's father, is it?" said Collins. "Oho!"

He heard Darcy sigh. Then Collins felt the man's fingers close around his forearm. When Darcy spoke he addressed the valet.

"No doubt you are longing for your bed, Mr. Holdsworth," he said. "I am able to see to Mr. Darcy's needs." He smiled ruefully. "In any case, I am likely to be in for a long night. There is no need for both of us to be up."

Trembling, Elizabeth stood outside her father's bedchamber door. How silent the house was! And yet, oh how she dreaded to hear sounds. Her father's struggle to breathe, for example, or Jane weeping. Or her mother's frantic fear.

Elizabeth pressed her palms to her cheeks. There would be that to face, come morning. It was unfair to her mother, if her father were truly in danger, to be left to sleep undisturbed, but for the sake of the household it must be so. As it was, poor Hill was looking unusually haggard. How long had it been since Hill slept? Elizabeth did not know. Hill and Ned had borne the brunt of her father's care, and all the more during Mr. Fleming's absence.

She heard movement inside her father's bedchamber: footfalls and the scrape of a chair. The door came open and her sister emerged.

"Jane," Elizabeth whispered, and held out her arms.

"Oh, Lizzy," she cried. "He is so pale and weak."

Elizabeth kissed her sister's cheek. "You must sleep. I shall stay with Father."

"Hill is a saint," said Jane, "but I know she is eager for Mr. Fleming. He shall come?"

"Yes and very soon. William left for Netherfield straightway. He would ride, which is only right, and I think he saddled the horse himself." She paused. "Our cousin knows a good deal more than we give him credit for."

"Dear Cousin William," said Jane.

"And oh, Jane," Elizabeth added, for how could she keep silent? "In the morning he intends to speak to Father."

Jane pulled away, and her eyes studied Elizabeth's. "And you do not mind?"

"Mind? I was never happier. Oh, how we have misjudged him!"

Jane gave a long sigh. "That will be a great comfort to Father," she confessed. "He is—" Jane hesitated and dabbed at her eyes with her sleeve. "To be honest, he is afraid, Lizzy. Of what might happen to us."

Elizabeth held her sister close. "Do not speak of it," she said. "We dare not abandon hope. Father is in God's hands, and Mr. Fleming will soon be here."

"And dear Cousin William," added Jane.

"Yes," whispered Elizabeth. "Dear, dear William."

Darcy removed the frock coat with none of Holdsworth's respectful care, and it soured Collins' temper. "Do you mind?" he complained. "Must you be so rough?"

"I thought you were too drunk to notice."

"I am no such thing," said Collins. "Bingley kept refilling my glass, that is all. Dashed good brandy, cognac. French, you know."

"Yes," said Darcy, "I know. Keep your mouth closed and listen, Collins. I have something to ask you."

Collins heaved a sigh, kicked off his shoes, and plumped down on the bed. "More talking," he complained, wiggling his stocking-clad toes. "First Caroline and now you."

"Miss Bingley," Darcy corrected. "You will refer to her as Miss Bingley."

"She doesn't mind what I call her. Good lord, Darcy, there's the clock chiming. Bless me if it isn't past two. Time to sleep."

"Not for you it isn't."

Collins yawned again. "Sleep," he repeated and lay back on the pillows. "Blessed sleep." He closed his eyes.

But someone was shaking his shoulder. "Collins," said the voice. "Wake up."

He attempted to turn over but was prevented by an iron grip. "No you don't," the voice warned. "Sit up or I'll douse you with water."

Collins struggled to sit up, shielding his eyes from the glare of the candle. "Are you still here?"

"Mr. Bennet," said Darcy, "is seriously ill."

"What has that to do with me?"

"If the man does not recover—if the worst transpires—it has everything to do with you."

Collins might be sleepy, but he was not stupid. He felt his lips curl into a sneer. "Not any more. Longbourn will be yours."

"You do not know that," said Darcy. "We could resume our true identities at any time."

"And if we do? What of it?"

"Only this. When you are master of Longbourn, what will become of your cousins?" Darcy's tone was insistent.

"The house and its income will no longer be theirs."

"You will cast them out?"

"How dramatic you are," Collins complained. "They must take lodgings in town. In keeping with their—what is the word?" He struggled to think. "Ah yes," he crowed at last. "*Milieu.* They must take lodgings in keeping with their *milieu.*"

"And what *milieu* would that be?" demanded Darcy.

"How should I know?" Something about Darcy's expression made Collins uncomfortable. "Do you expect me to support them?" he squealed. "Impossible! Out of the question!"

"Is it?"

Collins primed up his lips. "I am not," he announced, "nor will I ever be, my cousins' keeper."

"So you will not support the Bennet women in any way," Darcy said. "Even lovely Elizabeth, whom you claim to love."

The thought of Elizabeth brought a smile. If her father was dead and she was living in genteel penury, so much the better. Collins put up his chin. "In that case," he said, "Elizabeth will be eager to become my wife. And now, will you kindly leave me in peace?"

The iron grip was released, and Collins fell back on the pillows. Trust Darcy to slam the door when he left.

And wouldn't it figure? Collins was now unable to sleep. Visions of cognac, sparkling golden in the firelight, swirled through his thoughts.

Never mind common politeness, Collins deserved none! The tenuous truce, or whatever his *détente* with Collins could be called, was over. Down it came, falling like a house of cards.

Darcy strode along the upstairs corridor, the thick carpet masking his footfalls.

"Mr. Collins," called a voice, "is that you?"

Darcy came to a halt. What now?

Never mind that it was the middle of the night, there stood Anne de Bourgh, wrapped in a figured dressing gown. Anne would never be pretty, but her wan expression did inspire a stab of pity.

"I heard voices earlier," she explained, "and after that I could not sleep. Are-are you returning to Longbourn, Mr. Collins?"

"I am," said Darcy. He glanced toward the staircase. If they were seen together like this—

"I wonder if you might do me a little favor."

She drew nearer, and Darcy felt his eyes narrow. Anne had never bothered to converse with him while at

Longbourn. He might as well have been a piece of furniture! What reason had she to speak with him now? None whatsoever, unless—

Darcy waited, concealing an impulse to tap his foot, for Anne had no notion of time.

"Would you mind delivering a letter for me?" she said at last. "It is in my bedchamber. I will not be long."

Off she went before he could answer. Good manners compelled him to wait.

Anne must have known this, for she took full advantage. The longcase clock at the end of the corridor ticked solemnly, and still she did not appear. Darcy, who was falling asleep on his feet, found a chair. His head nodded forward on his chest, the muffler making a cushion for his chin.

At length he heard a door open and close. With a grimace he rose to his feet.

From the folds of her dressing gown Anne drew several sealed letters. "If you would deliver these, I would be most grateful."

Darcy examined them, squinting in the dim light.

"The names are clearly written," she said. "There can be no mistake." And then, perhaps because of nervousness, she continued talking. "There is one for Lydia and one for Kitty. And the last one—"

"—is for Mr. Wickham," Darcy finished for her. "Where am I to find him, I wonder?"

"I—am not sure, Mr. Collins. In Meryton? Or perhaps he will call at Longbourn? One never knows."

"Quite right," said Darcy. "With Mr. Wickham, one never knows."

Farther down the corridor a door opened. Anne swung round and gave a ragged gasp. "Oh," she faltered. "Why, good evening, Cousin Fitzwilliam." She attempted a smile.

Darcy said nothing. God only knew why Collins was not asleep. Then he noticed the empty glass. Was the man was in search of a drink?

And Collins was surly. "What have we here?" he growled. "An odd time of day for callers, Anne. You ought to be in bed."

"As should we all," said Darcy. He allowed his gaze to travel to the empty glass. "At this hour," he added, "Mrs. Nicholls will have locked away the spirits. A precaution against servants taking a liberty."

Collins' scowl deepened. "You are a fine one to talk of liberties." He rounded on Anne. "And what about you? Flirting with the rector in your night dress."

"It-it does look rather odd, I admit," Anne began.

Darcy interrupted. "Since I am returning to Longbourn," he said smoothly, "Miss de Bourgh has given me letters to deliver. I am about to bid her good-night."

"Letters?" Collins said, sneering. "Or is it a love note? A *billet-doux*?"

Anne gave a cry of dismay. "They are—for Kitty and Lydia."

"An honor for the Bennet family, to be sure," said Collins. "Your mother," he added, "would not approve. And neither do I."

Anne shrank against the wall. "I-I do not care what you think, Fitzwilliam. As for Mother, she can go hang!" Anne turned and fled. Her bedchamber door closed with a bang.

"Well done, Collins," said Darcy. "Now we'll have Mrs. Jenkinson on our hands, demanding an explanation. And Mrs. Nicholls too, once you stumble into the drawing room, looking for that brandy decanter."

"There is nothing wrong," Collins practically spat, "with a man being thirsty."

"Do not add drunkenness to your list of virtues, please. In a man of your rank, it is especially distasteful."

And before Collins could say another word, Darcy turned on his heel and left.

31 For A Kingdom

Although it was late when Darcy returned to Longbourn, his weariness made him reckless enough to tap on Mr. Bennet's door. It came open and Elizabeth's face peered out. When she saw him, her composure crumbled. "Oh, William," she cried and threw herself into his arms.

Darcy had not meant to interfere, but she came to him so trustingly, like a child. What could he do but hold her close?

"Thank you for bringing Mr. Fleming," she said. "His presence has been a godsend, and his composure has settled us all. Dear Hill has gone to bed at last." She pulled back to look at him. "Have you slept, dearest?"

"Have you?" he said gently.

Her face showed strain and her hair was disheveled, but Darcy did not care. She was beautiful, and she was soon to be his very own. Nothing else mattered. He kissed her cheek.

"I caught a few winks in a chair at Netherfield," he told her, "while I waited for Anne de Bourgh to finish her letters." He reached into a pocket of the overcoat. "You see? My patience was rewarded. One for Lydia and one for Kitty and one for..." Darcy paused.

"Not Mr. Wickham?"

"The very man. "And after we've slept," Darcy went on, "we'll lay our plans. I ought to make the delivery this morning. But enough of Wickham, how is your father?"

"Feverish and unsettled. Oh, William, he is so weak and in pain. Jane told me earlier, but I would not believe it. His breathing is shallow and that frightens me. But now that you are here, I can be easy."

Darcy did not see how his presence made a difference, but he did not quibble. "You need to know that Bingley has come; he would not let me walk. He has brought fruit for your father and has promised chickens, as many as you need. At the moment he is making up a bed in the drawing room. I have built up the fire and will fetch a blanket."

"But—will he not go home?"

"Bingley is a stubborn fellow, though you would never guess it, and he insists on serving your family. Thus, he has made himself available for any errand, night or day. I tried to make him leave, but he will not go."

"Bless Mr. Bingley. Such a kind and thoughtful man."

"I believe he has something to say to Jane and also to your father, come morning."

"Oh, William, truly?" Elizabeth's expression held something like wonder. "This is the best news in the world, the very best. After ours, of course."

"Yes," he said, stroking a lock of her hair. "After ours."

"He and Jane shall be happy together, I know it," she added. "For they are so well-suited."

"I did not always think so," Darcy admitted, "but I do now."

"But his sisters?"

"His sisters had quite another match in mind, one in keeping with their ambition. Like Jane, Georgiana is gentle and good, but she is much too young to be married. Bingley is merely her brother's friend, nothing more."

Elizabeth was smiling. "How much you overhear at Netherfield, sir. Should I be frightened?"

"Eavesdropping is my principal talent. Unfortunately," he added, "the Church of England does not make use of the confessional, or I would know more."

She laughed, as he hoped she would. Color returned to her cheeks.

417

Somewhere he heard a clock strike four. "Off you go," he said, "to watch and pray for your father. I shall do the same, while setting up a barricade before the drawing room door."

"A barric—oh! For Mr. Bingley."

"In a household of women, a fellow needs all the protection he can get."

A dimple appeared in Elizabeth's cheek. "Dear William," she said, "what an encouragement you are. No matter the circumstance, you always know just what to say."

"Not according to Lady Catherine." Darcy put a hand on each of her shoulders. "Now then, you are to wake me if I am needed, no matter how trifling the request. Am I understood?"

"But—" Elizabeth protested.

"This is not a suggestion. If I am needed, you know where I am."

"Yes, William."

"And," he added, because he could, "if Jane needs something, you know where Bingley is."

When Elizabeth returned to her father, she found Mr. Fleming asleep in a chair. She lit a fresh candle and settled in to wait. Her father's eyes blinked open. She took his hand in her own. "Father," she whispered.

"Dear—Lizzy," he managed.

"Don't speak, Father, until you've had a little water." She brought the glass and supported it while he swallowed. "You ought to be sleeping."

"I cannot sleep. If I do, my dear—I might not wake."

Elizabeth began to protest, but he interrupted. "Jane's Bible," he said, pointing. "Read me a text."

She found the Bible and opened it. She discovered that she was trembling. Never before had her father made such a request.

"The one about," he said, "the Father's house."

With a sinking heart Elizabeth turned to latter half of John's gospel. She could not be reading this passage, a comfort to so many, to her sweet and robust father. Was his time truly near?

"*Let not your heart be troubled; you believe in God, believe also in Me.*"

She paused and stole a look at him. The agitation in his manner had stilled.

"*In My Father's house are many mansions: if it were not so, I would have told you. I go to prepare a place for you.*"

Elizabeth heard a long sigh. He seemed to be breathing more normally.

"*And if I go and prepare a place for you, I will come and receive you unto Myself, that where I am, there ye may be also.*"

"A place for me," her father repeated. "The Savior has a place for me." Another sigh escaped his lips. "And

I, who for so much of my life—have had no place for Him."

"Dear Father," said Elizabeth, taking his hand again. "Do not reproach yourself."

His lips curved into a rueful smile. "A poor follower of Christ I have been, Lizzy. An even poorer father—to my children."

"How can you say so?"

"After I am gone, you will learn—the truth. The entail—"

"Never mind the entail."

"I—dislike discord in my home," he went on. "Especially when it comes to money. I set nothing aside—for my girls. For you, who were depending upon me."

"You have done your best," said Elizabeth loyally.

"False consolation does not become you," he said.

Elizabeth sat silent, wondering how much to say. The candle sputtered. Mr. Fleming stirred in his sleep. A log on the fire fell apart with a whispering sigh. "Our cousin, William Collins, desires to speak with you," she said at last.

"I imagine he does."

"It is my earnest wish, Father, that you will listen to him. And," she added, "that you will give us your blessing."

He gave a start. "My blessing? To you and William Collins?"

"He will be asking for my hand in marriage, yes."

"Not that," he said. "Anything but that."

Mr. Bennet broke out coughing. Mr. Fleming, startled awake, came out of the chair and bent over him.

After some minutes, Mr. Fleming exchanged a look with Elizabeth and withdrew to his chair.

Mr. Bennet spoke again. "Lizzy," he said, "have you not always hated Mr. Collins?"

"I have misjudged him. We all have. He is a sensible man, intelligent and capable."

"But the letter."

Elizabeth sighed. "I cannot explain that foolish letter, for it is at variance with the man I know him to be. I suspect that Lady Catherine dictated it. She has done so for his sermons."

"Paugh," said Mr. Bennet. "A coward."

"He has his living to earn. And it does no good to offend a person like Lady Catherine. Shall we say he dislikes discord?"

Her father looked unhappy.

"He is a good man, Father."

"But Lizzy," said her father at last, "will you marry a fool?"

"William Collins is no fool. And I love him, truly I do."

"He has bewitched you. With good looks and charm of manner."

Her father did not smile with her. "Life is short, my dear," he said unhappily. "Marry as you will—while there is time."

She kissed his forehead. "Thank you, Father."

"I am ill—and must rely on a man like Collins to follow through on my behalf. Bring your mother when Mr. Collins comes," he added. "She has been pining for this match."

"Please do not think that Mama had any bearing on my decision. My choice to accept William's proposal will come as a complete surprise to her."

Her father lapsed into silence. Presently he said, "There is no reason to—delay on my account."

"Father—" Elizabeth protested.

"Best to have the banns read before the bell tolls, eh?"

He was teasing her, and it nearly made her weep. For just a moment, his eyes held their familiar twinkle. The moment passed, and his eyes closed.

"I cannot tell you, Lizzy," he whispered, "how relieved I am to know that you will be provided for. I scorned William Collins, but God in His mercy had other plans."

32 Certainly Very Little

It was close on eleven when Elizabeth came down to breakfast. Sitting alone at the long table was William. He looked up; his eyes came alive with warmth. She slid into the chair beside his and as the room was deserted, kissed him tenderly on the cheek.

"Mama is taking breakfast in her bedchamber," she told him. "When she comes down, Father would like us to come to him together." She could feel her cheeks grow warm. "I—told him of our wish to marry," she confessed, "and he has given his blessing. Unless you have changed your mind."

He said, smiling, "I have not changed my mind. Allow me to serve you breakfast."

"Not just yet. Before my sisters come in, we ought to talk over Anne's letters."

Apparently he was prepared for this, for he drew them from a pocket. Lydia's and Kitty's he set aside. "These serve as a blind for this one," he said, placing Mr. Wickham's letter before her. "I have not had enough sleep for delicate strategy. How do you propose we should open it?"

"Do you truly believe he intends to elope?"

"I do, yes."

Elizabeth gave herself to thinking. "This is Anne's reply," she said slowly, "the first of its kind, and you are her courier. This, I think, is where you prove your trustworthiness. For who else will serve as Mr. Wickham's deliveryman?"

William's smile dissolved into a grin. "Wickham already thinks I am stupid," he said, "and Anne needs no convincing."

"Yes, a clever maneuver on your part. What I mean is, there will be no information in this letter, only affirmation and agreement—if his object is elopement."

Elizabeth felt her blush deepen, for William was beaming at her. "Wickham's reply," he said slowly, "will be the material one, yes."

"Do you agree, then, to leave Anne's letter unopened?"

"We'll risk it."

The door opened and Mary came in. While she busied herself at the sideboard, William pushed back his chair.

"To Meryton I must go," he said quietly. "No doubt our man is sleeping off the excesses of last night. He certainly did not come here."

"Not with Father so ill." Elizabeth rose and walked with him to the door.

At the threshold he paused. "I wonder," he said. "Would he dare to call at Netherfield? Lady Catherine would have his hide."

"But Mr. Wickham does not know Lady Catherine."

"Ah, but he does. As a boy he threw rocks at her coach and was soundly thrashed. He'll give her a wide berth."

"How do you know what Mr. Wickham did as a boy?" said Elizabeth, smiling. "Or were you listening at doors again?"

He looked surprised, but only for a moment. "Nothing so dramatic," he said. "Darcy told me, ah, when we rescued his sister. A cherished boyhood memory."

And it was. How Wickham had howled! Even as a youngster he was a sneak and a bully, and he knew just how to get round Darcy's old father.

Darcy discovered that he was smiling. There would be no getting round for Wickham this time.

The Rose and Crown smelled of stale smoke and was almost deserted. Darcy nodded to the barkeep and passed through the taproom. At the door to the inner parlor he paused. Sure enough, there was Wickham, nursing a cup of coffee. The buxom barmaid hovered nearby. Her glances in his direction left no doubt as to the nature of their relationship.

And it must have been quite a night, for Wickham did not look well. When he noticed Darcy, his bloodshot gaze was watchful.

Watchful, that was what Wickham had been as a boy. Alert to opportunity.

The man took another sip of coffee and licked his lips. "Hello, Padre," he said. "What brings you here? Have you come to hear my confession?" He turned to wink at the barmaid. She giggled.

"Merely a pedestrian errand," said Darcy, giving Wickham Collins' most bovine stare. "I am charged with the delivery of this."

When Wickham saw Anne's letter his eyes narrowed—like a snake's, Darcy thought. He held it out, and Wickham snatched it. Desperation made him greedy.

Here was evidence of the wisdom of Elizabeth's advice. Even hung-over, Wickham was sharply observant. He examined the seal before breaking it.

Deliberately obtuse, Darcy said, "Will there be a reply, sir?"

"Why, yes," said Wickham. "But I do not like to keep you kicking your heels here. Call for it in, say, half an hour?"

Darcy did Holdsworth proud. "Very good, sir," he said woodenly. "I appreciate your consideration."

"In fact, here." Wickham reached into a pocket and drew out several pennies. "Have a cup of coffee on me."

It took all Darcy's strength to appear grateful.

As he went out he heard someone say, "Good news?"

"Very good news." The exultation in Wickham's voice was unmistakable. "I mean to win at cards tonight, for there will be calls upon my purse."

And later, with his reply to Anne in Darcy's pocket, Wickham's laughter rang in Darcy's ears all the way to Longbourn.

Mr. Bennet had not withheld Elizabeth's news from his wife. And when she learned that Mr. Bingley had come to ask for Jane's hand, there was no containing her.

"We must have a dinner, Lizzy," she gushed, "to announce the engagements. So you must hurry and get well, Mr. Bennet. Mr. Bingley has promised chickens, as many as you can eat. So you may gorge yourself to your heart's content."

Her pent-up anxiety found relief in talk, and later that morning she filled the drawing room with it. "Two daughters about to be married; was there anything more wonderful? Such splendor for you, Jane. Carriages and gowns and pin-money! And a fine residence into the bargain. And for you, too, Lizzy," she added kindly.

"Thank you, Mama," said Elizabeth. If jubilation took her mother's mind from her father's illness, so much the better.

"Let me see," Mrs. Bennet went on, "we need three Sundays for the banns to be read—"

"But Mama," said Mary.

"Do be quiet, Mary! Your father and I have talked everything over. The banns are to be read as soon as may be, with no shillyshallying."

"Shilly-what, Mama?" said Elizabeth.

"It's an expression. It means delaying," said Mrs. Bennet. "Your father was most insistent."

"Mama, really," said Mary. "Given Father's condition—"

"Of course he shall recover. News such as this puts heart into anyone. Mr. Collins is nothing to Mr. Bingley, but we are no less pleased. We are settled at Longbourn forever!"

"Mama," protested Mary.

"Now that the threat of being driven from our home is past, your father will live for many years."

Mrs. Bennet paused, struck by a sudden thought. "Could Mr. Bingley or Mr. Darcy or one of Mr. Darcy's fine relations contrive to get a special license? Three weeks is too long to wait."

"Mama," said Jane.

Mrs. Bennet glanced at the clock. "What a shame that it is so early. I cannot wait to share the news with Lady Lucas. If only she weren't so ill. Perhaps I should write her a note, yes."

"All of Meryton will be buzzing," said Kitty, "once Lady Lucas gets wind of it."

Elizabeth heard her younger sisters laugh. It felt good to have laughter in the drawing room again.

"Jane must have clothes made, Mama," Lydia pointed out. "And Lizzy too, although the need is not so pressing. In Hunsford, who will there be to see her?"

"Mr. Collins' parishioners," said Mary loyally.

Lydia's comment sent Mrs. Bennet into a frisson of happy anxiety. How could not one but two sets of bridal clothes be made in so short a time?

How could they be paid for is what Elizabeth wondered, as her mother went out with Jane.

Sometime later Ned came in, looking ill at ease. "Miss Elizabeth," he said, "one of them officers—not one as is known to us—is asking for Mr. Collins. What do I say to him?"

"Oh, lord," said Lydia. "Tell him Mr. Collins is not at home."

Elizabeth set aside her mending. "I shall see him, Ned, thank you. Do show him in. And," she added, "if you could inquire as to his name?"

"Ah!" Ned's face brightened and he held out a card. "He did give me this, Miss."

Colonel Fitzwilliam, the card said—a beautifully correct card, with the name engraved on expensive paper.

The gentleman was just as correct and dressed in regimentals. His eyes, Elizabeth noted, were unmistakably blue. Immediately Lydia and Kitty began whispering.

He made a graceful bow. "I beg your pardon for intruding," he said easily. "My cousin Darcy has written the most shambling letter." He indicated a folded paper.

"Mr. Darcy?" said Elizabeth.

The man brightened. "Fitzwilliam Darcy, yes. Do you know him?"

"He is a guest at Netherfield Park. We have met on several occasions."

His smile widened. "Then I can be easy about forcing my presence upon you."

Elizabeth could not help but smile as she introduced her sisters.

Lydia interrupted. "Do call her Kitty. Everyone else does."

Elizabeth saw a twinkle in the Colonel's eyes. She invited him to be seated and cast a speaking look at Kitty. Ned would never remember to have tea brought in, but Kitty might. Unfortunately, she showed no signs of recognizing the hint. The lure of an unknown officer was too strong.

"It's the most confounded thing," said Colonel Fitzwilliam, settling into a seat opposite Elizabeth. "And quite unlike my cousin. Ah yes," he added, "Darcy is my cousin, you see."

Colonel Fitzwilliam unfolded his letter. "He tells me that I am to see Mr. William Collins, a man I wouldn't know from Adam. Apparently this Collins holds the key to some mystery."

"You're in luck," crowed Lydia. "Mr. Collins is our guest. Isn't it funny? He is also our cousin."

"Mary," said Elizabeth, "would you have tea brought in? I fear that Ned has forgotten."

She turned to Colonel Fitzwilliam. "We are rather out of sorts this morning. Our father is ill and so is our footman."

Colonel Fitzwilliam's smile fled. "No doubt you are wishing me at Jericho, Miss Bennet. I do apolg—"

"Mr. Collins," interrupted Kitty, "is probably at Netherfield Park. He usually is. Lady Catherine de Bourgh is there, you see. She is his patroness."

Colonel Fitzwilliam blinked in surprise. "My aunt is here?"

"She came when she learned of Mr. Darcy's injury," Elizabeth explained.

"Injury? When was this?"

"About a fortnight ago," said Kitty.

"He was struck by lightning," added Lydia. "But he has recovered, if one does not count his outrageous proposal to Lizzy." She broke out giggling.

"Proposal?" cried Colonel Fitzwilliam. "A proposal of marriage? Darcy?"

"Lizzy blames the laudanum," Lydia continued, "but we are not convinced."

"Lydia," warned Elizabeth. She turned to Colonel Fitzwilliam. "Mr. Darcy hit his head when he fell, sir. Mr. Fleming—Lady Catherine's physician—tells us that his prospects for recovery are excellent."

"Eventually," said Lydia.

"Poor fellow," said Colonel Fitzwilliam, shaking his head. "I am behind on every hand, it seems."

"Excuse me," said Lydia, "but have you lately joined the ____shire Militia? Your uniform is so very fine."

"And," added Kitty, "it is different than that of the other officers."

"I belong to the Dragoon Guards, 6th regiment. Not," he added, smiling, "to any militia."

"Oh!" said Kitty and Lydia. "The Dragoon Guards!"

Colonel Fitzwilliam was on his feet, making his bow to Elizabeth. "Apparently it is to—Netherfold?—that I must go."

"Netherfield Park," said Elizabeth, smiling. "I will ask Ned to direct you."

Mary came bursting through the door and nearly collided with the Colonel. "Elizabeth," she said, "you are wanted upstairs. At once."

"In a moment, Mary."

"Mama says you must come now. Father is asking for you."

33 BUT LOOK AT HOME

Darcy saw at once that Mr. Bennet's condition had worsened. Either Elizabeth had concealed the truth from him, or she did not understand what she was seeing. But of course she did not understand. Such knowledge was acquired only through experience. It was obvious, too, that the man was in pain.

"Elizabeth has told me," said Mr. Bennet, between breaths, "what it is you wish—to ask, Mr. Collins. You seek—my blessing—to marry my daughter."

"I have come to ask for Miss Elizabeth's hand, yes," Darcy said. "I quite understand your reluctance, sir."

Mrs. Bennet broke in. "Reluctance?" she protested. "Mr. Bennet is *not* reluctant, Mr. Collins, not at all."

How Darcy wished Mrs. Bennet were not in the room! But Mr. Bennet had insisted that she join them, so here she was.

"It is not my intention to upset you, sir," Darcy added.

But he had. Even a simpleton could see that Darcy was wresting the man's pet lamb from his bosom. Mr. Bennet was loath to give Elizabeth up, especially to someone like Collins. If their positions were reversed, Darcy would have felt precisely the same.

"Have I any choice?" said Mr. Bennet. "I am in no condition—to object. Indeed, I ought to be—grateful."

"And we are," said Mrs. Bennet. "Deeply grateful."

"I deserve no gratitude, sir," said Darcy quietly. "Nor do I deserve your daughter. There are few men in England worthy of so great a treasure. I ask only to care for her, to shelter and provide for her."

"You are—not her equal."

"Indeed, sir, I know it," said Darcy.

Mrs. Bennet interrupted. "What do you *mean*, Mr. Bennet? Mr. Collins is your relation. And while he is not precisely a gentleman, he has a gentleman's profession."

"Not equal in intelligence," continued Mr. Bennet, as if he had not heard. "Nor in spirit. Or insight."

Darcy squirmed under Mr. Bennet's gaze. The man made him feel like a schoolboy who had stolen an undeserved treat. And he was right, blast him. He was right.

The door came open, and Elizabeth entered.

A smile spread over Mr. Bennet's wan face. "Lizzy, my dear." He attempted to hold out a hand. "Mr. Collins has something—he wishes to ask you."

Elizabeth turned expectantly to Darcy.

"*Ask* you?" scoffed Mrs. Bennet. "Mr. Bennet, you told me that they were engaged already."

"Hush, my dear," said Mr. Bennet. "We must now listen to Mr. Collins' beautifully—" he paused to cough "—spoken prose."

There was a barb there; but Darcy paid it no mind. It was protocol to kneel, but even if it were not, his legs would not have supported him. Thus Fitzwilliam Darcy embarked on his very first proposal.

"Elizabeth," he began, all too aware of her mother and father and of the state of his nerves. "Dearest Elizabeth—Miss Elizabeth," he hastily amended. "So much has changed since I arrived at Longbourn. I myself have changed, in ways I cannot describe." He paused. "I wonder if anyone would believe how much."

"Much has changed for me as well," she said.

"I cannot begin to understand why Provi—" Darcy stopped himself. "—why God Himself has thrown us together in this extraordinary way, nor can I predict the outcome. Or rather, I should say, the future."

He was rambling, heaven help him. He ought to speak of his deep and sincere love for her. But to do so, as Collins, before her parents seemed selfish and grasping. Then he heard Mrs. Bennet give an impatient huff.

Elizabeth helped him. "We live day to day, dear William, do we not?" she said, smiling. "Walking by faith and not by sight. Who among us can see what the future holds?"

The future. Bless Elizabeth, he could see the future, at least for the short term. If Mr. Bennet lived out the week it would be a miracle. His duty was clear. He had become Collins for such a time as this.

"My earnest desire," said Darcy, over the hammering of his heart, "is to protect you, to provide for you, to walk by your side through life as—" he paused to take her hands in his own "—as your loving and adoring husband."

"And it is my desire," she replied, "to walk beside you as your loving and adoring wife."

Darcy closed his eyes and waited. No church bells rang, the heavens did not open, nor did a flash of lightning split the sky. The bedchamber remained solidly real, along with Mr. Bennet's labored breathing. He was still Collins and very much so.

"Trust a rector to preach a sermon," Mrs. Bennet remarked. "All that was required, Mr. Collins, was to ask a simple question."

One way or another Collins knew he must get round this cousin of Darcy's. For that was what Mrs. Nicholls had called him: your cousin, Colonel Fitzwilliam. Who was he and why had he come? Miss Bingley was not available for help.

With trepidation he followed Mrs. Nicholls to one of the small parlors and went in. He expected to see a man with Darcy's dark good looks and arrogance. But this cousin was built on more ordinary lines, and he was obviously pleased to see Darcy. Collins wondered how he ought to greet him, but the Colonel made everything easy—he simply held out a hand. Collins took it because he must (he was never eager to shake hands, as some were) and received a thump on the shoulder. "Darcy, old fellow. You're looking fit."

Collins sighed. Why did people tell lies to those who had been ill? "I have been better," he said, and he drew up a chair for himself. "How have you been faring? How is the family?"

It was Collins' experience that people liked to speak about themselves, and Colonel Fitzwilliam was no different. He launched into a recital about people Collins had never heard of and finished with his mother's latest whim, redecoration. "She would have a time with this old place," he added.

"Yes, Miss Bingley—do you know Miss Bingley? —is keen to have a go at modernizing it," Collins said. "She has schemes to redecorate Pemberley." He forced a laugh. So far things were progressing nicely. "And your father? How is he?"

Too late Collins realized that he did not know whether Darcy's uncle was alive—or even if Colonel

Fitzwilliam's father was his uncle. With cousins one never knew.

"You know how he is," said Colonel Fitzwilliam, and Collins breathed a sigh of relief.

"Coming the earl more often than not, ranting at young bucks like me. There's always some squabble in the House of Lords to get him riled up."

Collins flinched, he couldn't help it. "H-house of Lords?" he stammered. Were Caroline and his cousin in league together?

Colonel Fitzwilliam's bright gaze fastened on him, and it added to his discomfort. Collins crossed a booted leg over the other. His aim was studied nonchalance, but somehow he knew that he was not succeeding. He forced another laugh. "As long as I am not the one running for office," he quipped, "it really is no concern of mine."

Colonel Fitzwilliam flinched. Collins knew suspicion when he saw it. He'd made a blunder. Obviously Darcy took politics seriously.

"Lady Catherine—our, ah, relation—has been urging me to run for office," he explained. "And so has Miss Bingley."

Colonel Fitzwilliam's gaze did not waver. "From what you've let fall," he said, "Miss Bingley will not be satisfied until she 'urges' you down the aisle. So she has added Parliament to the list? What else, I wonder?"

"I am afraid to think of it," Collins admitted.

"You never could stomach her for long, as I recall. Myself, I would cut the connection with Bingley altogether. Unless, of course, the sister is pretty. You have never said—is she? She is obviously well-off."

Collins did not know how to respond. Raillery was never his strong suit, and he suspected that it was not Darcy's. But with this cousin would Darcy let his guard down?

And then Collins realized that he had lapsed into silence. Men of quality never allowed a conversation to flounder. "Perhaps you have heard," he bleated, "that I was injured."

"Ha, struck by lightning, if the ladies of Longbourn are to be believed. What actually happened, old fellow?"

Collins was rescued from having to answer by the appearance of Mrs. Nicholls. She brought a decanter and glasses. Was it sherry? Claret? What did one serve in the afternoon? Darcy would have known.

"Ah, here we are," he decided to say. "Dutch courage."

This was another term from his university days, but from the expression on Colonel Fitzwilliam's face it was not one that Darcy used. Mrs. Nicholls poured each of them a glass. Colonel Fitzwilliam thanked her charmingly. Collins was amazed to see her flush with pleasure. A man in regimentals, he decided, could get away with much.

Colonel Fitzwilliam leaned forward. "And now," he said, drawing a folded paper from his pocket, "will you kindly explain this letter? Who the devil is William Collins, and why should I speak with him?"

34 LET SOLDIERS FIGHT

"I am ashamed to admit how much I must rely on your expertise," William confessed, as he drew her to sit beside him. He was looking weary, with deep circles beneath his eyes. Elizabeth smoothed an unruly lock of his hair and tenderly kissed his cheek.

"Believe me, it is no trouble," she said. "Jane is with Father. I am able to be away for a few minutes."

She paused and then said, "He is happy, you know. About our engagement."

William's eyes met hers. "And so am I." He then brought out Mr. Wickham's sealed letter and together they examined it.

Presently she said, "This should not present too much difficulty. The seal is nicely formed. With a knife we should be able to lift it. The bright red of the wax will be difficult to replicate, however, when we reaffix it."

"I use—ah, Mr. Darcy uses—the same sort of wax," said William. "He would ape the man. Extravagant devil."

"Mr. Darcy?"

"I meant Wickham. See how crisp the stationery is? Hot-pressed and expensive. To outward appearances, he is a man of means. And why not? One must bait the hook well to land the best fish."

He passed a hand over his eyes. "Forgive me. I've had so little sleep that it is difficult to think. And it is at such a moment that the true test comes." He smiled a little. "Will you be shocked, my darling, to learn that I am tempted to deliver this as it is, and be done with it? To simply stand aside and allow Miss de Bourgh to reap what she's sown?"

"Not at all," said Elizabeth loyally.

"But that would never do," he went on. "It would save us a world of trouble, but she has no idea what Wickham is. And I most unfortunately do." He reached into a pocket and brought out something wrapped in cloths. "Here is my razor, as sharp as I can make it. Will you handle it or shall I?"

"I will, I think. My hands are smaller and accustomed to delicate work. If you will just fetch—"

But William was already on his feet. He brought the little table and placed it before her. Elizabeth dusted it carefully with her handkerchief. It would never do to dirty the paper.

"Now then," she said, unwrapping the razor. She placed it along the surface of the paper, just beside the seal. "This is rather exciting. "My first experience in—what did you call it?"

"Espionage."

And then it happened—her hand slipped. "Oh!" cried Elizabeth. For she had not lifted the wax at all, but instead had cut the paper. "Oh, William," she whispered, not daring to look at him. The silence was terrible.

And then he began to laugh.

"But I have spoiled everything," she cried.

"Not at all," he said. "You, in your wisdom, have made our way easy."

"Easy? How can you say so?"

"I have not been thinking properly, or else I have been thinking too much. But you—or your hands—they knew better." He leaned in, grinning. "What happens if I do not deliver this to Anne today?"

"I do not know." She thought for a moment. "I suppose nothing happens."

"Exactly. Nothing. Wickham's fine plans are therefore wasted, for at the specified time Anne will simply not be there."

"Is that the end of it?" It seemed so simple and yet

"And now," William went on, "let us have done with all this espionage and open the blast—er—blessed thing." He broke the seal and spread the page.

There was written only this:

Your will is my command, lady fair.
All praise and credit on the second morrow given
To Edm. Spenser, England's Arch-Poet
Just after moonrise.

Elizabeth read the words with astonishment. This was nothing like what she expected to see.

Collins put out his hand for the letter. Too late he realized that Darcy would have known what he'd written. Worse, Darcy had sent this letter after they had switched places. How much did Colonel Fitzwilliam know?

"H-have you seen Mr. Collins?" he managed to say.

"I have not yet had that pleasure," said Colonel Fitzwilliam. "The young ladies of Longbourn House—for that is where you sent me—told me that he is out."

Out? Trust Darcy to be difficult! Aloud Collins said, "Perhaps he is on an errand for Lady Catherine."

"That's the other thing. What is she doing here?"

Collins pursed up his lips. Did his cousin expect him to know all? "I might ask you the same about Anne."

"Anne?" The Colonel's brows knit into a frown. "Has Anne come as well? Why in heaven's name would she do that?"

"To marry me, presumably."

Colonel Fitzwilliam stared at him. "Marry you," he said blankly. "Anne has no desire to marry you. She has never shown the slightest interest." He leaned in. "Did Aunt Catherine bring her for that purpose?"

Collins knew the answer to this one. "Anne came of her own accord."

"Oh, please. Anne could no more come here than she could fly to the moon. She can scarcely sit through an evening at home, let alone a fifty-mile ride in a traveling coach."

"Am I responsible for what Anne decides?" Collins cried. "I was senseless to the world. All I know is that Lady Catherine sent for her physician, one Mr. Fleming, and that Anne compelled him to bring her along. And Fleming, being entirely without sense or backbone, acquiesced."

"Of all the mawkish, ill-considered—" A string of muttered oaths followed.

Collins was rather shocked. He reached for the decanter and refilled his glass.

The door opened and Miss Bingley looked in. "There you are, Mr. Darcy. Would you care to come with me to Longbourn House—?"

Colonel Fitzwilliam had risen to his feet. Caroline Bingley stood there gazing at Collins, a smile frozen on her lips. Too late he realized she was waiting for an introduction.

"Ah," he said, "Miss Bingley, may I present my cousin, Colonel Fitzwilliam. Colonel Fitzwilliam, Miss Caroline Bingley."

She smiled prettily, and the Colonel made a bow. "Since you are occupied, I will make my call alone," she said. "I do hope," she added, most certainly for the Colonel's benefit, "that there are no 'brother officers of the militia' lounging about. The Bennets are quite popular with the _____shire Militia."

"So I have been given to understand," Colonel Fitzwilliam said.

"In such poor taste, the militia," she went on. "Second sons, brought into prominence. Or commoners, who have no business wearing regimentals." She gave her nickering laugh. "When last I called at Longbourn, that odious Mr. Wickham was lounging about."

Colonel Fitzwilliam's expression changed. "George Wickham?"

Collins was on solid ground here. "Why, yes. He came into this district just after we arrived. Pleasant fellow, but talks incessantly."

"Wickham, pleasant?" cried Colonel Fitzwilliam. "Darcy, have you lost your mind?"

"Why, no," Collins faltered.

"Our aunt is here, our cousin is here, and Wickham is here. Is Georgiana here too?"

"Stop shouting," Collins complained. "How was I to know that you cannot abide Mr. Wickham?"

"How was I to—? After what happened? It was all I could do to keep you from murdering him!"

"Murder?" cried Collins. "I have no desire for the hangman's noose! Why would I murder Mr. Wickham?"

Colonel Fitzwilliam was muttering oaths again, with no regard for Miss Bingley's presence.

"Only consider," Collins said, in a desperate effort to lighten the mood, "what a sad loss that would be to the ladies. Mr. Wickham enlivens a party, as I recall."

"Oh, doesn't he just?" shouted Colonel Fitzwilliam. "Confound it, what is wrong with you, Darcy?"

"Nothing," said Collins, a bit too soon.

"Don't tell me you've lost your memory. I've been in battle, I know what cannon fire does to a man. You haven't the look of it."

Collins felt panic rising and it threatened to choke him. He covered his face with his hands. "My head," he wailed.

"Spenser?" Darcy said again. "What does Edmund Spenser have to do with anything? Wickham wouldn't read *The Faerie Queene* to save his life."

"Undoubtedly Anne has," said Elizabeth. "And I have misjudged her. We have opened the wrong letter, William. His held the invitation, yes, but hers gave the time and place to meet. This is not, I believe, the customary practice in an elopement, to have the lady take the lead—"

"Customary?" Darcy broke in. "No, nothing Wickham does is customary. He'll have her pay for coach and horses and the toll fees too. And why not? She'll end up paying for everything else in the end."

Darcy slid an arm round Elizabeth and drew her close. "Ah well," he said. "Mistakes happen. We must think, that is all."

But Darcy could not think. He closed his eyes and rested his cheek alongside hers. "The first thing," he said wearily, "is to list what we know."

Elizabeth reached for the letter. "On the second morrow," she said. "Would that be Monday?"

"Lady Catherine won't travel on Sundays; Anne knows that. By Monday, she and her mother could be gone from Netherfield."

"What time would moonrise be?"

"I think there was a half-moon while I was riding back with Bingley. But in all honesty, I was so tired it could well have been cloudy. So we'll hunt up an almanac."

"Father should have one."

"What do you bet it's early Monday, just after midnight? That seems to be the right time for an elopement. But where are they to meet? And why Spenser?"

"Edmund Spenser, England's Arch-Poet," echoed Elizabeth.

"There is a clue there, but for the life of me I cannot find it. At any rate, it's a great relief that Fitz has come."

"Who?"

"Colonel Fitzwilliam. I will need his help to thwart the elopement. I haven't the courage to do it alone."

She found his hand and held it. "You were courageous this morning," she said, "when you asked for my hand with my parents looking on."

"On one's knees, one does not shake quite so badly," he admitted, smiling. "And now I must send you back to him." He rose to his feet and offered a hand.

Elizabeth gazed up into his face. "William," she said, "what has Mr. Fleming said to you about Father?"

"Not a word. And yet—" He gathered her hands into his own.

"Father shall recover," Elizabeth said stoutly. "He must."

Darcy did not answer.

"William?"

"Spend all the time with him that you can," he said gently. "Indeed, I have been wrong to burden you with this business about Wickham. I have kept you away too long."

"But my place is also with you," she protested. "I wish to help you."

"Your place is with your father. I know of what I speak. I—have a little more experience with this." He kissed her forehead. "Every moment is precious. I did not understand this when my mother was so ill. I do not wish you to carry the same ache of regret."

"William?" Tears spilled onto Elizabeth's cheeks.

"We shall hope and pray for a miracle," he whispered.

"But you do not think one will come?"

He gathered her into his arms and held her close.

"Oh dear." Caroline Bingley crossed the room to the bell pull. "This continues to happen," she told Colonel Fitzwilliam. "Lady Catherine's physician has gone to Longbourn to tend a man who has a cold, whom I daresay is perfectly well."

Collins raised his head. "Which is where Fleming should remain," he said loudly. "We have no need for him here."

Miss Bingley looked to the Colonel. "Lady Catherine," she said in a whisper, "has plans to take Mr. Darcy to Rosings Park."

"I can hear you," said Collins. "I shall not go to Rosings Park. Or to London."

"Why Rosings?" said Colonel Fitzwilliam.

"To shield him from the world, poor lamb," said Miss Bingley. "I imagine your family—you are his cousin, are you not? —would dislike having his condition publicly known."

"Breathe the word madness and my father will explode," said Colonel Fitzwilliam. "Too many jokes about the mad earl."

"But Mr. Darcy is not an earl," said Caroline Bingley.

"No," said Colonel Fitzwilliam. "But my father is." He grinned. "I am one of those second sons you castigated earlier."

"Oh!" she faltered. "I—beg your pardon, sir. I had no idea."

"I am not," said Collins to anyone who would listen, "going to Rosings Park."

"Colonel Fitzwilliam," said Miss Bingley, "as you are Mr. Darcy's cousin, my brother and I would be honored if you would lodge with us at Netherfield for the duration of your stay."

"For the pleasure of my company?" said Colonel Fitzwilliam, smiling. "Or because I know how to handle Lady Catherine?"

"Do you?" she said. "Oh, you cannot imagine what a help that will be."

"Ah, but I think I can," he said.

35 Ranting, Roaring, Rattling Boys

"Spenser," Darcy muttered, as he trod the lane to Netherfield Park. That the idea originated with Anne, Darcy did not doubt. Wickham knew nothing of epic poetry, and he would have misspelled the name.

Was there anything at Longbourn connected with *The Faerie Queene*? Or with Elizabeth I? Not that Darcy could see. But he suspected that the reference to Spenser referred to a meeting place, so whatever it was must be out-of-doors. The trouble was, Anne never went out while at Longbourn. There had been too much snow.

So whatever it was could be seen, through the snow, from a window at Longbourn. Or else it was a landmark that Anne could identify. Whatever it was must be easy for Wickham to locate and also be near a road.

Darcy ignored the discomfort in his feet and kept walking. He ought to have borrowed a horse. Then again, he would need that horse tomorrow night, wouldn't he? Unless the family needed it to summon Dr. Bentley.

Or would Collins be called on to pray for Mr. Bennet and administer his last communion? So far Mr. Bennet had not, thank God, requested such a thing, but what if he did? Would God look with disfavor at his lack of ordination? Or at his lack of willingness to serve a dying man? Darcy was afraid he knew the answer.

He returned to the question at hand. *The Faerie Queene* brought to mind images of knights and ladies and sprites and nymphs and mythical beings. Any of these could be in the woods at springtime—the mythical woods, not Longbourn.

So it was at Netherfield Park, Darcy decided, that he would find his clue. Collins' shoes were a tattered ruin. Bless Mrs. Hill, she had done her best—the shoes reeked of polish. No workman at Pemberley, not the lowest stable boy, would be allowed to appear in such disgraceful attire. Never mind, Darcy told himself. Such things as appearance were no longer important.

He crossed over the border of the Netherfield estate without realizing it, and soon the mansion was in sight. But he should have known, for he was greeted by a distinctive sound.

"Hee-haw. Hee-haw-hee-haw-hee-haw."

Why couldn't Bingley have peafowl like everyone else?

A previous tenant had decided that a donkey and cart would be amusing, and when Bingley took possession there were a pair of donkeys wandering the estate. "I can't shoot them," Bingley said. "I don't know what to do with them."

Darcy now wondered if he would have to chase down Wickham and his cousin in a donkey cart.

As he neared the garden, he heard the ring of approaching hoof beats. Someone was leaving Netherfield. But when he saw the horseman's profile, Darcy's shoulders sagged with relief. At last Fitz had come.

"And here is Lizzy," said Mrs. Bennet, as Elizabeth entered the drawing room. "My dear," she added, "Miss Bingley has come, with *such* a lovely basket of hothouse fruit."

Elizabeth and her guest exchanged nods, and she slid into a nearby chair. She had come seeking Kitty, but it was obvious that she would not escape until Miss Bingley's quarter-hour was over.

Her mother fairly beamed with good spirits. "Congratulations are in order, my dear Miss Bingley," she said. "I daresay you have not heard that our Lizzy is to marry her cousin, Mr. Collins."

"How—nice."

Caroline Bingley's glance told Elizabeth precisely what she thought of her fiancé and also of her clothing and hair. Having come from her father's bedside, Elizabeth pushed Miss Bingley's shallow scorn aside.

"They will be married as soon as may be," Mrs. Bennet continued, "and then our Lizzy will be off for Hunsford. But she will return to us within a very short time, oh yes." She paused to simper. "We shall know more as soon as your brother finalizes his plans." And then she winked.

Caroline Bingley put up her chin. "My brother and I are for London as soon as may be," she said. "I know of no other plans."

"Oho," said Elizabeth's mother, "so you have not spoken with your brother this morning?" She was practically rubbing her hands with glee. "He will have news to be sure. I'll not spoil it for him by telling you."

At once Miss Bingley rose to her feet. "I'll not detain you, ma'am," she said crisply. "Please accept my best wishes for your husband's recovery. A winter cold is such a nuisance." And out she swept.

"Well I never," said Mrs. Bennet. "She did not stay even ten minutes. I trust my girls have better manners."

"Fitz," Darcy shouted. Collins' pulpit-trained voice carried beautifully, and Colonel Fitzwilliam pulled up. He wheeled and cantered over to Darcy. Darcy waved. "Hallo, Fitz," he called.

His cousin approached warily. "Should I know you?" he said.

Fitz was the most affable of men, but his voice held a ring of hauteur that was entirely new. As Collins Darcy was not his cousin's equal, but neither was he nobody. This new distance, so cold and impersonal, cut Darcy like a knife.

Collins' clothing was to blame and also his profession. On the other hand, who was Fitz to be so high in the instep?

Colonel Fitzwilliam sat on his horse, an imposing figure in uniform. Cloaked like that he resembled a Cossack commander, gazing with contempt at a serf.

"I believe you had a letter about me," was what Darcy said. He could not bring to introduce himself as Collins. Indeed, it was pointless to do so, since he would be at last confessing the truth.

At once Fitz swung out of the saddle. "Are you Collins?" he said. "My cousin said nothing about you being a curate."

"Rector," said Darcy, "of Hunsford Parish."

"Is that so?" said Fitz. He did not extend a hand or smile.

So it was to be like that, was it? "In point of fact," said Darcy crisply, "it was I who sent that letter."

"I daresay Miss Bingley did not wish to impose, Mama," said Elizabeth. "Kitty, Father has been asking for you. Shall we go up?"

Kitty did not look happy. "Oh," she said. "But—Mama, Lydia and I were hoping to walk to Meryton this afternoon. The weather is fine, and..."

"In all this cold? Certainly not. I need you here, Kitty. Your sisters' engagement dinner wants planning, for it must happen as soon as may be—especially if Mr. Bingley must go away to London. Hill is taken up with your father's care, and Jane and Lizzy are busy above stairs as well. Can you not send Mary with Lydia?"

"Mary," cried both Kitty and Lydia. "Mary will not do at all."

"Kitty," prompted Elizabeth, holding open the door.

"Oh, very well," she said. "Come with me, Lydia." They followed Elizabeth out.

At once they began whispering. "We shall have to find a way around Mama," said Lydia.

Elizabeth pretended not to hear. She began to mount the stairs.

"What I do not know," said Kitty, "is how we are supposed to raise such a whopping amount. It isn't like twenty pounds grows on trees."

"We must do our best. We must be resourceful, like women in novels."

"Elizabeth," called Kitty, "have you any money I can borrow? It's—for one of the shops."

Elizabeth stifled a sigh. "If you pay your accounts on time," she said, "tradesmen are willing to extend credit."

"Oh, ah, yes," said Kitty.

"But it's almost Quarter Day, Lizzy," said Lydia. "And anyway, it's not as if we are desperate. Such as Denny and Pratt, who must what-do-they-call-it with their timepieces and watch chains."

"Pawn them," supplied Kitty. "That's what they do, and that dreadful Mr. McCurdy gives them money."

There was a pause. "I wonder," added Kitty.

Open scorn was in Fitz's eyes. Never had Darcy been so close to disliking his cousin, and yet he must attempt to explain. "I came into this district with Charles Bingley," he said, "to assist him in selecting an estate."

"You?"

Darcy ignored his cousin's churlish tone. "Bingley wanted the advice of a resident landowner."

"He must be more of a numbskull than I thought to seek advice from someone like you."

Darcy kept his irritation in check. Yes, it was definitely the clothing. Who knew Fitz was such a stickler? Or that first impressions were so blasted difficult to overcome? Nevertheless, he must persevere. "Bingley decided to take the house," he said, "and a fortnight ago he hosted a ball. Collins was present—"

Colonel Fitzwilliam folded his arms across his chest. "Unless I miss my guess," he said, "Collins is your name."

"—and after supper he followed me into the garden."

"Collins followed you."

"Yes. And while we were arguing, a storm blew in."

"Let me guess," said Fitz. "Lightning struck. You sustained a direct hit."

"How do you know that?"

"Darcy told me, and so did the lovely ladies at Longbourn House. Yes, I have seen him, so I know more than you think. A likely story."

Darcy felt his eyes narrow. "It is the truth."

"See here, Collins, for that is clearly who you are, what really happened? Fisticuffs? Did Darcy clean your clock?"

"I did not brawl in the garden or anywhere else," said Darcy frostily. "The force of the lightning threw me to the ground."

"Or else Darcy's fist sent you there," said Fitz.

"Collins fell on top of me. And when I came to myself—"

"I'd like to see that, you falling on top of yourself. You likely cracked a few bones."

"Ribs, actually," said Darcy, with a rueful smile. "Hurt like Hades. When I came to myself, I was in this body." He indicated Collins' form.

Colonel Fitzwilliam gave a snort. "You are telling me," he said, "that you are Fitzwilliam Darcy? That you are—how shall I say it? Inhabiting Collins' body?"

"Yes. And William Collins is living in mine."

Darcy saw his cousin's lips twitch. Obviously he was working to swallow a guffaw. Then Colonel Fitzwilliam threw back his head and laughed. "Oh," he gasped. "This is rich. Upon my word, first-rate!"

"If you have spoken with your cousin," said Darcy evenly, "you must have seen the change in him."

"The best jest ever." Fitz doffed his hat. "I salute you. I don't know who put you up to this—Simmons? Was it Simmons? Very well played, Collins, or whoever you are. Very well played."

"Fitz, this is no joke. I am Darcy."

"Of course you are. And Darcy—is he supposed to be you? He played the buffoon to perfection. I can imagine my poor aunt's spasms, to discover that the heir to Pemberley is now an idiot."

"I wish to God this were a joke. As Darcy, Collins knows nothing of Pemberley," said Darcy. "Or of Georgiana, or of anything else."

"Ha," said Fitzwilliam. "He thinks Wickham a sprightly dinner guest. A clever rig, very clever. The rector's get-up was a stroke of brilliance. Lends credibility to an otherwise outrageous scheme."

He leaned in. "So if this is not a joke, what is it precisely?"

Darcy felt his cheeks flush. "My bungled attempt to explain an incomprehensible situation."

Colonel Fitzwilliam's brows descended. "Incomprehensible? I think not. What kind of a flat do you take me for?"

At all costs Collins must avoid another encounter with Colonel Fitzwilliam. And also with Lady Catherine and Caroline Bingley and Anne de Bourgh. He could find no refuge in his rooms upstairs, for Holdsworth was working there. How a man could find occupation in caring for clothing Collins did not know, but that was beside the point. Where in all this great house could he hide? And then he remembered how Mr. Bennet avoided his wife and talkative daughters.

Fortunately Bingley's library was empty. A fine fire crackled on the hearth, and Collins sank into one of the overstuffed chairs with a happy sigh. At last, peace.

Or perhaps not. What he'd assumed was the hearth rug was a sleeping dog, a liver spaniel. The animal raised his head hopefully.

Collins gazed at the dog with distaste. "Shoo," he said. "Go away."

But the dog would not be denied. "For the sake of all that is holy," Collins complained, "keep that tongue in your mouth where it belongs."

Of course the animal would not be satisfied until it had licked Collins' hand—and the shining surface of his beloved Hessian boots.

"I understand this no more than you do, Fitz," said Darcy. "But it's the honest truth. Question Collins, or should I say Darcy?"

There was a pause. "I already have. He has been well-coached. He knows his part perfectly."

"Blast it all, Fitz, the man knows next to nothing! Ask him to ride or to shoot, make him dance with Caroline Bingley—he cannot. He can do none of those things."

"You've had your jest," said Colonel Fitzwilliam. "But I'm not having any."

"Ask Darcy about your parents, Fitz, or your brother. Or his father. He knows nothing, not even information that could be gleaned from the social column in any London paper."

Fitz folded his arms across his chest. "As I say, a fine jest."

"Try me," said Darcy. "Ask me anything, anything you like."

"So that you can gather more information about me or my family? No thank you." He leaned in. "Who are you? What kind of rig are you running?"

"I told you. I am Darcy."

His cousin responded with a string of oaths. "Out with it," he said. "How much is this going to cost me?"

"Cost you?" said Darcy. "What do you think I am, Fitz?"

"Isn't that patently obvious? A dammed charlatan! A swindler and a blackmailer! Well? What's the figure?"

Darcy gave a curt laugh. "As if you had the funds to pay."

Colonel Fitzwilliam was shocked to silence.

"Let's be honest, shall we?" said Darcy. "You came here in answer to my summons. But you also knew that I would open my purse. Reimbursement for travel, a gift, a loan until quarter day. Call it what you will, it amounts to a handout."

"Hee-haw," came the distant bray of one of the donkeys. Its timing was excellent.

But Darcy did not laugh. "This time, my dear Fitz, you will find that the feeding trough is empty. As Collins I have no money, and as Darcy, Collins cannot sign a draft on my bank. So you, my dear cousin, are out of luck."

Fitz's face was dark with anger. "You—"

"Unless you decide to run off with Miss Bingley," Darcy went on. "She is worth at least twenty-thousand. Have you played the second-son-of-an-earl card? With her it might work."

"You," Colonel Fitzwilliam spat, "are a demon from hell. I don't know where you get your information."

Darcy was now too angry to care. "I tell the truth—for the first time in almost a fortnight—and what do I get for my pains?" he said, "Insults!"

Fitz looked an answer.

"Of all people," Darcy went on, "I thought that you—my friend, my own flesh and blood, a man I consider closer than a brother—would at least hear me out. Like a fool, I thought that you would have the grace to believe what I say. I am Fitzwilliam Darcy. I wrote that letter. And now I wish I hadn't."

"You are mad. And if my cousin will be shut up in a madhouse, as God is my witness, you will be there with him."

"And then what?" said Darcy. "As Georgiana's guardian, you will have oversight of Pemberley—including a generous yearly income—and sit on your hind end? Or fritter it away on tradesmen's bills and gaming debts?"

"What?" shouted Fitz.

"I seem to recall a dark-haired opera dancer several years back," said Darcy. "I, or more accurately, my purse, pulled you out of the River Tick. To the tune of several thousand pounds."

Fortunately Darcy's responses were not as bovine as Collins' body made them appear. Just in time he dodged the swing of Colonel Fitzwilliam's fist.

36 OF CHEQUERED FORTUNE

Elizabeth opened the bedchamber door for Kitty, who was crying softly. But where was Lydia? Mary was standing there, so Elizabeth motioned for her to come inside. A moment later she came back into the corridor.

"Do find Lydia," Elizabeth whispered to Kitty. "She ought to see him now."

"But Lizzy, surely—"

"Just find her, Kitty. And send Mama up as well. On second thought, I'll see to that myself."

Elizabeth sent a futile glance down the stairwell. If only William were here! "I think it is time to send Ned for Dr. Bentley," she added.

Kitty's face was pale. "Surely Father is not—"

"Go for him yourself if Ned cannot be spared. I must wake Jane."

Collins avoided the dog by paging through a London newspaper. Presently he heard the door open, but it was only Charles Bingley. The dog perked up and went to greet his master, tail held waving.

"Good morning," Bingley said. "Or should I say good afternoon? I daresay I've missed both breakfast and luncheon."

"I apologize for violating your inner sanctum," Collins said stiffly. "Holdsworth is working in my rooms, and Lady Catherine is lurking about, ready to pounce. Even Colonel Fitzwilliam will rant at me."

Bingley spread his hands. "Unnecessary to explain it, old man." A lopsided grin appeared. "You've forgotten that I often hide in here."

He took a newspaper from the table and slid into the chair opposite Collins. "So your cousin has come," he observed. "Heaven only knows what Caroline will say."

As if on cue, the door opened to admit Bingley's sister. "You will tell me this instant," she said, without preamble, "why Mrs. Bennet was winking at me. Winking, Charles, as if she was privy to a saucy secret."

Bingley lowered the newspaper, and as he rose to his feet Collins heard him sigh. "Surely you are mistaken," he said.

Collins knew he ought to stand as well. Instead he concealed himself behind the newspaper.

"Revolting creature!" Caroline Bingley said. "I take the trouble to bring fruit to her miserable worm of a husband, whom I daresay is not sick at all, and this is the thanks I get. She chortles—yes, chortles! —with secret glee. Worse, she implies that her secret involves you. Well?"

Collins shrank into the corner of the chair. In this mood, he would be next.

"I daresay Mrs. Bennet is not herself, for her husband is seriously ill," said Mr. Bingley. "Jane fears the worst."

"Must you use her Christian name? And what do you know about Miss Bennet's fears? Intimacy of that sort is most unbecoming."

The library door opened again, but Caroline Bingley did not notice. Collins swallowed a yelp of dismay and hid behind the newspaper.

"It does no good," Miss Bingley went on, "to encourage familiarity with lesser persons with whom one should not be connected."

"My sentiments exactly," said Lady Catherine, coming into the room. "Although I never expected a *parvenu* to say so."

She fastened her gaze on Charles Bingley. "I am looking for Colonel Fitzwilliam, whom I understand is here, and also for you, Mr. Bingley. It is high time to discuss my plans for my nephew, Fitzwilliam."

Collins repressed the impulse to inform her ladyship that he was in the room.

"Colonel Fitzwilliam has gone to Meryton, ma'am," said Miss Bingley. "I have no idea when he shall return. Charles, I have invited him to stay with us until we depart for London."

"Another feather in your cap," Lady Catherine remarked. "Best hurry and write to all your fine friends before he departs." She turned and made her way to the door. Caroline Bingley resumed her tirade, speaking low.

"I trust you are not encouraging Miss Jane Bennet to hope for more, Charles. We have been over this many times. Louisa and I—and even Mr. Darcy—believe that you can do much better."

Collins peered over the edge of the newspaper. The library door was open, but Lady Catherine had paused at the threshold.

"I realize that Georgiana is rather young," Caroline was saying to her brother, "however, both in temperament and fortune she is an excellent match for—"

"Georgiana?" interrupted Lady Catherine. She closed the door. Collins felt himself begin to tremble—he knew that tone of voice. "Young woman," she said, "I trust you are not speaking of Miss Georgiana Darcy as part of some scheme."

Caroline Bingley was struck speechless.

"Do not think that you can pull the wool over my eyes. You will do well to banish Miss Darcy from your plans. An alliance between your family and ours would be most unsuitable."

Caroline Bingley's cheeks were scarlet. "Upon my word," she sputtered.

Charles Bingley was looking rather pale. He drew himself up. "I might as well tell you—it will be public knowledge soon enough," he said. "This morning, shortly after dawn, I asked Mr. Bennet for Jane's hand in marriage. She has accepted, and we have her parents' blessing."

"Charles," wailed Miss Bingley. "You did not! The Bennets are nobodies."

"Mr. Bennet is a gentleman," said Lady Catherine crisply. "The favor, young woman, is being conferred upon your family, not hers."

"But they have no connections, no fortune!"

"And Georgiana Darcy has?" said Lady Catherine. "Is this a point in her favor?"

"I-I did not mean that," Caroline protested. She rounded on Collins. "Speaking of matrimony, Mr. Darcy, I've news of Miss Elizabeth," she cried, "whose fine eyes you once admired. Elizabeth Bennet is to marry that buffoon, Mr. Collins. A triumph indeed."

"What?" cried Collins.

"Most sensible," said Lady Catherine. "He has done precisely as I suggested. A rector ought to have a wife."

There was no reasoning with Fitz in this mood, so Darcy turned and stalked away. That swing revealed the state of Fitz's mind. He was angry, yes, but he was also frightened.

Darcy felt only the bite of disappointment. His cousin's presence brought to mind his old life, and most especially, his sister. How he had counted on Fitz's help to reestablish a relationship with Georgiana. There was no hope of becoming himself again, but through Fitz he had hoped to have some influence, to do her some good.

Darcy reached the Folly and took refuge behind one of the statues. He saw Fitz pause and look round several times, but he continued in the direction of the stables.

Darcy drew a long breath. He would speak to his cousin again, but only after he had had a chance to think. He raised his eyes to the heavens in a silent prayer for help. And then he noticed the stone arches. Of course. *Spenser the arch-poet.* His cousin Anne and George Wickham would be meeting here, at the Folly.

Again the library door opened, and again Collins cringed. This was becoming like a second-rate stage play. And who should come in this time but Colonel Fitzwilliam. It seemed to Collins that he was looking ruffled and out of sorts.

"Pardon the intrusion, ma'am," he said to Lady Catherine, "but the butler said you were here."

Caroline Bingley thought he was speaking to her. "Do come in, Colonel Fitzwilliam," she said.

"Aunt Catherine," he said, "within the hour I shall be leaving for London to retain the services of an expert. Until I return and he has made his examination, I insist that Darcy remain here."

"My dear nephew," began Lady Catherine.

"I am afraid I must insist, ma'am," he said. "Darcy tells me that you intend to take him to Rosings. There is no point in doing so if care can be arranged another way."

"Do you mean a place like Bedlam?" faltered Miss Bingley.

Colonel Fitzwilliam hesitated. "That is the general idea, yes."

It was these people who were mad, Collins decided, and not him. They had forgotten that he was present—except for Miss Bingley and that remark about Elizabeth Bennet. He would have plenty to say to Darcy about that!

Again the door came open, but only to admit the butler. "Mr. Collins' compliments," he said, "and is Mr. Darcy home to callers?"

A silence fell, during which everyone gazed at Collins. It took him a full minute to digest what was happening. Darcy had come, though of course as "Mr. Collins." Collins had no wish to see him, but neither did he wish to listen while everyone else decided his future.

Lady Catherine gave him no choice. "Off you go, Fitzwilliam," she said. "We have plans to discuss."

Collins made a face and heaved out of the chair. The door swung shut behind him. Voices resumed talking, but not distinctly.

A specialist from London sounded ominous. But then, so did London and the cellar at Rosings, which is no doubt what Lady Catherine had in mind. On the other hand, he had the Darcy fortune at his disposal. Perhaps the specialist could be induced to recommend a year's convalescence abroad, say, in Italy? Yes, Collins rather fancied Italy.

In the entrance hall sat Darcy in a chair. "Good lord," said Collins. "You look like death." Darcy's face was haggard and his clothes looked as if he'd slept in them.

"Not a social call," Darcy said, as soon as the butler was out of earshot. "I've come to write a letter. I need access to your writing desk."

"By Jove," said Collins, "I forgot. Georgiana has written again, and I have no idea how to reply. I'm half afraid she'll come."

"So is Fitz," said Darcy, mounting the stairs. "That is to say, Colonel Fitzwilliam. I take it you've met."

"We have," said Collins, following. "And might I ask, what business have you to be proposing marriage to Elizabeth Bennet?"

Darcy tuned, and it seemed to Collins that an ugly light came into his eyes. "That decision was made in response to yours. Namely that upon Mr. Bennet's death, you will cast your cousins—or are they mine? — into the street."

"I said no such thing."

"But you did. A remarkable revealer of truth, too much drink. You made your opinion unmistakably clear."

The trouble with Darcy was that he thought himself smarter than everyone else. "Taking an awful chance aren't you?" Collins taunted. "What if we change back?"

"That is looking less and less likely," said Darcy. "If we do, you are set, Collins."

They came to the landing. Darcy paused and looked Collins in the eyes. "To say truth, Mr. Bennet is dying."

Collins felt his face grow hot; his fingers clenched into fists. "Longbourn—snug, dear Longbourn, the desire of my heart—will be yours? Along with Elizabeth?"

"Keep your voice down. You will do well to remember that my fortune, my beloved sister, and my family honor, have been surrendered to you."

"It is not fair," complained Collins. "I do not wish to be you. Not anymore. Not when I can have Longbourn."

"And I," said Darcy, "have had to make peace with being you."

"You don't have Colonel Fitzwilliam on your heels, haring off to London to summon a specialist."

Darcy's eyes narrowed. "Fitz is leaving?"

"Within the hour he said."

"With intention to shut you—and me as well—away in Bedlam? I'll see that."

"I'd rather travel through Italy," said Collins.

"Fitz will never allow it. But take heart, Collins. All is not lost. I'll prepare you for Fitz's examination. But you must quit pouting and apply yourself."

Collins' lower lip protruded. "I am not pouting."

At Darcy's insistence, Collins brought him upstairs. "Holdsworth is working in the dressing room. If your business is of a private nature—"

"There is little privacy in a house of this size," said Darcy, "or I daresay in any other. Simply tell Holdsworth to take himself off and he will gladly comply."

Collins bristled. "I know how to give orders to servants," he said. "If you must know, I am trying to guard your dignity."

"My what?"

"It's—your clothing," said Collins. "How you can appear before a fellow like Holdsworth is beyond me. He is fiercely particular."

"My good man," said Darcy, "Holdsworth will not give a fig about what I wear. It's your appearance that showcases his skill as valet. And if you continue to put on weight, he will certainly give notice."

This caused Collins to suck in his gut. "According to Mr. Fleming," he said with a sniff, "a healthy appetite is a sign of recovery. But you are a fine one to talk. You have ruined my best frock coat and breeches."

Darcy located the box with his writing supplies, retrieved the key from a drawer, and unlocked the box. "If you will bring Georgiana's letter," he said, "I will answer it now."

Collins began patting his pockets. "I could have sworn—" he muttered.

"Try the drawer in the bedside table. If Holdsworth found it that is where it will be."

Sure enough, Collins found Georgiana's letter. "Do you think he read it?"

"Very possibly. Just as Mrs. Nicholls no doubt tried to hear what was going forward in the library."

"Good gracious."

"A large house is very like the nave of a church. Caroline Bingley made no effort to hide her irritation; I could hear her in the entrance hall."

Collins made grumbling noises and Darcy unfolded Georgiana's letter. He could not help sighing a little to see her familiar writing. "This message is innocent enough," Darcy told Collins, "and as I said, I have nothing to fear from Holdsworth. But you must learn to guard your privacy."

"I see no point in having a locked box if the key is kept in the drawer."

"But I had nothing to conceal. And the key is not always kept in the drawer." Darcy drew out a sheet of paper, trimmed the pen, and dipped it in the ink pot. "I have decided to mention your injury to Georgiana, albeit in the mildest of terms."

"Darcy—" protested Collins.

"My objective is to keep her from coming here."

"Please do," said Collins.

"The trouble is, sooner or later she will hear of it—from my aunt—so it is best to be straightforward."

"If that brute Fitzwilliam has his way—" Collins began.

Darcy gave him a quelling look. "If you insist on talking, I shall never finish this," he said. "Now then, in the wardrobe is a dark blue riding coat. The brass buttons have a military insignia—not authentic, but close enough. If you would be so kind as to bring it here?"

Collins shuffled off and Darcy wrote out a brief and affectionate message. Please God it would keep his sister in happy ignorance—for now. He folded the letter and wrote the direction.

"At some point you must learn to sign my name," he called to Collins. "As I have learned to sign yours."

Collins came out of the dressing room. "But that's—that's forgery," he spluttered.

"It is, certainly. But who will know?" Darcy propped Wickham's note to Anne and studied it. Collins came forward with the riding coat. "Now what are you doing?"

"Copying out Wickham's message to Anne. It was necessary to open his letter," he explained, "but I can more easily replicate it than repair the damaged seal."

Collins clicked his tongue "You, the upstanding citizen, the pattern card of virtue."

"You shouldn't believe everything Aunt Catherine says. But this is not for sport. The elopement is set for tomorrow after midnight. One way or another I must stop it."

"What elopement?"

Darcy laid down his pen. "Collins," he said, "you are not a stupid man; do you never listen? You will learn so much by paying attention. And do not give me the excuse that your head hurts."

"But it does," complained Collins.

"When it is in your best interest, your mental capacity is fine. And it is in your best interest to keep Anne from running off with George Wickham."

Collins gave a sniff. "What is Lady Catherine to me? Or her daughter?"

"Lady Catherine is your blood relation," said Darcy. "And while you are no longer dependent of the Rosings estate, you have a duty to protect them."

"Oh, lord," said Collins.

Darcy took up his pen and began to write. Fortunately Wickham's hand was not difficult to copy. "Tonight," he said, "after the family is in bed, you will go down to the library. In the right-hand side of Bingley's desk, bottom drawer, you will find a case with dueling pistols."

Collins fairly squealed. "What? You will fight a duel?"

Darcy just looked at him. "Any man worth his salt does not enact an elopement unarmed. And Bingley's pistols—a foolish and impulsive purchase—are the only ones I can lay hands on."

"Except that it is *my* hands that will be doing the deed," said Collins with another sniff. "I am reduced to stealing."

"Borrowing," corrected Darcy. "We'll put them back before dawn, nicely cleaned."

"Cleaned?" squeaked Collins. "Why cleaned, if you plan not to shoot?"

"Wickham could become difficult," said Darcy. "His need for money is desperate."

"Anne has money and he needs it—that sounds like a perfect match."

"Ah, but her inheritance is not settled absolutely," said Darcy. "That is to say, her mother could disinherit her from the bulk of her fortune. If that happens, then Anne will be your problem."

"Not if I can help it," said Collins.

"See if Anne and her new husband don't come begging," said Darcy. "They'll threaten to cause a scandal if you do not make them an allowance."

Collins actually snorted. "Let them threaten. What care I for scandal? The Darcy fortune is an impenetrable fortress."

"Hardly," said Darcy.

"I have seen men of rank at university. Their wealth protected them from a world of trouble. No," Collins said, "unlike you, I am not afraid of Anne de Bourgh."

Darcy felt his eyes narrow. "Whether de Bourghs or Bennets, you are not your cousins' keeper, are you? You will stand by while Anne is left destitute?"

"She should have thought of that before she disobeyed her mother," Collins said primly. "Anne gets what she gets for running off with a rogue."

"I marvel," said Darcy, "that you chose the church as your vocation."

Collins opened his mouth to answer, but Darcy cut him off. "Give the coat to me and go smoke a cigar. If there are any left."

"Of course there are," Collins said peevishly. "What is the coat for?"

Darcy decided to humor him. "The buttons." He indicated Wickham's letter. "Dear George used a uniform button to make the impression for the seal, and I shall do the same. Anne won't know the difference."

"What a devil you are, Darcy."

Darcy did not answer. Fitz had told him the same thing.

Collins settled into the sofa, and Darcy resumed his copying. At last he sealed both letters with red wax. Collins was enjoying his cigar, his feet propped on a low table.

Darcy gazed out the window at the bleak winter landscape. He'd expected too much from his cousin, and his disjointed explanation did nothing to help. If Fitz could not accept the truth, how would Elizabeth react?

Would she believe him?

But he must tell her—indeed, he would do better than he had with Fitz. He would state the facts, rationally and in sequential order, without dramatics. Elizabeth loved him; she would hear him out.

His gaze traveled to the table. Here were pen and paper. Yes, he would write a letter and explain everything. It was his best chance of being understood.

And if she did not believe him?

Darcy cast doubt aside and pulled out a fresh sheet of paper. He dated it and wrote the salutation.

Elizabeth, my Beloved,

An excellent beginning—except that he had written in his own hand.

Darcy frowned at the page, chewing his lip and thinking. Should he begin again and ape Collins' crabbed scrawl?

The bedchamber was quiet, save for the muted snores of Collins, who had fallen asleep. The cigar must have burned out, for there was no evidence of smoke.

What I have written, I have written drifted through Darcy's mind. Pontius Pilate again. Most definitely not a good sign.

But Darcy could no longer afford to wait for signs. Squaring his shoulders, he began to write.

37 FIELDS OF FROST

Collins slept on, and Darcy tore up another sheet. It was the preamble that was giving him fits. It now occurred to him that he had never written a letter to a woman he loved.

Once the beginning was in hand, the rest came more easily. Days of thinking, and the botched explanation to Fitz, worked in his favor. At last Darcy signed his name—his own name—and sat waiting for the ink to dry.

He rose to his feet and crossed the room to the sofa. There lay Collins, asleep. What an unattractive fellow he had become! The coat was creased, there was a stain on the waistcoat, and Collins had no idea that one's neck cloth would not remain in place without attention. His mouth gaped; the breathing was raspy.

Fortunately, the right hand was unimpaired. Should Darcy risk removing the signet ring? He hadn't used it for Georgiana's letter, and she was one of the few who would notice.

Collins gave a muffled snort and shifted his position. No, Darcy decided, it was not worth it. He returned to the desk, melted the wax, and sealed Elizabeth's letter with the riding coat button.

That coat brought a wave of regret, for it was beautifully made. On a whim, Darcy shrugged out of Collins' black frock coat. The cut of the riding coat was severe and the sleeves were not right, but in a pinch it would do. He would not wear a coat this fine for many years, if ever. Reluctantly Darcy replaced it in the wardrobe, shrugged into Collins' beetle-black, and quietly let himself out of the room.

The letter to Anne was delivered easily enough. As Darcy suspected, she had shut herself in her bedchamber, claiming to be ill. Her face appeared wan enough, until she caught sight of the letter. She could not conceal her eagerness—at least not from him—but she did try, with a sidelong look meant to put Mr. Collins in his place. She shut the door at once, leaving him standing there.

All that was left was to walk back to Longbourn.

The sun was low in the sky when the house came into sight. In the cold winter air sounds carried, and Darcy heard voices coming along the lane. He slowed his steps, reluctant to show himself. For unless he missed his guess, here were Kitty and Lydia.

"But we *cannot* tell her how miserably we have failed."

"It serves her right," said a second voice. "Where were we supposed to find *twenty* pounds?"

"We would have more if you had pawned your necklace like I did." This voice, Darcy decided, must be Kitty's.

"The amount that Mr. McCurdy offered was laughable. I am not such a flat as to be completely gulled."

And the second voice was Lydia—using cant she had picked up who knew where. Darcy came to a halt and waited.

"But what else have we to sell?" he heard Kitty lament.

"If I were allowed to sell my creations, we would have plenty," said Lydia. "My bonnets are always prettier than anything in the shops. The women of Meryton would be happy to pay."

"Anne is relying on us. How else will she escape her fiend of a mother? Without money for travel, Anne will never reach Pemberley."

Darcy stood very still. What a schemer his precious cousin was turning out to be!

"She is a fool to travel alone on the mail," said Lydia. "That's the first place they'll look."

"Which is why she must borrow my clothes. Hers are too fine—that is what her letter said."

"Not much of a compliment to you, is it?" said Lydia. "My letter said nothing about clothes, and I am glad. I'd rather not give up any of mine."

"Yours are the wrong size," Kitty pointed out.

"She will swim in yours. She is much too thin."

"That does not matter because she will be wearing my cloak."

"But it's red," said Lydia. "Not the color one wears to avoid being noticed."

"Then I shall have to lend her Jane's," said Kitty. "Jane will not mind, since Anne's need is truly dire."

"La," said Lydia, "when Jane marries Mr. Bingley, she will have heaps of new clothes. And so shall we, for Mama is eager for us to meet all of his fine friends. But look there," she added. "Someone has come to call."

"Has Mama invited Dr. Bentley to supper?"

"Nonsense, we are not that late."

"Perhaps he has come to call on Father," said Kitty, "for that is his chaise. Unless it is someone else. We could be mistaken."

And then, echoing through the winter countryside came the sound of the parish church bell slowly tolling.

Darcy concealed a groan. Its meaning was all too clear. Mr. Bennet had passed into eternity.

"Why are they ringing the bells now?" said Lydia. "There is no service."

Kitty gave a ragged gasp. "Father!" she cried.

"Of course it isn't Father," said Lydia roughly. "Someone else has died, someone in Meryton. People die every day."

"My necklace," Kitty wailed. "Oh, my poor necklace! Father gave it me for my birthday, and now it is gone. And so is he!"

Darcy strode forward and closed the gap between himself and the girls. They were now clinging to one another.

"Mr. Collins," cried Kitty. "Why are they ringing the bell?"

He offered an arm to each. "Shall we go inside? Your mother will be glad to have you home."

Kitty and Lydia went charging up the stairs, calling for Elizabeth and Jane. Darcy lingered alone in the vestibule. There was little doubt about why the bells were tolling. For the second time he felt the weight of inheriting a property. But there was no jubilation in it, as fools like Collins assumed. He would manage the Longbourn estate with the same care he had given Pemberley. And, God willing, it would prosper.

Mrs. Hill came into the vestibule, her demeanor deferential.

"Mr. Bennet?" he said gently, before she could speak.

"Yes, sir," said Hill "With the Savior in heaven he is, and out of his pain."

"I am so very sorry. You were especially fond of him, I think."

"It is kind of you to say so, sir."

"He was my relation, a man I should have spent more time getting to know."

"You'll care for his Elizabeth, sir, and his girls. Thank God you came when you did."

And then he remembered Elizabeth's letter. This was the wrong moment to deliver it, yet Darcy knew that if he delayed he might lose his nerve. This was a time for honesty. Elizabeth deserved to know the truth.

He called Mrs. Hill back. "If you would put this in Miss Elizabeth's bedchamber, away from prying eyes," he said, "I would be grateful. She—needn't discover it right away."

There was no hint of saucy coyness in Mrs. Hill's eyes. "The younger girls," she said, "mean no harm, but I understand your meaning, sir. I know just the place."

There was more to be said. "I ought to say a few words to the family after supper," he said. "I would like you to be present, Mrs. Hill. At some point we will go over the household accounts. I would like to have an idea of what is fair and reasonable."

Was it his imagination, or did Mrs. Hill's shoulders straighten? There was no mistaking the respect in her gaze. Darcy was no tyrant, nor would he evade his responsibilities. He had been running an estate for too long to toe the ground or appear indecisive.

"I would prefer not to disturb Mrs. Bennet. Although you might let her know, at a moment you think best, that I am amenable to making a reasonable allowance for the purchase of mourning garments."

"That is most generous, sir, but perhaps I ought to warn you—"

"Have no fear, Mrs. Hill. Your former mistress will learn to moderate her demands. I will not have the household staff tyrannized by emotional outbursts."

There was a short silence during which Hill dabbed at her eyes. "God bless you, sir," she said quietly.

There were voices on the landing above, and Darcy heard a beloved voice say, "He is?" He looked up.

Elizabeth's face appeared over the banister rail. "Oh, William," she cried, and she came hurrying down the stairs.

Mrs. Hill held out the letter, but Darcy shook his head. She went off at once, and Darcy held out his arms to receive Elizabeth.

"How I wanted you!"

"I am sorry to be away so long, dearest." He drew her close.

She settled her cheek against his shoulder. "I understand," she said. "And Dr. Bentley has been wonderful. But oh, how I needed you."

"I am here now," he said. "Whatever challenges come, we will face them together." He hesitated. "I have been through this a few times."

She pulled away to look into his face. "Your parents."

He dried her tears with his fingers. "And now your father," he said. "I am sorrier for this loss than I can say."

"Mama is wild with grief and worry," Elizabeth confessed. "She is fearful that you will cast us out, or else turn the household upside down. For that reason she wishes us to be married at once."

Darcy drew a long breath. Yes, he should have anticipated this. Mr. Bennet's death complicated things in more ways than one. "Your father deserves to be mourned," he said. "In six months' time, if you are of the same mind, we'll have the banns read and marry."

"And you will remain with us?"

"Not as a resident of Longbourn House," he said gently.

"But—"

He laid a gentle finger to her lips. "Whatever comes," he repeated softly, "we will face it together. But we needn't face every challenge just yet."

He heard her give a little sigh, and she again laid her cheek on his shoulder. "What a comfortable person you are, William," she said.

38 HE KNEW NOT HOW

Supper that night was simple and subdued: soup with bread and cheese. In silence Elizabeth and her sisters filed into the dining room and found their seats. A place was made beside Jane for Charles Bingley, their only guest. Dr. Bentley had kindly refused Elizabeth's invitation, thus removing the burden of conversation. Elizabeth was too worn to think, let alone talk.

Their father's place at the head of the table—and their mother's at its foot—were conspicuously empty. But as the soup was being served, the door came open and William brought in their mother. With gentle courtesy, he seated her in her usual place. Elizabeth knew that she did not wish to come down. But William was not to be gainsaid, and he had quietly won her over.

"Begin as you mean to continue, Mr. Collins," Mrs. Bennet said. "You are the master of Longbourn now and should sit at the head of the table." She dabbed at her eyes with a black-edged handkerchief. "Of this house, my much-loved home, I am no longer mistress."

He thanked her and slipped into a vacant chair, leaving Mr. Bennet's seat unoccupied. Elizabeth's heart warmed at this small act of thoughtfulness.

The soup and bread were good, the tea strong and bracing. How many hours had it been since anyone had eaten? The midday meal had been forgotten.

At last William Collins laid down his spoon and looked at each in turn. "I thought it best," he began, "to go over with you all, together, what will transpire to honor your father. I wish there to be no confusion. I have spoken with Dr. Bentley. The funeral service will take place as soon as we can arrange it, within a day or two."

"Mr. Collins," protested Mrs. Bennet, "you do not mean day, but night. For we must have a night funeral, as all the leading families do."

"We shall not imitate London practices, ma'am," said William. "We will do what is proper to honor your husband, but without needless display and extravagance."

Elizabeth heard her mother give a sniff. "Needless extravagance, he calls it. What do you know about family honor, Mr. Collins?"

He went on as if he had not heard. "To that end, I will be engaging the services of Mr. Willard. He will arrange for furnishing the church and the house, and will handle details such as transportation for the service."

The dining room became absolutely still. Mr. Willard was Meryton's funeral undertaker.

"Oh, but Cousin William," said Jane, "there is no need. For truly, we ourselves are able to—"

"No, Miss Bennet," he said. "You, your sister, and Mrs. Hill have borne the brunt of your father's care. I have no intention of saddling you with additional responsibilities. Tonight, Miss Bennet, you will sleep, as will Elizabeth. Our friend Mr. Fleming is no doubt sleeping now."

He turned to Elizabeth's younger sisters. "As for tonight, Mary, Kitty, and Lydia will share the vigil."

"The vigil?" Lydia burst out.

"That is the custom, yes," said William. "You may divide the hours among yourselves, or sit together if that is your preference."

"Do you mean we are to sit beside a dea—beside Father? All the night through? But that is—that is—"

"—customary," William finished for her. "It is also your duty."

Elizabeth found her voice. "Pray forgive my sisters," she said. "It has been a long while since we have experienced a death in our family."

"Close on ten years," Mrs. Bennet put in. "My great aunt Mary, though she can hardly be said to count, being at least eighty. Your father," she added, "inherited Longbourn as quite a young man."

"I still do not see why we must sit up all night while Jane and Elizabeth sleep," said Lydia.

"Because I require that you do," William said mildly. "Tomorrow you will sleep, and your sisters will take their turn, along with helping your mother with the correspondence." He paused. "Are you volunteering to write letters, Miss Lydia?"

"Oh lord, no," said Lydia. "I hate letters. Even so, I think it most unfair that—"

"Then kindly do as you are told. Miss Mary, I assign to you the task of selecting Scriptural texts, as well as a hymn, for the service."

Mary looked gratified, but Kitty took up Lydia's protest. "Must we sit up tomorrow night as well?"

William merely looked at her. "Of course," he said.

"I will have to get out of it," Elizabeth heard Kitty whisper to Lydia.

Meanwhile William was still talking. "Mrs. Hill will handle the after-funeral reception," he said, "with the help of Jane and Elizabeth and Kitty."

"What about me?" Lydia protested.

"I would like you to oversee tokens of remembrance for the mourners. I have seen how clever you are with ribbon. I daresay rosemary is customary."

At this, their mother raised her head. "Ribbon and rosemary for remembrance? Is that not rather paltry, Mr. Collins? We are, after all, one of the leading families in the district. It will never do to be thought stingy."

"As I am the one taking on the cost of the funeral," said William, "it is I who will be thought stingy."

Mrs. Bennet gave a mighty sigh.

"It has been my experience," he continued, "that an opulent, showy funeral is a means of assuaging guilt, or concealing a lack of affection for the deceased. Your father was much-loved by both his family and friends. There is no occasion for unnecessary pomp and ceremony."

"Of course we wish it to be done properly," Mrs. Bennet fretted. "I am forced to trust your judgment, Mr. Collins.

"What about tomorrow night, Mama?" said Kitty. "For the vigil, I mean. Lydia and I needn't sit up for a second night. Or perhaps Mr. Willard knows of someone who can."

"What about you, Mama?" suggested Lydia. "Will you share the vigil?"

"Me?" she cried. "Sit up all night? I am prostrated by grief, as Mr. Collins knows full well. Indeed, it is a wonder that I have joined you all for supper." She pushed back her chair and rose to her feet. Mr. Collins and Mr. Bingley did likewise.

"I shall force myself to make an appearance at the reception, as is my duty. But of more I am incapable.

Mr. Bingley, will you see me upstairs to my room? Hill, fetch the hartshorn."

Elizabeth caught up with William in the vestibule. He was putting on his coat and hat. "You are not going out?"

He smiled, and for a moment his face lost its pallor. "I must see Mr. Willard, who is expecting me. Dr. Bentley offered to stop by with my card."

"But William, you are exhausted."

"Ned is taking me in the carriage."

"Even so, you are far too tired to be doing business now. And when I think of that elopement—"

"Thank God for small wonders," he said, bringing an arm around her waist. "Were it taking place tonight, Wickham would have his way." He bent to kiss her tenderly. "I will come home as soon as may be. You are not to wait up."

"Indeed, I do not think I could, even if I wished it."

He released her, but as he put on his hat she saw him hesitate. "I hate to ask this of you," he said, "but—"

"Yes?"

"Would you be able to select your father's favorite suit of clothes?"

"For Mr. Willard," she whispered.

"I would not ask, but you will know what is exactly right."

"Yes," Elizabeth said. "I am willing." She raised her face for another kiss but it never came.

Instead she heard him say, "What the devil?" For outside there were the stamping of feet and also voices—merry voices. The cheerful rat-a-tat of the door knocker was an explosion of sound in the silent house.

Elizabeth gave William a startled look. "The officers?"

"Expecting cards and coffee, no doubt," he said.

"Obviously they have not heard."

The knocking sounded again. Behind them a door slammed, and Mrs. Hill came hurrying forward.

"I'll handle this," he told her, and with a swift movement opened the door.

There stood a cluster of uniformed men, half in shadow. Upon seeing Elizabeth their banter ceased.

"Hello, Wickham," said William, "and gentlemen." There was an edge to his voice.

Elizabeth came forward. "I daresay you have not heard. Indeed, how could you? For there has not been time—"

"Your father, Miss Elizabeth?" said a voice, Mr. Platt's she thought.

"I fear so."

The officers removed their hats, all traces of cheer gone. Elizabeth was touched.

Mr. Wickham stepped into the light. "My dear Miss Elizabeth," he said. "I believe I speak for all my brother officers, when I offer my most sincere and heartfelt sympathy. The world has lost a splendid fellow."

"If we can serve you in any way, Miss Elizabeth," added Mr. Platt, "you have only to let us know."

"Thank you, my friends," Elizabeth said. "Good night." She gave a look to William, and he quietly shut the door.

"Those poor fellows," she said, as soon as he had fastened the bolt. "I believe Mr. Platt meant it when he offered their help."

William was drawing on his gloves. "I suppose it would be bad form to ask them to mount a guard tomorrow night at Netherfield."

He was jesting, or was he? Could she enlist the help of the officers?

"A joke, dearest," he said. "There. I hear Ned with the carriage. Off to bed with you."

Such a comfort, his solid form and strong arms. And he was wearing the shaggy brown coat, the one that made him look like a bear. Elizabeth shed a few tears on his shoulder and then, very reluctantly, released him to his errand.

39 PAST ENDURANCE

The next morning Elizabeth and Jane went quietly to church with Mary. William slept until late in the afternoon, but evidence of his handiwork was everywhere. Mr. Willard's people had come and gone, and a room had been draped for the vigil. Elizabeth's father now rested in a coffin. Her mother could say what she wished, but Elizabeth knew that William had spared little expense. Her younger sisters did not like being up all night, but they were exempt from receiving the steady stream of callers.

Just now she and William were alone in the drawing room, a rare moment. "You have slept through Mr. Fleming's departure," Elizabeth said, pouring out a cup of coffee for him. "Unless Miss de Bourgh or her mother require his services, he will be returning to Hunsford."

He winced. "I meant to ask for his bill, to settle with him before he left."

"He mentioned that he would see you in Hunsford. I suppose you can arrange things then."

"That's another thing. My duties as rector are not arduous. Remaining for another six months might not be a bad idea."

"So long as that?"

"I am afraid so. Bingley won't like it any more than I do, but since the banns have not been read, we shouldn't proceed with the weddings. I understand that his sister is pining for London."

"That is hardly surprising," said Elizabeth. "But we must keep Mr. Bingley here, by all means."

William did not share her smile. Instead he lapsed into thought, frowning into his coffee.

"Is something wrong? Shall I have Mrs. Hill make a fresh pot?"

He looked up. "The coffee is excellent, thank you. It's just that I—have an awkward question to ask. And yet of all your family," he added, "you are the one who would know."

"Please," she said. "If I can be of service..."

"Has your father a money box?" he said at last. "That is to say, for incidental expenses?"

"Yes, in a drawer of his desk. Would you like to see?"

"Only if it will not give you pain."

It would, but Elizabeth was reluctant to say so. After all, her beloved father's bookroom, his private sanctuary, could hardly be kept as a shrine. Eventually it would become William's office. It was not surprising that he had need of funds, most likely for the funeral arrangements. She could see that he was embarrassed to ask. "I'll show you now, if you like," she said.

Even so, it took courage to open the door. Her father's presence was everywhere in this room; his empty chair tore at her heart. Elizabeth took herself in hand and drew back the draperies. Pale winter sunshine lit the surface of his desk.

"Just here," she said, speaking quickly so as not to cry, "he keeps money, usually not more than ten pounds." She brought out the box and, using the key her father kept hidden under the mantel clock, unlocked it.

"Thank you."

Elizabeth swallowed back tears and presented the key. "This is now yours," she whispered.

Instead of taking it, he enfolded her in his arms. "This was a bad idea," he said. "It is too soon."

"It must be faced, sooner or later," she said. "Much better to do so with you than alone. Now then," she said, turning to the box, "the latch is just there. Sometimes it sticks."

"Borrowed money from it, have you?" he said, smiling a little. But the box, when he got it open, was empty.

"What in the world?" said Elizabeth. "There was money here last week, I know it." She rummaged in the drawer. "He has a ledger to record what is taken out." But there was no fresh entry.

"Where can the money be?" she said. "This is terrible."

"I can think of several explanations. Your sisters might have needed to purchase something for the funeral or the reception. Or your mother might have wished for new gloves or a veil and sent someone to Meryton."

"Then why did they not record it? William, someone has stolen Father's money."

His arm came round her shoulders. "Who knows about this drawer and the box? Do any of the servants?"

"I am sure they do—we all do—but none of them would stoop to stealing. Unless—" An unwelcome suspicion crossed Elizabeth's mind. Kitty had been speaking about needing money. But Kitty would never steal.

"We won't make accusations just yet," said William. "After all, it is only ten pounds."

"Only ten pounds?" Elizabeth repeated. "William, that is no trifling amount."

He relocked the box and replaced both it and the ledger in the drawer. "The key hides under the clock, does it? I'll leave it there."

"This is terrible," Elizabeth said again.

"We won't fret over it. There is likely a reasonable explanation."

"Father was ill, and the loss would be undiscovered for some time. How could anyone do such a thing?"

"Come," he said quietly. "We have lingered here too long." He led her out of the bookroom.

The shadows had lengthened; soon it would be sunset. William consulted his timepiece. "I must go soon," he said reluctantly, "and it is not likely that I will see you again until morning. After everything is over."

"The elopement, do you mean? William, I do not like this. Why must you be involved?"

"Because it is my duty."

"What about Colonel Fitzwilliam? Why can he not do something?"

"He left yesterday for London to fetch a specialist."

"Is Mr. Darcy ill again?"

William hesitated. "After a manner of speaking," he said.

"Then what about Colonel Forster? If he knew what Wickham is up to, surely he could keep the elopement from happening."

"Wickham would likely deny it."

"What about Lady Catherine? She would see to it that Anne never left her sight."

"That's just the trouble," said William. "With her mother involved, Anne would never back down. The elopement would simply be postponed until another time and place. No, Anne must see George Wickham for what he is."

"And if she does not care? Perhaps having a handsome husband is enough. Perhaps she will not mind that he is expensive or a rogue or—"

"Elizabeth," he said softly.

"I know," she admitted. "You ought to help her. But I do not like it. What can you hope to do alone?"

"Ah, but I shall not be alone. I was hoping to enlist the services of Mr. Fleming. Barring that, I must be content with Mr. Darcy."

"Mr. Darcy!"

"You—haven't read my letter, I take it."

"Letter?" she said.

"I was afraid something like this might happen. I entrusted it to Mrs. Hill, who promised to put it in a place where you would find it. Sooner or later you will."

Elizabeth discovered that she was not only smiling but blushing. "You wrote me a letter?"

Outside came the sound of carriage wheels. Her time alone with William was almost at an end.

And yet there was something in his expression that raised suspicion. She faced him squarely. "Now William," she said, "if you are meaning to cry off, I won't have it. You can list a dozen reasons why you are not worthy to be my husband, and I will not care."

He looked uncomfortable. "There are some things you ought to know about me before—"

"I do not care," she said fiercely, as the knocker sounded. "Whatever your reasons are, they do not matter."

"I rather think they do."

"Have you another wife?" she demanded.

He blinked. "Why, no."

"A string of children born out of wedlock?"

"Certainly not!"

"Is there a warrant for your arrest?"

Weary though he was, his eyes begin to twinkle.

"Because for the life of me, William," she went on, "barring these I see no reason why I should not marry you."

The drawing room door was open, and Elizabeth saw Sarah come into the vestibule. "Letter or no letter, you have my answer," she told him. "And if it is, as I suspect, an exacting list of your faults, I might very well tear it up."

He bent to kiss her swiftly, just before Sarah had the door open.

The caller was Mrs. Niles, and she had brought not only her elderly mother but also all three of her daughters.

"I will see you in the morning," William said softly, and went out.

When Mrs. Niles and her talkative family left, Elizabeth went straight to Kitty's room. But it was no use, for her sister was fast asleep.

All that evening Elizabeth waited. Jane gave up and went to bed, but Elizabeth sat with her book. The drawing room was quiet, save for the hiss of the fire, and she made the mistake of drawing a lap blanket around her shoulders. Sometime later she awoke with a start. It was dark, for the candles had guttered.

What hour it was Elizabeth did not know, but someone else was in the drawing room—she could see the candle. Elizabeth was about to speak when she heard a whispered "Botheration! Where is that key?"

It was Kitty's voice.

Elizabeth heard a door open and close. She rose to her feet and followed Kitty, feeling her way in the darkness.

Kitty stood in vestibule, pulling on a pair of black gloves. Beside her rested a valise and a hat box. What was her sister doing with these? She then put on a cloak—not her own, but their father's dark cloak—and her black bonnet. Was Kitty leaving the house?

Elizabeth opened her mouth to speak but no sound came out.

There was a rustle on the stairs. "Are you still here?" Elizabeth heard Lydia whisper from above.

"I cannot find the latch key. You will have to let me in."

"For heaven's sake, be quiet! Do you wish to wake everyone?"

Surely her sisters could see her standing there! And then Elizabeth remembered that she too was wearing black.

"Leave the door unlocked then," said Lydia. "And hurry. You'll be late."

"I know," said Kitty. "Poor Anne!"

Poor Anne?

Lydia disappeared up the stairs, and the main door closed quietly behind Kitty. At once Elizabeth went rummaging for her own cloak and hat. She now knew exactly where Kitty was going—to Netherfield. Just how deeply was her sister involved in Anne's elopement?

A gust of wind sent Elizabeth's cloak billowing. She gathered her skirts and set off, running as fast as she dared. Clouds blew across the sky. There was a change in the weather coming; Elizabeth could feel it.

It was a long while before Elizabeth caught sight of her sister. She was walking now, being encumbered with the valise and hat box. Elizabeth cupped her hands around her mouth. "Kitty!" she called.

Kitty swung round and gave a cry. Immediately she broke into a run.

"Oh, no you don't," said Elizabeth, and gave chase.

The moon appeared low on the horizon, just beneath the clouds, and Kitty ran on. At length the lane dipped into a hollow, and Elizabeth saw Kitty lose her footing. With a cry, she fell.

With the wind whipping her skirts, Elizabeth stumbled forward. "Kitty," she called hoarsely. "This has gone on long enough."

Kitty raised a distraught face. Tears were rolling down her cheeks. "I have spoiled everything!" she cried.

Elizabeth knelt beside her. "Are you hurt?"

"My skirt is torn."

Elizabeth took hold of the corner of Kitty's cloak. "This is Father's. Why are you wearing Father's cloak?"

"You wouldn't understand." Kitty began to cry again. "My cloak is red, and I couldn't—" She paused and wiped her eyes. "I know it looks odd, Lizzy, but it's important."

"It had better be, since your gown is torn and Father's cloak is dirty. And," Elizabeth added, "his money is missing."

Kitty covered her face with her hands. "You don't understand," she wailed. "This is important."

"Important enough to become a thief?"

Kitty's hands dropped. "It is a matter of friendship," she said hotly. "True friendship."

Elizabeth felt her lips curl. She held out a hand and pulled Kitty to her feet. "Very well," she said. "I am listening."

"Anne is escaping—her only chance—from her tyrannical mother. Truly, you have no idea what she suffers."

Elizabeth chose not to answer. Kitty knew very well what maternal tyranny looked like. "And?" she said. "By what means is Anne de Bourgh escaping?"

"Why, by the Mail, of course."

"In the middle of the night? Do not be ridiculous. You know as well as I that the Mail leaves every morning at ten. Not in the middle of the night."

"But this is the only time Anne can escape from the house! While everyone else is sleeping."

"You mean to tell me that Anne will wait in the cold for hours?"

"It isn't very cold, Lizzy," said Kitty. The wind swirled an escaping tendril of her hair.

"After which time she shall walk to Meryton? Or is she planning to walk there now and wait in the market square?"

"I—I do not know."

Of course Kitty did not know. Who knew what story Anne had fed her? "A more sensible plan," scoffed Elizabeth, "would be for Anne to hide in your bedchamber until daybreak. But instead you meet her here."

Kitty reached for the hat box, but Elizabeth would not let go of her arm. "What is in the valise?" she demanded.

"Nothing—important."

"I thought you said that everything about tonight was important."

"It's only clothes. Two of my oldest gowns and some night clothes. Anne's clothes are too fine for the Mail." Kitty made another attempt to free herself. "Please, I am terribly, terribly late. I gave Anne my word."

"Night clothes?" said Elizabeth. "Surely Anne has her own."

"I—do not know. I put in a number of things just in case. It never hurts to have a spare nightdress."

The moon emerged from behind the clouds, giving Elizabeth a look at her sister's strained face.

"Very well," Elizabeth relented. "I shall carry the hat box." But she kept a firm hold of Kitty's arm.

"Can we not walk faster?"

"You are limping."

"I am—not. Not much." Kitty's expression was mulish. Elizabeth increased the pace slightly.

"So tell me," she said, "since Miss de Bourgh obviously has a plan, where is she going?"

"To her cousin's, of course. She does have some relations who will help her."

Elizabeth gave her sister a sidelong glance. "Why has she not applied to Mr. Darcy for help?"

"It's—it's to his sister that Anne is fleeing. She lives at a place called Pender-something."

"Pemberley," supplied Elizabeth. "It's curious that you should mention Pemberley in connection with Mr. Darcy's sister. I thought she lived in London."

"Does she?"

"According to Mr. Collins she does."

Kitty gave an impatient huff. "What does Mr. Collins know? Who made him an authority about everything?"

"Anne could have a very different scheme in mind."

"Really, Lizzy, you are becoming just like Mr. Collins. And furthermore—" Kitty broke off speaking. "What's that sound?"

Elizabeth came to a halt and so did Kitty. Over the rush of the wind came the clatter of wheels and horses.

"Unless I am mistaken," said Elizabeth, "that is a traveling coach. Now why would someone come to Netherfield at this hour?"

Kitty gave a nervous laugh. "It isn't even one o'clock. Perhaps Mr. Bingley and his sister are returning from a ball?"

"He had supper with us. And if there were a ball, don't you think we would have heard of it?"

Kitty tried to break free. "Let me go, Lizzy. I ought to have been there before this."

"Been where?" said Elizabeth.

"Oh, anywhere."

The approaching coach was not yet visible, but it was definitely nearer. "I think your instructions were rather more specific," said Elizabeth drily. "At the Folly, perhaps? Beneath the arches?"

Kitty gave a gasp. "How did you know that?"

"Perhaps I know more than you think." Lights appeared in the distance and then dipped out of sight. Within minutes the coach would be upon them. Elizabeth dug her fingers into Kitty's arm and pulled her from the lane.

"But we're almost there!"

"Quick," Elizabeth ordered, pulling Kitty behind a hawthorn bush. "Get out of sight."

Kitty was struggling with the valise. "For goodness' sake, leave that!" Elizabeth said. "It's not important."

"It is to Anne," protested Kitty.

"Anne is beyond our help now."

Elizabeth's heart was hammering. When she and William had read Anne's letter it had been a game, a shared amusement. But here in the darkness with the coach bearing down, it was all too real. Wickham was coming, and William was waiting at the Folly. What would happen when they met? William would be armed. Would Wickham fight?

"Ow!" cried Kitty, for there were thorns. "Stop pushing! If that coach is coming for Anne," she added, "shouldn't we stop it?"

The coach lights were again visible, and so were the horses.

"The driver could take the valise to Anne," said Kitty.

Elizabeth gave her sister another push. "George Wickham is in that coach," she said roughly. "And believe me, he would not be happy to see you."

"Wickham?" cried Kitty, over the thundering of hooves.

The horses flashed by and so did the coach. Once it was past Elizabeth staggered to her feet. "Four horses," she said. "Oh, William," she whispered, "he is planning to travel far."

"Who is?" said Kitty, extracting herself from the bush. "These wretched thorns! I have scratches everywhere, no thanks to you."

Elizabeth strained to see down the road. What was happening at the Folly?

Kitty gave a wrench and tore free from Elizabeth's grasp. She took up the valise and hat box and went running after the coach.

Elizabeth scrambled after, every sense alert. Soon there would be shouting, for Wickham would not easily surrender the de Bourgh fortune. And gunshots? Would there be gunshots?

Elizabeth already knew the answer. Her William would not give over an innocent woman to a man of Wickham's ilk, not without a fight.

To her left loomed the dark silhouette of the house, to her right were the gardens. There was no longer light from the moon, for the clouds had closed in again. The promise of rain was in the air.

Before the Folly stood the coach, the light of its lanterns glancing off the horses.

A gust of wind came rushing through the tops of the bare trees. Where was Kitty? Where was William? And where was George Wickham? She must not allow her sister to be seen by Wickham. Or by William, for that matter.

Elizabeth struck out in what she hoped was the right direction. She had not gone far before rain began to fall. A flash of lightning lit the sky.

It was then that she saw the figure huddled on the lawn. Elizabeth threw caution aside. "Kitty!" she called. "Are you hurt?"

Kitty was gasping for breath. "She is not here, Lizzy," she said. "I kept my promise and oh, she is not here."

Elizabeth put her arms around her sister. "Come," she said gently. "We must get out of the rain." For it was raining steadily now, the drops hissing into the lawn. A roll of thunder shook the ground.

"I brought everything she asked for, even the money." But the fight had gone out of Kitty. Another flash of lightning revealed the hat box and valise waiting forlornly near the Folly.

Elizabeth helped Kitty to her feet and together they stumbled toward an evergreen hedge. Too late she realized that it was holly. There would be more scratches here, but also shelter from the rain. She took a final backward glance at the coach.

But what was this? The door was now open. Was someone descending?

40 TUTOR OF TRUTH

As Darcy and Collins entered Netherfield's darkened kitchen together, the scent of rising bread came to greet them. Here was the true test of stealth. The cook's quarters at Pemberley were very near the kitchen, and intruders were roundly trounced. Tonight Darcy had no choice. One way or another he and Collins must reach the service door. Darcy kept a firm hold on Collins' arm, both to guide him and to keep him from running away.

"Confound it," Collins hissed, "let go!"

"Not on your life," Darcy whispered back, "since you are incapable of obeying even the simplest direction."

The fireplace coals were banked, and their glow served as a guide. The service door would be somewhere to the right.

"I have followed your instructions to the letter," Collins whispered savagely.

Darcy could not let this pass. "I told you," he said into the man's ear, "to wear black."

"But I am!" Collins squeaked.

Darcy's free hand found one of the offending buttons. "Of the half-dozen in my wardrobe, must you chose the coat with brass buttons?"

"But it's my favorite."

Darcy tightened his hold and propelled Collins to the door. "Here," he said. "Unfasten the bolt—quietly."

Reluctantly Collins obeyed. With care Darcy opened the door and pushed Collins out into the night air.

"Kindly remember," he said once the door was closed, "what we are up against tonight. Stay silent, and if you value your life keep those buttons covered."

Collins gave a loud sniff. "Why I allowed you to talk me into this I'll never know."

"Because," said Darcy, "you need to prove that you are me. Therefore you must rescue your cousin."

The paddock was deserted, eerily unfamiliar in the darkness. A gust of wind sent dead leaves scuttling across the gravel.

Darcy pulled his hat well down and struck out in the direction of the gardens. Collins had no choice but to trot along beside. The gravel served to amplify their footfalls.

"For heaven's sake," Darcy growled, "pick up your feet. That noise is enough to wake the dead." Then, remembering that Collins cared nothing for their mission, he added, "You'll ruin your shoes."

"I hate these shoes. They pinch."

Darcy came to a halt. "They did not do so when in my possession. If you insist on stuffing yourself like a hog, Collins, you will grow fat. Even your feet."

At last they rounded the corner of the mansion. Before them lay the garden, its shrubs reduced to blackened mass and form. Overhead towered bare trees, their branches whispering and rattling in the wind. Darcy left the gravel path and trod on the lawn.

But of course Collins must talk. "I do not see why," he began primly.

Darcy rounded on him. "Can you not keep silent for two minutes? This is no May-game, Collins. We are defrauding Wickham of thousands of pounds, money to which he believes he's entitled. He won't surrender Anne without a fight."

Collins' cloak had fallen open. "Those buttons," Darcy added, twitching Collins' cloak into place, "guarantee that you will be shot."

Collins recoiled "Why? What have I done?"

Darcy felt his lips curl. "It's what I have done. I foiled Wickham's plot to elope with Georgiana. The man despises me."

Darcy turned his attention to the lane. Of a travelling coach there was no sign—yet. "Come along," he said to Collins. "It looks like we're in luck."

The path led through the rose garden. It was on a night much like this that Collins had followed him. Bingley's ball—could it have been little more than a fortnight ago? It felt like a lifetime.

Again Collins broke the silence. "How much?" he said.

"How much what?"

"How much money did Georgiana have?"

"Thirty thousand," said Darcy shortly.

It was some time before Collins replied. "That is quite a sum," he said. "One can hardly blame a man for—"

Darcy turned on him. "Money," he fairly spat. "With you it's always money. Have you no morals, Collins? My sister was but fifteen, defenseless against a brute like Wickham."

"Of course I have morals! I am a man of the church, after all."

"Not anymore," said Darcy. "Come along, we're wasting time. Keep your eyes and ears open. Wickham should arrive soon."

Collins fell into step beside him. "Anne de Bourgh," he said, "is not fifteen."

"In some ways," Darcy retorted, "Anne is even younger."

DARCY BY ANY OTHER NAME

The Folly loomed before them, and Darcy gave a sigh of relief. "We're in time."

Collins resisted. "The place is deserted. You have the wrong night."

Darcy mounted the shallow steps. "Now we settle in and wait."

"In all this cold?" The wind came howling through the arches; Collins shuddered. "A storm," he lamented. "Beastly luck, what with the wind."

The wind would be an excellent cover for the noise of a traveling coach. "The question is," said Darcy, "will Wickham come alone? Or is one of his so-called brother officers in on the plot?"

Collins gave a snort of dismissal.

"Oh yes," Darcy went on. "Where large amounts of money are involved, men will do much. My sister's companion was in Wickham's pay. Now that you are me, you will learn that knowing whom to trust is anything but easy."

Before long Darcy saw what he was looking for—a coach and four, its lights bobbing as it crossed the lawn. It came to a halt not far from the Folly. Darcy saw the postilion dismount and climb up to join the driver. Apparently they were expecting to wait.

Collins shuffled his feet unhappily. "Bother this wind."

Darcy could have said the same, but his attention was directed at the coach. Wickham was within, warm and snug, while the men he'd hired sat out in the cold, smoking.

The men he'd hired. This gave Darcy an idea.

"Remain here," he told Collins. "Do not move or make a sound."

"As if I could," Collins muttered. "I'm nearly frozen."

Keeping to the shadows, Darcy made his way to the coach and four. On the back was strapped a trunk—Wickham's, he assumed. The man was clearing out of Meryton.

How best to approach the driver? For once Darcy was thankful for Collins' parson's hat—and for the fact that the wind had dropped, making conversation possible. If only the rain would hold off.

"Evening," he said, lifting his hat to the men on the box. He allowed a Derbyshire lilt to creep into his speech. "Rough night to be traveling."

"Aye, that it is," said one of the men.

"If I weren't a man of the cloth," said Darcy, borrowing Collins' expression, "I'd be carrying a flask to offer. As it is, I'll give a bit of advice."

The driver puffed on his pipe. The ashes in the bowl glowed red.

"I've had dealings with the man you're toting. He's a fine one for talk. I see he's traveling far tonight—clearing out, as it were."

"I wouldn't know," said the driver guardedly.

"Has a habit of leaving debts behind. He'll chouse a working man out his due without batting an eyelash."

"Is that so?"

"If I were you, I wouldn't budge an inch until I was paid in full. Cash, not promissory notes and fine talk. Especially on a night like this."

The two men on the box exchanged glances, and Darcy hid a smile.

"I'd best be off before the rain sets in," he said. "A good journey to ye." He sauntered off down the lane—and none too soon, for as he reached the shadows he heard the door to the coach come open. How much of their exchange had Wickham heard?

Darcy stepped behind a hedge and carefully retraced his steps to the Folly. Collins was almost beside himself.

"There," he whispered urgently, "do you see? Out of nowhere someone came and left those." He indicated two dark shapes near the steps.

"And you did not apprehend him?"

Collins drew himself up. "I was instructed," he said primly, "not to move."

"Did you see who it was?"

"Of course not. I think," Collins added, "that it was a woman. But not Anne, because she ran away again."

Rain was now falling, and over its hiss came the sound of voices—Wickham's and the driver's. Darcy's lips twisted into a smile. So Wickham hadn't paid up. Was he counting on Anne to provide the money? As if that would happen! Anne, like most young women of rank, never carried cash.

But where was Anne? And then light—brilliant and white and blindingly intense—illumined the scene. A moment later everything was black.

Thunder growled and rumbled, and it brought Collins to life. "Lightning! Lightning!" he crowed, and he began to dance about. "Longbourn shall be mine, all mine. Beautiful, beautiful Longbourn!"

Darcy made a lunge for Collins. He must keep the man quiet!

"I shall be a gentleman," Collins rattled on. "I'll have cigars, and a wine cellar, and a man to look after my clothes."

Another flash of lightning. Darcy strained to see. Was someone leaving the house?

"Lightning, beautiful lightning," sang Collins. "O munificent providence, Longbourn is mine." He paused to suck in a breath. "And lovely Elizabeth as well."

"Stow it, Collins," said Darcy curtly. "You aren't back to being yourself yet." He pulled Bingley's dueling pistols from the pockets of his overcoat. "Here," he added. "You might need this."

Collins was shocked to silence. "But," he stammered, "that is a pistol."

Darcy cast his gaze heavenward. "Haven't you heard a word I've said tonight? We aren't playing huzzlecap."

Rolling thunder served as punctuation. "We're going in," said Darcy. "And for once in your life, Collins, be a man and not a mouse."

41 Perils of Men

"Look there!" squealed Collins.

Sure enough, a woman was hurrying from the house. She cast a worried look behind her.

Darcy left the Folly, keeping to the shadows. Slowly he worked his way nearer to the coach.

Wickham was continuing to argue with the driver. Darcy saw him smile and spread his hands, a characteristic gesture. "All in good time, my friend," he heard him bleat.

"There's no time like the present," the driver countered. His stance was aggressive.

The postilion had his hands on his hips. "Do you mean to tell me," he said, "that you won't pay?"

"Have patience," said Wickham. "You're a testy fellow, aren't you?"

"On a cold night in all this rain?" said the postilion. "I should say so. We expect to be paid." He turned to the driver. "Had enough, Bob?"

Apparently the driver had. He grunted assent and stumped to the rear of the coach.

"Hang on," cried Wickham. "What are you doing?"

"Removing your trunk, sir, as you will not—or cannot—pay up."

"No, wait! I-I—"

"George?" said a voice.

Wickham spun round. "Anne!" he cried.

Darcy saw Anne come forward and slip her hand under Wickham's elbow. She gazed trustingly into his face. "We must hurry," she fretted. "Why are we standing here in the rain?"

"Hold a minute, Bob," called the postilion. "Well?" he said to Wickham.

Anne looked from one man to the other. "Is something wrong?"

Wickham moistened his lips. "Anne, dear," he said. "Have you brought the money?"

Darcy saw Anne's smile slip. "Y-yes," she said. "Kitty promised it would be in the satchel. You do have Kitty's satchel?"

Wickham was at a loss. "What satchel?"

Anne began looking about. "She said it would be here at the Folly. Have you—there it is! Over there!"

"What are you—?"

But Anne was running across the lawn. She returned, lugging a valise and hatbox. At once she had it open, digging through the contents. "It's here," she said. "It's got to be. But—"

There were paper banknotes all right, and Anne began to count them. "Ten," Darcy heard her say. "Eleven, twelve..." She turned to Wickham. "There were supposed to be twenty, not twelve. Is it...enough, dearest?"

Wickham did not return her smile.

Anne returned to the valise. "Perhaps the rest is in coins. That must be it—they've fallen to the bottom."

By the light of the coach lamp Darcy could see the panic on Anne's thin face. This comedy was about played out. Darcy stepped into the light and addressed Wickham.

"Quite the romantic gesture, making the lady pay," he remarked. "But then, that is your usual style."

"What the devil?"

"Mr. Collins," cried Anne. "What are *you* doing here?"

"I should be asking the same question," said Darcy. "Kindly return to the house."

Anne stood her ground. "Never!"

"Save your sermons for Sunday," said Wickham.

Darcy turned to face him. "One would think," he said, "that a fellow who is so in love would have found something to pawn." Wickham's watch chain and fob were in clear view. "Once again you're out of luck," Darcy continued. "Anne has no more access to ready cash than Georgiana."

"Georgiana?" said Anne.

Darcy turned to her. "Your intended bridegroom has rather a bad habit of living off of other people's money. Usually women's."

"How dare you!" said Wickham.

He took a swing at Darcy, but the postilion caught his arm. "Strike the Rector, will you?" he growled.

"Mr. Collins," pleaded Anne. "Please go away! What is this to you?"

"Give me the money, Anne," shouted Wickham, attempting to shake free. "For pity's sake."

She tried, but Darcy was too quick. He snatched the banknotes and held them out of reach. "The roads are in foul shape," he remarked. "Were you planning to travel all the way to Gretna? Or was it to be London?"

"Certainly not London," said Anne. She lifted her chin. "Mr. Wickham and I intend to be married, Mr. Collins. Whether you like it or not."

Wickham's ready smile appeared. "Do you know," he said, "you could save us time and trouble by doing the deed for us, Collins."

"Not unless you have a special license," countered Darcy. "But then, you wouldn't. Such a thing is beyond you, both socially and financially."

DARCY BY ANY OTHER NAME

Wickham's insolent smile slipped. Darcy turned to Anne. "And what happens when your mama cuts you out of her will," he said, "which she shall certainly do."

"She would not dare," Anne said hotly.

Darcy turned to Wickham. "You had a sure thing with Georgiana; her inheritance was settled absolutely. Anne's parent, on the other hand, is very much alive. And vindictive, bitterly vindictive."

"Indeed she is," said Collins, stepping forward. "I am in a position to know. And may I say that eloping," he added primly, "is most undignified. What a way to enter a family! Your mother, Miss de Bourgh, will be greatly displeased."

Wickham laughed. "As always, the master of understatement," he said. "Never make a scene, that's your motto. Very well, Darcy," he added, and his eyes narrowed. "How much?"

Collins blinked in surprise. "How much what?"

"How much will you hand over to make me—how shall I say it? Disappear?"

Collins put up his chin. "I do not understand your meaning, sir."

Darcy kept his gaze fixed on Anne. "What Mr. Wickham means, Mr. Darcy," he said distinctly, "is that if you wish to halt this elopement, you must pay him off."

Collins appeared stupefied. "Pay him?" he repeated. "Do you mean with money? Not on your life! If he wants money," he added, "he should work for it."

"Ah, but acquiring money without labor is Wickham's principal talent," said Darcy. "A desire for entitlement, nurtured from infancy. A man born on the manor, but not," he added, "to the manor born."

Wickham rounded on Darcy. "This," he said hotly, "is not your affair."

"I am to stand aside while you defraud yet another relation of Darcy's, is that it?"

Anne looked from one to the other in obvious dismay.

"Might I remind you," said Darcy, "that envy is a sin? A besetting sin in your case, for it persists in spite of the generosity shown you by the Darcy family."

"What generosity?" shouted Wickham.

"Your education, your allowance," Darcy shouted back. "The compensation for the living you refused."

"You call that compensation?" Wickham sneered.

"Do you know," said Darcy, sliding a hand into his pocket, "I ought to have shot you at Ramsgate when I had the chance."

"Ramsgate?" cried Wickham. "What do you know about Ramsgate?"

"More than you think." Darcy brought out Bingley's pistol and cocked it.

"Who are you?" demanded Wickham.

Thunder rumbled, and again the rain began to fall in earnest.

"Collins," ordered Darcy, without taking his gaze from Wickham, "take Anne to the house."

DARCY BY ANY OTHER NAME

Instead of obeying, Collins made a grab for Darcy's arm. "Darcy, no," he cried. "Don't shoot!"

A flash of lightning illumined the garden.

Wickham licked his lips and glanced at the coach. Darcy guessed his thought. "Left it behind on the seat, did you?" he said. "Pity."

"You-you wouldn't shoot an unarmed man!" cried Wickham, his face wet with rain.

"Darcy, no!" cried Collins, above the hiss of the rain. "That's murder."

Darcy cursed silently. The firepan was soaked, meaning that Bingley's pistol was as good as useless. But that did not keep him from leveling it at Wickham.

Anne screamed and so did Collins. Darcy laughed and tossed Bingley's pistol aside. "Firepan's wet, Wickham," he said. "Don't you know anything?"

Nevertheless Wickham made a dive for it.

"We'll finish this," said Darcy, "the old-fashioned way." He took hold of Wickham's lapel and hauled him to his feet. As Collins, Darcy outweighed the man. And as himself, Darcy knew a thing or two about pugilism. The jaw? No, he decided. The nose.

Wickham guessed his purpose. "Not the face!" he screamed.

Darcy kept hold of Wickham and punctuated each blow. "You predatory—rapacious—wastrel," he shouted.

"Help me!" Wickham gasped, looking to the driver and postilion.

But help was not to be found. "Nice right hook, Rector," the postilion remarked.

Wickham kicked at Darcy's shins and worked to squirm out of his coat. Anne began beating Darcy's back with her fists. "Stop, you brute!" she screamed.

A memory flickered, and Darcy's grip tightened. "When were you planning," he shouted to Wickham, "to tell your bride about the tavern girl?"

Anne's assault on Darcy's back ceased. "Tavern girl?" she echoed. "What tavern girl?"

"The one who shared his bed the other night."

Wickham's face was pale, and his nose bled freely. His breathing was labored.

"No doubt he intends," Darcy added, "to finance his by-blows with his wife's money."

"By-blows?" cried Anne. "What do you mean, Mr. Collins?" She clung to Darcy's arm.

He shook her off. "Give me one reason," he shouted at Wickham, "why I should allow you to live."

"Darcy," screamed Collins. "You're a clergyman! A clergyman, not a murderer!"

The air was crackling with energy. Darcy could feel the hair on the back of his head stand on end. There was a roaring sound.

"Darcy!" he heard Collins scream, and the man's fingers tore at his coat. Darcy recoiled for another blow, but lost his footing in the mud. Wickham wiggled free from his grasp.

The sky ripped white. Cannon fire shook the earth in an explosion of sound. Darcy felt his body stiffen. Someone screamed, and something hit Darcy on the back of his head. Down he went, with Collins collapsing on top of him.

There was pain—as if he had been punched—and lightheadedness, but this time Darcy did not lose consciousness. And yet it was odd, for he discovered that he was lying on top of Collins when he could have sworn it was the other way round. Darcy rolled off and staggered to his knees. He realize that he held something—fabric from Collins' black coat.

In the dim light Darcy stared at his hands. These were his own fingers, not Collins,' and there was his signet ring. Darcy released the fabric and out of habit moved the ring to his left hand.

He turned to see Collins' wet and frightened face staring up at him—a face Darcy had seen only in the looking glass.

Darcy felt his insides turn to jelly. He was himself. It was done.

Meanwhile he could hear Anne crying out for George Wickham. Apparently the man had run off.

The driver and the postilion bent over him. "By Jove," one of them said. "You're alive! You're both alive!"

"Never seen anything like it," said the other. "Not in all my days."

Darcy marshalled his wits. The sooner the coach was gone from Netherfield, the better. "You deserve—to be paid," he managed to say. Sure enough, there in the mud were Kitty's fallen banknotes. Two one-pound notes were all that were left. Trust Wickham to land on his feet! But two pounds were enough. "If you will kindly remove the person's trunk," Darcy said, and held out the notes. "I take it he is no longer here?"

The driver did not need to be told twice. "He's gone all right," he remarked. "Went haring down the lane."

"Thank God for that," Darcy said.

Anne now stood beside the coach, wet and forlorn and weeping. Darcy gathered his strength. It would be up to him to see her safely into the house.

Collins, meanwhile, had scrambled to his feet. As Darcy looked on he patted his stomach, his cheeks, and his thighs. Right there in the mud he spun in a wobbly circle. "Oh, joy!" he sang to the heavens above. "I am myself!"

Lightning flashed and in the distance, thunder rolled. The storm was moving on.

"Yes!" screamed Collins to the clouds. "Go, go! Wreak your havoc on someone else!"

Out of the gloom of the garden a figure came rushing forward—a woman, hampered by sodden skirts. "William," she called out. "Oh, William!"

Darcy turned, stunned to hear his beloved's voice. "Elizabeth," he whispered.

"Oh, that this should happen twice!" she cried, and she ran straight for Collins.

Like a dazed man Collins opened his arms and received her eager embrace. Above Elizabeth's bowed head Darcy caught a glimpse of Collins' face and quickly looked away. The man's smug expression was a punch to the gut.

Yes, it was done; he was himself. But his part was not played, was it? For Darcy now discovered that Kitty stood beside Anne, comforting her.

Kitty and Elizabeth. How much had they seen?

Darcy approached the driver. "Take these women," he said, "and this gentleman to Longbourn House."

It was on the tip of his tongue to order the men to remain silent about this night's events. On second thought, why conceal Wickham's infamy?

"You did a good deed tonight," he added, "in thwarting this elopement. The young woman is an innocent, and Wickham a rogue."

"No need to tell us that, sir," said the postilion. "The Rector, he's a bonny fighter."

"Always enjoy a good mill," the postilion added. He indicated Wickham's trunk. "Want anything done with that?"

"Not a blessed thing," said Darcy. "Let it lie in the mud until it rots."

All that was left was to part Kitty from Anne, and then to lead Elizabeth, who was arm and arm with Collins, to the waiting coach.

Elizabeth was scrupulously polite. "Thank you, Mr. Darcy," she said crisply, without meeting his eyes.

Darcy looked away. "I—am sorry about your coat, Collins," he said. "I'll have Holdsworth send another."

It took effort to ignore the man's answering smirk.

"Dear William," he heard Elizabeth say, "are you much hurt? Oh, your poor, bruised hands!" The door was pulled to, and the driver climbed onto the box.

As the coach moved away, Darcy held back a sigh. "Come, Anne," he said to his cousin, offering his arm for support—a heroic gesture, considering how poorly he felt.

"Oh, Fitzwilliam," she said, collapsing against him. "George is not gone, not altogether. He is waiting for me. He shall come back, he shall!"

"I'm afraid not, my dear."

"But he loved me! He said so many times!"

"Did he?"

There was a pause. "He did—once or twice. And it was true, I know it! He could not have been lying!"

Darcy put an arm around Anne's thin shoulder. "He said the same to Georgiana."

"Georgiana?" faltered Anne. "Then it was true?"

"He was after her fortune," Darcy said gently. "And yours."

Anne began to cry.

Bless Holdsworth, in a pocket Darcy found a clean handkerchief to offer Anne. "At the time," he said, "Georgiana thought her heart was broken. She has since recovered, and so shall you."

"Never!" There was a pause. "What will Mother say?"

"Not a thing, if I can help it."

Anne looked up at him with wide eyes. "But—"

"You've learned a painful lesson. I do not see where Aunt Catherine comes into it."

"But if Mother were to find out," Anne said. "If she were to discover us tonight, together like this..."

Anne fell silent, and then added, "Do you—think we ought to marry after all?"

Darcy drew a long breath. "No," he said quietly. "We do not suit, Anne. As for your mother, in truth there is nothing to discover."

42 Give Me Leave

William slept late that morning, and Elizabeth felt his absence keenly. The funeral would take place in the afternoon, and until that time she knew to expect a steady stream of callers. Eventually, however, she sent Ned to check on him. He returned with the news that Mr. Collins was snoring heartily. "Rattling the windowpanes he is," was the way Ned put it.

Lydia dissolved into giggles. "Poor Lizzy," she said. "That does not bode well for your married life. Bedchambers at opposite ends of the house."

None of the others laughed.

Kitty drew near "Last night, Lizzy," she whispered. "You remember, when Mr. Darcy tore Mr. Collins' coat?

And because of the rain he was covered with mud? Perhaps Mr. Collins has not come down because, why, he has no clothes to wear."

"Kitty, "said Elizabeth warningly.

Lydia pounced on this. "Do tell," she cried. "Don't keep secrets!"

Elizabeth swallowed a sigh. Could not Lydia moderate her behavior for even one day?

Fortunately a package arrived to divert Lydia's interest. It was wrapped in brown paper and addressed to Mr. Collins. There was also a flat packet for Kitty. Mrs. Hill disclosed that both had come from Netherfield Park.

Of course Lydia was intrigued. "A love note?" she cried. "From whom? Not," she added laughingly, "from Mr. Darcy. And what is this? Mr. Bingley has sent nothing for Jane?"

"Mr. Bingley is coming to the funeral, Lydia," Kitty burst out. "What more do you want?"

Elizabeth took hold of the packet and guided Kitty out of the drawing room. "Upstairs," she ordered. "Into my bedchamber."

"But—!" protested Kitty. "You must give it me! It's from Anne, I just know it."

"The less anyone hears about Anne, the better," said Elizabeth, following Kitty up the staircase. "I meant what I said, not one word about last night. Especially to Lydia."

Kitty looked unhappy. She went into Elizabeth's room and sat on the bed. "I do not see why," she said.

"It's not like Mr. Collins killed anyone. And Mr. Wickham ran away."

Elizabeth closed the door. "Think of Anne's reputation," she said. "That mother of hers is sure to hear of it. How would you feel if you were the source of her information?"

"But—!" said Kitty.

"Then too, your part was hardly honorable. Stealing the household money for Anne."

"I did not steal," Kitty protested. "I merely...borrowed." She paused. "All the same, I do hope we shall see Mr. Wickham again. Do you think he will call after the funeral?"

"No," said Elizabeth. "I expect that he has left Meryton for good." She passed Kitty the packet and stood by, with her arms folded across her chest.

To Kitty's wonder, the packet contained four five-pound banknotes. "They're from Anne, bless her," Kitty cried. "I knew she would pay me back."

Elizabeth was not so sure. How had Anne come by twenty pounds?

Kitty was searching through the banknotes. "I was hoping she would send me a note. Although," Kitty went on, "isn't it odd? This is not Anne's handwriting."

Kitty gathered the banknotes and went out, and Elizabeth wandered to the window. How weary she was of Anne and Mr. Wickham and all the rest. She had been able to explain away the wet clothing, although she doubted that Hill was fooled. William had been no help.

He'd stumbled up the stairs to bed with scarcely more than a hasty good night.

Then again, she could hardly blame him. After his angry confrontation with Wickham and the nearness of the lightning strike, he must have been as spent as she.

A shaft of sunlight came through the window glass. It would be a dry afternoon for the funeral.

Elizabeth felt her throat constrict. How she longed to hear her father's voice, or to trip into his bookroom to ask a question or share a wry observation!

As it was, she was needed downstairs. The last thing she wished to do was converse politely with callers, but she must support her sisters. Weary though she was, she could do that much.

As she was leaving the bedchamber, Elizabeth remembered her book. She could not bear to open one of her father's books, but perhaps her half-finished novel? She found it in the top drawer of her bureau. Wedged between its pages was a folded letter, well-sealed.

Elizabeth's heart gave a thump. William's letter! Eagerly she broke the seals to find three pages in beautiful, precise writing. At once she began to read.

Elizabeth, My Beloved,

Will you take it amiss if I confess that what you hold in your hands is my very first love letter?

Elizabeth could not help but smile, picturing this reserved and private man bashfully writing of his love. Was he blushing as he wrote the words?

Be not alarmed. I do not intend to plague you with an execrable sonnet (which you will be obliged to admire) nor will I burst into song.

She nearly laughed for joy. Today of all days she most needed his sense of humor.

I simply want you to know, my dear, that in these precious weeks you have come to mean more to me than life itself.

Such delightful words. Even when the door banged open and Mary came in, Elizabeth continued to smile.

"It's Mama, Lizzy," said Mary in a rush. "She's asking for you and for Hill, and she does not wish me to read to her or anything!" And then Mary did the unthinkable, she burst into tears.

At once William's letter was put aside. "Never mind Mama," Elizabeth said gently. "This has been a trying day for all of us. Aunt Phillips will soon be here. Have you had breakfast?"

"Not yet, but—"

"Go down at once; you'll feel better after you've eaten. And send Hill up with a fresh pot of tea for Mama." Mary did not need to be told twice.

Sometime later, with Aunt Phillips installed in her mother's bedchamber, Elizabeth came down to find Jane alone in the drawing room.

"Mr. Collins has come down at last," Jane said, speaking low, "but I must warn you, Lizzy, he is not feeling well. I heard him complain to Mrs. Hill about breakfast."

This did not sound like William. "What could be wrong? Did he say?"

Jane looked reluctant. "Something about a lack of variety on the sideboard. I daresay he slept poorly and has a head-ache."

Elizabeth remembered William's flaming row with Mr. Wickham and his bruised and battered hands. Of course he was not feeling well.

"I ought to have relieved Mary," Jane went on, "for you know how Mama is. But I did not like to leave Kitty and Lydia to receive callers."

"One can see why," said Elizabeth wryly. Her youngest sisters were nowhere to be seen.

Her gaze dropped to William's enticing letter. She found a seat on the sofa and drew it out.

"Lizzy!" whispered Jane.

Elizabeth looked up. The drawing room door was open and William stood at the threshold. "Good morning, fair ladies," he said.

Elizabeth's brows went up. A formal greeting to be sure, but why did his smile seem forced?

"You look very smart this morning," she told him, for he wore a new blue coat. In fact, all of his clothing was new. Not quite appropriate for a funeral, but he did look well. "Have you been shopping?"

He wrinkled his nose at her. "Certainly not."

"Your coat is very fine," she said.

"Yes," he said, "it is, rather." He was now circling the drawing room, taking in the way it had been draped for mourning. Elizabeth heard him click his tongue. "I see that no expense has been spared here."

Elizabeth was stung into replying. "There is nothing of which you did not approve."

"Apparently I was in a generous frame of mind."

"I am sorry you are feeling poorly," Elizabeth said. "Would you care for coffee? It often helps with the headache."

"If what is made here can even be called that," he grumbled.

"You are a grumpy bear, aren't you?" said Elizabeth, and she came over to plant a kiss on his cheek.

He made a sound that was rather like a giggle. "What's all this?" he said, pointing to the book she held. The pages of his letter were clearly visible.

"A book."

"No, this." His fingers ruffled the letter's pages. Surely he was funning, surely he could see that it was his own! But although his lips smiled, there was no sparkle in his eyes.

"A letter from a gentleman," Elizabeth teased.

"Which gentleman would that be?"

"Does it matter?" she said playfully.

Apparently it did, for his brows descended. Almost she confessed it to be his own letter, but something held her back. He just stood there, looking at her with unsmiling eyes.

Elizabeth felt her head swim. "If—you will excuse me, please," she stammered. Her father's bookroom adjoined the drawing room. Elizabeth walked away from William, opened the door and went in. Just as quickly she closed the door behind her.

The fireplace was cold, but as before, her father's presence was everywhere. This room had now become her sanctuary—but from what? Surely not from William! Wearily she slipped into her father's chair and unfolded her letter.

At its essence love is truthful, and I will now disclose a circumstance that I can neither understand nor change. I have made several paltry attempts to speak of it, but how can anyone explain the incomprehensible?

Yes, William had hinted at some mystery. Perhaps he was impatient because she had not yet read this. She continued reading.

I shall do my best to present the facts as I experienced them and must trust you bear with my inadequacies.

Someone was scratching at the bookroom door, probably Lydia. Elizabeth ignored this and read on.

To begin, I must take you back to the ball at Netherfield and the storm...

The door was pushed open, and reluctantly Elizabeth looked up. It was William.

"I—am reading my letter," she said lamely.

His brows went up. "As I see." He closed the door behind him and came to stand before the desk. Apparently he was still unhappy. Elizabeth folded the letter and pushed it under the blotter.

"I would like an explanation, if you please, as to your presence at Netherfield last night," he said. "A deplorable happenstance, I must say, and *most* inappropriate for my affianced bride." Incredibly, he began making a clucking noise.

Elizabeth could only stare. "How was I to know that Kitty was pledged to help Anne? I could hardly allow her to tramp all the way to Netherfield, at midnight, alone."

"You ought to have thought of my consequence, dear Elizabeth. After all, I am now an influential member of the community."

"I did what I thought was best. I am sorry that you do not like it."

"Moreover," he continued, as if she had not spoken, "you put yourself in grave danger of illness. It is most unwise to be out on a cold and rainy night, drenched to the skin as you were."

"As we all were," countered Elizabeth. "Given your mood, I am surprised that you were present at the elopement at all."

"It was Darcy," he protested. "He compelled me. You cannot think," he added, "that I would demean myself by being party to such a scheme."

Elizabeth raised her chin. "I thought your purpose was to rescue Anne de Bourgh. And besides," she added, "doubtless you have earned the gratitude Lady Catherine de Bourgh."

"But that's just it! Darcy insists that her ladyship must never know! My effort was therefore wasted."

"Unless you count as unimportant Anne's rescue."

He hesitated. "Of—course not."

"And is it not best to do the right thing in the eyes of God?" she went on. "Even if your good deed is never acknowledged by others?"

She saw him bristle. His eyes, which she once thought to be so large and expressive, held no warmth.

"I do not see why we must argue," she added crossly.

At once he put out a hand. Elizabeth was at a loss. Was she supposed to take hold of it? She remained where she was.

"Indeed, I do apologize," he said, and he made a little bow. "That wretched breakfast put me out of temper."

He had many reasons to be irritable, but instead of sympathizing with him, Elizabeth said, "What was wrong with breakfast? It was no different today than any other."

He did not reply to this. And then, as she looked on, his fingers began to twine and twist together in a hand washing motion. Elizabeth was struck by a vague memory. He had done this when he first came to Longbourn. Yes, and her father had remarked on it.

What was wrong with William?

The look in Elizabeth's eyes was distinctly unfriendly, calling to mind Caroline Bingley's acid glare. He was relieved when Elizabeth went out of the bookroom.

But Collins had no intention of leaving. He'd long wished to examine Mr. Bennet's inner sanctum, but the man had never invited him in. Wasn't it interesting how events had turned out? Mr. Bennet's coffin would soon be taken to the churchyard, and this room was now Collins' very own.

Even so he hesitated. He'd heard the sound of carriage wheels earlier, and there were voices in the drawing room. He put a cautious ear to the door. Yes, here were callers, a windfall. His cousins would be occupied for at least a quarter of an hour.

Collins cautiously lowered his bulk into Mr. Bennet's desk chair. He'd felt this same exhilaration when he took possession of the Hunsford parsonage, before Lady Catherine put her oar in and began ordering him about. But her ladyship had no claim on him now. He was a gentleman indeed, answerable to no one.

There would be time enough when he was feeling stronger to rearrange furniture or take stock of the titles on the shelves. But here was a prime opportunity to examine the contents of Mr. Bennet's desk.

What interested Collins was the amount of Longbourn's income. He'd seen the table Mrs. Bennet kept and the quality of the family's apparel. Surely Longbourn brought in two thousand a year, a heady thought. He began to open drawers.

Presently he discovered the money box and ledger. The box was unlocked, and at once Collins counted the banknotes. Twenty pounds, a boon! He ran a finger down the ledger page and discovered that there was too much money here. Surely the household budget would not miss five pounds?

Then again, whose money had Darcy been spending? His! The remaining banknotes beckoned, and Collins surrendered to impulse. After all, who would question the master of Longbourn? He rolled the banknotes and put them in his pocket.

As for the rest, there was nothing of interest. Mr. Bennet's will, an enticing document, was surely kept at his solicitor's office. Collins closed the final drawer and sat back. To inaugurate his possession of this room he would smoke a cigar. Sadly, he had brought none with him from Netherfield. If only he had known how last night's events would turn out!

Yet for the most part Collins was satisfied. He'd seen the way Elizabeth had looked at Darcy, and it was thrilling to think she had such passionate feelings. It was her father's death that had her out of sorts, that was all.

Collins pushed back the chair and was about to stand when he noticed the blotter and the folded pages beneath. Elizabeth's letter! Moistening his lips, Collins unfolded the sheets. The hand he recognized at once as Darcy's. Quickly he turned to the last page and swore under his breath. Darcy had signed it as himself!

Collins read the letter through three times. A detestable account and one that would ruin his plans for matrimonial bliss. It was abundantly clear that it was Darcy she loved, not him. And if she read this letter she would know that.

But had Elizabeth read it?

No, he did not think so, nor did he think she should. Why burden her with information that was no longer true?

At once he pocketed the letter, but it made a bulge. On second thought, why carry it on his person and risk discovery?

A scraping of chairs in the drawing room confirmed his decision. Collins scanned the bookroom for a hiding place. Not in a drawer or in a book, it must be somewhere she would not think to look. For Elizabeth would search for the letter, of this he was certain. And then

Collins noticed that one of Mr. Bennet's framed prints was off-kilter. The corners of his mouth turned up.

With a swift look to the closed door, Collins removed the picture from the wall. The back was not sealed with paper, and he found a way to wedge the letter into the frame. Again he looked over his shoulder. The voices in the drawing room were louder; the guests were leaving. He must hurry.

Just as he returned the picture to the wall he heard the door come open. He hastily arranged his features in time to greet Elizabeth. She went at once to the desk.

"Have you seen my letter?" she said.

The anxiety in her voice was not pleasing, but Collins had his answer ready. "Of course I have," he said. "You were reading it."

"I—seem to have mislaid it."

"Perhaps it is in your book?" he said. "If you will excuse me, I have something to talk over with your mother."

Elizabeth did not lift her gaze from the desk. "Mama should not be disturbed."

"I have something of a private nature to discuss," he said, "and it cannot wait."

Before she had a chance to ask more questions, Collins went out of the bookroom. And when he knocked at Mrs. Bennet's door he was as polite as he knew how to be. Mrs. Phillips answered, looking harassed.

"If you please," he said, "I would like a few minutes of Mrs. Bennet's time. Just a few minutes, mind."

"Who is it?" he heard Mrs. Bennet shrill.

Mrs. Phillips turned. "It's Mr. Collins," she whispered.

Truly, if the need were not urgent, Collins would certainly go away. But the growing crisis lent him courage. He pushed past Mrs. Phillips and boldly walked into the room.

Mrs. Bennet let out a scream of protest. "Mercy, Mr. Collins, this is my bedchamber! Is nothing sacred?"

"I apologize for the intrusion," said Collins, wringing his hands in spite of himself. "I have something of a private nature to discuss with you."

"Can it not wait until after the funeral?"

"I fear not. You see, I must write to the Archbishop of Canterbury this very afternoon," he said.

Up came Mrs. Bennet from her reclining position. "What did you say?"

Collins looked significantly at Mrs. Phillips. "As to that, I would prefer to speak with you privately."

"My sister," said Mrs. Bennet, "is not to be sent out like a dog. I demand that she remain. Now then, what have you to say?"

He drew a long breath. "Merely this: Elizabeth and I must be married as soon as possible."

He knew to expect a wail of protest. "So soon after Mr. Bennet's death?" she cried. "Impossible!"

"Of course we must be married," he said crossly, "and it is for that reason that I am sending for a special license. How else can we continue to live in the same house?"

"But your engagement has not been announced," protested Mrs. Bennet. "There will be talk if you marry without a proper period of mourning."

Collins heard the door come open. "What talk is that, Mama?" Elizabeth said.

"Nothing that you need worry about, my darling," Collins said hastily.

"Six months is not too long to wait," Mrs. Bennet insisted.

"Jane and Mr. Bingley should certainly do so," Collins agreed. "But we cannot, nor should we continue to share the same residence. If you are concerned about the cost or inconvenience of the license," he went on, "I am well able to afford it. Nor is procuring a license as difficult as it appears. If the full amount is remitted with the request, the Archbishop of Canterbury's office has been known to grant favors for clergymen."

"What sort of favors?" Elizabeth wanted to know.

"Mercy, Lizzy," Mrs. Bennet cried out. "Mr. Collins wants you to be married by special license! This very week!"

"Or sooner," said Collins. He gave Elizabeth his best smile.

"No," she said flatly. "That will not do at all."

Collins' smile grew taut. "I beg your pardon," he said politely and turned to Mrs. Bennet. "I had no idea that you and your daughters were prepared to live elsewhere."

"Live elsewhere?" shrilled Mrs. Bennet. "Why, where would we go?"

Collins spread his hands. "You could take rooms in Meryton," he suggested. "Or your sister will surely take you in." He gave a friendly nod to Mrs. Phillips.

"All of you?" Aunt Phillips sputtered.

"William," said Elizabeth, "I thought you were to return to Hunsford for six months. That is what you told me."

That was what Darcy had told her; it sounded like something he would say. But Collins was not Darcy. Moreover, he did not care for Elizabeth's tone of voice. "Even the best of plans change," he pointed out primly.

"Do they indeed?" said Mrs. Bennet. "Then perhaps you can change Lizzy's mind about attending the funeral."

Collins could not believe his ears. "You shall do no such thing." A show of authority was important, especially with a fiancée.

"But we already agreed that I would," protested Elizabeth. "Jane and I shall be seated in the church before the procession even leaves the house. No one will notice us."

By now Collins was angry. "I am the head of this family," he said. "And I will not have you bring reproach on my name. Especially since it is about to become yours."

"But Father deserves to have someone from his family present at his funeral."

"And what am I?" said Collins. "This is my final word, Elizabeth. I am extremely displeased."

And with that he took himself out of the room. A lesser man would have slammed the door, but Collins was mindful to shut it with a civilized click. He heard their voices within, arguing. It would be some time before Elizabeth could extricate herself.

Down the stairs to the bookroom he went, taking the treads two at a time. Before he sent his request to Doctor's Commons—by express, it could not be helped— there was something he must do.

There was no fire in the bookroom, but Collins had seen a tinderbox. He removed a spunk and went into the drawing room for a light. Mary and Jane were there, but Collins ignored them.

Back to the bookroom he crept, as anxious thoughts multiplied. Were there footfalls on the stairs? Would he be interrupted? With trembling fingers he removed Darcy's letter from its hiding place. He gave an uneasy glance over his shoulder. Should he blockade the door? Or would that give a misleading impression?

For he was guilty of nothing, nothing at all. And this letter could do a world of harm.

With a hammering heart Collins knelt before the hearth, crumpled the pages, and threw them in.

"Hurry, hurry," he whispered, with beads of perspiration gathering on his brow. It took some time for the flame to catch and gain strength.

He would have remained to watch the pages burn to ash, but he had a letter to write.

43   Tolling the Bell

The morning wore into afternoon. Mr. and Mrs. Gardiner arrived from London, much to everyone's relief, and now Elizabeth and her sisters had only to wait. Soon the bell would begin to toll, summoning the mourners, and the procession would begin. Even now the funeral hearse with its black horses waited discreetly in the paddock.

William Collins stood before the fire in the drawing room, warming his hands. "Gloves and cloaks and who knows what else," he muttered. "Such expense."

Elizabeth pretended not to hear. Of course these must be provided for the bearers. Why must he complain? She kept an eye on the front windows. If only Mr. Bingley would come!

Her uncle had also heard, and he stepped forward. "I have you to thank, Mr. Collins, for seeing to the arrangements. If my business affairs had not been so pressing, I would have handled them myself."

Mr. Collins' cheeks turned pink with pleasure. "It was nothing," he said, stammering a little. "The merest exertion. You must understand that a man in my position," and he paused to indicate the cassock and surplice he wore, "is not precisely a novice in these matters."

"You spared our ladies much trouble and worry," said Mr. Gardiner. "I commend you."

"Anything for the ladies. Within reason, of course, that is to say, within the bounds of common sense and practicality. Not that I mean anything against my cousins, but really. The expense!"

"In my opinion, a worthwhile outlay," said Mr. Gardiner quietly.

Conversation moved on to the dry weather and the condition of the roads. "A very good thing for my surplice," said Mr. Collins, "if the roads are free of mud."

The sound of the chaise-and-four was almost a relief. "Come, Jane," said Elizabeth, rising from her seat. "I believe Mr. Bingley is here."

Mr. Collins made a noise. "You insist on attending the funeral?" he said. "Even though you know my opinion?"

"I shall attend, just as we agreed."

Mr. Collins turned to Elizabeth's uncle. "Reason with her, convince her," he said. "For she refuses to mind me."

"Lizzy," said Mr. Gardiner, "do reconsider. You have been through so much already. You must be worn to the bone."

"Jane and I shall arrive at the church long before the—" Elizabeth broke off. How could she say the word casket? "Before anyone else," she finished.

"Dear Uncle," added Jane, "we shall come directly home after service. Here is Mr. Bingley. We should not keep him waiting."

"Elizabeth," said Mr. Collins, "I demand that you remain."

She gave him a look, took Jane's arm, and went out. Nevertheless, her hands were shaking as she drew on her gloves and fastened her cloak.

"Poor Mr. Collins," said Jane. "He must be nervous because of the eulogy."

Elizabeth was out the door almost before her sister could finish her sentence. "Lizzy," cried Jane, "you've forgotten your hat!"

"Good afternoon," began Mr. Bingley, but Elizabeth stalked past him to the chaise.

"The nerve of William Collins!"

Jane came rushing after with the hat. "Mr. Collins is making a fuss," she told him. "We'd best be on our way."

At once Mr. Bingley called an order to his driver, stepped in after Jane, and pulled the door to.

Presently Jane said, "Let me help you with your hat, dearest. You've tied the ribbon all wrong."

Elizabeth surrendered it to her sister. "It does not matter how I look," she said. "Why must William walk to church with the mourners? Why must he deliver the eulogy?"

Mr. Bingley said nothing, looking from Jane to Elizabeth.

"Because of his position as rector," said Jane mildly. "It is only natural that he join the processional with Dr. Bentley. After all, this could well be his last act as a clergyman."

"I sincerely hope so," Elizabeth flashed. "And I hope he mires his precious cassock in the mud."

She saw her sister and Charles Bingley exchange a look. "Surely you do not mean that," said Jane.

Elizabeth felt her throat constrict. "Why should he suddenly care for pomp and ceremony?" she said roughly. "When he specifically promised—"

Elizabeth could not continue. William had promised to sit beside her during service, to be a support. Why had he suddenly changed his mind?

The remainder of the drive was accomplished in silence. As they pulled up before the church, the bells began to toll.

Elizabeth fled from the chaise as soon as she was able and hurried inside. She stood shivering in the narthex.

Surprisingly, Mr. Bingley took the lead. "Come," he whispered and led them up the side aisle.

He was particular about the seating. He went in first, placing himself on the center aisle, then Jane, and then Elizabeth. Elizabeth understood it. He wished to be a support to Jane by sitting beside her, but neither did he like to separate Elizabeth from her sister. Such kindness! And then she recalled that Charles Bingley had lost both father and mother.

They sat quietly for some time. The rays of the late afternoon sun lit the stained glass windows. Elizabeth studied the colored patterns as they traveled across the walls and pews and floor.

The sanctuary was cold but not silent. Above the tolling of the bell Elizabeth could hear the organ being opened. She squeezed her eyes shut. By now the mourners would be departing from the house and with them her father's casket.

He was leaving his beloved Longbourn for the last time!

Elizabeth could scarcely breathe. Perhaps her uncle had been right, perhaps this was too much. But there was no turning back now. She stole a glance at Jane. She and Mr. Bingley sat shoulder-to-shoulder, talking somberly.

Elizabeth's eyes found the floor. The space beside her on the pew was conspicuously empty. The bells continued to toll, louder now, clanging with a new intensity. Of course. The doors in the narthex were open.

Presently the organist began to play, and Elizabeth steeled herself for what was to come. After a long while there was a muffled commotion. Down the center aisle came Dr. Bentley and Mr. Collins. Behind them would come the cloaked bearers with the casket.

There was a movement; she saw Mr. Bingley reach to cover Jane's black-gloved hands with one of his. Elizabeth's gaze slid to her own lap, and her fingers laced tightly together. If William would not be here to hold her hand, then she must hold her own.

Down the aisle came the casket bearers, shouldering their burden, and after them the pall bearers. With solemnity the black velvet pall was laid across the casket. Elizabeth wished to look away but found that she could not.

Even though he had been lying in state in the parlor, this was different. A cold sensation sent icy tendrils curling round her heart. Soon her beloved father would be laid to rest in the churchyard. Would William Collins, a man her father cordially disliked, be the first one to toss soil into the grave? Would he be the one to say, "Ashes to ashes, dust to dust"?

Behind her the mourners filed in and took their seats. Elizabeth did not turn to see, but she could sense that there were many. Her father was both liked and respected.

DARCY BY ANY OTHER NAME

She now discovered that tears were rolling down her cheeks; she dried them with gloved fingers. Her handkerchief was in her reticule, but in her haste to depart it had been left behind.

Something white appeared at the corner of her vision. A folded lawn handkerchief, held by a black-gloved hand.

The space beside her was no longer vacant. Startled, Elizabeth looked up to discover Mr. Darcy sitting there. He appeared pale and unwell, but there he was. How mortifying for him to find her like this!

"Please, Miss Elizabeth. Take it."

Was Mr. Darcy whispering? Here in church the man was whispering to her?

"*I am the resurrection and the life,*" Dr. Bentley's voice called out. "*He that believeth in Me, though he were dead, yet shall he live.*"

The service was beginning. Wordlessly Elizabeth took the handkerchief and dried her eyes.

"*Blessed—are those who—mourn,*" another man called out, with careful intonation. This was William Collins' pulpit voice, heard for the first time. Elizabeth found that she much preferred Dr. Bentley's simple declaration. But Mr. Collins was not finished. "*For they— shall be—comforted.*"

Oh, she could not bear it, she simply could not! How could she sit and listen to him speak about her father, a man of whom he knew nothing? And in such condescending tones! Her breathing became labored; she struggled to conceal it. Not only from the congregation, but most especially from Mr. Darcy.

Dr. Bentley bid the mourners welcome and led the first prayer.

Elizabeth bowed her head, but when the prayer was over her gaze slid sideways. Mr. Darcy held a prayer book and it was open. This was a surprise. She never thought of Mr. Darcy as devout. Perhaps he was merely dutiful. Yes that was it, he was dutiful.

And yet like Charles Bingley Mr. Darcy had lost both parents. For some reason Elizabeth had the impression that he had been fond of them. But that could not be right. How could she know such an intimate thing?

"And now," she heard Dr. Bentley say, "we shall hear from the Reverend Collins, late of Hunsford Parish, who shall be residing among us at Longbourn House."

"Dearly—beloved," said William Collins in unctuous tones.

Why must he pause so often?

"We are here today—to commemorate the life—of—of—"

Why had he stopped? Elizabeth glanced up, caught by his expression of uncertainty. Did he not remember her father's name?

"—Mr., er, Bennet. And to commend his soul— to the Almighty, the Maker—of heaven and earth."

There was more, much more. What was worse, she could feel Mr. Darcy's searching gaze. Why was he staring at her? Abruptly she rose to her feet.

"Miss Elizabeth," he whispered. "Is anything wrong?"

"Lizzy?" whispered Jane.

Elizabeth pushed past Mr. Darcy, knocking the prayer book from his lap. It hit the floor with a bang. She could feel the gaze of everyone present.

She fled up the side aisle. After a pause Mr. Collins continued with his message, his elongated vowels echoing from the walls. At last Elizabeth reached the narthex, pulled open the heavy door, and stumbled out.

Now she had done it, the very thing she did not mean to do. She had called attention to herself and made a scene. She pressed her back against the outer wall of the building. It would be dark soon. If only she could stop shivering!

She heard the door open and close, and she resolutely turned away. This would be William Collins come to scold her.

"Miss Elizabeth, are you ill? May I see you home?" The voice was gentle, and it belonged to Mr. Darcy.

Elizabeth was struck speechless. "I—am well, thank you," she managed to say. Polite, she was honor-bound to be polite. He was only Mr. Darcy, but he deserved that much.

"You do not look well," he said. "And you are cold." He began to strip off his coat. Was he planning to give it to her?

"Stop!" Elizabeth cried out. "I have shamed my family enough without you adding to it."

"But you are cold." His voice was surprisingly compassionate, and somehow this was familiar. But that could not be right. Mr. Darcy was never kind.

"I care nothing for the cold," she nearly shouted. "Nothing, do you understand?" She moved away.

He followed. "Let me take you home," he said. "You should not remain out here."

"Nor should I be seen in your carriage! Please, I must go back inside. He will have finished by now."

"He?"

There was a pause. How could Elizabeth answer? She closed her lips and turned away.

"Do you mean Mr. Collins?"

There was an edge to Mr. Darcy's voice now, and Elizabeth bit back a smile. She'd been mistaken about his newfound compassion. He was now his usual self.

"Of—course not," she told him. This was a lie, but she could not bear to say the truth.

"If you will kindly excuse me?" Elizabeth turned on her heel and pulled open the church door.

This time Mr. Darcy did not follow. Just before the door swung shut she thought she heard a sigh.

44 My Reasons I'll Own

"Your cigars, sir," said Holdsworth. With precision he placed the humidor at the corner of the bureau.

Darcy turned sharply in his chair; the sudden movement made his head swim. "So early in the day?"

Holdsworth hesitated. "Just so, sir," he said and went out.

Darcy compressed his lips. Collins and his smoking habit. What else had the man managed to do, besides drink the wine cellar dry? Within a short time, the man had alienated almost every member of Bingley's staff.

And then there were the friends Darcy had made as Collins. Last night he took dinner in his rooms, prompting a visit from Fleming. The man's examination was precise and thorough, and he'd taken his leave with a tight, polite smile. This from a man who had been his friend!

Collins' friend, Darcy reminded himself. Gilbert Fleming was Collins' friend, not his.

Darcy returned to his letter, a message of condolence for Mrs. Bennet. He would deliver it later, after he redeemed Kitty's necklace.

Presently he pushed back his chair and stretched his stiff limbs. If only his mind were not alive with scenes from Longbourn! Kitty's wan face and Mary's solemn grief; Lydia's noise and Jane's gentle patience. And Elizabeth? Yes, Elizabeth. His one and only love.

What pain was in her eyes last night! How he longed to enfold her in his arms and protect her! But irritation was present in those eyes as well. What had he done to enrage her? Why did she treat him with coldness? Hadn't she read his letter?

Of course she had, but how could he be certain? He could scarcely ask such a thing at her father's funeral. For if she had not read it, how could he confess that he was Collins?

Or rather, that he had been Collins.

If, on the other hand, she had read it, there were two possibilities. Either she did not believe him, or else she had decided to wash her hands of him.

The latter was all too likely.

The somber reception following the funeral he had avoided. He knew what those were like. Elizabeth was already fatigued, and he did not wish to add to her discomfort.

As for the immediate future, God only knew what Collins would do. It was too much to hope that he would allow a decent interval before taking possession of Longbourn. Would he make good his threat to send his cousins away?

If this were so, would Elizabeth feel obliged to marry the man? The woman Darcy knew would never do this. But Elizabeth was now vulnerable in ways she had never been before.

Just as he'd been vulnerable as Collins.

Darcy's eyes found the floor. Mrs. Bennet's five thousand pounds, invested at four percent, would bring an income of two hundred a year. How would so little support Mrs. Bennet and her daughters?

There was a rattle of the door latch, and before Darcy could respond Caroline Bingley came in. Behind her was a footman with a loaded tray.

"Good day, Mr. Darcy," she called, pushing the door fully open. "Time for our morning tea!"

Darcy glanced at the clock and then at Miss Bingley. Tea in his bedchamber? He politely rose to his feet, hating the way even mild exertion made his head throb. "Rather early, is it not?"

"But such is our custom," she said smoothly. "Do you not recall?"

Collins again. What more had the man done?

From the corner Miss Bingley boldly brought forward a dumb-waiter. Darcy gave a start. What was that doing here?

"Do sit down," she said. "Mr. Fleming tells us you are very much better. He says you are like your former self."

What did Fleming know about his former self? And what was behind Miss Bingley's coy smile?

"I have brought the latest London papers for your perusal," she added.

"Thank you," said Darcy. "But I prefer to read them in the library." In truth, he did not feel up to reading anything. If only he could shake this cursed weakness!

He saw Miss Bingley hesitate. "What you need," she said brightly, "is a nice cup of tea." She selected a cup and saucer. "Yes, a nice cup of tea to settle your stomach."

Did she think him a child? With growing annoyance Darcy watched her pour out. "Less milk, please," he said. "And no sugar."

Miss Bingley gave a forced laugh. "Now, now, Mr. Darcy," she said. "As if I do not know how you take your tea these days."

Darcy narrowed his eyes. "No sugar, please," he repeated.

Her response was to shake out a napkin and spread it on his lap. "Now then," she said, hovering over him like a mother hen. "Shall we count the lumps together? One-two-three..."

DARCY BY ANY OTHER NAME

Darcy leaned forward and took hold of the cup. "Thank you," he said. "We'll save the sugar lumps for the horses, shall we?"

Confound it, now he was speaking with a nursery voice!

Caroline Bingley dimpled. "You cannot fool me. I know how you dislike horses."

She turned to the footman. "If you will just bring in the other things?" she said. "That will be all."

Caroline Bingley resumed smiling in a way that Darcy did not trust. "It is time for some serious study, Mr. Darcy," she said. "Colonel Fitzwilliam will soon return, and he shall bring with him a man who will ask you questions."

A memory stirred. Ah, yes. Fitz and his medical man from the asylum.

The footman returned and deposited a stack of books beside Miss Bingley. "Have no fear," she added brightly. "I shall be your tutor."

"Surely you are jesting. How can you be of help?"

"This," said Miss Bingley, opening a book, "is the Baronetage. Will you tell me, please, your cousin's Christian name?" She began turning pages.

"My cousin Fitzwilliam?" said Darcy. "Hudson."

Startled, Miss Bingley looked up. "What—did you say?"

"His name is Hudson," said Darcy. "Hudson Richard Julian Fitzwilliam, after his mother's father and our great-grandfather. Naturally you will have no occasion to refer to him in this manner, unless you wish to see him lose his temper. The family refers to him as Fitz."

It took some time for Miss Bingley to locate the listing for his uncle and the names of his sons. "Very well," she said uncertainly. "Let us go on. What are your parents' names?"

Darcy told her.

"And your sister's name?"

"Shall we dispense with all this?" said Darcy. "I daresay the examiner will ask questions that are more to the purpose."

"I—have no idea what you mean," said Miss Bingley.

"My housekeeper is Mrs. Reynolds; my steward is Bellowes." Darcy counted off the names on his fingers. "The cook—let me see, is it François? No, that was the other one. It's Henri. Henri Bernard. The farm manager is Gibbs. The farrier is Percy; the gamekeeper is Ewan. The head parlor maid—"

"Good gracious, how am I to verify these?"

Darcy felt his lips twist into a smirk. "You'll just have to trust me," he said. "But my cousin will know the answers."

With reluctance Miss Bingley closed the book. "Lady Catherine has postponed her journey in order to be present at the examination."

"I expect she will have questions of her own. I am not afraid of her."

Miss Bingley looked worried. "I should warn you," she said, "that Lady Catherine intends to compel you to return with her to Rosings Park."

"As her prisoner? I'll see that."

Somewhere a clock began to chime. Ignoring his weakness, Darcy rose to his feet. "If you will excuse me," he told her, "I must now depart for Meryton. Thank you for the tea."

"Meryton? What can you want there?"

Darcy opened a drawer and removed a pair of gloves. "A moneylender by the name of McCurdy," he said. He went into the dressing room and selected a hat and an overcoat.

Miss Bingley did not disappoint. "Moneylender?" she demanded, as soon as he returned. "What can you want with a moneylender?"

Her shrill tone made his head hurt.

Darcy took his letter, closed the writing desk and locked it. "After that," he said, "I intend to call at Longbourn House."

"Longbourn House!" she cried. "You have no business at Longbourn House."

"Ah, but I think I do."

Her eyes narrowed. "With Miss Elizabeth Bennet?"

"Now that you mention it, yes," replied Darcy, and he smiled a little. The mention of Bellowes' name had reminded him of something.

"My main objective is to see William Collins," he said. "Do apologize to my cousin if he arrives this afternoon. I do not wish to miss the interrogation."

Elizabeth followed Mrs. Hill into the drawing room. "Letter, do you say?" said Hill. "I haven't seen a letter." She began sorting through the fashion periodicals piled on one of the tables. "Where did you see it last?"

"I was reading it in Father's bookroom," Elizabeth explained. "And then—something happened. Callers came, I think. I recall sliding it under the blotter on the desk." She hesitated. "No, I did that before Mr. Collins came in."

"Mr. Collins." Hill gave an unhappy huff. "You'd best ask him yourself. He's in there now, settling in, so he says. I don't call it that."

"Where is Will—er, Mr. Collins?"

"In your father's bookroom, turning things topsy-turvy. If your letter is there, it will be a job of work to find it." Hill went out, leaving Elizabeth frowning after her.

"If my letter is there," she repeated. She hoped it was not. For some reason she did not like to think of Mr. Collins finding it. Which was nonsense, for he had written it in the first place.

It was that mood of his. She went to the bookroom door and opened it. "William?" she said softly.

At once she saw that the position of the desk was changed. Moreover, her father's framed prints and paintings had been taken from the walls and were now stacked against a chair. There was a scuffling noise.

"William," she said, smiling in spite of herself. "Why are you on the floor?"

His head appeared from beneath her father's desk. "Yes? What is it?" He sounded unhappy.

"I—see that you are settling in."

He scrambled to his feet. "Speaking of which, I shall have something to say to Mrs. Hill about the condition of this room. The amount of dust beneath the desk is a scandal." He began brushing at his breeches. "We pay these people to clean."

"Hill was occupied with Father's care," Elizabeth protested, "as well as with the arrangements for the—funeral."

"A convenient excuse."

"Also, Father disliked being disturbed. He thought dust to be—" Elizabeth found it difficult to continue. How she could picture her father saying that dust was healthful! "To be—of no consequence. Sarah is good about keeping the hearth tidy," she added.

"Slipshod housekeeping," said Mr. Collins, "is a thing I shall not tolerate."

"Then you'd best be prepared to hire another servant or two," Elizabeth flashed. Her gaze swept the room. It was anything but tidy now, no thanks to him.

"Nonsense. Those we have must work more efficiently instead of lounging about. Such as that footman who has managed to disappear."

Where was William's gentle smile, his ironic sense of humor?

"James has been ill, as well you know," Elizabeth said, eyeing him with growing resentment. "Haven't you something else to do?"

"I am now a gentleman of leisure," he told her. "Your uncle and Mr. Phillips have the legal niceties in hand. They are now at his office in Meryton. I saw no reason to accompany them."

Elizabeth's gaze found the hearth and held. There was ash in the firebox. And yet there had not been a fire here for days.

"Was there something you wanted?" he said.

"I am looking for my letter."

"Still?" The exasperation in his tone was unmistakable.

"You have not seen it?"

"Earlier, when you were in the drawing room. Really, Elizabeth, you must be more careful."

Elizabeth put her hands on her hips. "And you," she said, "must be less rude."

His mouth opened but no sound came out.

"See here," Elizabeth went on. "Can we not put pique and ill-feelings behind us? Simply because I attended my father's funeral is no reason for you to nag at me."

"I am not nagging."

"We have all been under a great deal of strain," she began.

"Me in particular," he retorted. "Especially when you chose to bolt from the sanctuary. Dr. Bentley was most concerned."

"As he should be, for I was grieving, William."

"You were making a scene, the very thing you promised not to do."

"Have the goodness to kindly—" Elizabeth closed her lips in time.

"To kindly do what?" he taunted.

She looked away—away from that face with the curling lip. "Why do you not have a fire here?" she said. "Shall I ask Ned to start another?"

"Another?" he squeaked. "Why do you say that?"

Elizabeth indicated the fireplace. "It looks as though you attempted it."

She saw him flinch, and he would not meet her eye.

"Why, look there," he cried, pointing to the window. "If I'm not mistaken it's Mr. Darcy coming up the lane—on that beastly horse."

"You sound as though you dislike horses," said Elizabeth.

"I do, and Mr. Darcy as well. Yes, I want a word with him."

"Pray do not tarry on my account."

William Collins wasted no time. He pushed past her and left the bookroom. Through the window Elizabeth watched him come out of the house and approach Mr.

Darcy, without having bothered to put on a hat or overcoat. Would he argue with Mr. Darcy as well?

Elizabeth turned away. She had no wish to see him make a fool of himself, which surely he would do in his irritated state.

Arguing! She and William never argued! Now it seemed that nothing she did or said was right.

Her gaze swept the room. So many changes! He had every right to make them, but so soon? And why was he defensive about starting a fire? Her eyes found the hearth, and she went to investigate.

Yes, there was ash here, and in flat sheets, as if pages had been burned. Which pages? Was he burning papers of her father's?

After an anxious glance to the window, Elizabeth knelt on the hearth. Her hands would be blackened from the ash, but no matter. She must discover what William had burned.

"Now see here!" Collins shrilled. "I have no business with you. You should not have come."

Mr. Darcy swung from the saddle, a skill that was not lost on Collins. "Keep that brute away," he added. "I've no wish for another lesson."

"Nor have I an interest in teaching you," said Darcy.

"Then why have you come?"

"To see if you open your letters, Collins."

DARCY BY ANY OTHER NAME

"What letters? Why should I receive letters? Save for bills sent by that funeral undertaker."

"I am not here to listen to your complaints."

"It is most unfair," Collins said. He was about to say more but he discovered he was shivering. It was all because of the cold, and yet he dared not invite Darcy into the house.

"I suggest you keep watch for the post," said Darcy. "You will find something there to lighten your burden. An annuity in the amount of one thousand pounds per annum for the support of your Bennet cousins."

"Support?" cried Collins. "Do you know that Mrs. Bennet is searching the neighborhood for a place to live? Haye Park or the great house at Stoke or who knows where else. Without the means to pay!"

"And now you are able to do something for her."

Collins folded his arms across his chest. "Your generosity is appreciated, but it is nowhere near enough."

This remark hit home; Collins could see it. Darcy was now angry. "Do you think money appears like magic?" he demanded. "Do you think I never feel a loss?"

Collins had to laugh. "One thousand pounds is not one-tenth of your income."

"Shall I remove one-tenth of yours and see what tune you sing?"

Collins gave a snort. "I'll be paying at least that amount to the funeral undertaker," he snapped. "Expenses that you authorized."

"Did you not wish to honor your cousin, whose passing has granted so many material blessings?" Darcy leaned in. "Have you learned nothing, Collins?"

It was on the tip of Collins' tongue to reply in kind. How dared Darcy correct him? But his teeth were chattering from the cold.

"The letter should arrive by Quarter Day," said Darcy. "Bellowes is both precise and thorough in carrying out my instructions."

Collins saw Darcy's eyes grow hard. "And you will spend that amount, in its entirety, upon support for Mrs. Bennet and her daughters. Is that understood?"

"As well as to pay for the special license," quipped Collins. "My request will be sent by express messenger today."

Darcy's brows descended. "What need have you for such a thing?"

"Why, to marry Elizabeth," said Collins. "We plan to have the wedding as soon as the license arrives."

"If you live," said Darcy. He turned and, without the aid a mounting block, swung into the saddle. "Oh, and one more thing."

Darcy held out a wrapped package. "If you would kindly return this to Miss Kitty?"

Collins was suspicious as he took it. "What is it?"

"Nothing to do with you," said Darcy.

"See here. I am not your errand-boy—" Collins began.

DARCY BY ANY OTHER NAME

"Can you not find room in your common, narrow soul for even one simple favor? One act of kindness?" said Darcy. "It is as I said: you have learned precisely nothing."

Before Collins could reply Darcy wheeled the horse and rode away.

45 'Tis Certain So

Alone in her father's bookroom, Elizabeth studied the unburned bits of paper she'd rescued. The largest held what was surely a closing signature: *illiam Darcy*. Had Mr. Darcy written something that had angered him?

On the other hand, William had looked so uncomfortable when she mentioned her lost letter. Why?

She returned her attention to the fireplace. What he had burned was no short note. She placed her findings side-by-side on the hearth:

>*s never my inten*—was never my intention?
>*facts as I experie* –facts as I experienced?
>*ound myself trapp* –found myself trapped?

Who was trapped, Mr. Darcy? How could Mr. Darcy be trapped?

And then Elizabeth became aware that it was quiet. She could no longer hear voices outside—and was that the sound of hoof beats? Hastily she gathered the fragments into her handkerchief and carefully swept the hearth.

Her fingers were covered with soot, but there was no chance to clean her hands. She brushed them against her skirts, trusting the stiff black silk to hide the evidence of her deed.

Darcy's accusation was like a slap, and yet Collins could not put it out of his mind. In spite of the cold, he walked back and forth in front of the house. Had he learned nothing?

But what was there to learn?

Longbourn, delightful Longbourn, was now his—he had learned to appreciate that. The life of a modest country gentleman suited him perfectly.

Freedom from Lady Catherine's dominance was another reason for gratitude. He might not be Darcy of Pemberley, but he was his own master.

And by Jove, he was free from Caroline Bingley and her political ambitions. No more fear of Parliament. No more fear of being elevated to the peerage, with its incumbent duties. He was free to settle here, take a wife, and enjoy the remainder of his days.

And he would provide for his cousins, now that it cost him nothing. Darcy owed him that; he could take Darcy's money without a second thought. Yes, Darcy owed him and Darcy could afford it.

And could he squeeze the funerary expenses from Mrs. Bennet's allowance? Why not?

As for Elizabeth, well. He ought to apologize, yes. He had been too harsh with her, too overbearing and demanding. The shine had gone out of her eyes, and he was to blame for it. A man ought to be patient with his future wife.

Collins squared his shoulders. So Darcy was wrong; he had learned something. He'd learned gratitude and also to be kinder to Elizabeth.

He found her in the vestibule, along with Kitty. Not the most conducive setting for an apology, especially with Kitty looking on. Then Collins remembered Darcy's packet. Without a word he presented it to her.

"What is this?" Kitty exclaimed, but Collins said nothing. Of course she must open it right away. Collins was just as curious to see the contents, but instead he studied the ceiling.

"My necklace!" she cried. "Lizzy, look! The necklace Father gave me!"

Collins felt a hand touch his sleeve. "Mr. Collins, how did you know?" He saw tears in Kitty's eyes, and he dipped his head modestly. "Was Mr. McCurdy very angry?" she asked.

"Who?" said Collins, before he could stop himself. The name meant nothing to him.

"Why, the man who, to whom I—" Kitty broke off speaking.

"I have no idea whom you mean," Collins said primly.

"I—see," said Kitty slowly. "Yes, he is best forgotten. But oh, I *thank* you for redeeming this, Cousin. I was at my wits' end over how to come up with the money. But I won't say another word. It will be our secret."

She went skipping up the stairs, and Elizabeth turned to him. "You visited the moneylender, William."

"I—why, no. Of course not," stammered Collins.

"You are altogether too good," she said. "As well as too modest. And here I thought you were angry with me."

"Not angry," protested Collins. "Merely—concerned. Too concerned, perhaps. As the new master of Longbourn, I wish above all to do what is right and proper. Tell me," he went on, "are your mother and sisters reconciled to living elsewhere?"

"Why can they not continue here?"

Collins had thought this one out, and he had his answer ready. "What woman would like to be a guest in a house where she has once been mistress?" he said. "Your mother deserves her own residence, just as you deserve to be mistress here, without interference."

"I—" said Elizabeth.

He interrupted. "I know all about interference and meddling, and I tell you it will not do. Lady Catherine held the upper hand at the parsonage, and I did not like it."

"Mama is hardly Lady Catherine," began Elizabeth.

Again he interrupted. "I have set aside one thousand pounds for the support of your mother and sisters. Do you think they shall be able to make do with that?"

Her surprise was everything he hoped for. "I daresay they can," she said, "but William, how shall we live?"

"I believe we can manage nicely on what is left." He paused to take in the glow of admiration in her eyes. "Sacrifice on behalf of family," he added, "is important."

"You are very generous, and their need is sincere. But such an amount!"

He waved a careless hand. "Unimportant."

"I—could not help but notice Mr. Darcy's attitude when he came. Is he angry with you?"

Collins shrugged this aside. "Who can say?" he said. "The man's a proud devil."

"Was it necessary to burn his letter?"

He blinked. "Ah—his letter."

Collins willed down panic; he must brazen it out. "He had no business writing the things he did," he said. Anxiety made his tone shrill. "I—did not wish anyone else to find it. No good would come, believe me."

She drew nearer. "Since we are confessing, I too have a confession to make. I cannot find the letter you wrote to me."

She thought there were two letters? She did not realize what he had done? "Well," he said, more gently. "It is no great loss."

"But it is! You said it was your very first love letter— I read that much." A dimple appeared in her cheek.

This was more like it! Emboldened, Collins said, "But you have the original before you." He puffed out his chest and even remembered to smile. "Behold the man!" he said.

Her smile slipped and so did Collins' confidence. Perhaps this was not the best expression to use. Darcy could be charming; perhaps he should try to do likewise? But charm was not as easy as it looked. If only he could remember his carefully-crafted compliments!

Then again, a man in love was supposed to speak from the heart. He must trust himself.

And so he drew nearer. "After all," he said, with another smile, "we shall be man and wife in not too many days." His fingers found her shoulders. "Which is rather wonderful. We are perfect for one another." In spite of himself, Collins giggled.

For some reason Elizabeth did not return the smile.

"Do you know," she said, "perhaps you ought to tell Mama about what you intend to do for her. She has been dreading the worst."

"But I would rather remain here with you," he said coyly. Beneath his fingers he felt her shoulders tense. "Do not run away," he added.

Her eyes would not meet his. "I—there are things I must attend to above-stairs."

"Not before you kiss me."

Her cheeks flushed scarlet. "William, really. Here?"

"Yes, here," he said. "I am the master, and you are the future mistress. What could be more natural?"

"It—is not like you to insist," she said.

"Nor is it like you to be stingy. Come, enough with maidenly reserve." Collins leaned in, closed his eyes, and placed his lips firmly on hers. He felt her hands move to his chest. Yes, this was very nice.

And then she pushed—hard. Collins' eyes came open. Elizabeth's eyes were open too. Why, it looked as though she meant to strike him!

Instantly Collins released her and took a step back.

"Good—night, William," she said.

He could not allow her to part with him thus! Should he follow? What would Darcy do?

Chagrin and shame made Collins' cheeks burn, but he remained where he was. He watched Elizabeth mount the stairs, but she gave no backward glance.

Elizabeth shut the bedchamber door and stood with her back pressed against it. What had happened to William Collins? That sickening kiss! She wiped her mouth with the back of her hand.

Presently there were footfalls on the stairs and muffled laughter. She heard a door open and close, and then silence.

Soon there came rapping on her door. "Lizzy!" she heard her mother say. "Lizzy, open this door at once."

Elizabeth did, but only a crack.

"What do you mean by quarreling with Mr. Collins?"

"We have not quarreled—"

"According to Lydia you have. And now Mr. Collins is upset."

Elizabeth sighed. How could she expect her mother to understand? How could she expect anyone to understand? The kiss was not the same. It simply wasn't.

"I'm sorry, Mama," she said. "I need time to think."

"Think?" cried Mrs. Bennet. "What is there to think about?"

What was there to think about? She loved William. In the presence of her dying father she had pledged to spend the rest of her life with him.

"You are to march yourself downstairs and apologize," her mother said. "Before Mr. Collins decides to start thinking—thinking that he should not marry you!"

"I—would prefer to be alone just now," Elizabeth said.

"Very well," her mother shrilled. "Then stay there. Nobody wants you!"

DARCY BY ANY OTHER NAME

Collins would much rather be in his bookroom, but he did not like to give over the drawing room to the younger Bennets. It was high time these girls realized that he was master here. If they wished to remain in this room, they would have to put up with him.

And must they chatter endlessly? They were like noisy black-clad starlings.

Presently their neighbor—was it Miss Lucas? —came to call. Kitty and Lydia, being ill-mannered, fell to whispering. Even so, Collins was able to hear.

"Such a to-do, you'll never believe it," Lydia was saying. "Lizzy and Mr. Collins have quarreled." Lydia paused to look in his direction. "And now Mama fears he'll break the engagement."

"Are they engaged? The rumors are true?"

"Of course they are true," said Lydia. "Rumors always are."

"You can imagine our surprise," said Kitty. "Lizzy falling in love with Mr. Collins of all people. A man she hated, right from the first. It came about," she added, "during the snowstorm."

"Father gave them his blessing before he died," said Lydia.

"And Mr. Collins has sent for a special license," said Kitty. "By express."

More looks were cast in Collins' direction.

"And now they have quarreled," said Lydia. "Lizzy has shut herself in her bedchamber."

Collins gave a loud harrumph. He was rewarded with Lydia's muted giggle.

Mrs. Hill came in, along with James (the do-nothing footman) and the tea tray. This set the girls into motion. Collins watched them with narrowed eyes. Would anyone bother to bring him tea?

"Lizzy will have no objection to seeing you, Charlotte," said Lydia.

"No indeed," said Jane.

Collins looked up. When had Jane come in? She poured out a cup and brought it to him.

"Would you care for cake?" she inquired. When he answered in the affirmative, she brought him two pieces. Elizabeth might be the beauty of her family, but lovely Jane was certainly the kindest.

The talking continued, and eventually Miss Lucas was persuaded to speak with Elizabeth.

From behind the pages of his book, Collins gave an audible sniff. He thought better of Miss Lucas, for she seemed a sensible creature. Collins also knew that there was no counting on women; they must be loyal to their kind.

As for Elizabeth, she could stay upstairs all night. The push to his chest and the disdain in her eyes were burned into his memory.

Charlotte sounded amused. "You have barricaded the door?"

Elizabeth removed the chair and let her friend come in. "It's Mother. She must fuss and fret, fearing that I will do something drastic like end the engagement. My father's passing has been very difficult for her."

"Do you intend to end it?"

"Of course not," said Elizabeth. "It's just that—"

Charlotte found a seat on the bed. "Has Mr. Collins behaved badly, Eliza? He seems perfectly ordinary to me."

"That's just the trouble," said Elizabeth. "He is ordinary. And he—wasn't."

"I see no evidence of a change."

"But you have not been here for weeks."

"Two weeks," replied Charlotte promptly. "I was here just before Mother became ill. And I must say, I was quite impressed with Mr. Collins. He asked about Meryton and my family and all the neighbors. His interest was sincere."

"It's as if he has become a different person."

"People do not transform in to someone else," said Charlotte. "It must be a mood."

"But how can I marry—"

Charlotte interrupted. "Not marry someone who has moods? Nonsense. Everyone has moods, even you." Her tone softened. "Imagine what your marriage will mean to your future and to your family."

"I am imagining it," said Elizabeth, around a sigh

"My father is sometimes foolish, but he means well. Mr. Collins is not a bad man, Eliza."

Elizabeth got up and hunted in a drawer for a handkerchief.

Charlotte went on. "Is romance as important as stability and a secure home?"

"Secure until he dies!" flashed Elizabeth. "Who knows, perhaps he will be struck by lightning again."

"Supposedly struck by lightning," said Charlotte. "I never did believe that story. It would have made an exciting end to Mr. Bingley's ball, if anyone had seen it happen. But no one did." She paused. "You are altogether too hard on him."

"Perhaps you are right," Elizabeth said slowly. "He did redeem Kitty's necklace. And he will be giving my mother and sisters generous financial support."

"There, you see? How a man spends money is an indication of his character."

This was true. Hadn't William said the same thing? After all, he had been injured. It was no wonder that he was out of sorts.

"Charlotte," said Elizabeth, "would you care to go with me to Netherfield? I would like to consult with Mr. Fleming."

"Today? I am afraid not. Is your business so urgent?"

"Tomorrow, then," said Elizabeth. "And yes, I believe it is."

46   Fain I Would

The fine weather held but it was cold, and Elizabeth could sense that her friend's patience was wearing thin.

"I had no idea," Charlotte was now saying, "that you meant to walk all the way to Netherfield."

"I did not like to ask for the carriage," Elizabeth explained. "William might have need of it."

"Did not like to ask?" echoed Charlotte. "Did you think he would refuse?"

How should Elizabeth answer? "It is not the same as asking Father," was the best she could do.

"I should think not. I daresay a fiancé would be fonder than ever a father could be."

Elizabeth attempted a reply but was unable.

At once Charlotte linked her arm through Elizabeth's. "I spoke without thinking just now," she said quietly. "You father was very fond of you indeed."

"Yes," Elizabeth managed to say. "He was."

"And you are a credit to him in every way. Always, he was proud of you."

"I fear he never understood my engagement."

"That, I believe," said Charlotte, "could be said of most fathers."

"Perhaps," said Elizabeth.

How she longed to confide in Charlotte! About last night's awkward supper, with William sitting in her father's place, silent and withdrawn and disapproving. And how she had come down to breakfast today well before his usual time. Was it to avoid seeing him? Or was it simply because she did not know what to say?

Not know what to say to William? A man with whom she had discussed everything, and without reserve of any kind?

Elizabeth walked beside her friend for some minutes in silence. "If you must know," she said at last, "I did not tell Mr. Collins about my plans today because he would not understand. About consulting Mr. Fleming, that is."

"Why are you consulting him?"

"I have questions pertaining to William's injury."

"Resulting from the so-called lightning strike? My dear Eliza—"

"It did happen," said Elizabeth. "In fact, I saw—"

"You saw?" Charlotte said. "What did you see?"

Elizabeth thought quickly. "The—Folly. I saw—the damage to the Folly."

Charlotte said nothing, but she gave Elizabeth a knowing look.

"It is not far from the house," said Elizabeth. "If you like I will show you."

"I know where the Folly is. I can only hope that it is not surrounded by mud. You might care nothing for a dirty hem, but I do not share that opinion."

She sounded annoyed.

"I am sorry for making you tramp all this way. Indeed you are a true friend to bear me company. I only hope that Mr. Fleming has not left for Hunsford."

Charlotte came to a halt. "After an hour's walk we might discover that he is not there?"

Fortunately the Netherfield mansion was in sight. Elizabeth urged Charlotte forward. "I daresay he will travel with Lady Catherine in order to look after Anne. And I cannot imagine that they would simply leave without a word to us. After all, Anne was our guest for almost a week."

"Dear me," said Charlotte. But she voiced no objection to seeing the Folly. Together they left the lane to enter the garden.

There were memories here, along with evidence for those with eyes to see. The wheels of the traveling coach had left scars in the lawn. And there was the hedge, behind which Elizabeth and Kitty had found shelter. In her mind she could hear William's voice, ringing through the night air, as he confronted Mr. Wickham.

He had not wished to fight, but his fine sense of honor demanded it. Anne de Bourgh was no favorite, and yet he risked his life to protect her. And then Elizabeth became aware that Charlotte had asked a question.

"I-I beg your pardon?" she stammered.

"I said, is that not Mr. Darcy?"

Elizabeth gave a start. Sure enough, standing before the Folly was the man himself.

"I must say," Charlotte added in a lowered voice, "I had forgotten how handsome Mr. Darcy is."

Elizabeth drew a long breath and let it out. There was no disputing the truth of this. Even clad in a somber greatcoat, he was the picture of elegance. There was something familiar in his stance, in the way he was frowning down at the fallen stones. But no, how could that be? She must be imagining things.

"Are you not a little sorry," Charlotte added, with a smile in her voice, "that you spurned his attentions so decidedly?"

Elizabeth's gaze traveled to the patch of ground where William had stood up to George Wickham, and her heart swelled. She had learned a thing or two since that night at the ball. Looks were not the measure of a man, nor were his attire or his position or his wealth.

"My dear Charlotte," Elizabeth said, and her lips curved into an answering smile. "I fear that Mr. Darcy is still not handsome enough to tempt me."

"Perhaps that is just as well, then" said Charlotte. "For it looks as though he means to speak with us."

Darcy felt as if his features had become etched with a permanent scowl, for his time at Netherfield had been anything but pleasant. He'd addressed directly his aunt's matrimonial scheme, a thing he should have done years ago. By the look on her face, she might well consign him to Bedlam! He'd also had the footman remove the dumb-waiter from his rooms. There would be no more intimate tea-drinking with Caroline Bingley.

And he had torn up pages of perfectly good paper in an attempt to write to Elizabeth Bennet. As if another letter would do any good.

And then there was Fitz and his scheme. Yes, Darcy would relish setting his cousin straight.

If only he could regain his strength! Even now he felt as weak as a cat.

To escape the house he'd come out to the Folly, though God alone knew why. There was no longer any mystery to unravel; he was again himself. And yet here he was, pacing back and forth to keep warm, halting to examine the inscriptions. Presently he glanced toward the house—and realized that he was no longer alone.

"Elizabeth," he said aloud.

For there she stood, wrapped against the cold in a plain black cloak. Her face looked unusually pale, no thanks to an ugly black bonnet. Beside her stood Miss Lucas.

A heaven-sent opportunity! How long had Elizabeth been here? And how would he tell her of what had taken place? Speak, he must ignore his dizziness and speak!

"Mr.—Darcy," he heard Elizabeth say. The reluctance in her voice was unmistakable.

Darcy nodded to Miss Lucas without taking his eyes from Elizabeth. "Rather cold today," he said. Not the most brilliant conversational opening, but he had to say something.

He knew she thought him arrogant and aloof. He must somehow counteract this impression.

"A curious structure," he went on, "What do you know about it?"

"About the Folly?" said Miss Lucas, before Elizabeth could answer. "Only what I have heard, that it was built by Lady Mustow."

As Collins Darcy knew that Miss Lucas and her family were relative newcomers. He turned to Elizabeth. "A prideful sort of woman, would you say?"

Her eyes met his. "Why do you ask?"

He caught himself shrugging, as Collins would do. "I have been studying the inscriptions on each keystone," he said. "I suspect that Lady Mustow must have struggled with pride."

"Or else her husband did," said Elizabeth. "I have heard that he had a temper."

"Yes, that would explain a few things."

Darcy saw Miss Lucas give Elizabeth a look. He decided to ignore her.

"Perhaps the Folly was meant as a message," he said. "A sermon in stone if you will. Allow me to show you."

Would Elizabeth follow? Would she converse?

"Between Cain and Abel, just there," he added, "can you make out the inscription? The stone has been worn by the elements."

Elizabeth's gaze was intent. He had aroused her interest.

Darcy drew the Bible from his pocket and found the book of Proverbs. "*Seest thou a man wise in his own conceit? There is more hope of a fool than of him.*"

"There is nothing unusual in that," said Miss Lucas. "It seems perfectly reasonable, considering Cain's attitude."

"And all the more if Sir Mustow was a braggart," said Darcy.

"I daresay," was Miss Lucas' only comment.

Darcy coughed. "I was thinking, Miss Elizabeth, that this text might also have a present-day application. Such as, for instance, my own conceit."

Against the white of her skin, Elizabeth's eyes were large. "Yours?" she said.

He felt his lips curve into a smile. No, a grin—Collins' foolish grin! "I am beginning to wonder," he said, "whether I have inherited more from my Aunt Catherine than I know. Namely, her fondness for always being in the right."

"Have you?" she said.

"That's the rub, isn't it? For you see, so often I am right."

"A happy thought."

Darcy bit back a laugh. "Isn't it just? Over there, between Peter and Judas, is the next inscription."

Elizabeth walked with him to the next arch.

"I've always had a soft spot for Peter," Darcy admitted.

"But not, I hope, for Judas," said Miss Lucas.

"And the inscription?" said Elizabeth.

"Short and to the point," said Darcy. "*Pride goeth before destruction and an haughty spirit before a fall.*" He paused and then added, "Rather like old Nebuchadnezzar."

This was something he'd pointed out as Collins. Would she make a connection? She was thinking, he could see that.

"And yet," Elizabeth said slowly, "Peter and Judas were not damaged by the storm. It was Moses."

So the leap was too great. But they were conversing, that was something.

"He lost a hand, I believe," Darcy said. "Moses is on the other side. Would you like to see?"

"Eliza," he heard Miss Lucas whisper.

"Come and see," urged Darcy.

"Eliza, our errand?"

"In a moment, Charlotte. I would like to see the damaged statues."

"I thought you said you'd seen them," Miss Lucas said.

"Yes, but I would like to see them again."

Darcy knew better than to appear too eager, and so he strolled away. Elizabeth followed.

"See here," he said, indicating the fallen keystone and the inscription. "It's Matthew VI," he said. "Not the fifth chapter as I originally thought. And here is something else I did not see, a small letter i. Which would make this Matthew 6:1."

Again Darcy brought out the Bible, but his fingers were awkward from the cold.

Then too, his attention was distracted by the appearance of a chaise-and-four coming along the gravel drive. Behind it lumbered an enclosed wagon, painted black, pulled by horses of a more rugged breed.

His jaw tensed. Unless he was mistaken, here was his cousin Fitz.

"If you please," said Elizabeth, "I will gladly read it for you."

He passed the book to her and she found the text. "*Take heed that ye do not your alms before men, to be seen of them*," she read. "*Otherwise ye have no reward of your Father which is in heaven.*"

"An unusual choice for Moses and John," Darcy observed, keeping an eye on the wagon.

"And does it have a present-day application?"

"Meaning me?" said Darcy, smiling. "Very probably, although I have tried to do otherwise. On the other hand," he added, "it perfectly describes Coll—" He caught himself.

Elizabeth appeared lost in thought, gazing at the Bible.

Miss Lucas spoke up. "I wonder if you can tell us, sir, whether Mr. Fleming is at home."

Elizabeth closed the book and returned it. "We were afraid that perhaps he had departed for Hunsford," she said. "But you were saying? About the inscription?"

"Mr. Fleming is here," said Darcy slowly.

Fitz and another man had climbed out of the chaise and were approaching the house.

"And do you think he is available to see Miss Elizabeth?"

"That I cannot say, Miss Lucas."

Darcy had a sudden thought. "Has someone at Longbourn become ill?"

"Not precisely," said Elizabeth. "I have several questions to ask him of a medical nature. In reference to a friend."

Did she mean Collins? Darcy felt his lips twist into a rueful smile.

"Unless I miss my guess," he said, "Mr. Fleming will be occupied for some time. But you are most welcome to wait."

An expression of reluctance crossed Miss Lucas' face but she said nothing.

"Thank you," said Elizabeth. "I believe we shall."

47 Jump at the Sun

Elizabeth knew she ought to leave the Folly, for Charlotte was cold and impatient. But there was something about Mr. Darcy—as if an unasked question hung between them. But that could not be right. She had no question to ask!

"Eliza," she heard Charlotte whisper. "Shall we go?"

"In a moment," Elizabeth whispered back. "I feel as if I ought to speak with Mr. Darcy."

Charlotte's face was pinched with the cold. "You already have."

"Yes, but I feel as though he has something to tell me, something more about the stones, perhaps. Something that will shed light on a mystery."

There was a pause. "What mystery would that be?"

Elizabeth had no answer. Of course there was no mystery. All the same, something was not right.

"To be honest," Charlotte continued, "I suspect that Mr. Darcy would prefer us to leave. He's done nothing but scowl since we arrived."

"Has he?" It seemed just the opposite to Elizabeth. There was something about his faint half smile and the shine in his eyes, as if they were friends sharing a secret. But Mr. Darcy was not her friend. She scarcely knew him!

And yet Elizabeth knew she must speak with him.

Mr. Darcy looked surprised, but not at all displeased. She said nothing and waited for him to speak. He did not disappoint.

"I apologize for provoking your cousin yesterday," he said. "I ought to have known he'd become upset."

"Do you mean Mr. Collins?"

"Since he has complained about expenses to me, no doubt he has expressed the same to you."

Elizabeth felt her cheeks grow warm. "Forgive my cousin's manners," she said. "Lately he has been short with everyone."

"I most pity Mrs. Hill," he said. "For it is she who must bear the brunt of his temper."

What did he know of Mrs. Hill? Elizabeth's gaze became intent. "To be fair," she said slowly, "I believe Mr. Collins' head pains him."

Mr. Darcy's response was immediate. "Too much thinking, perhaps?"

Before Elizabeth could reply, he cut in. "Forgive me," he said. "That was uncalled for. I have not been well myself."

"Was it the lightning strike?" she said. "On the night of the elopement there was another." Mr. Darcy did not respond, but she persisted. "I know what I saw."

"There was another, yes," he said slowly. "And therein lies the crux of the matter, Miss Elizabeth—" He broke off speaking, his gaze arrested.

Elizabeth turned to see a group of men walking toward them. Their gait was purposeful.

Mr. Darcy made a sound—was it a chuckle? That could not be, for he was not smiling. His face was pale and set.

"What has Collins told you about the lightning strike?"

"Not a thing. He has forbidden me to mention the subject. But those men," she added. "Are they coming to speak with you?"

"I fear so," he said. "A bit of a surprise to see footmen. I was expecting Fitz to recruit fellows from the stables. In case rough-and-ready measures were needed."

"What do you mean?"

Mr. Darcy smiled a little. "My cousin Fitz has become concerned about the state of my health. He has brought a physician to, shall we say, take me into custody if necessary."

"Custody?"

"A simple misunderstanding," said Mr. Darcy.

"But that wagon—"

Elizabeth's gaze returned to the men and then shifted to the gravel drive. A chaise-and-four was approaching at a clip. "What in the world?" she heard Darcy say. He made a movement.

The chaise drove past and then drew up, the steaming horses stamping and tossing their heads.

Seeing it, the men broke into a run. "Halt, sir!" one of them called to Darcy.

The door of the chaise opened and a slender young woman descended. "Fitzwilliam?" Elizabeth heard her call. "Is that you?"

"Upon my word," said Darcy. "Georgiana!"

The young woman, with bonnet askew and cloak flapping, came running across the lawn.

"Hi, now, Miss," shouted one of the men. "Best to keep your distance. Things could get ugly."

Georgiana Darcy stumbled ahead and cast herself into Mr. Darcy's arms.

"Pray do not be angry," Elizabeth heard her say. "I had to come. That is to say, we had to come."

"We," repeated Mr. Darcy. "Whom do you mean?"

"Mrs. Annesley and Mr. Bellowes and I."

DARCY BY ANY OTHER NAME

"That'll be enough of that, Miss," said the same man who had shouted. "Step away from the patient. Gentle-like."

"Fitzwilliam?" said Georgiana.

The man put a heavy hand on Mr. Darcy's shoulder. "We'll be taking you along with us, sir," he said. "No funny business, mind."

The menace in the man's tone was unmistakable. Two of the footmen took hold of Darcy's arms. Georgiana Darcy looked to her brother in alarm.

"These men have some questions for me, dearest," he said. His eyes met Elizabeth's in silent appeal.

At once she stepped forward. "We will wait for your brother together, Miss Darcy," she said brightly. "Shall we go into the house? I believe your cousin is there. Why, no, here he is."

Sure enough, Colonel Fitzwilliam was striding across the lawn.

Georgiana ran to meet him. "You cannot be serious, Fitz," she said, with surprising fierceness. "Tell these men to release Fitzwilliam."

Colonel Fitzwilliam put her aside. "Did you summon her here?" he shouted at Mr. Darcy.

"Of course not!"

"I came of my own accord," said Miss Darcy. "In part because of your letter, Fitz. Why are these men behaving so strangely? There is nothing wrong with Fitzwilliam."

"My dear," began Colonel Fitzwilliam. "I fear he has not been himself."

"Nonsense," said Miss Darcy.

Over Georgiana's head Colonel Fitzwilliam glared at Mr. Darcy. "It is pointless to resist," he said.

"I am not resisting," came the answer. "Shall we get this over with?"

"Indeed, that is why we have come."

There was steel in the Colonel's voice. In spite of herself, Elizabeth shivered.

Elizabeth and Charlotte followed closely behind the others. In the cold air, their voices carried.

"It's Collins I'd like to nab," Elizabeth heard Colonel Fitzwilliam tell Miss Darcy. "As for Darcy—"

There was a pause. "This isn't your brother, Georgie. He isn't right in the head. That Collins fellow is behind it." He cast a sidelong look at her. "Have you heard your brother mention Collins? Podgy fellow with a pugnacious streak."

Pugnacious? William Collins was anything but pugnacious! Elizabeth strained to hear more.

"He says he's the rector at Hunsford," Colonel Fitzwilliam continued. "I cannot see Aunt Catherine offering the living to someone like that."

Georgiana Darcy hung on her cousin's arm. "Will those men harm Fitzwilliam?"

"Honesty is not easily come by, my dear. They'll get the truth out of him and no mistake. If you had heard how he talked the other day, Georgie, the things he said about Wickham."

"Wickham?"

Elizabeth could not mistake the shock in Georgiana's voice. Colonel Fitzwilliam's manner became gentle. "I might as well tell you," she heard him say. "The man's been seen in the neighborhood." He gave Miss Darcy's arm a pat. "No need to be distressed. He won't come within miles of this place."

Miss Darcy walked in silence and then said, "Did you arrange this? These men, coming for my brother?"

"If you had heard him talk—"

"I did hear him—today. You are making a mistake. Fitzwilliam is as he has ever been—kind and honorable and good."

"His illness is in the mind, my dear."

"None of his letters indicate illness," she said. "I have had several."

"The changes are subtle, Georgie."

"Not according to what you just said," she protested. "You described a madman. My brother is not mad."

"We'll know soon enough. I'd like to have the hide off Collins, though."

Charlotte drew nearer. "This sounds very odd," she whispered to Elizabeth. "Not at all like the Mr. Collins we know."

But Elizabeth's attention was taken up with Mr. Darcy, and she studied his face as the men marched him into the house. His sister was right. He looked gray-faced and ill, but certainly in his right mind.

"Why does this man see Mr. Collins as a criminal?" Charlotte went on.

Elizabeth gave no answer. Indeed, what could she say? William Collins had a temper, but was never violent.

Into the mansion they went behind Colonel Fitzwilliam and his cousin. There was some disturbance when Miss Darcy insisted on remaining with her brother. Colonel Fitzwilliam would not be moved. He left them standing in the entrance hall and went with the men into the library.

Caroline Bingley came rushing forward. "My dear Miss Darcy," she said, taking hold of the girl's hands. "We shall not allow harm to come to your brother. I have devised a plan."

"Do you think Fitzwilliam is mad, Miss Bingley?"

Elizabeth saw Caroline Bingley hesitate. "Of course not," Miss Bingley said stoutly. "But there have been changes."

"What sort of changes?"

"I would rather not say."

"What is your plan?"

"Why, to marry your brother myself. I can then return with him—and you—to Pemberley. We shall arrange to have him cared for there."

DARCY BY ANY OTHER NAME

Miss Darcy pulled free and faced Caroline Bingley squarely. "My brother is not a lunatic."

"Of course not," soothed Miss Bingley. "Although your cousin Anne says—"

"How would you know what Anne says?"

"I am here, Georgiana."

Elizabeth turned to see Anne de Bourgh descend the staircase. "And so is Mother."

"Shall we go into the green salon?" said Miss Bingley brightly. "It is very much warmer there."

As the others moved off, Charlotte began whispering again. "Your sisters told me that Miss de Bourgh was engaged to Mr. Darcy."

Apparently Charlotte's voice carried, for Elizabeth saw Miss Darcy glance back at them.

"Is this true?" Miss Darcy said to Anne. "Are you engaged to my brother?"

Anne colored up and said something that Elizabeth could not hear.

Caroline Bingley led them to chairs before a cheerful fire. "Do make yourselves comfortable," she said. "I'll just ring for tea."

"I am sorry to disappoint you," Miss Darcy told Anne, "but Fitzwilliam has never expressed an interest in marrying. Although he did mention Miss Elizabeth Bennet in one of his letters." She offered a shy smile to Elizabeth.

"I fear he and I did not get on," Elizabeth confessed. "I was deliberately provoking when I ought to have kept my peace."

"Must we speak of Miss Elizabeth?" Caroline Bingley broke in. "Your brother's opinion of her makes no difference, for she is engaged to be married."

"To Mr. Collins," added Anne, with a sly smile. Elizabeth now realized that she thoroughly disliked Anne de Bourgh.

"The man my cousin mentioned?" said Miss Darcy. "Dear me."

"You needn't bother with him," said Miss Bingley.

Georgiana gave her a look. "My cousin also mentioned Mr. Wickham."

Anne looked up, and then averted her face. "Mr. Wickham," she said unsteadily, "is a lying beast."

"Do you know him?" said Georgiana. "I had no idea. He is—not the sort of man your mother would like."

"It matters not. I shall never see him again." Anne de Bourgh disappeared behind her handkerchief. Elizabeth felt an unexpected stab of pity.

The door opened and Lady Catherine came into the room, propelled by Colonel Fitzwilliam. "I demand to have my part in this examination!" she told him.

"Indeed, ma'am, I think not."

"Not only am I a member of the family," she said, "but I am the eldest member present. I refuse to be shut out!"

"This does not concern you, ma'am. Please wait here with Georgiana and the others."

"How dare you exclude me, simply because I am a woman! Your father shall hear of this!"

Lady Catherine's threats had no effect on her nephew. Out he went, closing the door.

"Oh, dear," said Miss Bingley, with a sigh. "What a turn of events! Poor, dear Mr. Darcy! How he must be suffering!"

"We have had this conversation before, Miss Bingley," said Lady Catherine bitingly. "Must I remind you of the impropriety of such a match?"

"Aunt Catherine," said Georgiana softly.

"Do not 'Aunt Catherine' me. You have no business being here. Fitzwilliam ought to marry Anne, not a common upstart."

Caroline Bingley gave a loud sniff.

Refreshments were brought in and silence descended. Elizabeth strained to hear—what? Shouting from the other room? The sound of a scuffle? There was nothing.

Presently Miss Bingley rose to her feet. "I cannot bear it," she cried. "I must know what is happening." She crossed the room and went out. Lady Catherine did likewise.

Elizabeth and Georgiana Darcy exchanged glances and put their teacups aside.

"We might as well wait with them," said Anne, around a sigh. Never had she sounded so melancholy.

Sometime later the library door burst open and Mr. Darcy came striding out.

Colonel Fitzwilliam was hard on his heels. "Darcy," Elizabeth heard him say.

Mr. Darcy turned. "Mathematics, Fitz? You demand that I calculate the area of a circle, a thing I have not done since I was nine?"

"If you could have seen yourself the other day," Colonel Fitzwilliam protested. "I needed something that involved reasoning. I—could think of nothing else."

"Because it represents the sum of your education! Really, Fitz. Did you truly think me mad?"

"Lady Catherine did."

"I most certainly did," Lady Catherine shrilled.

Mr. Darcy winced, as if her voice hurt.

"What you need," said Mr. Bingley, "is a drink. Come back into the library."

"Not just yet." Mr. Darcy turned to Elizabeth with a look of entreaty in his eyes. "Miss Elizabeth, might I have a word?"

"Whatever for?" shrilled Lady Catherine.

In spite of herself Elizabeth took a step forward.

Georgiana came rushing forward and took hold of his hand. "Is all well, Fitzwilliam? Have those terrible men released you?"

"They have, dearest."

"And may we now go home?"

He said something in her ear that Elizabeth did not catch.

"Disgraceful," said Lady Catherine to no one in particular. "From start to finish, a degrading, unmannerly exhibition. Where did you find this physician, Hudson?"

Elizabeth saw Colonel Fitzwilliam flinch. He became red in the face.

"As for you," Lady Catherine went on, addressing Mr. Darcy, "out of Christian charity I shall attempt to forget your denial of my daughter's claim."

"There is no claim, Mother," said Anne.

"None at all," said Mr. Darcy, but kindly.

Lady Catherine drew herself up and glared. "Come, Anne," she said. "It is high time we left this place. Mr. Fleming will accompany us and watch over your health. Where is he?" And she stalked off, leaving Anne to trail behind.

Elizabeth became aware of Charlotte's gloved fingers on her arm. "Perhaps we should go as well?" she said.

Mr. Darcy stood his ground. "Miss Elizabeth?" he said. "A moment of your time?"

Elizabeth looked from Charlotte's set expression to Mr. Darcy's unwavering gaze. She heard his aunt give a derisive sniff. "I fail to see what business you could possibly have with this person, Fitzwilliam," she said.

This was all the encouragement Elizabeth needed. Without a word she walked into the small parlor. Mr. Darcy followed.

"Fitzwilliam!" his aunt shrilled. "I have not finished speaking with—" The closing of the door shut out the rest of her speech.

Here Elizabeth was, alone with Mr. Darcy.

Alone! Memories of a similar occasion came surging forward, unbidden and unwelcome. This man, rocking back and forth as he stood before the mantelpiece at Longbourn. His lips compressed in a simper as his fingers twined together. Elizabeth's heart began to hammer. Surely he would not make another declaration!

He placed a chair; what could she do but sit? He took a seat opposite, and Elizabeth put up her chin. She had no recourse but to hear him out—and then, God willing, she would never see this man again.

Mr. Darcy's head was bowed, and she was left to confront the top of his head. Of course his thick hair was beautifully arranged. His hands, she noted, were elegant—unlike poor William's. Thank goodness his fingers remained still.

Abruptly Mr. Darcy looked up, and his eyes met hers with surprising frankness. "I have long been wishing to speak with you on this subject," he began.

"Indeed," she interrupted, "I quite understand your position, Mr. Darcy, and I beg of you to consider mine. We have nothing more to say to one another."

His brows went up. "I beg your pardon?" His surprise was almost comical.

Another wave of memories: William, hiding behind the sofa. William, half-choked with laughter, holding Mr. Darcy's arms and demanding an apology.

"You are feeling well today, sir?" said Elizabeth.

"Forgive me, but when I saw you last..."

"I am not dosed up on laudanum, if that's what you mean."

Elizabeth felt her cheeks grow hot. "Of course not," she said hastily. "It's just that you are so pale, sir. I fear you are unwell."

"Rather worse for wear," he said. "I daresay Collins and I are in similar shape. If I may continue?"

"Certainly," she said politely.

Again Mr. Darcy steepled his fingertips; the gold of his signet ring flashed. "How I ought to begin this conversation has proved elusive. I had hoped to introduce it along more natural lines. I fear that only a frontal attack will do."

An attack? Elizabeth found her voice. "Must we reopen a chapter that is best left closed?"

Very slightly Mr. Darcy winced. "Forgive me for causing you pain. I have no defense; my cowardice is largely to blame. I kept silent when I should have spoken."

"You were anything but silent that day!" Elizabeth flashed.

A bashful half-smile appeared. "That I am a bungler is hardly a surprise," he admitted.

Elizabeth had no reply. This was the sort of thing William would say. And his hands—Mr. Darcy was steepling his fingertips just as William used to do. The tilt of his head, the shine in his eyes...

Elizabeth averted her gaze. What right had he to adorable mannerisms? She had every reason to dislike this man!

"You asked about the lightning strike," Mr. Darcy said. "You were correct in your assumption: both Collins and I were hit during Bingley's ball. I attempted to explain in my letter, but I rambled quite a bit." His smile became confiding. "I am not surprised that you were confused."

"What letter do you mean? For I—"

The door opened to admit Charlotte. "Eliza," she whispered. The warning in her voice was unmistakable.

At once Mr. Darcy rose to his feet. Elizabeth did the same, but more slowly. "I received no letter, Mr. Darcy."

"Eliza," whispered Charlotte. "Do have a care."

There was some commotion outside. "Mr. Collins," Lady Catherine's voice called out. "A moment of your time, if you please!"

Charlotte was flushed with embarrassment, but not Elizabeth. Of what should she be ashamed? William ought to laugh at finding her alone with Mr. Darcy. Instead he stood scowling in the doorway.

Elizabeth put up her chin.

"Might I ask the meaning of this?" William demanded.

"Mr. Darcy and I were conversing about the storm," she said. "I was about to take my leave."

"What are you doing here? You have no business with Mr. Darcy."

Oh, hadn't she? Elizabeth kept her temper in check. "I came to see Mr. Fleming," she said.

"Have you no consideration for my feelings? I was sick with worry when you could not be found."

"And yet you live," Elizabeth pointed out.

His expression became peevish. "Ned saw you leave," he said, and he pursed up his lips.

"With Charlotte Lucas!" said Elizabeth.

"I took the trouble to find you," he countered, "because the special license has come." He looked beyond her to Mr. Darcy. "We are to be married tomorrow morning."

Elizabeth could not miss the triumph in his tone. She took a step back.

"You do not seem pleased," William said.

Elizabeth opened her mouth to speak, but no sound came out. Would William embrace her? Here, in front of Mr. Darcy?

Charlotte broke the silence. "What very good news! Might we impose on you, Mr. Collins, to take us home in your carriage?"

"I am leaving at once, for there is much to do."

"Miss Elizabeth," said Darcy. "If I might have a moment more of your time."

William Collins gave a loud harrumph.

"About my letter," continued Mr. Darcy.

"Never mind the letter," said William. "As my connections with your family have been concluded, I bid you adieu, sir."

Mr. Darcy ignored Mr. Collins. Indeed, his gaze never left Elizabeth's face. "Miss Elizabeth?" he repeated.

Elizabeth felt William Collins take hold of her arm. "Another time, perhaps," he said and pulled her away.

"William," whispered Elizabeth, once they gained the entrance hall. "Must you cause a scene? It was never my intention to speak with Mr. Darcy."

"I should hope not. Mr. Darcy," he said, "is an idiot."

Elizabeth held back the obvious retort. "I daresay your head pains you, but must you be so grumpy?"

"You do not know the half of it," he said. The butler opened the main door and out they went, with Charlotte following.

"And yet you blame me for being concerned," Elizabeth flashed. "And for wishing to discover if there is a remedy that could be helpful."

"The most helpful thing," he said, "is for you to never again mention Mr. Darcy. Or his aunt."

"With pleasure!"

He opened the door of the carriage, none too gracefully.

"A happy serendipity, this," remarked Charlotte, as she took a seat opposite Elizabeth. "We needn't walk home after all."

Elizabeth did not answer. Through narrowed eyes she watched William Collins climb into the carriage and arrange the lap robe over his legs. Tomorrow morning she would marry this man.

48   Turn of the Tide

The next morning it was snowing, which seemed appropriate for the occasion. Darcy had pressured Bingley into arriving early. There was no sense in taking chances.

Yesterday he had seen Collins' face, gloating over Elizabeth as if he were a greedy child with a treat. Did Collins love her? No, it was lust, the desire to possess her beauty.

Or perhaps it was because Darcy loved her, and his love fueled Collins' twisted revenge.

Bingley's chaise came to a halt before Meryton's parish church. "Here we are," said Bingley, probably to break the silence. "Let's hope the door is open."

Darcy followed, his mind taken up with Collins. What reason had he for revenge? What had Darcy ever done to him?

Except to be everything that Collins was not.

Was Collins another George Wickham, then? Driven by jealousy and greed?

Bingley tried the church door and turned to Darcy with a smile of triumph. Darcy remained where he was, with the snow falling round him.

Collins hadn't Wickham's roving lasciviousness—he considered himself a moral man—and yet his motives were just as base. He would deceive Elizabeth in order to have her.

But she had not been warm toward Collins yesterday. Something did not ring true, and she knew it. Bless her, her loyalty would not allow her to repulse Collins.

He would see that happen today.

The door opened and Bingley put his head out. "Are you coming?"

Darcy gave a start, brushed the snow from his shoulders, and went in. He walked past Bingley to the front of the church and sat in the first pew—on the groom's side.

"We are in no one's way here," Darcy explained. And they wouldn't be. The entourage from Rosings was gone. Collins would have no friend to stand by him.

Bingley gave him an odd look. "Gad," he whispered. "It's even colder in here. Where is everyone?"

"A private ceremony, apparently," said Darcy. "Immediate family only."

"Which explains your presence."

Darcy could not help himself; he felt a smile tug at his lips. "Perhaps," he said, "I am about to become just that."

He heard Charles sigh. Poor fellow, did he think 'Mad Darcy' had returned? But Darcy was feeling better than he had in days. The ringing in his ears was gone, and he no longer felt as if he had Serson's Speculum spinning in his head. He could think clearly. Better yet, he could act.

A door opened and closed, and Collins came mincing down the center aisle. He halted when he noticed Darcy. "What are you doing here?"

Darcy's brows went up. "I might ask you the same thing." He rose to his feet and looked Collins over. "Wearing my coat, but not my breeches. An unusual combination, blue and black."

Collins' eyes narrowed. "Can I help it if you destroyed my only presentable frock coat? Moreover, thanks to you and that interfering Mrs. Hill, none of my clothes fit properly."

Darcy could see the buttons straining to hold the waistcoat closed, but he made no comment. He could feel Bingley's interest.

Collins did not bother to lower his voice. "You are not welcome here. You need to leave."

"This is a public service of the church," said Darcy mildly. "All are welcome, as you know."

Collins brought his hands to his hips. "Not you. This is my wedding, and I will not have you present."

"A penitent sinner, denied? By a minister of the church? But not," Darcy added, "by God."

"You are anything but penitent!"

"It happens that I am. And what about you? Are you a sinner, Collins? I say that you are."

Collins opened and shut his lips like a fish. His chest swelled. "How dare you," he said between shut teeth. "How dare you!"

In the back of the church a door opened; there was a commotion in the narthex. Without taking his eyes from Collins, Darcy said, "Off you go, Charles."

"Huh?" said Bingley.

Darcy lowered his voice. "Unless I miss my guess, Miss Bennet and her sisters are here."

Charles Bingley stood there, blinking at him. "Go on," whispered Darcy. "You remember."

With that, Bingley turned and went up the aisle. Collins' gaze shifted to the narthex, where the girls were brushing snow from their cloaks.

"Has Miss Elizabeth come?" said Darcy politely. "With brides, one never knows."

"How dare you," repeated Collins.

"I heard you the first time. Were you planning to marry Elizabeth without telling her who you are?"

Collins put up his chin. "She sees nothing amiss. And neither do I." He moved as though to follow Bingley, but Darcy pulled him back.

"No, you don't," he said. "It is bad luck for the bridegroom to see his bride before the wedding. I thought you knew that."

"To Hades with bad luck!" spat Collins. "I want a word with her, and by all that's holy I intend to have it."

Again Darcy pulled Collins back. "Swearing in the church," he said, shaking his head. "Standards for clergymen have certainly slipped."

Collins attempted to shake free.

"No doubt you wish to inform Miss Elizabeth that I am off my head," continued Darcy. "You won't get anywhere near her, Bingley will see to that."

Collins muttered an oath.

"If she comes to the altar, that is," continued Darcy. "She might not."

Mrs. Bennet's voice could be heard, mingling with the others. How familiar these voices were to Darcy; he could distinguish each one.

"Now you see, girls, there he is. You-hoo, Mr. Collins!" Mrs. Bennet waved a black-gloved hand.

Darcy saw Collins stiffen. "One of the guests is eager for this marriage," Darcy remarked. "I wonder if she is the only one."

Dr. Bentley came rustling forward to shake Collins' hand. "All set, are we?" he said kindly. "You are now on the other side of things, Mr. Collins, no longer the officiant. Never mind the nerves. All bridegrooms are nervous."

Darcy saw Collins force a smile.

"And how very good to see you again, Mr. Darcy. And in such fine form, too. I take it you are to be best man?"

Oh, the irony! Darcy's eyes met Collins.' "That is for Mr. Collins to decide."

"Ah," said Collins. "I—ah."

How would the man answer? He would not dare be seen snubbing Mr. Darcy of Pemberley! Darcy hid a smile and waited.

Dr. Bentley's smile grew wide. "Take no offense, sir," he said to Darcy. "It's only nerves."

"Now mind you take care of the ring," Dr. Bentley went on. "I'll ask for it at the proper time. Your job as best man," he added, "is to keep Mr. Collins standing upright."

"May the best man win," murmured Darcy, before he could stop himself.

Collins gave him a dark look.

Dr. Bentley merely smiled. "You will have your little joke, sir." He turned aside to greet Mrs. Bennet and Mr. and Mrs. Phillips.

Darcy watched the rest of the Bennet family file down the center aisle: Bingley with Jane, and Mary with another woman whom Darcy did not know. Kitty and Lydia brought up the rear. There were no others—no 'brother officers' from the militia, no friends to support Collins.

Darcy thought that perhaps Mrs. Hill would attend, but no. Collins must have offended her thoroughly.

And then his eyes found Elizabeth, standing at the back of the church with a man—her uncle? Yes, Darcy remembered seeing him at the funeral. He was speaking earnestly to her. Bless him, did he sense that something was amiss?

Elizabeth's face was drawn and unsmiling. Poor darling, to be married in a stiff black dress and a dreary black bonnet! She wore a black cloak too, which her uncle now helped her to remove.

Was there a flash of faded pink? Was Elizabeth wearing Sir Magico's cloak?

Darcy's heart was wrung, for he understood it. She was clinging to a precious memory: their midnight kisses in the parlor. It was him she loved, not Collins! His lips parted to speak, but no. He must bide his time.

Meanwhile the bridegroom was fluttering and clucking. "The ring," Collins squeaked. "I-I haven't got a ring."

Darcy ignored him. Elizabeth's uncle was continuing to speak with her. Her face, though pale, was set.

Darcy turned back to Collins. "Can you send someone to fetch it?"

The man's face was twisted with anguish. "If only it were that simple!" he whispered. "Blast it all, can I help it if I forg—"

Comprehension dawned. "You paid out for a special license," said Darcy, speaking low, "and yet you *forgot* to purchase *the ring*?"

"I was—detained! Preoccupied! Busy!"

"The most important commitment of your life," Darcy went on, "and it slipped your mind?"

"It was a natural mistake! Under the circumstances, *most* understandable. I was quite overcome with the management of Longbourn House."

Darcy just looked at him. Surely he could not be serious.

Collins fell silent. It took Darcy a moment to realize that he was staring. "I say," said Collins, "since you are Best Man, would you mind...?" He indicated Darcy's hand.

Immediately Darcy covered his signet ring. "Never," he said. "Not in a million years."

"You know the state of my purse!" hissed Collins. "Why, I had to borrow from the household money for the special licen—" He broke off speaking.

Darcy did not bother to disguise his contempt. "Borrowed?"

Collins was breathing unevenly. "I will give her a ring later. Yes, that's it, once her father's affairs are concluded. We shall choose it together, and all will be well."

"Do you know, Collins, there is not much difference between you and Wickham."

Collins was kept from replying by the approach of Elizabeth and her uncle. She was clinging to his arm as she trod the aisle, and the sprigs of winter sweet she carried trembled. As she neared, Darcy could see circles beneath her eyes. How many sleepless nights had she endured? Darcy fought the impulse to push Collins aside and enfold her in his arms.

Dr. Bentley came surging forward. "All set, Mr. Collins? Miss Elizabeth?"

"I will say again, dear Lizzy," said her uncle, "that you needn't go through with this."

"I am—ready," said Elizabeth in a small voice.

"It is only nerves, good sir," said Dr. Bentley. "There is nothing new in that."

Elizabeth's mother spoke up. "You might smile a little, Lizzy. You will frighten your poor bridegroom."

There was a pause. The smiles were all Dr. Bentley's as he opened his book.

"Dearly beloved," he said. "We are gathered together here in the sight of God, and in the face of this congregation, to join together this Man and this Woman in holy Matrimony..."

Dr. Bentley went on, and Darcy became occupied with his thoughts. He had learned a thing or two as Collins about humility. And now he was about to do something that his dignity would find abhorrent.

Dr. Bentley paused to turn a page. "I require and charge you both," he said, "as ye will answer at the dreadful day of judgment when the secrets of all hearts shall be disclosed..."

Secrets of the heart.

Darcy's gaze transferred to Collins. The man's eyes would not meet his.

"Well?" Darcy murmured into Collins' ear.

"Shut up," he hissed.

So much for common honesty!

Darcy shifted his stance, and Collins gave him a sidelong look.

Dr. Bentley went blithely on. "...that if either of you know any impediment, why ye may not be lawfully joined together in Matrimony, ye do now confess it. For be ye—"

Darcy's head came up. "I beg your pardon, good sir," he said crisply.

All heads turned.

"Since Mr. Collins will not speak," Darcy went on, "I fear I must. There is, most definitely, an impediment."

Someone gave a gasp, but Darcy did not look in Mrs. Bennet's direction. Any minute now he knew Lydia would begin to giggle.

In this he was disappointed. There was only silence, taut and anxious. Dr. Bentley stood holding his book and blinking. "But, sir," he said at last.

DARCY BY ANY OTHER NAME

Beneath the black bonnet Elizabeth's face was pale, and her eyes were wide.

Meanwhile Collins was shaking like a teakettle on the boil. "Are you out of your mind, Darcy?" he hissed.

Darcy felt his lips curve into a smile. "Perhaps I am," he said, gazing at Elizabeth.

"There is no perhaps about it," cried Collins. "The man is mad."

"Or perhaps," Darcy went on, "I am in my right mind and, more to the point, in my right body."

"What do you mean?" said Elizabeth.

"Do not listen to him! Whatever he says, do not listen! The age of miracles is past! His claim that the Almighty exchanged our bodies is nonsense! Utterly false!"

"Exchanged your—" Into Elizabeth's eyes came a spark of comprehension. "Is that what happened?" she whispered.

"Of course not," Collins fairly screamed. "It's that letter. He had no business writing that letter."

Mr. Gardiner stepped forward. "What letter would that be, Mr. Collins?"

Collins glared at Dr. Bentley. "Proceed."

Dr. Bentley looked to Darcy. "My good sir," he said. "Have you a legitimate objection?"

"No, he does not! Kindly get on with it. We do not have all day."

"The game is up, Collins," said Darcy quietly. "Elizabeth knows. She sees the change in us—she has always seen it. She cannot marry you, for you are not the man she loves."

"Oh, and I suppose she loves you?" Collins challenged. "Nonsense. She hates you."

There was a murmur among those assembled.

"She has every reason to," said Darcy.

His eyes found Elizabeth's, and he laid a gentle hand on her shoulder. "I ought to have told you at once, but I did not know how. Later, I began to doubt that I would ever be myself again. It occurred to me that becoming Collins might have been, shall we say, divinely orchestrated? As a means of provision and protection for you and your family."

"Protection?" cried Mrs. Bennet. "You call breaking up a wedding protection? A fine thing!"

Elizabeth turned to Collins. "That letter you burned," she said. "It was mine?"

Collins made a series of inarticulate sounds.

"Was it *my* letter, Mr. Collins?"

"It—depends upon how one looks at it," he stammered.

"Answer the question!"

"Lies, all of it! Preposterous untruths!" Collins turned to Elizabeth's uncle. "Surely you see that Mr. Darcy is mad."

"I see nothing of the sort. I am aware that my niece is reluctant to enter into this marriage. She will do so over my objections."

"Brother!" wailed Mrs. Bennet.

"And mine as well," said another voice—Elizabeth's aunt?

"The bride must answer for herself," said Dr. Bentley.

"Lizzy!" cried Mrs. Bennet. "You cannot *jilt* a man at the altar! What will people say?"

Collins opened his mouth to speak, but Darcy beat him to it. "Well, Miss Elizabeth?" he said gently. "What say you? Will you have Mr. Collins—the real Collins—as your husband? Or," he added, "will you have me?"

Dr. Bentley closed his book.

"That letter," said Elizabeth, "was written by you?"

"A poorly-worded expression of my regard, and a shambling explanation. I do not wonder that you were confused."

"I read only the first half-page. How did it begin?"

Collins stamped his foot. "Of course he does not remember."

Elizabeth's uncle held up a quelling hand. "I believe Mr. Darcy has the floor." He turned to Darcy. "Are you able to answer, sir?"

Darcy's lips twitched into a smile. "I fear so, for I rewrote it several times. The greeting is: *Elizabeth, my Beloved.*"

He heard Elizabeth's intake of breath—she remembered!

"Then the preamble, something about this being my first love letter, which I shall not repeat here. And then this:

Be not alarmed. I do not intend to plague you with an execrable sonnet (which you will be obliged to admire) nor will I burst into song.

Darcy paused. "I hope you will not ask me to prove this by singing," he told her. "Collins has the better voice; I was only borrowing it."

"What?" squealed Collins.

"Which song, Mr. Darcy?" demanded Elizabeth. "Which song did you sing?"

"Why are you asking *him* about something that I did?" cried Collins. "Er, that is—"

"Yes, Collins, tell us," said Elizabeth's uncle. "Which song did you sing?"

Collins shifted his weight. "I, ah, sang a hymn, of course. I forget which one. We shared a hymnal together in church, did we not?"

"No," said Elizabeth flatly.

"It was in the drawing room at Longbourn," Darcy said. "You played as I sang Purcell's *I protest against cringing and whining.*"

"I did no such thing. I do not know any songs by Pur—" Collins stopped.

"Yes you do," Mary burst out. "And you recited Shakespeare as well. We heard you, Mr. Collins. We all heard you."

And then there was silence.

Darcy's bashful smile returned. There he stood, gazing at Elizabeth, his hand on her shoulder, waiting for her to say something. A delicate blush now colored her cheeks; her eyes no longer held a hunted look.

"Who *are* you?" she whispered.

"I am your William," he said simply. "Fitzwilliam Darcy. And I am entirely yours, if you wish it."

The seconds ticked by.

"Body and soul," Darcy added, unable to help himself. "Right down to the dimple in my chin."

He heard her slight gasp.

"No!" cried Collins. "William is *my* name, not yours!" He made a lunge for Elizabeth, but her uncle held him back.

Darcy's gaze never left Elizabeth's face. Hesitation was in her eyes, along with disbelief—or was it wonder?

"The man is lying," cried Collins. "You are betrothed to me! To *me*!"

Elizabeth gave a start and turned to Collins.

"That's better," said Collins. "Now then, shall we dispense with this foolishness?" He snatched her hand, causing the sprigs of winter sweet to fall to the floor. "Continue," he told Dr. Bentley.

Elizabeth pulled free of Collins' grasp. "No, sir," she said distinctly. "I cannot—and will not—marry you."

Mrs. Bennet gave a faint scream.

"But—" sputtered Collins.

Elizabeth's uncle stepped forward. "The lady has spoken, Collins," he said. "Kindly stand down."

"But—she is mine!"

Dr. Bentley cleared his throat. "Dearly beloved," he announced, "let us pause for a moment of silent prayer. For it seems that the bride has had a change of heart."

There was some noise as Collins was escorted from the sanctuary. Darcy's attention remained fixed on Elizabeth.

"William?" she whispered. "You were—William—all the time? The snowstorm, the foiled elopement, the—kisses?"

Darcy enfolded her hands in both his own. "I fear so, my love."

Elizabeth did not pull away. She lowered her gaze, studying their entwined fingers. Darcy felt the seconds pass. Would she believe? Would she dare to trust him?

And then she lifted her eyes. "You are a stranger to me," she said slowly, "and yet—and yet I know you very well."

"You do, yes." Darcy found it difficult to continue. "Would you—care to have me as your very own?"

"*Would I?*" she said.

And with a cry, Elizabeth released his hands and threw her arms around him.

"Lizzy!" cried her mother.

But if Mrs. Bennet had anything more to say, Fitzwilliam Darcy did not hear.

49 Epilogue:

Upon A Summer's Day

When they reached Lambton, Darcy ordered the top taken down, and the horses now traveled at a leisurely pace. Majestic oaks and beeches, clothed in the tender green of spring, created an enchanted world of dappled light and birdsong. The Pemberley Woods were beautiful in any season, but this glorious June day was beyond compare.

Even so, as they turned in at the Lodge, Darcy found himself on edge. Was he nervous? What a thought! And yet he had seen the effect that Pemberley had on people, Caroline Bingley in particular.

But what did it matter? Elizabeth had loved him when he'd been Collins, and she trusted him even when he'd been called 'Mad Darcy.' Her family never believed the story of the exchange, nor had Fitz. Only Elizabeth. Darcy studied his bride's upturned face, so lovely in the subdued light.

"Such an ancient, beautiful woodland," said Elizabeth softly. "Is the house much farther?"

An innocent inquiry and yet Darcy hesitated, for the estate was extensive. By comparison, Longbourn's park was miniscule. "I am afraid it is," he said.

She smiled. "Then I shall not be walking to Clarke's—or its equivalent—to exchange a book."

Was there a lending library in the village? Darcy had no idea. And how could he explain about the extent of Pemberley's collection of books?

"I ought to have shown you Lambton more closely," he said. "It's just that I wished—"

"—to be at home," she finished for him. "And so do I."

He cleared his throat. "You will find the house rather different from Longbourn," he said. "Not as, how shall I say? Cozy?"

"I expect it is like Netherfield, only better—because it is yours."

"Ours," Darcy amended.

He noticed the faint blush on her cheeks and a shy smile of pleasure. "By the goodness of God," he went on, "we take our place as stewards, you and I."

This was the honest truth, a thing Darcy had not taken to heart until recently. He and Elizabeth were

Pemberley's caretakers, not her owners. In this there was room for pleasure, but not for pride. After all, he hadn't earned God's favor, and he certainly did not deserve it. Collins might strut and crow over Longbourn House, but to what end?

The road descended deeper into the woodland, where the shade was cool and welcoming.

"This is delightful." Elizabeth unfastened the ribbons of her bonnet and laid it aside. "Just listen to the birds."

Again Darcy was struck by her expression of wonder. This lovely woman, who had so thoroughly captured his heart, shared a sincere love of nature! He must teach her to ride. By heaven, he would do better than he had as Collins' teacher!

A tendril of Elizabeth's hair escaped; Darcy leaned forward to gently tuck it behind her ear. "Just beyond that rise of land lies a bluebell wood," he said. "There are several on the estate."

"I would love to explore each one." She dimpled. "You know how fond I am of woodland walks. And of mud."

Yes, he did know; he knew it as himself, as Darcy. Without meaning to, he bleated out his thought. "I am sorry that you had to leave your family home."

She looked her surprise.

"You did say once, when I was Collins, that you were relieved to be able to remain."

"Nonsense," she said cheerfully. "Pemberley is very much better!" And then she added, more seriously, "I always knew that I would leave one day. We all did. But I have memories."

And Darcy had memories too. "Do you know," he said, "there are times when I rather miss being Collins? His singing voice, for one. And his ability to enter a room unnoticed."

He saw the ghost of a smile. "And don't you dare agree," he added.

"*I* always noticed you," she countered. "As for the voice, when Mr. Collins sings words penned by others, perhaps he can be pleasing. But the mouth that sings also speaks what is in his mind."

"Or what isn't," quipped Darcy.

"And therein lies danger! It is a great relief to be away from Mr. Collins. I cannot think why Charlotte accepted his proposal."

"For the same reason a certain young woman, who shall remain unnamed, would gladly have accepted mine: the lure of a landed estate."

"But Charlotte does not love Mr. Collins," Elizabeth burst out. "She does not know what love is, not as you and I do! And when I think of being his wife, of—!"

They shared a look.

It was all Darcy could do not to laugh. In the past six months, Collins had become even more peevish—and fatter, too.

"She must therefore learn to love Longbourn House instead," he said lightly. "I believe children are counted as consolation."

DARCY BY ANY OTHER NAME

"Children" Elizabeth repeated. "With Mr. Collins."

They shared another look. "Best not to think of it, my love," he whispered.

"Indeed. Are we now nearer to the house?"

"Ah, no," he said.

"It is through the woods?"

"And over this set of hills. We need to cross the river as well. The house is on the opposite side of the valley."

"The valley," he heard her whisper.

Elizabeth grew quiet for the next half mile, as they made the gradual ascent. At last they emerged from the woods, and Darcy told his driver to pull up. He slid into the forward-facing seat beside his wife.

Across the valley stood Pemberley House, large and handsome, its stone walls golden in the afternoon light. Behind it rose a ridge of high wooded hills; wide lawns swept down to the lake. The lake was blue today, Darcy noted, as blue as the cloudless sky.

He put his arm around Elizabeth, enjoying her warmth against his side. "Do you like it?" he whispered into her ear.

Elizabeth did not answer right away, nor did Darcy press her. There were swans on the lake today, unusual for this time of year.

"I have never seen a house so perfectly situated," Elizabeth said at last. There was another pause. "I was wrong. Pemberley is not at all like Netherfield."

Darcy breathed in her scent as he drew her closer. "I am glad you approve."

"Approve?" Elizabeth turned to him. "You were willing," she said slowly, "to give up all this to live at Longbourn?"

"To live at Longbourn with you," he amended. "And the answer is yes, absolutely." He felt his lips curve into a smile. "Love does not count the cost, and neither did I."

"Oh," she whispered.

And because her soft lips were invitingly near, Darcy kissed her—kissed her in spite of the driver and footman—just as he had done when he was Collins. Simply because he could.

The End

WORKS QUOTED

Chapter 1
Jane Austen. *Pride and Prejudice*, 1813
(bits of dialog from Mr. Collins, Mrs. Bennet)

Chapter 2
Twa Corbies (Scottish folk ballad)

Chapter 17
William Shakespeare. *Sonnet 51, 73*
Henry Purcell. *If Music Be the Food of Love*
Henry Purcell. *I Resolve Against Cringing and Whining*

Chapter 20
William Shakespeare. *Othello*, Act 3

Chapter 30
With Women and Wine I Defy Every Care
(18th century drinking song)

Chapter 49
Church of England. *Book of Common Prayer*, 1662

Scripture quotations are from *The Holy Bible:* King James Version, 1611

ABOUT LAURA HILE

Thank you so much for reading.
It is a pleasure to write for thinking readers.

Darcy By Any Other Name is a surprise, a novel I never thought I'd write—because surely every *Pride and Prejudice* variation has been explored!

Ah, but then I stumbled upon a most intriguing idea...

I live in the Pacific Northwest with my husband, sons, and a collection of antique clocks. One day I hope to add a cat or three.

The comedy I come by in my work as a teacher. There's never a dull moment with teens!

Visit me on-line at Laurahile.com
Do stop by. I'd love to meet you.

Join my mailing list about new releases.

You can also find me on Facebook and Twitter.

ALSO BY LAURA HILE

*Laugh out loud, fall in love,
be swept away by...*

MERCY'S EMBRACE

Readers are loving Laura Hile's joyous *Mercy's Embrace* Regency novels, which feature the so-arrogant Elizabeth Elliot from Jane Austen's *Persuasion*. But Miss Elliot is not as smart as she thinks, and that's where the fun begins.

Come discover Jane Austen's 'Other Elizabeth,' as she plunges headlong into love with a dashing naval officer who is so much more than her match.

"...enjoyable from beginning to the last page of the third book. This treasure should be read sooner than later."
~Austenprose.com

"The world of Jane Austen's Persuasion *fairly sparkles under Laura Hile's deft and humorous touch."*
~Pamela Aidan, author, *Fitzwilliam Darcy, Gentleman*

"I am greatly enjoying Ms. Hile's respectful renderings of these beloved Austen characters, and I relish her fast-paced and thrilling style."
~Austenesque Reviews

Made in the USA
Middletown, DE
24 June 2023